TIME TRIAL

T0078297

TIME TRIAL

REG BULL

ARCHWAY
PUBLISHING

Archway Publishing books may be ordered
through booksellers or by contacting:

Archway Publishing
1663 Liberty Drive
Bloomington, IN 47403
www.archwaypublishing.com
1-(888)-242-5904

ISBN: 978-1-4808-0389-3 (sc)
ISBN: 978-1-4808-0390-9 (e)

Library of Congress Control Number: 2013920674

Printed in the United States of America

Archway Publishing rev. date: 11/13/2013

Chapter 1

No passion so effectively robs the mind of all its powers of acting and reasoning as fear

: *Edmund Burke*

THE DESK SERGEANT PRODDED DISTASTEFULLY AT THE crumpled *KFC* napkin. 'It's the mugger's finger', explained the disheveled man. 'I grabbed his arm and bit it off. That's blood - not ketchup. Should be able to get DNA from that, huh? And I don't mean the Colonel's.'

Scooping the mangled flesh into an evidence bag with a pen soon destined for the trash, the Sergeant dialed for an officer to attend. Just another ordinary day in the human enclosure of New York's Zoological Gardens, his eye perusing the menagerie of plaintiffs waiting on the bench at Precinct 19 on the Upper East Side. The sergeant buzzed the man through a door while beckoning the next in line to his pedestal. A tall, white male with a neatly trimmed crop of silver hair pushed back from a sun-tanned forehead. The light angling in through the station's blue painted windows picked him out like a solitary figure in an Edward Hopper canvas. An elderly man in good shape below a white polo shirt tucked into a pair of crisply pressed chinos. To the sergeant's seasoned eye he was aged close to seventy, though he moved across the hall like a man half that age.

'So how may I help you, sir?' meticulously recording the time in his bursting notebook: April 3rd, 1142 a.m..

'My name is Thomas Paine - with an 'e'. I live out of state and I'd like to report a crime.'

'So what brings you to New York, Mr. Paine?'

'Work.' Up close the sergeant saw the delta of wrinkles around his eyes, rendered deeper by sunnier climes.

'And the crime, sir?'

'A murder. Or maybe murders.' The older man's face remained impassive as he pondered this question of plurality.

'Murders, huh? So who're the victims?'

'I don't know, it hasn't happened yet.'

The sergeant squeezed his ketchup-smeared pen. 'So do you know their names, Mr. Paine?'

'No, they'll be random. But it'll be an Alice this, a Mohammed that, and a John who-gives-a-shit', observed Paine, hands in pockets like a man advising a neighbor on the re-painting of his picket fence. 'As for the perpetrator - well that would be me.'

The sergeant stopped writing. Paine held up a hand to stem the deluge of enquiries. 'To save us both the energy, why don't you just summon the shift detectives who'll be handling my case. You see we don't have a lot of time.'

The sergeant held the man's gaze but was met with an impassivity bordering upon disinterest. He flicked a glance at the long queue of people waiting on the bench. A baby had begun to mewl, the noise reverberating around hardened walls like bellowing into an oil drum. He reached for the phone.

Paine sat upright on a battered aluminum chair, his astringent aftershave filling the interrogation room almost as much as his aura of confidence. Anyone looking through the observation window might have presumed the two detectives present were speaking with their superior officer.

'So, you want to be a sexagenarian Ted Bundy', began the morose-looking detective. 'So let's jump right to the conundrum, Mr. Paine. If that were true - since you've been public spirited enough to hand yourself in - you'll be getting a life term in one of our infamous correctional facilities which would mean you couldn't then commit the crimes, yes? So are we in some wacky Alzheimer's loop here, sir?' Paine's took a long look at his watch. One of the digital types made by *Texas Instruments* in the 1980's, with eye-straining red LCD numerals. Quite the antique nowadays.

'Believe me, I'd like to explain further, Detective, but in under fifteen minutes a modest explosive device planted "somewhere in New York City" will detonate. Though admittedly I can't guarantee you the *exact* body count.'

'I think you're shitting us, Mr. Paine', said the thin detective, avoiding his partner's eye. 'We've been working this City a few years now and you don't strike us as the type.'

'But I'm not from this City', came the calm reply. 'Listen, I told the Desk Sergeant I didn't need to speak with him, and frankly gentlemen, I don't need to speak with you either. Can I suggest you get on to the FBI's New York office and alert them to the situation. Other than that, there's really nothing more you can do.'

'That's for us to decide, Mr. Paine', said the morose detective peremptorily, perching heavily on the creaking table's edge. He glanced at his partner who slipped out of the room. 'And as for the FBI, you clearly don't watch enough TV otherwise you'd know all murder falls under the jurisdiction of the relevant state', he bluffed.

'Well there are several reasons to contact them,' sighed Paine, leisurely clicking his thumbnails together, 'but only one of them is relevant for now.'

'Yeah, what's that?

'Because within the next few hours there will be two further explosions: one in Minnesota and one in Florida. Then a handful more in the next few days. So I'm guessing that qualifies, yes?'

Smiling, she held the deli door open for the au pair with the twin boys to exit, her own daughter skipping lightly ahead of her into the intoxicating aromas. The little girl stuck her nose to the cabinet's glass front. 'Cannoli, mommy – pleeeease!'

'The usual, please', said the mother smiling at the assistant in the icing-white smock.

'And how long will these last before they're all gobbled up by the little Senorina , eh?' he asked, snapping open a bag and winking as the little girl nuzzled into the front of her Mother's coat.

Afterwards, when she was being interviewed by the police, all the mother would remember next was that - as the assistant had bent down - she had suddenly been aware of the screaming glass from the storefront window sleeting into her back. Thank the merciful heavens her daughter had been shielded from the shrapnel that had peeled her own hands and scalp. She would recall the clear topographic line on the shop assistant's face where the half above the pastry cabinet had been bloodily eviscerated by slivers of glass, the undamaged half below set in a rictus of surprise. She would explain that, pulling the shards of plate-glass from her weeping back, she had seen the pall of smoke rising from the broken windows of Precinct 19 opposite the deli. Then groggily she would hear the paramedics confirm that the blast had been in the Precinct's reception area.

And then she would remember the people lying shattered in the road. Too many for her to count. And at this point she would be thinking again about her daughter who was being looked after by a kind paramedic at the adjacent ambulance. One with kind, dark eyes. Eyes a little like the deli assistant's had been, before one had been sliced open by the dagger of glass now stabbing into his brain.

———

The thin detective moved as fast as he could across the tiled floor, the sprinklers having turned it into Vaselined glass. Smoke from downstairs was hemorrhaging through the corridors as the interrogation room's door opened.

'He's bombed the fucking Precinct!' squeaked his sad faced partner, the comb-over on his balding pate washing away in the drizzle of man-made rain. 'I'll evacuate the son-of-a-bitch down to the car', he croaked as his thin partner tip-toed gingerly down the miniature waterfall that now constituted the main stairs. Loafers leaking stale water onto three day old socks.

From the landing he could survey the whole Reception area. The gently arched window above the visitors' bench was now completely missing, the gaping hole throwing grainy light upon the powder-covered bodies of people strewn groaning across the puddled floor. The Desk Sergeant was on his knees administering mouth-to mouth, his deep blue uniform now a Confederate grey as dust from the blast went into solution. Outside sirens moaned, cars returning home to a crime scene they had just left. The bedraggled detective spotted the precinct's Captain frantic on the phone, squelching across to mumble an urgent explanation.

The crumpled frame of the sad detective and the lean figure of Paine sat wet and silent in the back of an unmarked car as the equally soaked Captain slid into its front.

'So, is that it or are there more?' craning his head round to stare violently at the elderly man.

'Now might be a good time to alert the FBI about Florida and Minnesota, yes?' Paine's dolorous reply.

'But what about *here*? Are there any more *here*?'

'Would you *like* more?' said like a parent asking a child if they wanted more chores. 'So, while you make up your leaden mind, let me clarify some points.

First, my future cooperation in this case is contingent upon you not processing me into the system. If you try to fingerprint me, take my photo, or stick me in one of those natty orange overalls, I'll shut up forever. Believe me, you *really* don't want that', smiled Paine as if only he knew the safe route out of the quicksand.

'*Natty*. Is that some Canadian word?' rumbled the Captain.

'I read widely', quipped Paine. 'Second, I have a list of names in the back pocket of my pants.' The sad, gently steaming detective shoved him over to fumble for it. 'These are the people whom I require to join the FBI team assigned to my case. If they're not allowed to participate then, once again, I'll shut up forever. I'd be obliged if you'd pass those two pieces of intelligence onto the FBI'.

The Captain's reading glasses were inside, glistening on his half-submerged desk, but he could still make out the names hand-written in bold script. 'Let me get this straight. You want these three people to work your case?' Paine twitched a lip in mute confirmation. 'Detective Sergeant David Song? I don't recognize the name.'

'And I doubt he's heard of you either, mediocrity being the bitch it is.'

Scrunching the damp piece of paper in an angry hand, the Captain popped the door and hurried out as if mustard gas had just been introduced to the AC.

'Oh, and how is that very helpful Desk Sergeant of yours? A survivor I hope.'

The Captain glanced back at the smile permanently pinioned to this man's face. 'He's just fine, motherfucker. He's just fine.'

———

Detective Sergeant David Song brushed the fingerprint powder off his light grey suit as his partner TK Bloomfield threw their San Francisco Police Department's Toyota around a corner, scattering a bevy of pedestrians. The two of them looked odd together. Bloomfield was a six foot six behemoth from Norwegian stock earning him the nickname Big Bird. While Song, the progeny of a small Vietnamese mother and a taller Caucasian American father, stood equidistant between them at five foot eight without a haircut.

'Does this old powder wash off?' he asked, massaging the stain he had picked up at the Case Evidence Archive. Two days ago a work crew replacing a pylon on the 880 had drilled through to find an air-pocket in the shape of a male curled in the fetal position. Song had seen pictures of the moulds of people caught in Pompeii's volcanic pumice, leaving a mirror-image of themselves at their moment of death two thousand years ago. Back then people had attributed it to the work of angry Gods, but here Song rather suspected angry Dons. A wrist watch found at the bottom of the human bubble looked like a roulette ball that had come to rest.

'1971 was when that pylon was built. Fuck, I was only sucking my mom's tits back then', grumbled Big Bird, depressed at the thought of trawling round urine perfumed seniors' homes searching for witnesses. Those people could hardly remember their own names now, let anyone from forty years earlier.

Song smiled patiently back at his long-time partner before turning to watch the trees roll by on Folsom Street in this his favorite month. Bloomfield took another corner as though driving a dodgem, slewing a pile of ancient papers with completed crosswords across the back seat. Song's phone burst into life with the intro to *Layla*.

'Song, it's Captain Romero. Where are you?' A phone call direct from the brass? Song instinctively straightened his tie. This pylon case must be attracting some serious shit.

'Captain Romero, sir', saying his name out loud to attract Big Bird's attention. 'Detective Bloomfield and I are on our way back to the Station.'

'Don't bother. Come asap to see me downtown. Bloomfield can wait outside to drive you to the airport.'

'The airport?' Song's eyes widening, his partner shrugging as he always did when it came to the mysteries of the command structure.

'You're going to New York City. Special request of the Federal Bureau of Investigation. Just what the fuck have you been up to, son?'

⁂

Sitting in her chocolate-colored cubicle, Agent Nevada Townsend lifted her arms in a classic high-diving pose and stretched. Her first FBI trainer had said the job was "20% at the scene and 80% at the screen", but today he had wildly underestimated that last part. She had just completed a tricky case involving allegations of corruption in the allocation of gaming licenses to a Navajo businessman. She knew she had been assigned to it because of her part Native American background, though that wasn't the reason she had been given by her streak-of-piss supervisor. Attached to the Las Vegas field office for two years now, Townsend felt she had been forced to survive on a thin gruel of second rate cases doled out by her third rate manager.

Depressed, she toggled to the resignation letter she had written a fortnight ago. Reading it for the fiftieth time, she swapped back the comma for the semi-colon she had inserted yesterday. Townsend was pondering whether she would ever have the guts to hand it in when she spied her idiot boss striding towards her, ID pendant clacking noisily against an overly large Bald Eagle belt-buckle.

'I should have the report finished by noon tomorrow, okay?' she beamed.

'Nope. I need it in the next three hours', he growled back. Townsend's chin dropped onto the neckline of her fake D&G blouse. Normally she could bend him like the spineless pond-life he was.

'Whoa - what's the rush?'

'Because by midnight I'll be sending you off with my good wishes and a mildly positive review for your personnel file.'

'Sending me off?' repeating his words, momentarily lost for her own. 'Where am I going?' fingers suspended uselessly above her keyboard.

'The city where everyone's so fucking dumb they named it twice in the song to facilitate its recall.'

'New York! What for?'

'I'm just a lowly field coordinator, princess. All I know is that when my boss gets a direct call from the Deputy Director of the Bureau instructing him to release one Nevada Townsend, I jump like a white Bob Beamon. So punch those keys, then saddle up and get your part-Apache ass out of here.'

———

Gabriel Fernandez threw the *New York Times* onto the mahogany dinner table in his Greenwich Village apartment. 'Talentless hack', he tossed in the same direction. He had just read a piece comparing America's diplomatic stance towards North Korea with that towards Cuba. Fernandez wasn't sure whether it was the piece he disliked or the journalist who wrote it. There had been a time when he himself might have been asked to author something like this. But that was long ago. He stomped into his designer kitchen past his imported Regency furniture, muttering as he crossed his 19th century Flemish rug. It was the industrious grinding of the Krups coffee maker that almost obscured the trilling of his apartment's phone.

'Gabriel, hi, it's Alan Hammond here, is this a good time?' asked the *New York Times'* Editor as if participating in some vast experiment on coincidence. Fernandez's legs were suddenly bored hollow. He had never spoken with the man before except as part of a group introduction.

'No, it's fine Mr. Hammond, just fine!' quickly recovering his equanimity and straightening his back as gentlemen should do when in good company. 'To what do I owe this inestimable pleasure?' thinking of that North Korean article, his mind racing to the possibility of a follow-up piece, the chance for two journalists to dual across the pages before a knowledgeable audience.

'Call me Alan, please. Listen, we've just taken an urgent call from the FBI who're looking for you. We said we'd go through our archives but they're probably zeroing in on you now anyway.'

The FBI, thought Fernandez, lamely followed by a pang of hurt that the *Times* had consigned him to their archives. 'How extraordinary! Did they say what about?' flopping onto a reproduction Chippendale chair with the headiness of it all.

'No, but my instincts are hollering there's something brewing. So can we agree that whatever it is, the *Times* will get first refusal? I'm taking dinner at my club tonight; would you care to join me?'

'I'd like that, Alan, I really would', replied Fernandez, grateful that his blushes could not be seen. 'So is there an FBI number to call?'

'No need. They'll come knocking any time now.'

Fernandez instinctively listened for a rap on his oak apartment door. But now there'd be no chance of him hearing it on account of the monstrous noise of the police sirens that had just this second so inconveniently pulled up outside.

———

The groundsman climbed down from his John Deere to stretch his back. The smell of the freshly cut turf, and the immaculate precision of the candy-stripe lines always gave him a sense of accomplishment.

At first he thought it was a clap of thunder, looking towards the powder blue sky for a clue. But his elevated gaze caught the bolus of smoke from up high at the back of the empty Ben Hill Griffin Stadium in Gainesville, Florida. At his age it was as much as he could do to jog the length of the pitch like a geriatric punt returner and climb the barrier where the smoke persistently hung on this windless day. Cautiously he closed in on the location as if cornering a drunken spectator. A chunk of the back row had been torn out of the ground. Fragments of smoldering orange seating were burning themselves black along clearly numbered aisles, filling the chemical air with an acrid cocktail of polypropylene and blistered paint.

———

The bread baker clicked crisply as it transitioned from kneading to rising. A rare stillness becalming this oft bustling Minnesota home.

The next click came from the attic, the roar of the percussive blast that followed careering like Pamplona Bulls through the suburban streets around. Within seconds the wood paneled house was crackling at the center of a huge ball of raging flame.

A mile away a mother doing the school run knew how much the screaming freckled kids in the back of her *Landcruiser* would be looking forward to their peanut butter and jelly snack when they got home. But in her kitchen, the bread baker itself was now baking.

— · — ·—

The Southern flight to JFK remained stubbornly unallocated to a gate at the top of the Departures screen. Detective Sergeant David Song was perched uncomfortably atop a bar stool swirling the remains of a flat, dusky amber liquid, which was pretty much how he himself was feeling right now. The initial adrenalin rush of being summoned to New York had since been vanquished by a dull, persistent foreboding. Captain Romero hadn't helped the situation by enigmatically confirming he had been sworn to secrecy for reasons of National Security. Song instinctively grimaced as he pondered that phrase, aware of both the honor and the horseshit it could be used to disguise. On the adjoining monitor, *Fox* was covering the bombing of a New York police station with eight now dead. Thankfully none of them from the Force thought Song selfishly. More explosions in Florida and Minnesota but the details were still hazy. So far no terrorist group had claimed responsibility, with *Fox* parading a series of experts each with their housetrained pet theory.

Song fished out his iPhone for the eighth time that hour. There were fifteen texts from Josie who he'd been dating for nine months and sleeping with for ten. It had been a tolerable period of mildly engaging conversation, but with sex like the 4th of July on PCP. Then two weeks ago he had come to the realization that – once more in the line of his many relationships - he didn't really care for her. Deep down he was looking for something more than just the sweaty horizontal, or in Josie's case every perspiring angle in Euclidian geometry. Song had talked it through with Charleen, his Vietnamese lawyer friend who everyone called Charley.

'I guess I'm becoming that hopeless romantic', he had confessed over pizza.

'No,' she had replied through her bubbling laugh, 'just the hopeless bit.'

'Are you Vietnamese?' asked a voice, dragging Song from his contemplation of the swirling liquid in his glass and the whirling Josie in his bed. The questioner was in his late sixties wearing an ageing *Zeppelin* T-shirt and a pair of *Levi's* struck in antiquity. But it was the Vietnam veterans' cap that told Song what was about to pass. That war had finished before he had been born and he had never even visited his mother's country. Nevertheless, for some his mere presence seemed to provide a conduit back to their past.

'Yes, sir. Half Vietnamese, half American.' There was a short silence which Song noticed happened a lot in encounters like this. In their minds were they back in flack-jackets scything across tree-tops in a Huey once again?

'My mom escaped in '76 and met my dad here in San Francisco', Song clarified, the man nodding, thoughts elsewhere in both time and space.

'Where are you heading, son?'

'New York. On business - I'm a police officer.'

'My son-in-law's in the Seattle Fire Department. My daughter was born when I got back in '69.'

Song's eye flicked to the Departures monitor where they had at last published his gate. 'You have a good journey, sir'. He made a fuss of collecting his things, allowing the man time to say what he had really wanted to all along.

'Sorry. I just wanted to say I was sorry.' A flight announcement did its best to drown him out, while teenagers wirelessly playing each other on a combat game nearby were hollering who should pick up the ammo. Song laid a calming hand upon the man's shoulder thinking that a priest might say something in Latin now.

'You have nothing to be sorry for, sir. On the contrary, I want to thank you. Without your sacrifice my mom wouldn't have escaped from Vietnam, never made a life for her family in this great country, and I wouldn't be here talking to you today. So would you do me the honor of letting me shake your hand?' The veteran rose stiffly from his bar stool, Song looking deep into rheumy eyes that were still scanning the tree lines of forests far away.

Chapter 2

Fear is not the natural state of civilized people

: *Aung San Suu Kyi*

AS SOON AS THE DOOR CRACKED OPEN AT JFK, FOUR AGENTS stepped in asking for Detective Sergeant David Song by name. They marched him through a series of back doors directly into a waiting SUV with wrap-around tinted glass, shooting out of the parking lot at a blood curdling speed. Tossed around in the back, Song had ventured the open question as to what the fuck he was needed for in New York, but he could have been alone in the vehicle for all the good this had done him. The explosions in New York and Florida had been breathlessly leading the news on Song's phone as he did his best to navigate the touch controls in this vehicular centrifuge. Words like Al Qaeda, Oklahoma, Boston, and inevitably 9/11 obliterating the tiny screen. The image of a bandaged woman injured in a delicatessen near Precinct 19, grasping her frightened daughter to her bloodied blouse, was the lead photograph on most sites.

When he had exited Captain Romero's office a few hours earlier, Song's commanding officer had offered some kindly words of support. "Remember, you're representing the San Francisco Police Department and more importantly you're representing me.

Fuck this one up and I'll fuck you up, Song." The sagacity of those words were still having their physical and metaphysical affect upon him at two o'clock in the morning Eastern when his NASCAR chauffer skidded to a halt outside the Marriott on West Street. Song was just thinking that this was an unusual place to stop for gas when the door violently slid open and he was half helped, half yanked out and shoved through the hotel's revolving doors.

Waiting for the elevator between his guards, Song pulled up a hotel app and perused the Marriot's write-up, glad that he wouldn't be picking up any checks here tonight.

A bedroom door on the fifth floor opened without the need to knock, revealing two agents in identical white shirts. One's athletic frame filled the entrance, while the older man remained seated.

'Sit down' said the younger, blond haired one waving off Song's chaperones with a studied, hostile interview face. The Californian smiled to himself for the first time in hours, knowing he had an identical professional mask in his own kit-bag. A file was slapped onto the oval glass table, its contents spilling out to reveal material from Song's personnel folder.

'So, Mr. Song, how do you know Thomas Paine?'

'Thomas Paine? I don't know anyone with that name', noting the agent had deliberately used the appellation of Mister, rather than Detective Sergeant. All part of the ritual of unsettling an interviewee, whereas its workman-like familiarity was actually serving to calm the Californian's nerves. But why would the FBI want to do this to him anyway?

'I believe you do,' pursued the young agent, 'so please do me the professional courtesy of not wasting my fucking time.'

'I don't know that name,' repeated Song calmly, 'other than the eighteenth century political philosopher. But I guess you're not alluding to him?' The young agent brushed away the enquiry, veering off on a different approach.

'I see you have a Vietnamese mother and a Caucasian American father, yet your family name "Song" is Chinese, yes? Tell me about that.'

'How about you tell me your name first?'

'You understand you're now culpable for nine fatalities, and that this state still has the death penalty?' he intoned changing tack yet again, his hard eyes locking onto Song's. The detective motioned with his hands to convey he knew that New York didn't, and what was all this shit about anyway? Meanwhile his stomach turned sickeningly with the realization that they seemed to think he was implicated in the precinct bombing incident.

'Will you submit to a strip search?' asked his inquisitor in a tone implying there was only one answer.

Song dragged himself back from worried thoughts, his patience thinning with this puerile approach. 'That depends. If you're searching me for a missing asshole, I can assure you it's not on *this* side of the table.' Song thought he saw a smile pass over the older agent's lips, silent in his bedside chair. The youthful Witchfinder General spent the next few minutes spitting questions of fact across the table, each requiring either a yes or no answer. Song felt there was neither art nor science in his approach, and if the idea was to lure him into swinging at impossible balls he had seen better in Little League.

'So if you don't know any Thomas Paines, why the fuck do you think you're here?'

Song shrugged his own bemusement. 'Maybe you just wanted to see me naked? If not, I'd be happy to return to San Francisco as I *do* have some homicides there that I *am* responsible for.'

The blond agent barked a laugh. 'You won't be seeing the Golden Gate for some time now, Mr. Song. Under the provisions of the Patriot Act and subsequent legislation we have the power to hold suspected terrorists indefinitely.'

'Terrorist?' Song rolled his eyes to the stippled ceiling to signal his contempt, but also to hide his growing dismay. 'If you really thought that, we wouldn't be sitting in a four hundred bucks a night suite talking all chummy now, would we?'

'Hold on Nate, thank you', interjected the silent agent from his chair. 'I don't think we're in the presence of a major threat to the American way of life. Detective Sergeant Song, my name is Special Agent Alex Corbyn of the Counter Terrorism Unit of the National Security Branch within the Federal Bureau of Investigation. It's a mouthful and the acronym's equally unpronounceable. This is Agent Nathanial Benjamin from Homeland Security who accidentally neglected to introduce himself earlier. Nate reports to me for the duration of this case, as does the rest of the team both here and in Quantico. I hope you'll forgive us this first encounter, but it's been helpful in getting an initial read.'

Song shook the hand of greeting before proffering his own to Benjamin who was noticeably slower in taking up the invitation.

'And in such an elegant location, Special Agent Corbyn. I'm impressed', Song replied, wondering how much more of this small talk would be necessary before he could get to his single point of interest: *why did they think he was involved in all this shit?*

'The Marriot was stipulated by our chief suspect, Thomas Paine, as his preferred residence for interrogation. He likes the way they dust an 'M' onto their cappuccinos', offered Corbyn flatly. This was okay for now, thought Song; easy concessions to the perp leading hopefully to an easy conviction. He would have done the same.

'I know you have an avalanche of questions, David, but I need you to get some sleep ready to meet Paine in a few hours. So can I invite you to stay here in one of New York's finest hotels - all expenses paid?'

Something about the senior Bureau man's demeanor told Song there'd be no point in resisting.

On the way down to the meeting room at seven a.m. with barely three hours sleep to his name, Song's phone hosted pundits and bloggers trading apocalyptical thoughts about the bombings, their motives, and the next targets. He was met in the lobby by Agent Kamamalu in charge of Paine's security, the FBI man's Hawaiian warrior heritage displaying itself proudly in a fifty two inch breasted suit and a handshake that could pulverize a walnut. They were joined by the young agent who had blundered though Song's interrogation just a few hours earlier.

'Just in case you missed it, the name is Agent Nathanial Benjamin, Homeland Security, assigned to work the case by Deputy Director Dawn Sharper in person', holding out his ID, seeming to set his face to mirror its photo.

'Yes, that's certainly you', confirmed Song.

Inside a well-guarded Marriot conference suite, walls scarred by the sticking tape from countless flip-chart sheets, Corbyn looked as though he hadn't seen a pillow in the last twenty-four hours. Song's quick scan of its diverse inhabitants reminded him of a packed trolley-bus back home. Quick-fire, Corbyn introduced Song, FBI Agent Nevada Townsend, Gabriel Fernandez - whom he described obliquely as "a member of the press" - and an older man in the garb of a catholic priest named Monsignor Patrick O'Brian. Everyone nodded blankly, Song taking comfort from what appeared to be their platform of shared ignorance.

'Let me begin by apologizing for yesterday's unilateral changes to your plans. Sorry to you all with the exception of Agent Townsend who does what the Bureau goddamn wants her to do', Corbyn shooting her a thin smile. 'Sorry for the "goddamn" there, Monsignor. The habits of a latter-day agnostic.' Song took this opportunity to appraise this young woman with a detective's eye. If she too had been travelling for most of yesterday, it didn't look like it. She caught his glance and smiled; eyebrows rising as if to say, *this looks interesting, huh?*

Corbyn gave an erudite autopsy of the events of the past day and his meetings with Paine. All attempts at interrogation had proven utterly fruitless though they had spent six intimate hours together. 'He wants to speak with Nevada, David, and Gabriel before he'll cooperate, and he insists there be a representative from a religion present, hence your participation Monsignor.'

'Whoa! He specifically gave you my name?' blurted Song out of heart-stopping surprise. 'I thought it was the Bureau who'd asked for me', understanding now the reason for last night's *Twilight Zone* pre-interview. 'Do you have this asshole's photo?'

'Only this snap on my cell which I sneaked without his permission. We haven't processed him yet, partly because that was a condition to maintain his cooperation, but also because we need to get the jurisdiction right. So the man you're about to meet is merely helping us with our enquiries and this photo doesn't exist.'

'I don't understand', said Monsignor O'Brian, dressed like Johnny Cash but for the blanched collar. 'Didn't you say he'd owned up to the bombings in advance?'

'Yes, but for complex legal reasons, Monsignor, we're characterizing him as a witness for now. Which brings me back to this photo - if the Bureau's attorneys were here they'd tell me to delete it.' Song noticed that Corbyn seemed to be answering O'Brian but speaking to Fernandez. What the fuck was a reporter doing in here anyway, he wondered?

Corbyn's cell passed around like a communion cup, each scrutinizing the photo for personal meaning. In turn each shook their heads, bemused by the image of the gaunt, white haired man. Song's mind shuffled through the IDs of his perps over the years drawing a complete blank. He just looked like a harmless old guy.

'In San Francisco, if a suspect — sorry, a witness - starts naming people to assemble around him, my first instinct would be to assume they're involved. So are we all under suspicion?' piped Song.

Corbyn peered again at Paine's photo, searching once more for revelation between its pixels. 'In some respects, yes, you are. But Paine appears to be intelligent, and clearly there's some game in play, so why imperil it by naming his co-conspirators? Therefore on balance - until proven otherwise - I'll assume you're all just cogs and wheels.'

'Until proven otherwise', echoed Townsend with portent. Song glanced again at this female FBI agent who like him had been inexplicably summoned to this place. Late twenties, mixed race heritage, well dressed but not impractically so. No jewelry except for a half-string of colored beads laced onto a silver neck-rope. No ring and, despite being exercised by his current situation, Song had noticed she was extremely pretty.

'Excuse me Special Agent Corbyn, what does "getting the jurisdiction right" mean?' enquired Fernandez. Song frowned at this man in his late fifties, hair darker than was natural, thirty pounds overweight, a Breitling under the cuff of a well-cut sports jacket, shoes individually crafted to slip deftly onto each unique foot.

'Forgive me', Song interjected again, 'but is it normal Bureau practice to give a member of the press – and indeed a man of the cloth – such privileged access to a case?' wrapping his question in as much decorum as he could muster.

'I repeat, you are *all* here at Paine's invitation' replied Corbyn, indulging the Californian. 'The Bureau has agreed with the *New York Times* that - in return for exclusive inside reporting on the case *after* its completion - Gabriel will not disclose any contemporary details.' Fernandez's face had a confirmatory look. That's one of his faces, thought Song.

'What about motive?' pursued Song, his detective's instincts reasserting themselves after the shock of hearing that his own invitation had been personal.

'Other than not being officially processed, Paine's asked for nothing. Hundreds of Bureau staff in D.C. and Quantico are blitzing possible links, but so far it's a bust.'

'And what do we know about Paine himself?' asked Townsend, Corbyn holding up an encircled thumb and index finger in reply.

'I guess water boarding him is out of the question, Nathan?' enquired Song to his young Homeland inquisitor from last night, only to be rewarded with a cold stare.

'In the Bureau we use electric shock and dental drills, isn't that right Nevada?' smiled Corbyn in an attempt to ease the tension for O'Brian and Fernandez's benefit.

'That's why we have such a large utilities bill', she grinned back.

'Finally, in our meeting with Paine please refrain from asking him the "why me" question. Because our primary goal this morning is….?'

'Discovering the whereabouts of the next devices', finished Townsend with an ironic flourish.

'Outstanding, Nevada. Hey, if this goes well maybe we'll all be back in our regular jobs tomorrow!'

But Song had a growing and uncomfortable suspicion that they wouldn't.

Agent Kamamalu led the column of invitees into a lemon and caramel bedroom suite on the ninth floor, with a ring of cherry-wood chairs hastily assembled round a table too small for their number.

Every eye was on the elderly man sitting with his back to the closed drapes, the early morning April light vanquished by their heavy weave. Song usually encountered people of this age as victims, rarely as the perpetrators, adding piquancy to the fractured surrealism of his past twenty four hours.

'Ah, now we are One! Welcome everyone, welcome! Especially Nevada, David, and Gabriel', gushed the silver haired man offering his hand. The three of them looked on uncomprehending. Song's cheeks were burning red with a compote of embarrassment and frustration; the absence of his guilt doing nothing to relieve the feeling of it. Corbyn had stepped back to observe this theater, Benjamin too flicking inquisitive eyes from face to face.

'And you must be Monsignor O'Brian', observed Paine. 'So you didn't opt for a Muslim, Alex, just in case that's what I'm all about? Ha! That would make my actions easier for everyone to understand, wouldn't it? The perfect symmetry of prejudice and convenience. Well, the Constitution may be color blind, but that doesn't equip us for today's complex theological challenges, does it, Monsignor?'

'Eh, no. I'm glad to help out, Mr. Paine', stumbled O'Brian. 'And if you need anything from me personally that doesn't interfere with the investigation's workings, please just ask.'

'Generous of you, Monsignor, I'll bear that in mind.'

As if the room were not crowded enough there were two video-cameras positioned to capture the circle. Song knew they would be carrying a live-feed somewhere, and that scrutiny would fall upon Townsend, Fernandez and himself as much as it would Paine.

'Well, we've met your request to assemble this specific group', interrupted Corbyn, lassoing the proceedings. 'Now we require you to deliver upon your part of the bargain, Thomas.'

'Business, always business with you', laughed Paine. 'We have time to spare, and I'll give you the exact locations of the devices once I'm satisfied, so don't worry. David Song! How very good it is to meet you in the flesh and to see that you are indeed your father's son. Nevada Townsend, looking at you brings back so many memories, both good and bad. Gabriel Fernandez, my, my, you've put on some weight since I last saw you.' Townsend caught Corbyn's eye as if to say, *I have no fucking idea what he's talking about*, while the throw-away reference to Song's father had at the same time chilled the detective's blood and equally heated his temper. Fernandez just looked puzzled.

'May they call you Thomas, or is there another name they should use?' asked Corbyn, directing everyone to sit. In Song's career he had seen many naked power gambits from interviewees but Paine's opening had been more accomplished than most.

'Thomas will do just fine. Now aren't you going to ask if I want an attorney present?'

Corbyn raised an eyebrow, 'Do you *want* an attorney present?'

'Do I *want* cancer?' with a wry grin.

'Yesterday was a busy one for you and your accomplices', picked up Corbyn. 'First you arrive in the City from – well, we're not exactly sure - then the bomb in New York, followed by Florida and Minnesota, just to cement our attention.'

'I like your style, Alex; it's not at all patronizing', enthused Paine. 'If you pass my interview I'm sure we're going to have fun working together.' Song was raking through everything Paine said: every inflection, every adjustment to tone. *How did this man know him?* It was beyond irritation.

'Your accent is American but your choice of vocabulary is more cosmopolitan', sallied Corbyn.

'*Cosmopolitan?* Look who's talking! No, I'll confess to you that I was born and bred under the broad stripes and bright stars. I have an interest in language, that's all.'

'So what else is it you want now?' Corbyn continued to probe, showing the kind of limitless patience Song knew was beyond his own compass.

'I don't *want* anything, Alex.'

'There were no casualties in Florida as the stadium was predictably empty, which makes me wonder why detonate at that time?' interjected Song, unable to contain himself. Corbyn strafed him with an icy glare, while in counterpoint Paine rewarded his guest with a smile, as a grandparent might humor a finger-painting child.

'The body count's not really my concern. If you're expecting some lame speech about big government versus the inviolate rights of the individual, I'll have to disappoint you. Hopefully you're going to find me less superficial than the 5th Volunteer Alabama Red-Necks. Of more importance to me at the moment are Alex and the Monsignor.'

'How so?' enquired Corbyn, making a point of taking off his jacket.

'We have quite a journey ahead, and the purpose of today's interviews is for me to decide whether you're the two to share that ride with the rest of us.'

'That's novel; I've never been asked to interview before', smiled Corbyn.

'I can see your ring, so start by telling me about your wife.'

'Tell me about yours first', Corbyn's retort, the entranced audience watching the ball fizz back and forth across a taught net.

'Never had one, and that wasn't some Jungian thing about my mother's tit. I've just been too busy, as you're going to find out. Feel free to keep probing around for emotional triggers, but this isn't *Silence of the Lambs*.' Paine opened his arms as if to apologize for letting everyone down. 'You look very sour, Agent Benjamin. Is there anything wrong?'

'I'm thinking about the kids who'll be attending their parent's funerals this week. How do you feel about that?' the growled reply. Corbyn glanced down at his paperwork, annoyed Benjamin had taken Paine's bait.

'I don't *feel* anything. It just is. But let's return to the subject of our interview, Alex.'

'There's that word again. Okay, what do you want to know about me?'

Paine shuffled forward on his seat, intensity etched into his wrinkled face. 'I have three questions for you. Answer them honestly and you'll pass, otherwise you've a long journey home.'

Corbyn took a calming breath. If he had understood correctly, Paine really was about to interview him for the post of lead investigator. He nodded his agreement, knowing that Time was wearing the other team's shirt for now.

'Question one. What's most important to you, justice or mercy?' enquired the old man.

'Justice', Corbyn answered without hesitation.

'Why?'

'Because it precedes mercy. A decision needs to be made within a just framework in order for mercy to have a context.' For Song looking on, part of him still wanted to pull back this guy's fingers until he whimpered the next device's location, but the other part was enthralled by the theater.

'Interesting, but derivative. Question two. Guevara once said, "I would rather die on my feet, than live on my knees". Which would you choose, Alex?'

'It was Zapata, not Guevara, and I'd choose my knees.'

'Why?' enquired Paine, gently swinging an arm over the back of his chair, the Dean of Humanities toying with a freshman.

'When up against insurmountable odds, play the long-game and wait for opportunities to retaliate. Patience over pride.'

'What's your view on that, Agent Benjamin?' Paine threw out, Corbyn hoping the Homeland agent would duck the punch this time.

'I'd stay on my feet,' he grizzled, 'and I'd have no intention of dying on them either.'

'Ah, the hubris of youth', winked Paine. 'Last question, Agent Corbyn. If your wife had been one of yesterday's fatalities in New York, what could I have expected from you: justice or mercy?'

'Neither.'

'How's that?'

'Because I'd have handed in my badge and hunted you down with a ruthlessness that would chill the souls of thoughtful men. And when I'd cornered you in a lonely place I'd have dug my thumbs right through those blue eyes of yours.' There was a perfect silence in the room. Song daren't flick his eyes to Paine lest they make too much noise.

'I believe you, I really do', whispered Paine in mock-awe, rhythmically tapping a finger on the table's mahogany-inlaid rim. 'Congratulations, welcome to my team, Alex!' proffering a hand that Corbyn shook with forced camaraderie.

'After that resounding success, let's begin O'Brian's interview by also asking a question about relationships.'

'I'll try my best', croaked the Monsignor receiving a tight smile of encouragement from Townsend. Paine shifted his weight as if carefully selecting his words.

'Have you ever sodomized a choir-boy?'

Fernandez's pen raced scratchily across his reporter's pad. Just exactly how do you spell *Pulitzer*, Song wondered?

'I have never... no. I don't ... no.'

'So have you ever masturbated in the shower?' Paine asked with spirit-level sureness. Song darted a glance at Corbyn who was like a man watching a felled tree lurching the wrong way towards his house.

'Thomas', interrupted the special agent, 'you asked for a member of an organized religion, and Monsignor O'Brian has been good enough to oblige. I don't think ….'

'It's all right,' interjected the Monsignor with a thin and increasingly pallid smile. 'I remember why we're here. No, Mr. Paine, I have not.'

'So no Y chromosomes doing the backstroke through the rectory plumbing?' Paine pulled a vinegary face. 'The final question. If nuns are married to Jesus, does this mean he can have coitus with them singly and in groups?'

'Oh really, I must protest!' exploded Fernandez rising from his chair, Song eyeing the reporter once again. A Spanish accent, therefore probably a catholic, interceding on behalf of the church responsible for his moral wiring.

O'Brian took his protector's elbow, guiding him back down with a thin lipped smile. 'I'm sure you already know that the marriage of our sisters to Christ is metaphorical, Thomas.'

'So that's a no then.' Paine had pressed his palms together as if in mock prayer. Who's this show for, wondered Song, and how does any of this pantomime speak to motive? Meanwhile Fernandez was angrily squeezing his pen as if the act alone could extrude words from it. The Bureau's team looked on, law enforcement antennae raking the scene for clues about their quarry.

'Monsignor, thank you for coming' said Paine as if this were his dinner party. 'Alex, I regret to inform you that O'Brian has failed his interview.'

'So what does this mean?' asked the special agent cautiously.

'It means we don't have the full team present so I can't divulge the whereabouts of the next detonations. It's very disappointing to end on this low note and – quite frankly – I'm at a bit of a loss what to do.'

The doorbell rang announcing the arrival of coffee. Song hoped it was going to be strong.

Corbyn took O'Brian aside in the corridor to commiserate with him. Song wondered how many religious piñatas they would need to go through before Paine found whatever he was looking for, and with what damage to the clock?

'Fuck! What did you think about that?' Townsend asked returning from the wash-room, a fresh waft of *CK Shock* accompanying her.

'We appear to be losing precious time on an ecumenical beauty contest. It's bizarre', said Song.

'Very John Wesley of you, but I agree', she replied through a mouthful of fresh *Wrigley's*. 'And his questioning was so different between the two interviewees. The Behavioral team in Quantico will be buzzing like a toddler on a sugar-shunt at the end of the video feed. Experts will be shredding every syllable and facial twitch for clues. Both ours and his.'

When they resumed thirty minutes later, the suite had been reset minus one seat. During the intermission, Kamamalu had escorted the old man into his bedroom where the TV was carrying an update on the death of New York's tenth victim.

'Did you get much sleep here last night, Gabriel?' small-talked Townsend as they re-entered Paine's suite, shuffling onto the seat next to the reporter.

'Regrettably, no. Whenever I'm working a story every fiber of my being is bent in sacrifice to the creative process.' Across the circle Song snorted his disdain.

As their curious host retook his chair a flash of pain swept across his wizened face, the first time Song had been able to view him as just an ordinary guy getting on in years.

'I've been ruminating about the completion of our team over an excellent double espresso,' announced Paine, 'and whether it's a Mullah, a Rabbi or a Pastor, they're all going to be establishment dumb fucks, aren't they? Here, hand me your list,

Alex. Yes, as I suspected: dull, unimaginative, each emasculated by their dogma's history. I should own up to this being my first miscalculation. I insist on there being some religious representation in our team, but without the dead-hand of an institutional God throttling every conversation. So what can we do - any suggestions team?'

With a start, Song realized they had just been asked a serious question. Paine really did not seem to have an answer. Is this what he had meant by them all working together?

'I'm well versed in the shamanistic rituals of Native American people. No reason why I can't represent both the Bureau and Faith', offered Townsend with an iconoclastic smile.

'So you want someone with a religious calling, but not so close to the church's bureaucracy that they'd be constrained by it?' chipped in Song. If this was the game Paine wanted to play, so be it, but he wanted to help win it - and fast.

'Precisely, David. But how do you find such people?'

'I don't know how many John the Baptist's there are in New York anyway,' shrugged the Californian.

Paine squinted at Song, his brow furrowing as he pursued a fugitive thought. 'I was at home a while ago when a young man came collecting food for the poor', he said eventually. 'When I told him hunger was God's way of thinning his itinerant crop he told me – what did he say exactly? – that I was a "shameful motherfucker who'd spend eternity sucking the Devil's cock." Ha! Can you imagine Monsignor O'Brian saying that? Now you find me an *enfant terrible* like that guy in New York and I'll take it from there.'

'We could do that', replied Corbyn slowly, casting a line into treacherous waters. 'But that's going to take time, and what happens if he fails your interview? So how about us recruiting that guy you met back home?' Song's eyes widened at Corbyn's cunning. If they found Paine's religious firebrand then they would also discover where he lived. Benjamin too was looking on through predatory eyes. A long minute passed as the old man worked through the implications.

'You've caught me unawares, Alex, I must admit. I'll need to make a few adjustments to my plan, but - oh what the hell - okay, I agree!' nodded Paine. 'I'm irritated I didn't think this through properly beforehand, so I'll have to live with the consequences.'

'So what's his name?' asked Corbyn, his voice tight with anticipation.

'I can't remember. We only spoke for a minute, most of which we were cursing each other.'

'So how the hell are we supposed to find him?'

'That's easy. I stuck his calling card to my refrigerator. I'd said his organization could come and collect my peach crop for their soup kitchen. Man cannot live by bread alone.' Song felt the air pressure drop as people held their collective breaths. Was Paine really about to tell them where he lived?

Corbyn formulated his next question as if aiming the last bullet in his gun. 'So where can we find your refrigerator?'

'I'm going to tell you', smiled his tormentor, 'but you've caused me to make a last minute change to plan, so bear with me. First, David, Gabriel, and Nevada will need to take a flight. Once they've arrived I'll give them my address.'

'So where are they going?'

Paine smiled, revealing a palisade of well-kept teeth. 'Have y'all ever been down to North Carolina?'

Chapter 3

A man who has been in danger, when he comes out of it forgets his fears. And sometimes he forgets his promises.

: Euripides

'WHAT ARE YOU THINKING, NEVADA?' ASKED SONG AS THE FBI's chartered jet screamed its way south.

'That Corbyn's a special guy. I've worked with Bureau bosses so jazzed on testosterone they couldn't come up with an interview strategy even if you stapled one to their dicks.' Song gave a mock grimace. 'So what do *you* think?' she asked, daintily wiping a latte moustache from her upper lip.

'I think that I'd like to know what the hell I'm doing here.'

'Ditto. It's driving me crazy. But beyond the narcissism of it all being about you and me, Detective, what else?' Song blushed; she was right, he needed to get beyond this for now. 'Do you *really* not know why you're here, surfer-boy?' she pressed. Song shook his head and shrugged, knowing the importance of responding quickly. She might be in the same situation as him, but she was also Bureau.

Across the aisle Fernandez sat alone, the constant chatter of his keyboard interrupted only by him staring out at the checkerboard of landscape slipping beneath them.

The fuselage door opened and a sandy haired agent wearing a beige wool jacket and a coffee bean colored tie entered. Blessing them all with a wide smile, he introduced himself as Ezekiel Burke, Head of the North Carolina FBI field office.

Exiting the Arrivals Hall, Song was aghast at the huge cavalcade of law enforcement vehicles awaiting their tiny party. 'Welcome to the Confederacy!' quipped Burke chuckling, Townsend raising an eyebrow as she dialed Corbyn's cell to be passed over to Paine.

'I just wanna check the three of you are really there', squawked the old man. 'So humor me by walking over to Courtesy Bus stop B.'

The travel-worn passengers in its queue scattered in dismay as a wedge of three dozen uniformed officers barreled towards them. 'Okay, I'm there', Townsend switched to speakerphone, cranking up the volume.

'Can you see the gum on the timetable?' Paine's voice crackled through the blaring device.

'It's round here!' shouted a state trooper.

Townsend twirled round to the other side of the board, bumping a feverishly scribbling Fernandez out of the way. 'It's on the back of the timetable positioned at three o'clock.'

'Well done!' Paine applauded drily. 'Now make sure you get some of our delicious pecan pie while you're down there, Nevada. My address is 83, Orchard Road, Pender County. Head for Burgaw and then turn east. To save time you're probably thinking of calling Sheriff Le Bon and having his boys turn the place over for you. But if you want them to get home in one piece tonight you should resist that temptation. Call me again when you're there. Oh, and one domestic chore: I don't remember turning off the power before I left, so take a look for me please. Have you seen the price of utilities nowadays?' Then her phone went dead.

The caterpillar of cars swept south from the airport round the southerly tip of Durham. The GMC's security glass made it difficult for Song to see much of the city, their hundred mph speed doubling that problem. Song was alone in the car with Burke who had majestically engineered Fernandez into another. It had been decided Townsend would remain at the airport just in case the address they sought was in the opposite direction to Paine's.

'I know Sheriff Le Bon a little', proffered Burke in his burnished accent. 'He's a good man, but I've found it helps move things along if you show people in the rural communities a little respect.'

'Well', said Song checking caller ID on his vibrating phone, 'in San Francisco the Feds normally get jack-shit from me if they don't bend over and take one from time to time, so we're in agreement on that.' Burke beamed an appreciative smile. 'Big Bird, you missing me already, or is there a crossword clue I can help you with?' shouted Song to his San Francisco partner above the modulating siren's din.

'It's only been a day and I can hardly remember your butt-ugly face', came the instant reply. 'And since when have you ever helped me out with a crossword clue, dumbass? I'm with Hardiman today and he buys me donuts and crap, so I don't care if you never come back. Just thought I'd let you know I'm being grilled by the Bureau. I don't know what you've been up to Davey boy, but it better be worth the shit I'm taking from these fuckers.'

'Thanks TK, but don't get too close to Hardiman. I'll be back soon and if I find any donut sugar on my seat there'll be words between us.'

'If it's just sugar on the seat you're worried about....'

Raleigh quickly disappeared in the rear view mirror, the highway now flanked by emergent wheat fields on either side. Song couldn't see a crop of any variety without recalling his mother's black and white pictures of her family's rice fields in the north of Vietnam before they had moved down to Saigon. It was that initial proximity to the Chinese-Vietnamese border which meant she had been able to teach Song both those languages. His mind was still lost in those grainy images when the siren's blare was punctuated by a helicopter's unmistakable chatter.

'What's happening?' enquired Song, peering skywards.

'I figured all the commotion might attract our flying media friends' answered Burke. 'Our vehicles will peel off as decoys at each exit to take the choppers with them. We should be unobserved by the time we get to Burgaw. Though there's nothing to stop Mr. Fernandez from making a call to keep his aerial brethren on track.'

'Yes there is - it's called greed', snorted Song. 'He won't want to share this scoop with anyone else.'

At just after three that afternoon, unobserved from above they pulled off the I40 at the junction with the 53 at Burgaw. Up ahead two of the Sheriff's vehicles accelerated off in a cloud of dust providing an escort to Orchard Road. Song knew they would be shitting themselves, as yesterday he too would have been if all this commotion had happened in his back yard.

The approach to Paine's house was down a two hundred yard dirt track flanked by peach trees sprouting the season's new leaves. In a few months their ageing boughs would be straining under the weight of plump fruit playing host to the hungry ballet of dancing wasps. At the drive's end stood the frontage of a cream painted, clapboard building already illuminated by the red and blue pulsating lights of six police vehicles.

Standing hunched in front of them, Sheriff Ritchie Le Bon was a seriously worried looking man. 'Agent Song, I've established a perimeter around the property', shaking the Californian's hand with one just dried on his pants.

'Thanks, but it's Detective Sergeant. I'm with the San Francisco PD, and please call me David.' Song swore he saw Le Bon grow an inch with the relief. Fernandez stood silently close by, an unused pad in his hand. Song looked down and spied a concealed recorder. There was nothing he could do about any of this bullshit; he would just have to let the Bureau's lawyers sort it out later.

'Begging your pardon, but what is it that Tom's supposed to have done?'

'All I can tell you, Ritchie, is he's helping us out with a case. The CSI's are on their way from Durham, but time isn't on my side so I'm going in there alone right now.'

'What exactly are you looking for?'

'I need to get to the refrigerator.'

'Jeez, there ain't no body parts in it, are there?!' blurted Le Bon.

'No,' or at least Song hoped not, 'I just need something that's on it.' Song strode towards the still house through the phalanx of police officers that parted unasked. A two-person swing hung from the porch ceiling, its chains looking freshly oiled. The drapes were open, but nets occluded the view inside. It was the picture of normality. The perfect subject for a Norman Rockwell study of a traditional rural home nestled in a sleepy farming community. Its owners out in the bronzed fields that stretched into the horizon, threshing corn with century old implements.

Song noticed the claustrophobic silence, peeking round to check everyone was still there. They stared back at him, their curiosity stilling the natural agitation of professionals at a crime scene. In the absence of the spoken word, Fernandez had taken to writing on his pad again. The surrealism of the situation welled up once again in Song. Yesterday he'd been staring out towards the Pacific. Now he was in spitting distance of the Atlantic having been invited there by a bomber to look at his refrigerator. Completely insane. Song dialed Corbyn who answered on the first ring before handing it to Paine.

'I'm standing outside your house, so what is it you wanted to tell me?'

'First, I need to check you're really there. Move onto the porch.' Song climbed two scuffed wooden steps that amplified the tap of his heels. 'There are numbers scratched into the side of the doorframe at head-height, what are they?'

'One hundred and sixty seven – or one, six, and seven', replied Song, the bare wood beneath the freshly scratched paint rendering them clearly visible.

'Correct, welcome to my home! Now I don't want you to get nervous, but I rigged a little anti-personnel device just inside the front door to deter unwanted visitors.' Song shivered as a freeze spread across his limbs. Yesterday one of this man's "little anti-personnel" devices had shredded ten people. 'I didn't expect anyone to be getting there so soon, and just to look at my refrigerator for Christ's sake! Door's not locked, so open it about five inches and un-hook the wire at knee height. Don't push too far or you'll be raining down on Burgaw in chicken-nugget sized pieces.'

Song's training told him he should really await the arrival of the Bomb Squad, but time wasn't his friend right now. The speaker rustled, as Corbyn retrieved the phone from Paine's hand.

'Don't go in, David. That's an order. Agent Burke will contact the Squad.'

Song had never thought of himself as a hero, but he wasn't a coward either. He had learnt from Sun Tzu's *Art of War* that the greatest skill of battle was how to avoid one. But today – on this prosaic North Carolinian porch - there was too much at stake for faint hearts. He looked down at his white knuckled hand wrapped around the door knob. All this shit for a scrap of cardboard on a kitchen appliance. Unbelievable.

'Step away from the door, Detective Sergeant. That's a direct order', adjured Corbyn in a stentorian tone.

'Sorry, Alex - no can do', Song replied at last, disconnecting the call. Immediately he punched the speed dial for Burke's number, hearing the chimes of Vivaldi's *Four Seasons* to the rear of him followed by the Agent's voice strangely in his ear and behind him at the same time. Corbyn couldn't reach either of them now.

'Stay on the line with me, Zeke. Tell the boys to get behind anything shrapnel proof.'

Song was crouching now, one hand holding the phone, the other about to twist the knob as multiple pairs of feet scrambled for cover. Song peered at the door frame as if the flood of adrenalin might have miraculously endowed him with X-ray vision. Interesting: why leave the door unlocked but then rig it to deter intruders? His hand tightened, the porch creaking as he rocked back and forth. Song thought about the emerging pathology of Paine. A calm man, very comfortable in control, un-hurried in everything he did, quite playful in his own way.

Playful.

He thought back to Nevada's airport call, something scratching at his instincts. Song let go of the handle, stepping back a pace. 'Ritchie, can your men scout round for the power junction please.' A shout came up to the right, Song walking round to a gaggle of officers in a half circle around a grey painted box. Fernandez was there sketching the scene. Hadn't he heard of phone cams? Song eased his way through the crowd, giving the switch a quarter turn to the *Off* position before returning to the front door, as did the men to crouch again behind their cars.

'Be careful, David', offered Fernandez with the slight hint of a Spanish accent as he scuttled to the rear of the biggest SUV, his handmade shoes powdered with farm dust.

Song caught Burke's eye, the Agent holding the live phone uselessly to his ear. 'Just how long is this call going to take, David? There'll be some people in New York trying to reach me on this phone, I'm sure', he said, grinning. Song returned the compliment, placing his hand back on the door knob, still wet with his sweat from before. He thought of the Vietnamese kitchen god, Ong Tao. If he was present in Paine's, Song hoped he was smiling on him today.

He snicked the door open five inches. The thin piece of twisted wire was exactly where Paine said it would be. Song stared at it for a few seconds, drew in a pearl-diver's breath and then lifted the hooked end out of its eye on the door frame. Gently he pushed the door open. Five inches at first, then twelve, until finally it stood fully ajar. Exhaling at last, Song took one stride into the musty hall.

If it had been preternaturally quiet outside, there was a mortuary stillness inside. Motes of dust lazily intersected stilettos of light streaming in through the parlor window. He stood, feet together like a man retreating onto the last cube of a once vast ice sheet. Behind him the wire and tangle of electrical cables disappeared into a freshly drilled hole in the oiled wooden floor. Song terminated the now redundant call to Burke, taking big steps to minimize his forensic footprint. Pushing through a battered door he entered a standard country kitchen with a worn pine table, a stone work surface, and a large porcelain sink looking out onto the back yard. Hand towels were draped neatly across rails, and there in the far corner stood a cream *GE* refrigerator, its usual comforting hum killed now by the recent absence of power.

In four long paces he was there, eyes hunting the magnetic buttons for their target. There, underneath a water bill, was his prize. Song took a photo of it and dialed Townsend.

'The name is Bradley Scott, written by hand on a business card printed with the address of the *Raleigh-Durham Christian Fishermen*'. Song heard her issuing instructions to a driver followed by the heavy rev of an engine and the familiar sound of sirens as they sped on their way.

'What was that stuff about no-one getting hurt?' she asked, Song explaining about the trip wire. 'Son of a bitch! This guy's a piece of work. But at least he was good enough to give you the warning', she opined.

'Maybe, but remember his quip to you about not running-up the utilities bill? It got me thinking, so I killed the power before I entered. I'll be interested to hear from the Bomb Squad what would have happened if I hadn't.'

⸺

Corbyn's face had the color of a tornado sky after Song had hung up on him. 'Let's see how good a detective he really is', Paine had observed laying sprawled on the bed, surfing the wall-to-wall TV coverage of yesterday's events.

Hitting the redial to the Californian for the eighteenth time Corbyn finally go through, stepping out into corridor trailed by a cloud of his own invective.

'David, I can't tell you how monumentally pissed off I am with you,' the Special Agent barked. 'This asshole already has ten deaths to his account and I'll be fucked if I'm going to be part of making it eleven. When you get back here we're going to have as serious a fucking talk as you've ever had.'

'Sure, Alex, I understand', Song's patient reply, knowing that he couldn't fault the man's anger. 'Meanwhile, is Paine there with you?' Corbyn stalked back to the old man whose nose was deep into a well-read *Washington Post*. 'Tell Paine thanks for the utilities tip, and that I owe him one.' Corbyn conveyed the message, puzzled at what it meant.

Paine smiled knowingly. 'Heck of a detective you've got there, Alex. He'll prove to be a great asset to our team. If he can only keep himself alive...'

⸺

Half an hour after Song had exited the building the Bomb Squad drove up cussing openly about the insanity of him entering an unsecured building. Le Bon had found a set of garden furniture for them to sit on at the side of the house, Fernandez preferring the company of the local officers. Song stared at this literary peacock strutting around the back yard, pecking at the grains of information dropped by honest police officers.

'I've told my boys to be polite to the reporter - but not too polite. Don't want him knowing more than the investigative team, do we?' shared Le Bon, following Song's gaze.

'So what can you tell me about Tom?' Song re-directed, taking a swig of bottled water brought from the Sheriff's car. Not for the first time that afternoon Le Bon removed his wide brimmed hat to wipe his forehead.

'Not much. He was here when I moved over from Piedmont County. I've seen him around town, ooh, maybe half a dozen times? I'm thinking he lives on his own on account of me never seeing anybody else, except for his two dogs. Yep, never had any trouble from Tom, and he never reported no trouble neither.' Song hadn't noticed any trace of dogs in the house; no food bowls in the kitchen or any other canine paraphernalia.

'Is there anyone around here who might be looking after them?'

'None that I can think of. Reckon I never heard anybody speak of Tom much.'

'Word of today is going to travel quickly,' observed Song, wondering if Paine had taken the dogs with him to New York, 'so here's the cover story: Thomas Paine is currently out of state helping law enforcement agencies with a case. He is not under arrest, and his assistance is proving invaluable to our investigations.'

A look of mystification settled on Le Bon's face. 'Who's Thomas Paine? The Tom who lives here is called Thomas Lane.'

'What?' exclaimed Song, 'Are you sure?'

'One hundred percent. I can't explain the explosives and shit, but are you sure you've got the right man?' The moment was interrupted by a uniformed man from the North Carolina Bomb Squad, playfully tossing something in the air.

'We've removed the device', he confirmed in clipped tones, 'and our dogs have been through the house. It was clean except for this charge', holding up a cube four inches on each side. 'It's C4, and the detonator's inserted here', pointing to a gash. 'Nothing fancy', he explained flatly, as if defusing a bomb was about as dangerous as programming a DVD recorder. 'The trigger was the wire attached to the doorframe. The detonator looks at first glance to be standard military issue from some time back. We also found a can of fuel under the porch which would have combusted making for a very effective fire bomb.'

'Holy Mother!' muttered Fernandez in studied shock, attracted to the Bomb Squad as any moth to the promise of a flame. 'And what kind of damage can that amount of C4 do?' licking hungrily at his nib.

'Terminal. The blast would have obliterated a good portion of the front, the fire torching the rest.'

Including me, thought Song, trying to stay focused enough to ask his next question. 'Triggers of this sort deliver an electrical charge to the detonator, correct? So what was the power source for this one?'

'This received its juice directly from the mains. There was no battery. I don't know what prompted you to turn off the power, Detective, but it most definitely saved your life.'

Townsend's four car convoy screeched to a halt in a herringbone pattern outside a warehouse located four miles from the airport. A plywood sign painted bright red proclaimed the *Raleigh-Durham Christian Fishermen* in daffodil yellow, the crude logo of a net boasting a single fish completing the design. She pushed open a rasping swing door leading into a large space dotted with decrepit furniture. In the far corner several tables supporting huge pans were surrounded by people mopping the floor.

'Agent Nevada Townsend with the FBI', she shouted, ID waving above her head. 'We're looking for a Bradley Scott?'

'That - that's me. Is there some kind of trouble, Officer?' said a crumpled looking young man rising from a battered old chair. His face was all surprise, the one Townsend had come to recognize whenever the FBI came calling.

'A private word with you over here please', she indicated with her head. The dozen people spread across the warehouse's expanse pretended to resume their manual work. 'Do you know a Mr. Thomas Paine?' observing up close that this man in his early thirties could do with a hot bath. Scott looked naturally thin-framed, but she suspected some of the missing pounds might be related the irregularity of his meals.

The grubby man looked up at the muddy windows as if their insipid light might help illuminate his memory. 'Nope. There's only a handful of Tom's around here, and I don't think none of them's called Paine. Why, what's he done?'

'He's not from around here. He lives down in Pender County. You *have* met him because you gave him this business card', holding up Song's relayed picture, Scott squinting to recognize his own handwriting.

'Shit lady, I've given thousands of these away to homeless people. Does he have a street handle?'

'He's not a homeless person. He says you exchanged words when you visited his house. You called him something abusive?'

'I can't recall cussing anyone in particular, and why's the FBI involved in something chicken-shit like that anyhow?' Scott protested, eyeing the burly men either side of the diminutive agent.

'We just need to know if you remember him.' Settling down again, Scott stared vacantly at the image on the phone. Not too quick this one, thought Townsend just before his face registered a glimmer of recognition.

'Oh yeah! Some old guy; lived on a farm down Pender way. Apples or peaches; a year or so back? Some of the farmers let us have crops close to spoiling and we bring them back to our soup kitchen', he waved his arm indicating the makeshift canteen behind him. 'Old timer really pissed me off. Didn't catch his name though.'

'He says you called him a motherfucker?'

Scott looked at her as though this was something he would not have expected to hear from a female FBI agent. 'If he says so, and as he has my card then I probably did, yeah. When I get antsy I have a wide vocabulary. Why, is he dead or something? Ain't nothing to do with me – I got witnesses!'

Townsend surfed the adrenalin of success. 'No, not dead, but you do need to come with us.'

'Shit, I ain't got time to go down to Pender. There's evening meals to prepare here for the homeless.'

'No, not Pender County, Mr. Scott. New York City.'

The Squad had departed, promising to send an urgent report on the C4. It was common knowledge that each batch carried a distinctive chemical marker and it was this they would be looking for. Le Bon's team was sweeping increasingly wider concentric circles around the house through the orchard and beyond, trailed by a sweating Fernandez taking his incessant notes. Song dialed Corbyn, hoping he had calmed down. The Lane identity was explained and within minutes thousands of Bureau personnel across the nation were crawling all over it. Then Song screwed up his eyes and told Corbyn about the power.

'So if you hadn't turned it off, you'd be dead? And you only worked it out because of some oblique reference Paine made at the airport?'

'Correct.' Song's replies were deliberately economical, wanting to see if Corbyn ended up in the same deductive place as him.

'But Paine wouldn't have known he was on speaker-phone when he was talking to Nevada, so you really could have died down there', the Special Agent's mind laying down the track of his thoughts just ahead of the wheels. 'Is this the reason he's brought the three of you together – so that he can walk you into his traps? It's way too convoluted. And this one's come faster than planned because of O'Brian's failed interview.'

Song had been pondering the exact same puzzle. 'It feels more about a Rites of Passage deal than a serious attempt to take me out. He's enjoying the chase as much as the kill. We should use that to our advantage.'

'Maybe. But I'm still going to tear you that second asshole for disobeying me.'

There was a shout from the officers searching the back yard. Song hung up and walked across the manicured lawn to join the huddle underneath the boughs of an old beech tree. Everyone was staring down at two cuts in the ground covered by a shallow heap of spoil. Perched on top of each was a white stone the size of a side plate.

'Sheriff, I'd appreciate you finding out what's underneath these stones.'

It was nine thirty that evening when the weary travelers ran across the apron at JFK. Kamamalu greeted them with cold pepperoni pizza which they gobbled down as though it were *Michelin* starred fare. Fernandez behaved as though this were the first time he had ever consumed something quite so proletarian.

'I've never been to New York before', stated Scott, nose super-glued to the SUV's window as it hurtled through phosphorescent-lit streets, his torn shirt riding-up to reveal submarine grey underwear that had once been white.

'Well, he certainly ain't no Monsignor O'Brian', Song whispered to Nevada.

'Do we go past the Twin Towers?' Scott asked disingenuously.

'No one goes past them anymore', replied Townsend quietly, silencing further conversation.

It was a Friday night and the Marriott had emptied its cargo of businessmen back to tidy suburban homes across this and other continents. Song whisked Scott into an elevator held gaping by three impassive agents.

Corbyn had found the time to shower and change between his continuous pressing of their guest and his equally pressing discussions with senior political stakeholders. In the corridor he shook Scott's limp hand and thanked him for coming, avoiding eye contact with Song. Benjamin too just glowered at the Californian. Wow, thought Song, they really were pissed with him.

'Paine's focus will be on you, Bradley, but please don't react, no matter what he says', Corbyn cautioned in his most honeyed tones.

'Then we can all go home?' asked the Fisherman of Galilee, pacing back and forth across the passage as if in a cage.

'We don't know yet', replied the Special Agent kindly.

'Shit, I wish I'd never knocked on his door to ask for those peaches. It sure doesn't happen this way on TV.'

It never does, thought Song, but at least *you* know why you're here.

———

At midnight Song was finally feeling the effects of two days of high drama, broken sleep, plane-hopping, and near death when Paine entered the room. He had dozens of personal questions to rattle off at this man, the rodeo in his stomach still bucking with multiple theories as to why he had been summoned, but these would have to wait.

Scott was the only one to look directly at this old man who had torn him from his beloved soup kitchens in North Carolina.

'Ah, is this the angry apostle?' enquired Paine, extending a hand that was studiously ignored.

'Bradley Scott's the name, and why have you brought me here?' barked the Fisherman, instantly forgetting Corbyn's plea for restraint.

Paine eased into his seat, nursing some weakness in his back. 'That's a fair question, Brad, but this gathering's not about you, my young friend.'

'It's not Brad, it's Mr. Scott to you, and I'm not your fucking friend', as though Corbyn had never briefed him. The cameras whirred, relaying every breathtaking second to enthralled audiences in D.C. and Quantico. 'The man I met in Pender was a proud farmer with opinions he was prepared to defend. Whereas you - you piece of shit - are a cowardly fucking murderer', fists balled, face cinnamon red. Not only hadn't he understood Corbyn's briefing, reflected Song, but he was even beginning to make Monsignor O'Brian look good.

Paine smiled thinly, locking his eyes on the Fisherman's. 'You credulous, God-fearing, shit-for-brains '.

'You soulless, motherfucking, ass-wipe', spat back Scott. Song wondered what the Monsignor would had made of this erudite theological exchange.

Paine rewarded Scott with a graveyard grin. 'Congratulations Alex! You've found the right man and thus completed my requirements. The team is formed and I'm prepared to disclose the whereabouts of the three devices.' He looked at his watch. 'Let's reconvene at ten hundred hours and I'll tell you then.' Song rolled his eyes and sucked in the room's stale air.

Corbyn scrambled for dry land. 'Hold on, Thomas! Given the extraordinary efforts we've made today, I really need those locations now.'

Paine made a show of thinking about it before shaking his head. 'No, I'm tired, and you'll still have plenty of time, trust me on this.'

'Alright, give us two now and one later', burst in Song unasked, Benjamin throwing daggered looks in his direction. Paine hesitated, hands on knees. 'Come on, Thomas, help Alex out here. His Boss is at the other end of these cameras so he badly needs a win. It would be the *team* thing to do', entreated Song.

'I'm not interested in his Boss. Our team's me, Alex, Gabriel, Nevada, you, and - as of tonight - Mr. Scott. Everyone else is irrelevant. But to prove to our new recruit here that I'm not as small minded as he thinks, I'll give you one location now.' Paine paused, deciding which to nominate, spinning the revolver's chambers. 'Go to St. Bartholomew's Elementary School in Spokane, Washington. Look at the ceiling in the refectory. Good night and good hunting, ladies and gentlemen.'

As the old man's bedroom door closed, Song heard Fernandez's incredulous whisper. 'Holy Mother, he's bombing the children.'

Song rose at six thirty a.m. that Saturday and took a long shower, slowly broiling the skin between his shoulder blades. It was beginning to grow uncomfortable, which was exactly how he had felt last night as the meeting broke up. Corbyn had taken him to the emergency stairs for privacy where he had proceeded to tear him that promised second asshole, and then a third just for luck.

'I gave you a direct order at Pender and you disobeyed me. You don't officially report to me, so in the absence of any command relationship I have to rely entirely upon your professionalism.'

'I understand your concerns,' Song had replied down the echoing stair-well, his own temper rising, 'but it seems to me Paine will allow his invitees more latitude than he will you and the Feds. Nevada, Gabriel and I are here for a reason and I refuse to believe it's just as bomb fodder. You saw how he reacted when I played this "team" thing with him earlier; we got St. Bartholomew's as a result. So if you think I'm just gonna sit around this group therapy circle reading exclusively from the Bureau's script, then you'd better ship me out and get a replacement. Oh, that's right, you can't do that, can you?'

At breakfast Song heaped plates high with food he knew he would never finish. Booting up his iPad he reviewed his mail. There were four from Charley. Although not his sister by blood, she was the daughter of his mother's closest friend and they had grown up together in the tight Vietnamese community of San Francisco. There were no secrets between them, and over his third cup of coffee he wondered what he could tell her now. He looked down at his screen-saver: a smiling picture of them both atop Coit Tower, with San Francisco's golden vista the perfect backdrop for her raven hair. Was that the sea air he could still smell from that day, or the intoxicating perfume on her neck?

She wrote: *Answer your goddamn cell! Seriously - what are you doing in Carrie Bradshaw's neighborhood? Got anyone pregnant back here brother?*

He wished he had - but not just anyone.

Charley's real brother, Gary Dok, had sent mail from the MIT address where he was a Professor in Information Systems. Gary was at the academic razor edge of internet innovation, the virtual metropolis that was, as Gary said, truly the only City That Never Sleeps.

'How much mail did you get and what have you been telling people?' probed Townsend creeping up from behind.

'Morning to you too. Fifty eight and nothing in that order. You?'

'Five. Some of my relatives still use fires and blankets to communicate, don't you know. Now shut up honey and get me some coffee while I catch up on events.'

The bombs' aftermath was still dominating the news above and below the fold, or rather the scroll line. However, there was one item conspicuously missing: St. Bartholomew's.

Googling it had only thrown up the usual listings of school theater productions and fund raising events. Handing Nevada her drip coffee, Song clicked the photo of its Principal, a smiling woman with political eyes. She would need those today, he thought.

'They're not gonna try and cover the school up, are they?' Song asked, fishing for Townsend's Bureau insight.

'It's a school for Christ's sake - you can see why they might', she ventured. 'Just look at Fernandez's instinctive reaction last night. Paine's in the barn that stores the country's seed corn, and he's carrying a tinderbox. There'd be wholesale panic.'

'And we're just about to find out Paine's final two locations. The cop in me senses we haven't seen the worst of it yet.'

Three new women were busying themselves on a bank of PCs and phones in the hotel's make-shift operations suite, each scanning different sites boasting FBI banners. 'Corbyn insists we keep the team here to a minimum, but don't be fooled by the paucity of resources' explained Townsend. 'Outside this room virtually every jarhead in the Bureau and Homeland is working the case. We're just a few corks bobbing on top of an ocean of national activity.'

Karen Oppenheim, a Senior Analyst with the Bureau, introduced herself as their back-office's team leader. She was around the same age as Song and Townsend, with bottled blond hair, wearing a dark grey pantsuit and a Celtic ring. 'So far only nine content-rich comments across two hundred Red Flagged sites,' she explained. 'Over there,' she pointed to a woman speaking to Corbyn, 'we have a third level monitor running on the thirty six Red Flagged people who've expressed an unnatural interest in the case. But that's just thirty six out of the thirty three million people who've commented about the incidents in mail, texts, or some other format.'

'Thirty three million!' repeated Song, impressed.

'After 9/11 the number of comments logged over one week was 3.3 billion in the USA alone,' shared Oppenheim, her hands ghosting across the keys.

'Any patterns developing?'

'To generate a pattern we need nodal data points, and we simply don't have any. This Paine/Lane guy's a mystery. If there are others out there working with him they'll be off line for now, maybe forever.'

At 0300hrs a SWAT team in Washington state had entered St. Bartholomew's under a strict blanket of secrecy, explained Corbyn to the team. They found a wooden plate screwed across two concrete supports in the ceiling space, careful removal of which had exposed a hole containing a pine box nursing a slab of C4. They found a detonator but no evidence of a trigger: no wires, no battery, no radio receiver. The business end of a bomb, but stripped of any command device. But that didn't matter, thought Song. In cases where children were involved the ability of adults to imagine the horrific worst was almost as corrosive as the act itself. Had this been Paine's intention here?

Homeland Security Agent Benjamin's briefing confirmed that the C4 at Precinct 19 had been placed in the wall space above the reception's window, designed to create a percussive blast propelling brick-work and glass shrapnel into both street and building. The Homeland man read their blank faces.

'I know what you're thinking. Until now we'd assumed he walked in off the street with the bomb, so how the fuck did he manage this?'

'Do we have anything more on the device at Paine's house?' asked Song, not liking this attenuated line-by-line briefing of events. It felt as though he was being treated like Fernandez, not as a cop.

'I was getting to that', snipped Benjamin with a flush of irritation. 'Lab confirms the C4 was manufactured in 1987. The military detonator originating from a batch made in 1999.' He looked up knowing their minds would again be grinding as much as his had done. How could a man in his sixties get his hands on high grade munitions, let alone get the opportunity to plant them in such a wide range of targets?

'Tell them about the search, Nate', encouraged Corbyn, as if coaxing a misdemeanor out of a child.

'Paine's house has yielded nothing further of interest. No bomb-making materials, no relevant literature - nothing. It's completely clean, completely normal.'

'What did they find in the back yard?' pursued Song, forcing Benjamin to turn laboriously to another page.

'The cuts in the ground contained the bodies of two Labradors buried two feet down: one black, one yellow. Presumably these were the dogs your Sheriff Le Bon mentioned.'

'Aw no. The bastard!' yelped Townsend involuntarily, Benjamin continuing unabashed.

'Dead no longer than four days, as though he didn't want them to suffer while he was gone. How very thoughtful. They also found a garbage can used to burn garden waste. In it were the charred remains of a desktop PC, but there was nothing left to salvage.'

'We're checking all his net presences and general documentation. So far nothing relevant', added Oppenheim.

'What about news coverage of St. Bartholomew's?' pressed Song.

Corbyn shifted nervously onto one leg. 'The school's been closed while officials investigate a possible asbestos problem.'

'And this is to prevent the spread of further - ', Song searched for the phrase, 'public destabilization?'

'Yes, but panic is the word you're looking for.'

'Do you think Paine will be okay with that?'

'What do you mean?'

'Well, it strikes me that – apart from the Precinct – he's chosen targets and times that haven't maximized his kill potential. The causality isn't casualties – forgive me the word game – it's more about his choice of targets and what happens in advance of the detonations. In the absence of any demands we can still only guess his motive, but I predict he won't be pleased we're covering-up the school.'

Corbyn nodded as he thought. 'You may be right, which is why I've focused Quantico on working up his personality profile. Kamamalu tells me Paine slept little last night, and they had to replace the remote's batteries given his constant channel surfing for news about his acts. He'll know about St. Bartholomew's now, so how he reacts will tell us more about him.'

'Okay, but it's going to leak eventually – it always does', commented Song. 'And then people are going to wonder if they can trust the authorities.'

'It's not "the authorities", Detective Sergeant', put in Benjamin sharply. 'It's *us*. We're all on the same team here. And if questioned you'll be expected to support the decision made on our behalf. Same rules as when you're back in Fruit and Nut Land and it's your Bosses there taking the hits to protect your ass.'

Song held Benjamin's eye. 'You're right, Nate. I apologize', he said at last. 'It *is* one team and I consider myself a member of it. But if I can behave that way, why can't you?'

'When I'm satisfied you're beyond suspicion, I will', shot back the Homeland Agent. 'Until then I have no other option but to regard you with caution. And if you were me you'd do the same.'

Benjamin was right, and therein lay the heart of Song's frustration. He knew he was innocent, but his invitation to this macabre piece of street theater was an hourly reminder to everyone that maybe he wasn't.

As the meeting broke up, Townsend pulled Song aside. 'If it's any consolation I'm in the same situation. I may be Bureau, but I've had that same bullshit from Benjamin in private. The good news is that Corbyn's already beyond it. Letting us out of the cage yesterday was his way of showing it.'

'Interesting, I didn't realize we were in a cage.'

'Then try booking a flight back to San Francisco on your lonesome and see how far you get. Make no mistake about it, Paine's not the only one under lock and key in this hotel.'

The *Detroit News'* Sports Editor was late in that Saturday morning, shouldering his way through darting interns to his cluttered desk. Last night he had returned from vacationing in

Aruba, the excruciating lobster-redness from those first days on the lemon sand now peeling away. His interior lineman's frame flopped onto his much abused chair. The desk was covered in Post-its and snail mail, some helpfully opened by the Sports Desk's PA, and some unhelpfully not.

'Nice tan', shouted a colleague from across the way. 'If I throw you my bagel can you toast it for me on your gut?'

'I'll stick it between my butt-cheeks and do both sides for you at the same time, jerk-off!' he growled back, the purple ink on an A4 envelope catching his attention.

Strictly Personal, to be opened by the Sports Editor only. His lump hammer fingers tore it open, yanking out a single typed sheet of paper.

'Son of a bitch!' he said out loud. 'SON OF A BITCH! Hey, you! Anyone! How can I reach our esteemed owner on a Saturday morning?'

As they entered the room, Paine was standing with his back to the window on this bright April morning. Song pondered that a man in control would deliberately position himself there. He allowed Paine's daguerreotype image to burn into his mind in remembrance of a man he hoped never to see again after today. In the corridor Fernandez had been trying to interview Scott as unobtrusively as possible but the ragged North Carolinian had been monosyllabic in his responses, escaping into Paine's room before Kamamalu had fully opened the door.

'Good morning', began Paine, again hijacking the meeting. 'Before we begin, I wonder whether Bradley could start us off with a prayer?' Scott's features were a mask of disgust but Corbyn had been coaching him, so with a sigh of irritation he bowed his head.

'Heavenly father we ask that You look after the innocent souls of those who've died in these tragic bombings. We ask Your help in closing this case quickly and we pray for the soul of Thomas Paine. We know he won't be joining You up there, but hope You'll help this cock-sucker see the error of his ways before his appointment with Lucifer. Amen!' Corbyn was going to have to spend more time with this young man thought Song smiling, as Fernandez delightedly filled another page in his pad.

'I promised to give you the location of the two devices', observed Paine, paying no attention to Scott's imprecations. 'However, I couldn't help notice St. Bartholomew's absence in the news?'

Corbyn had already run his intended reply past a dozen people at Quantico. 'That's right. An executive decision has been taken to avoid any unnecessary disruption.' Song noting the use of "executive" as a not-so-subtle way of flagging that the decision had been made elsewhere.

'Very well, that's your choice and ultimately your responsibility', replied Paine, Song not liking the sound of that. 'So, ladies and gentlemen, I would advise you to get to these next locations before midnight.' A slight hesitation, purely for effect. 'You'll find one in a crematorium. The other you'll find at 520, 12th Avenue, in this fair city of New York'. Song and Townsend looked mystified at each other, turning imploringly to the whirring cameras for the identity of that address. Song imagined a vast army in D.C. and Quantico on the fast-draw to Google it.

'A crematorium', repeated Corbyn, allowing them time to do just that. 'Where exactly?'

'I had intended to tell you, but this "executive decision" to hush-up St. Bartholomew's is not in-keeping with how I want our relationship developing, so this is the consequence. Start looking now in the thousands of crematoriums across the U.S.

and you might get lucky in the next few hours. If not, the bonus is that any fatalities won't have far to travel.' Corbyn made to protest, Paine interrupting with a raised index finger. 'While your minions search for that other address, I have one thing further to add.' The cell in Corbyn's pocket rang unanswered.

'Furnishing you with these two locations concludes the first chapter of our work. If you want to discover the whereabouts of the device detonating next Wednesday – in four day's time –this team needs to meet with me again at 1000hrs that day in a location I'll notify you of later. It's been fun so far, people, but now it gets really interesting.'

Song's mind was overwhelmed by new questions giving way to half-answers, each then evicted by new questions. *So this wasn't the end of it?* In truth he had suspected it wouldn't be. For one, the mystery of his participation in this curious morality play wasn't even close to being understood yet. As Corbyn distractedly took the insistent call, Song caught Townsend's eye, each staring impassively at the other. Looking now to Fernandez, Song could have sworn he saw a flash of relief on the man's closely-shaven face. That this shooting star of a story might yet turn out to be a lengthy media comet. Then finally on to Scott whose simple face just looked as confused as ever.

'Okay, you know who to contact', instructed a shocked looking Corbyn, reminding Song of the DUI victim's he had seen. Corbyn looked levelly at his entranced audience and then at his grinning tormentor before clearing his throat.

'Number 520, 12th Avenue, New York City is the consulate of the People's Republic of China.'

'Correct!' erupted Paine, flicking his hands into the air like an amateur magician. 'Now does anyone here speak Mandarin Chinese?'

Chapter 4

What we fear comes to pass more speedily than what we hope

: Publilius

THEY RAN ACROSS THE MARRIOT'S FOYER SCATTERING bellhops and marooned businessmen alike, SUV engines purring ready to accelerate. Song veered towards Corbyn's vehicle, Benjamin half-turning to find him on his six.

'Not this ride, Song.'

'*Wei shen ma?* Why?' barked Song, continuing again in Mandarin. '*How's your knowledge of Chinese culture, shit-head?*' Benjamin looked back blankly at him before sourly ordering out one of the agents to make room. The doors hadn't closed properly before they were screeching into the stream of traffic, sirens wailing in a pattern that seemed to have repeated itself time and again over the past forty eight hours. Just two days, thought Song. Incredible.

Corbyn hung up on his ninth consecutive conversation, his normally crisp white shirt with its perpendicular blue tie respectively looking grey and crooked. 'Bombing a sovereign piece of China on American soil. Very clever, Thomas,' he said out loud about the man who had been whistling David Bowie's *China Girl* as they'd sprinted from his room. 'What are you thinking, David?'

'That no one's wanted to use the "terrorist" word until now. People have referred to the incidents, the attacks, the devices, and virtually any other word except terrorism. Since 9/11 we've focused on some foreign nemesis out there somewhere, in a cave or a training camp. But now we have Paine. One of our own is bombing America, and we still don't know why. We've been unable to protect people in their homes, at work, at school, and now with the crematorium not even in death. Hell, it seems we can't protect our diplomatic guests either.'

Corbyn's answered yet another call in monosyllables. 'The Consul-General's at a golf tournament in The Hamptons and a rule of the competition is that everyone turns off their phones. Frigging unbelievable! His deputy is a Mr. Zhang Win Fen. State are sending over translators, but please stay close just in case, David.'

Two minutes out from the Consulate, Corbyn's phone rang yet again. Corbyn listened intently before hanging up wordlessly. Even Kamamalu risked a quick glance at his Boss in the rear view mirror. 'This morning the *Detroit News'* Sports Desk received a letter signed by a Thomas Paine detailing attacks upon all six locations, including St. Bartholomew's,' Corbyn paused to shake his head, 'the Consulate, and the crematorium. So in addition to the helpful people from State, the press are already there to greet us too. Welcome to Purgatory, gentlemen.'

Flinging open the door, Corbyn was immediately engulfed by a crowd of agents and officers, Benjamin elbowing his way through to stand at the Special Agent's side. The police were enforcing a blockade one hundred yards either side of the consulate, while others poured into neighboring buildings sending weekend personnel running for cover. Overhead two media choppers vied for airspace like insane adornments on a crib mobile.

'So we were right about not hushing up the school', opined Townsend appearing at Song's side. 'The press are gonna shred us: Kindergarten Killers, Terro R' Us.'

'And Paine says there's a seventh device in four days time. Son of a bitch! Any thoughts about that?' added Song.

'Only bad ones', she replied, peering glumly at the gathering throng of cameras at each of the barriers.

'I've never been to New York before', interrupted Scott, as if nothing were happening. 'Say, is this place close to Central Park?' Townsend looked levelly at Song, calling up *MapQuest* to entertain their grown-up child.

At the Mobile Control Room Corbyn stood flanked by men from the State Department. Alongside them hovered three nervous Chinese, two with hand-guns barely concealed under ill-fitting jackets. Corbyn waved Song over. 'The interpreter's not here yet and Deputy Consul Zhang's wound up tighter than a Baptist in a brothel. Translate for me!'

'*Wo hen gaoxing ren she ni*,' bowed Song, irked by his sudden appointment as interpreter. "I am pleased to meet you."

'Is there a political element to these attacks? Tibetan or Xinjiang separatists?' shot back the Deputy Consul in Mandarin with a voice close to cracking. If Zhang had understood the situation so far, then clearly he did speak English but wouldn't admit to it. Song patiently ran him through the story in near-perfect Mandarin, remembering long hours spent in his mom's store with Chinese neighbors playing mahjong for matchsticks.

'Tell him we need immediate access to his fucking building', blurted a man from State unaware Zhang was bilingual.

'I apologize for the foolishness of my colleague', Song ventured in Mandarin, throwing State a withering stare. 'It would of course be imprudent for you to allow access without the prior agreement of the Consul-General.' Zhang's features remained immobile, though it was clear he appreciated Song's delicacy.

'Are you sure this guy gets it?' said another square faced man from State.

'Oh, I'm quite certain that *he* gets it', clipped back Song in high irritation. Thankfully the interpreter arrived and Song retired with a bow. Walking back to the car he took in the crush of reporters steadily multiplying at the cordons. Whatever disjointed PR mosaic Corbyn had been able to create was splintering asunder.

In the slot between two hastily parked Bureau vehicles Fernandez was using a hood to steady his notebook, the only journalist within the cordon sanitaire. Scott was languidly kicking at an imaginary stone.

'I saw you speaking to that Chinese guy. Do you know they have over a million people there and they're all godless Communists!' whined the Fisherman, Song electing not to put him right on either error. Accessing the net, Song flicked to an influential conservative blogger's site to be greeted by the heading *Murder of the Innocents* about the St. Bartholomew's misinformation.

> *"The fundamental discussion concerning Big Government is not only about the constant march of petty laws seeking to regulate the minutia of our lives. It is about the suppurating arrogance of apparatchiks who at their patronizing worst presume to 'protect us' from the Truth. The potential danger of the asbestos (sic) at St. Bartholomew's was that it might shred our children's lungs, whereas the real danger of Big Government is that it does the same to the respiratory organs of Democracy. Strangely enough, we should look to former President Clinton for counsel on what to do at this difficult time: let none of us inhale."*

Whichever politician had made that St. Bartholomew's decision, Song would rather be a Bomb Squad officer right now.

The aged widow glared at the man whose coughing fit had interrupted the Pastor's eulogy. Her deceased husband's best friend was doing his best to cough up the one lung that remained after his cancer. It was another interruption she could do without. Upon their arrival at the Crystal Peace Crematorium everyone had been given a hastily printed waiver absolving the management of any responsibility should a bomb go off. Everyone had signed - what else could they have done in the circumstances?

'As I was saying, the deceased was blessed with four children and eleven grandchildren, all of whom are with us today. He worked long hours in his job as a mechanic in Baltimore, putting food on the table for his loving family before retiring here to Tucson eleven years ago.....'

In the seat behind his weeping mother her dry eyed son peered at his watch, worrying about making it in time for his family's flight back to Pittsburgh. As the Pastor droned on about the bastard who had been his father, he gazed coldly up at the kitsch plastic chandelier gently swaying in the AC's current.

And that was where he was looking when the blast wave killed him, three of his siblings, and seven of their children. The ceiling bulging down to slap them with its cruel concrete and steel, followed by a spray of flaming gasoline that welded man-made fabric to blackened skin.

Miraculously the grieving widow survived, though she was unable to wear that scorched mourning dress to the multiple funerals she would attend in the week that followed.

Song was slumped in the SUV, eyes closed as if to shut in his frustration. Townsend was piggy-backing off an unsecured network, State television in China confirming that its sovereignty was under attack from "unknown" forces the American authorities were struggling to control.

'Struggling to get into the fucking building more like!' she protested. Song was just drifting into a light sleep when Corbyn called.

'It seems you made quite an impression on the Chinese. Your presence has been requested.'

'They don't want the official translator. It seems you're the one they trust', he confirmed to a baffled Song in the stale fug of the Command Room. A still nervous Zhang relayed through Song the three provisos Beijing had set for them entering the building at ten o'clock that evening.

First, only three members of the Bomb Squad would be allowed access. Second, they must be under the scrutiny of a Chinese Official. 'That person will be myself', explained Zhang in a voice so brittle it might shatter. 'Third, to facilitate communication, Detective Sergeant Song must accompany me.' Song was lost for words, be they English or Mandarin. Twice in under two days he would be within the blast radius of an explosive device.

Corbyn whispered into Song's ear. 'Yesterday I instructed you not to enter a booby-trapped building. Today, I'm requesting that you do.'

At ten p.m., Song and Zhang were pinioned to the sidewalk, corpulent Goth samurai in the Squad's ill-fitting black armor. Their nervous faces thankfully obscured by thick, hardened visors. The recent news from Tucson had confirmed eleven fatalities and Song was hesitant to make it twelve for the day. Standing at the Consulate's threshold the Squad Captain's briefing was simple: stay out of the fucking way.

Moving through vacant corridors like nighttime security men, the five heavily breathing men were soon crowded into the target office. 'This is a variation of a ground penetrating radar we use to find cavities', said the captain, though Song forgot to translate this and Zhang didn't seem to be in the mood to protest about it. Within a minute it had detected an anomaly in the offending wall. 'Same dimensions as St. Bartholomew's. About eight pounds would be my guess. More than you'd find in a Chinese firecracker', with a grin. The captain's two sweating guests stood still and humorless, all movement suffocated under the weight of their layered protection.

A square outline was sprayed onto the wall, one of the Squad methodically chipping at its center with a deafening power tool. Song could feel rivulets of sweat running down his heavily beating chest.

'That's the box front exposed. We'll continue with a hand-chisel now.' None of them needed the skill of a Rodin, but Song guessed each was acutely aware of the consequences of an overly enthusiastic clout. The captain scrutinized the monitor again, beckoning them over.

'It's a clear shot', he pointed, black gloves stubby and immense against the image's fine detail. 'Here's the ordnance, which I'll bet my handsome life insurance policy is C4. This slim little fellah here's the detonator. Over here's a hunk of metal, but none of us knows what it is.'

'Where's the power source and trigger?' ventured Song.

'There aren't any. No timer, no radio receiver, no battery - nothing. It's like a vasectomy; the business end of the kit's there, but it only fires blanks. Just as we suspected.'

'Just as we suspected?' parroted Song.

'It looked from the first radar shot it was going to be a dud. You didn't think we'd take a power tool to the wall if it was live, did you?'

Having dropped his armor as he walked, just like on a TV lingerie commercial, Song fumbled for a bottle of water lying under a fold-up chair outside the Command Center.

'I guess you're looking for a high five or something?'

Dropping exhausted into it, Song finished the bottle and looked up at Benjamin, the flood-lit consulate frontage his backdrop. 'Sorry - what did you say?'

'I guess you're looking for some praise; some "at-a-boy, David!"'

Song was tired. Not just from the weight of the kit, or the long hours, or the tensions of this extraordinary day, but also from an overall sense of disconnection. He had access to every conceivable technological link but still the overwhelming feeling was one of separation, of being out of control. It was not something he was used to, nor comfortable with. He gave a long sigh, rubbing his neck to massage away the fatigue.

'If you think today has addressed my concern about you being in league with Paine, it hasn't. If you already knew this device wasn't primed then it was all up-side for you. Just like the one under the porch. No pain, but lots of credibility gain. And as for the cozying up to the commies, well that's someth-'

Exploding out of the spilling chair, Song's fist caught Benjamin under the chin, snapping his arrogant jaw shut, making him swallow that last insulting sentence. The agent fell with a dull thud onto the asphalt. Breathless and groggy he rose from the ground, turning to engage.

'Whoa! Whoa!' shouted someone, throwing himself between the sparring males. It was Bradley Scott.

'People are dying out there and this is how you two wanna spend your time? You – Agent Benjamin – get over there and do whatever it is you do. You – David – over there. Now!' Benjamin's brooding figure towered over Scott, rotating his jaw for a few seconds before moving off without looking back. Song shook his head in disbelief. Outside of resisted arrest, he hadn't hit anyone in a fight since high school. Scott picked up the toppled chair.

'*Corinthians 4.9*. "We are made a spectacle unto the world, and to angels". Having said that, Agent Benjamin sure is an asshole.'

'Thanks Bradley. I'm embarrassed. I don't know what got into me.'

'It was the Devil. Maybe not the big-ass Devil, but one of his chicken-shit minions', grinned Scott.

'You're pretty handy at breaking up fights', Song observed, aware of the pulsating ache growing in his fist.

'Experience. Hungry people will fight for the last crust of bread if they don't know where the next one's coming from. And it's Armageddon if someone tries to touch their sleeping bag!' The Fisherman took Song's hand, squinting at the knuckles. 'That's a puff pastry punch you have on you, boy. Not even a cut', he laughed. Song smiled back at this unusual man, wondering if he had read him incorrectly.

Later, back in his hotel room with the TV muted, Song flexed his bruised knuckles in front of the bathroom mirror, again shocked by how he'd reacted to Benjamin. But the exhausted face staring back at him from the hardwood framed glass still didn't know why he was here.

Meanwhile, on Song's muted TV screen two political analysts were opining about the implications of this for Sino-U.S. relations as a tame State Department aide was lionizing the gushing support offered by the Chinese consular staff. Anyone who had been asleep for the past sixty hours could have been forgiven for thinking that the country was now at war. But with who?

Drained both by the day's events and by the frustration of his circumstances, Song sought the refuge of his bed without checking voice-mail, text, or logging on. To friends and family alike, David Song had disappeared from cyber view.

Only disconnect.

At noon the following day Song sat outside the Virginia office of Jack Greene, Corbyn's boss at the National Security Branch of the FBI, racking up his fourth state in as many days. Now he knew how Presidential candidates felt.

Quantico: much storied, rarely exaggerated. Stacked with conspicuously intelligent people who would not have been out of place in the Board Rooms of Corporate America, the principal difference here being the substitution of hollow-point for PowerPoint.

Song noted that 'Scoop' Fernandez was on-site with the Bureau's attorneys while Scott had stayed in New York courtesy of some Bureau babysitters. Benjamin had spoken to Song twice that morning in an accomplished act of civility that the Californian had tried to mimic. The only flaw in their Alpha Male pact of silence was the livid bruise along the Agent's jaw line. Song wondered which piece of furniture Benjamin would tell people he had hit it on.

A thick maple door opened, Townsend beckoning him in with a private wink.

'What an eventful few days you've had, Detective Sergeant!' asserted Greene glancing over drug store spectacles. 'Let's start with a refreshing departure from protocol by giving *you* the opportunity to ask *me* the first question.'

'Great - how do you know for sure you can trust me?' Song blurted, grateful at having the chance to rebalance this lopsided story.

'Bull's-eye', replied Greene flatly, jotting a flowing note with his fountain pen. 'Actually, we don't. Sorry - that was tautological – I mean we don't know *for sure* we can trust you. Yet.

We've conducted toe-in-the-water interviews with colleagues, bugged your phone, reviewed your bank details, and scrutinized your parents' IRS returns. The real good news is we've found nothing untoward. The real bad news is that we looked', discarding his fountain pen to sharpen a pencil instead, contrails of wood-shavings spilling onto his cherry desk.

'And I can respect that. My mother's Vietnamese and their laws used to be modeled upon the Napoleonic Code where prisoners were presumed guilty before proven innocent. I'd have been disappointed if you hadn't assumed the same about me.'

Greene chewed lightly at the pencil's end, mulling this over. 'Your file's exemplary. No disciplinary investigations - with the exception of course of that one fatality', peering over his glasses again, making Song feel like his soul was being scanned. 'Enlighten me.'

'He was a Haitian immigrant named Marcus de Montford and he'd just knocked over a liquor store', explained Song, immediately worried that Greene had chosen this of all things. 'I was leading my partner in foot pursuit when de Montford veered down an alley before turning to fire three rounds at me from a distance of approximately twenty yards. Two streetlamps were busted so we were both in shadow as we exchanged fire, and after my sixth round he fell to the ground dead. Later investigation revealed that my first two rounds had struck him directly in the heart inflicting mortal wounds. So his last shots had been fired harmlessly into the ground, probably induced by the muscle spasms of a dying man. Due to the poor visibility I thought he was still aiming for me, hence my additional four rounds which appeared gratuitous in retrospect.' Song stopped, knowing this was word for word what he had said to the investigators.

'And the interesting twist to this otherwise unexceptional story?'

Song shuffled on his seat. 'My last four shots also struck his heart, making six hits within a tight circle four inches in diameter.'

'That's a marksman's shooting, isn't it?' asked Greene, already knowing the answer.

'Yes, but I'm no William Tell. And it's that "twist" which had people asking whether I'd been using a black man for shooting practice? Anyway, the investigation exonerated me.'

'And how did you feel about the incident?'

'Wretched.'

'Interesting word. Why so?'

'Because I didn't join up to kill anyone, no matter the circumstances. Taking a life also took something from me', replied Song without the emotion he still felt.

'I see you made full use of the department's counseling services. Seventeen visits to be precise.'

'I'd rather talk to a Psychology MA immediately than an *AA* buddy forever.'

'Point taken. And you were ordered not to make contact with the deceased's family. Why on earth would you even want to do that?' asked Green shrugging his substantial shoulders.

'de Montford had a young daughter, and I wanted to see if I could help.'

'That's a little naïve, isn't it?'

'Naive is one word, accountable another. Just because I wasn't criminally responsible doesn't mean I'm not socially.'

Greene massaged the corner of Song's salmon pink file, eyes raking the detective's face. 'But you were ordered not reach out.'

'That's correct', the worry beginning to scratch harder at Song's intestine with its porcupine quills.

Greene sniffed at a non-existent odor. 'And in the end you didn't. But a close friend of yours did. One Charleen Tran Dok

- Charley I believe you call her. Each year Charley deposits $3,000 into a trust fund set up for de Montford's daughter, just a week after $3,000 arrives into her account from yours. Is this an example of Californian philanthropic money laundering, Detective Sergeant?'

'It's the *Beach Boys* influence, Jack; it's why we call it the Golden State.'

'So,' burst out Greene, animatedly closing Song's file, 'do you feel that same sense of moral accountability for our current situation?'

'Insomuch that I'm responsible for delivering the tasks Special Agent Corbyn entrusts to me, yes. But with regards to Paine's actions, none whatsoever because I'm not involved. I haven't got a damned clue why he's implicated me.'

'Not *implicated*, David. Involved', corrected Greene, lightly drumming the table. 'It's an important distinction. The safe option for me would be to lock you in a windowless room and grill you like a cheap cheeseburger. That would be the Napoleonic way, yes? That's what a lot of people up there want me to do. They're just like the people who didn't want you taking an interest in the de Montford girl.' Greene let the allusion sit on the table before continuing. 'But Alex thinks that would be a criminal waste of your talents. And since the FBI is all about catching criminals, not joining them, we've decided we want you on the inside. From now on you'll be joining all the relevant meetings and you'll also need to investigate your own background to discover the reason for your involvement. You'll recall Paine's oblique reference to your father, I'm sure. Any questions?'

But Song was too relieved to have any. Had the lights just turned from red to green?

'David, a private word', said Greene drawing the detective close as the room emptied. 'Six shots within a four inch diameter?' he whispered. 'If it wasn't marksmanship, do you know what it was?'

'Fear', replied Song as a cold sweat returned to his forehead.

The Bureau man nodded. 'Clearly those seventeen counseling visits weren't wasted. In stress situations some people go all to pieces, while others excel. That can be a very powerful asset, but it can also be very dangerous. You need to know which it is for you, son.'

Song thought back to his opening of Paine's front door and the gentle lifting of the wire within, not really sure if he would ever have the wisdom to distinguish which was which.

Chapter 5

You can discover what your enemy fears most by observing the means he uses to frighten you

: Eric Hoffer

QUANTICO'S POLISHED OAK CONFERENCE TABLE GROANED under the welter of reports. To Song's left sat Dawn Sharper, Deputy Director of Homeland Security. The detective whistled silently to himself; when Greene said he was inviting him inside, he hadn't been kidding. Sharper thanked everyone for their hard work.

'Detective Song', she barked, startling him in his leather padded chair, 'we'd particularly like to praise your contributions in Pender County and at the consulate. The Chinese Ambassador has also singled you out for special attention.'

'You're welcome', croaked Song in a squeaky voice, flushing strawberry-red at the inanity of his reply.

'America's response to terror requires a fully integrated enforcement approach', she droned on, 'which is why we are happy to have a celebrated member of an august Police Department join our team as a fully-functioning member.' Greene fiddled with his pen, Corbyn stared at something invisible above her head. Perhaps this woman was standing for some election Song didn't know about?

'Thank you, ma'am. Happy to help', squeaked Song again, realizing this wasn't much better than his last offering. Across the table, Townsend swallowed her laughter. Motivational speech over, Sharper departed leaving Greene to offer a grim overview of the death toll, the claustrophobic tension smothering the nation, and the truth about how little they still knew about the perpetrator.

'People are looking up at their attics wondering what's up there; looking under their bus seats wondering what's down there; passing public buildings wondering what's in there. In three short days Mr. Paine has got everyone looking everywhere without him even stepping outside the Marriott. Today we need to get ahead of the curve, people.' Greene invited Special Counsel Samantha Franks to speak, in her early fifties, mousy grey hair, her wedding ring sporting a diamond the size of a glass eye.

'To be crystal clear, you must treat Paine as someone helping us with our enquiries. He is *not* a suspect. This is very, very important because we haven't mirandized him for the reason's you already know. I will not tolerate any creative freelancing on this point. We need to ensure that his eventual prosecution sticks like shit to Linus' blanket.'

'Amen to that', said Greene. 'Although I'm in overall charge, I expect to follow the advice Alex's team offer as it'll be them who're in day-to-day contact with Paine. This way I can get to spend more time on the golf course.' Everyone laughed appreciatively, though Song doubted this impressive man saw many putting greens unless they were in an aerial reconnaissance photo.

'So what is Sauce-per-eel-a anyway?' asked the six year-old of his father, swiveling back and forth on the bar stool. His seven-year old sister echoing that question while pulling a face at herself in a huge mirror boasting the hand-painted words : *Joe's Soda Shop*. Her dad said the fittings here were like the 1950's, and got real excited about something called polished chrome. She wasn't sure why he was getting so worked up as he had been born in 1972 which she was pretty sure came later. She watched the man behind the counter pulling levers on a machine that gurgled and coughed to his touch.

'Sarsaparilla was the favorite drink of Woodrow Wilson. Makes you grow up brainy and strong', he said, from underneath a funny hat that had no peak.

'*McDonalds* have banana milkshakes. Do you make *McDonalds*, mister?'

'Button it, Ronald', said his dad, playfully pulling down his son's *Falcons* cap, their stadium not a mile away. 'Your Grandpop bought me sarsaparilla when I was your age and look how big and strong I am now, just like The Hulk', adopting a muscle-man's pose and roaring.

The boy's sister laughed, so she must know what a Hulk was because he certainly didn't. And anyway, what was that loud bang just then and why had his dad just knocked him onto the floor? Why couldn't he hear anything now except a loud whistling, and why was his forehead wet? Why was his dad slumped motionless and heavy on top of him - had someone knocked him down too?

And why was his sister lying half in and half out of the broken storefront window? Bloodied knees bent neatly over the jagged glass.

Although a Sunday, Quantico was full to capacity, the only clue to the day's identity an occasional sighting of jeans as people bobbed across cubicles.

'What did the Bureau's background investigation find out about you?' Song asked Townsend.

'Nothing except an ancestral link to the Little Big Horn. But that's okay because the Bureau likes winners. Forget about me though, what about you, you dog?'

'Six rounds in a four inch diameter? It's no big thing.'

'Not that, dummy! The deal with the daughter and the three big ones each year? If the single gals here knew about that, you'd be dating until Thanksgiving! That's most women's definition of a "real man" you know.' Song wondered if that were true, and if Townsend was hitting on him.

'What's the story on Benjamin's bruise?' he asked, fishing to see if news of their altercation had leaked.

'It looks really painful', she replied, smiling. 'Karen Oppenheim said he'd hit it on a chair. Man, I sure hope the chair's okay.'

The next two hours consisted of a stream of specialist presentations, leaving Song breathless at the end of each immaculate one. Specialist Billy-Jo Spearing pointed to eighteen inches of reports as she ran through the executive summary of each on screen.

The deeds to Paine's Pender County house were in the name of Thomas Lane, bought in 1992, and the name on every scrap of paper was exclusively Lane's. Spearing's team had tracked down two financial identities: one for Thomas Lane, via a *Visa* card, the other for Thomas Paine via a current account at the *Bank of America* in Durham. In total he had savings of $13,831 which he topped-up in $5,000 chunks of cash whenever it ran low. He hadd never reported any employment income to the IRS but never drawn social benefits either. Based upon an approximation of his age they had found 2,126 people with one of his two names, all painstakingly being tracked down by field agents. He owned a 1999 Ford pick-up registered in the name of Lane for which they were still searching. While she spoke someone entered to pass Greene a message. He read it with an expressionless face before handing to Corbyn.

'We're receiving reports of an explosion at a soda shop in Atlanta at 1300hrs local time. Three dead, thirteen wounded. Nate, find out what's going on.' The audience was grimly silent as the Homeland man edged out of the room and the next speaker made his way to the front. Song had that terrible feeling again of a battle being fought in a neighboring field, spiky brambles frustrating his participation in it.

Agent Archie Margolis, a weapons specialist, explained that the various C4 charges had weighed between six and sixteen pounds and were manufactured between 1980 and 1995. That was when the peanut farmer was still President, thought Song.

Two of the detonators were military, manufactured between 1978 and 1992. As for their trigger devices they were assumed to have been vaporized, a detailed combing of the sites yet to discover anything of use, though there had been a power source within easy reach of them all. 'So, in other words,' Margolis summarized, 'we can't say whether they were detonated remotely, or by an in-situ timing mechanism.'

'But if you had to guess, Archie?' pressed Greene emerging from a prolonged silence.

'For the consulate, school, and stationhouse, we know they were secreted in the fabric of the building, so I think he had the whole show wired up some time ago, sir.'

'And what about the age of the kit?'

Now it was Margolis' turn to arch his eyebrows. 'Well, C4 has a very long shelf-life and it's extremely robust.' Song thought back to the Bomb Squad captain casually tossing his slab like a relief pitcher. 'But we shouldn't confuse that fact with the time it's taken to use it. So, yes, I'm surprised we're seeing assets dating back to the late 70's. I mean, where've they been hiding all this time?'

'Just because the ordnance is old doesn't mean it was deployed back then', added Corbyn. 'He could have planted it a few months back.'

'Which is why we have people crawling over the building records to find the last structural work at each target.' Finally Margolis pulled up a slide of a silver cigarette lighter. 'This was found in the wall at the consulate.' Song remembered the Squad mentioning seeing something metallic in it. 'The lab say it's a plain ol' cigarette lighter, albeit a stylish one. It has prints, but they're not in the system and they're different to the ones from Paine's house. It's unlikely he would have interred it there by accident, so we must assume some intent.'

'How were the dogs killed?' interjected Song, wanting to ponder the lighter's significance later.

'Judging by the crushed trachea, the pathologist's view is they were manually strangled.'

'*Manually* strangled?'

'Yep, Paine killed the dogs with his own bare hands.'

Agent Michelle Denny of the Behavioral Unit wove an intricate pattern of Paine's personality type. An inventory of his house suggested complete normalcy, while a general fastidiousness pointed to a penchant for order over chaos. Cable preferences placed him in the middle of his demographic, while limited access to his IP records - being duly cautious as the Special Counsel required – looked like Snow White's. He had an eclectic collection of books, many of which would be considered highbrow. Song perused the list as she spoke, spotting many in his own e-collection.

'Looking at his performance so far, Paine's remained assured and dominant, but not hectoring. There may be control issues here - namely he's always had it. Turning himself in indicates a man comfortable behind the wheel. And when he lost that control for a while by rejecting O'Brian, far from panicking, he asked "the team" to brainstorm an answer with him.

We have absolutely no clue on motive. I know this'll disappoint you, but he's no psychopath, and without any demands we can't fathom any causal factors. It's immensely frustrating.

With regards to his concept of the "team", that could also be a control issue, but it could equally be one of affiliation. He's remarkably relaxed – you've all seen that – and though exercised by O'Brian it never spilt into anger. Paine's ugly questioning of the Monsignor might suggest a religious component, as would his demand to have a church activist present.' She paused just long enough to draw Greene's attention.

'But you don't think that, Michelle?'

'It'd be tempting, but let's not rush the beaches yet. If someone says they don't like apples, can we assume they nearly choked to death on one? Maybe as a kid he was beaten with a rosary, but I don't think so.

He's extremely playful. His half-jokes, the way he's teasing us with time, the delayed letter sent to the Sports Desk, these are indicative of a man with a sense of humor - no matter how perverse. So whatever his motive really is, he seems determined to enjoy himself along his leisurely way.'

'If you had to put money on it,' sallied Greene, 'do you believe he's a lone wolf?'

'Yes, he's a single agent pursuing a single but as yet unclear agenda. A man of ability with the characteristics of a natural leader. And why would someone of that caliber turn himself in leaving lesser accomplices to continue the campaign in absentia? Also we have the invitations issued to his three "guests". No credible terrorist organization would countenance such a display of personal preference. He's a lone wolf, for sure, and a hungry one at that.'

Devaughan Wallis' comprehensive overview of the media situation was simultaneously compelling and chilling. Serially unfaithful baseball players, kiss and tell au pairs, and DUI footballers proving no match for the hypnotic appeal of this terrifying national emergency. The inescapable conclusion of the editorials was that America had in three days moved from an attitude of easy peace to one of bristling defense. But against whom, or what, they were as clueless as the authorities.

Benjamin cracked open the door. 'Atlanta death count's at five, including a seven-year old girl and her father.' Corbyn dialed the number Kamamalu had given him.

'Thomas, is there something you want to share with me?'

'Like Ray Charles, I have *Georgia on my Mind*', said the old man above the TV's noise in his hotel room.

'You said the next device wasn't due until Wednesday.'

'No, I told you to meet with me on Wednesday to discuss the device due to detonate then. I never said there wouldn't be one before then. I wasn't trying to be clever - you just fucked up. Today's was five-pounds located behind the soda shop's mirror if you need to validate.'

'Does this mean there may be others before Wednesday?'

A moment's pause. 'Tomorrow, 3 p.m. Eastern time, and I've nothing further to say about it. Now if you'll excuse me, *ABC's* running an interview with a weeping Georgia Congresswoman.'

Greene called a ten minute break while he and Corbyn made some calls. On the conference room's TV, Song watched a medic loading a tiny body bag into an ambulance. It seemed that watching was all he was required to do.

This had got to stop.

'Turning now to the Minnesota bombing,' continued Wallis half an hour later, 'this paper in Connecticut's reported domestic fire alarm sales jumping 900%, while plasterboard sales are rocketing because people searching attics are putting their feet through ceilings.' Song would have smiled except Charley had just texted to say her landlord had visited to "check out the attic".

'The hostile column inches devoted to the St. Bartholomew's cover-up have now become column miles. Putting it simply, we're fucked and I'm advising full disclosure going forward. This isn't Afghanistan; everything's in full view here every day. For instance, this paper in Mississippi is running photos of the botched Beslan rescue in North Ossetia in 2004 next to St. Barthlomew's. And take a look at this.' Wallis toggled keys, bringing up live footage from *ABC*. 'This news stream is from the Rosa Parks High School in Indiana where their PTA asked for volunteers to conduct a search. Over nine hundred people turned up at six a.m. today, a Sunday! That number grew by three as the cops monitoring the situation lent a hand with the hunt. Their unwitting participation is now being portrayed as the authorities having sanctioning the search in the first place! Now police stations across the country are being inundated by requests for help.

This is the *Facebook* page of a parent at Rosa Parks, and here's a picture she uploaded.' Song saw a dozen smiling parents posing like an ice hockey team around a make-shift poster reading, *Vigilante Angels – protect and survive*. 'This is what she said on *CNN*:

> "*The government and the FBI don't seem to be able to stop them. So if every parent checks their kid's school, checks their home, checks their car, that's how we can keep our children safe. We don't want to be seen as vigilantes like in the movies. That's why we came up with Vigilante Angels.*"

Finally, following the incident at the Consulate, State has received requests from nine other – how shall I put it – "unfriendly" legations for us to begin an immediate sweep of their premises. They're trying to make us look real bad, and at the moment that's not too difficult.'

'Any hint in the media of the Pender County device?' asked Song.

'Nope, the boys down there have throttled that one. Not even a Tweet. Which brings me to some figures regarding Joe Public on the net. We've identified 287 million comments …'

'Wow, that stood at 33 million yesterday,' interrupted Townsend.

'We'll pass half a billion by OJ and bagels tomorrow. It's an extreme level of engagement, almost unprecedented in our experience. Oh, and this is just the USA. We had some spare capacity so we ran a search on Chinese sites and picked up 202 million references on the Consulate alone.

It's one hell of a big Global Village, and *all* the natives are getting restless. Not bad for a seventy-year old retiree stuck in a hotel bedroom.'

'This is the full inventory of Paine's house,' explained Agent Benjamin brandishing a thick document. He went on to explain that only one set of prints had been lifted from the premises and there was no match with any on record. DNA would take longer, but no one was expected anything useful from it.

As the agent sporting a purple bruise ran through a litany of facts leading nowhere, Song quickly scanned scores of pages detailing everything from the dimensions of each of Paine's rooms through to the number of cans in his larder. Paine had a well-equipped tool area but nothing you couldn't find in any suburban home. The appendix held sheaves of pictures. It was like peering through a dollhouse window, too frightened to touch its fragile exhibits with Brobdingnagian fingers.

As Benjamin droned on, Song flicked through a selection of the folder's photographs, finding one of the crowded kitchen table he had spied when giant-stepping towards the refrigerator.

Song froze.

In blow-up shots of the table-top there was one of a local newspaper, in another a fork and spoon as if awaiting Goldilocks' arrival, and in the last the image of several carefully laid out envelopes. Benjamin was explaining that the graves of the two dogs had been aligned East-West and whether there might be some Christian significance to that when Song began to rise in reflex from his chair.

'Sorry to interrupt, but project photo 783 onto the screen please, Nate.' All eyes were on him, Benjamin hesitating for a moment before complying. 'Scroll down to the third envelope from the top', everyone watching the image caterpillar-jerk to a stop. The magnified envelope's script was now easy for everyone to see - but impossible for anyone to read.

Except for Song.

Blurred but elegant pictographs filled the screen. The envelope was addressed in Chinese.

Corbyn cleared his throat. 'What does it say, David?' Song was still standing but he wasn't sure how, as if his legs had been de-boned by a professional butcher.

'It says in Mandarin, *For the urgent attention of Detective Sergeant David Song.*'

———

'As I said, he's playful', shared Denny knowingly to Song, squeezing past him in the corridor to the coffee station. The meeting had rapidly adjourned while one of Le Bon's team sped back to find the envelope. Special Attorney Samantha Franks agreed a legal case could be marshaled for it to be opened on Song's behalf given it was addressed to him.

'Of course people might conclude I already knew about the envelope because I conspired with Paine to put it there', he commented gloomily to Townsend. 'One man's insight is another man's subterfuge.'

She took a deliberately long look at him. 'But I distinctly heard Greene say we're both on the inside now. So if anyone – let's say Benjamin for argument's sake – is still thinking that conspiracy shit, then they need to take a walk outside with me and my service automatic.'

Song wondered how long it would take for one of Le Bon's black and whites to bust their suspension hurtling along those dirt roads. 'Is this the whole team working on the case', he asked to distract himself, waving an arm to indicate the cubicles around them.

'Are you shitting me? This is 0.001% of the resources at Greene's disposal! We're the Alpha Team with the job of working Paine and examining our own links to the case. Meanwhile the grown-ups are orchestrating the huge Beta, Delta, and Gamma teams you and I will never see. They number over fifty thousand heads if you count anyone with a badge. It's an immense exercise, a full national mobilization. We're just the rounding errors. And the only reason both our families haven't been thrown into the back of an unmarked van for blindfolded interrogation is as a mark of respect to us. We have to deliver the goods from them otherwise someone else will.'

As the meeting reconvened, Corbyn called for their attention. 'During the break I took a call from Paine. He's been specific about the new "more permanent" location he mentioned yesterday. It's to be in New Jersey. If we don't facilitate his transfer there then he won't feel obliged to share any more information with us.'

People spoke at the same time: 'Why New Jersey?', 'Let's re-focus the identity search there', and 'What the fuck does more permanent accommodation mean?' Distractedly, Song flicked another look at his phone. Just how big was Pender County anyway?

Specialist Javier Santos was two minutes into his review of Paine's accent as a means of triangulating region of origin when Song's cell trilled loudly. He had the feeling everyone else had been waiting for it too. The file Le Bon's man had sent of the envelope's message bloomed onto the tiny screen, and once again it was in Mandarin.

'What is it now?' asked Corbyn, almost afraid to know.

Song cleared his throat to relieve the tightness in it. 'It's probably pasted from an online translation but in essence it says: *Best avoid going to church next Sunday.*'

Greene left immediately as Corbyn summoned the meeting back into order. A church. It was difficult not to admire the simple brilliance of Paine's targeting.

'Being the only linguistic geek in the room', intervened Santos above the racket, 'may I point out he didn't say house of worship. That implies a Christian facility. Also the note says "next Sunday", but of course it could mean today if the envelope had been opened earlier....'

Someone gasped in the room. 'Shit! I'm on it', hissed Benjamin, flicking open his cell. Song shook his head. This wasn't them getting ahead of the curve, it's was more like them flat lining. He pulled at a hanging fingernail, ripping it unevenly down to its delicate bed.

Before Corbyn dismissed the meeting he had one last depressing thing to say. 'I'm sure it's occurred to you all that if there's no church bombing today then Wednesday's device clearly won't be Paine's last.'

Song thought depressingly of the one suit and three work-shirts he had hastily thrown into his bag back in San Francisco, typing *JC Penney* into his phone.

In the airport van that evening it was Townsend who asked the inconvenient question that had been on everyone's mind. 'When does someone warn the churches?'

'Indeed, Nevada, when?' Corbyn's mind was processing. He had just come off the phone to Greene who had been patched into some seriously powerful conference calls. 'The White House's view is we have five more days to go at Paine before we have to break the news.'

'That's the politically astute thing to do,' she agreed, 'but that's five precious days pissed away. Look what the Rosa Parks PTA managed in just one!'

'I'm not sure anyone's up for creating more nationwide panic right now, Nevada. And do we really want Church members clambering around explosives with gasoline lamps and snagging trip wires like the one in Pender? No, the President's relying on us turning up something beforehand.'

'So, no pressure then', huffed Townsend as the harsh airport lights drifted into view.

At ten p.m. back in the Marriot, Song took a quick circle through the depressing media coverage of Georgia. Once again Paine had accessed America's psyche with his deft choice of target. Two clips on *YouTube* had been removed, and Song knew why. He tracked one down on an indie site to be greeted by an image of a girl's broken body hanging out of the store's window, her puny arms listless above her head in a ballerina's pirouette of death.

The heartbreaking shot left him in need of hearing familiar voices. 'Have you called your parents yet?' quizzed Charley. Song's mind could see her thin waist swiveling to pull a book of case law off a precariously balanced tower at her legal aid center, each strand of her black hair flowing in perfect symmetry to caress her elegant neck.

'No, I was just going to', he answered dishonestly.

'Your mom will be so pissed she'll drive a T-54 onto your front lawn. Go do the loving son thing.' She rang off with a tinkling laugh, leaving him again smelling sea air and Chanel. So finally, unable to delay it any further, he rang his parents for the first time since leaving. Song's mom had obviously been coached by his father to dial it back.

His father. The man Paine had glibly referenced during their introduction. Song was sweating just thinking about how he was going to raise the issue. 'Hey mom, I'll be coming back soon and I'll need to speak with you and dad about something. Nope, nothing to worry about.'

Nothing to worry about. He wished.

That night he dreamt of crooked church steeples studded with blood-stained glass, and a spiraling fire on its vertical pilgrimage towards the heavens.

———

The next morning Fernandez was on a conference call to the *Times'* background team of eight freelancers. There were stories to be had in every device's location and, once the case was concluded, there was a premium on getting the book to market fast. Amongst all this death Fernandez hadn't felt so alive since the 1980's.

Scott was wearing Bureau bought clothes. He had insisted on getting them from a charity shop, the agent accompanying him having to spend a whole $38 on a complete wardrobe. Another thirty had been spent on disposable cameras with which Scott had annoyingly snapped his way around Manhattan.

The authorities in the Garden State had just come into possession of a property in Mountain Lakes, New Jersey, and that was to be Paine's new home. The house had been part of a narcotics assets harvest, and in addition to large communal spaces, ten bedrooms, and a cottage out back with a further three, it also had the type of stellar security system of which any wannabe drug lord would have been proud.

'So what can we do about today's 3 p.m. device?' enquired Townsend.

'Nothing', replied Corbyn with a coldness everyone knew he didn't feel. 'I'll pump Paine but he's vowed to keep silent.' The meeting broke up in somber mood with Corbyn taking Song and Townsend aside. 'David, for today I'd like you to review the background checks conducted on Fernandez. Nevada, take a look at Bradley's, and for God's sake find me something to help manage him better than I've done to date. Otherwise there could be a homicide on this case that Paine isn't responsible for!'

Song was in the lobby waiting for his ride when Benjamin strode up proffering a file. 'State's translation of the Mandarin is identical to yours, but you should see it anyway. Meeting the Editor of the *Times*, huh? Don't be surprised if he invites you for golf; you're going to feature large in Fernandez's book so he'll be looking to snuggle up.'

Song was worried that this looked suspiciously like small talk from Mr. Hostility. He repaid the compliment. 'I worked a case once where the wife killed her husband with a five iron. From the blood spatter you could tell she had a kink in her backswing.' Benjamin smiled back, the blue stain under his chin darker now. He stood immobile, staring out at a concierge expertly cramming a family's improbably sized luggage into a taxi's impossibly sized trunk.

'I apologize again for the punch', Song continued, trying to break the awkward silence. 'That level of confrontation isn't like me.'

'Understood', responded Benjamin robotically. 'But it *is* like me; it's how I got where I am. I'm smart, but there are people in Federal much smarter. So what I can't deliver in IQ, I compensate for in KQ – kinetic quotient. I work eighteen hour in-your-face days, with four for sleep, leaving two for the gym and eating. The trick is to know all your own failings, all your fears – and defeat them. Take a five iron to their heads, yeah?' Song's car had pulled up but he wasn't going anywhere just yet. 'And that's why I'm giving you a hard time. Because that's what I do', he subsided, not looking at Song once throughout. 'So are we good?'

'We are', replied Song, though not so sure about the "we" part.

With a little bit of furniture shifting you could play a game of tennis in Editor Alan Hammond's capacious corner office at the *New York Times*. 'Welcome, Detective Sergeant – may I call you David? You must give my EA your numbers so we can get you into a round of golf.'

'Maybe later', replied Song, chalking one up for Benjamin on the golf call. They were joined by Cal Spinelli, the *Times'* Deputy Editor, as Song explained the Bureau's attempt to discover why Fernandez had been chosen by Paine.

Spinelli confirmed he had worked alongside Fernandez back in the 1980's when they were both junior hacks. 'It was a great time for Gabriel because he had a link into Reagan's White House. His grandfather had been a player in Franco's government and the Spanish diplomatic connections had passed on to him. Through these he got to know someone in Latin American affairs and onwards to Jim Baker, Reagan's

Chief of Staff. Gabriel contributed to policy documents for the Administration and that earned him some juicy interviews. He did some other pieces on the Warsaw Pact and a couple of things on Mitterrand. Hell, he even got to meet with Kissinger whom he sucked up to big time! He did a big retrospective of Nixon's policy in the Far East: Agent Orange, the Mao visit, that sort of thing. He was really moving up the ladder for a while, but post-Reagan he started shimmying back down as fast as his ascent. Soon after he dropped off my radar.'

Song drilled-down, trying to conjure up an image of Paine and Fernandez crossing paths. It must have been fleeting, otherwise Fernandez would have remembered him. 'I know you've had some time to think about this, so can either of you guess why Gabriel's been selected?'

'Absolutely none', replied Hammond definitively. 'Like you we've been looking at his work for specific commentary on terrorist events but there's nothing lighting up the pinball table.'

Song moved to another tack. 'Forgive me but he doesn't seem to be – how can I put it – the journalistic type. I've met a few back home and it's not unknown for them to be real assholes', he smiled, to be rewarded by two in return. 'Whereas Gabriel seems to be more, more-'

'Academic, bookish, scholarly, desiccated?' rattled off Hammond with a grin. 'Yes, Gabriel could never be described as a journalist's journalist. Give him a lead and he'd wonder which dog to put it on! He's more of a feature writer; a work-horse, not a stallion, and – with respect – not necessarily the best one of those either. We've given him a team to help cover the case's geographic spread, but just between the three of us it's also to support him with some more accomplished writers than himself. If Paine wants Gabriel on his team, it's for personal reasons, because it certainly isn't for his journalistic talents.'

'So if his work is so pedestrian and his contributions so sparse since the 80's, why is he still working for you guys?'

Hammond beamed a lottery winner's smile. 'In truth, we'd forgotten he was still on our freelancer books. He just fell between the administrative cracks.'

'So let me get this right, a simple clerical error has resulted in you getting the most sensational inside-story of the decade?'

'And if we listen quietly for a moment,' laughed Hammond, 'we might just hear the rustle of God's silken robes as He moves to and fro in His mysterious way.'

'Alex wanted you to see this,' said Oppenheim flourishing papers above her head back at the Marriot. 'Check out page eighteen.' Song poured himself some java, only to spill it over the doughnut box as he hit the relevant paragraph. Swearing to himself he put the dripping pot down and read it again. From the assayer's mark and the initials *PCF* stamped into its base, the cigarette lighter found next to the consulate's device had been manufactured in 1976 by a luxury accessories business with offices in New York. *PCF* was owned and run by one Phillipe Carlos *Fernandez*.

Song hurried to one of the communal computers. *PCF's* elegant website proclaimed an *Old World style for a New World life*. Accessing their online store there were no signs of any lighters, but Song found the name he was looking for in their list of advisory directors: Gabriel Jesus Fernandez.

He searched *eBay* for every conceivable permutation of the lighter but came up with nothing. Calling over to Oppenheim he asked her to conduct a historical search of their online presence.

'Sure, but there are already two hundred Agents crawling over that particular angle. You just need to access their reports and look for links they can't spot. You don't need to do the grunt work yourself, Detective Sergeant.' Song knew this, but he was a beat cop at heart and he had to get into the dumpster himself rather than reading reports about its odors. Pulling out his cell he dialed the number he had hoped never to call.

'Gabriel, it's David. Are you free for coffee? There's something we need to discuss. By the way, are you a smoker?'

—•—

They met at a family run coffee shop named *A Shot in the Dark*, round the corner from Gabriel's apartment. Dark green leather chairs punched through with quarter-sized brass rivets were clustered like a coven around black mahogany tables. Fernandez sat in his favorite corner, an espresso cup in his dainty hand.

'I'd like to show you something', Song pushed the lighter's photo past twin latte glasses.

Fernandez donned old-fashioned spectacles but still held it at arm's length. 'My goodness! It's one of our old lines. Where did you get this from?'

'Have you ever owned one of these?'

'Yes, thirty-six of them to be precise. I gave the last one away – oh, ten years ago. My family runs a luxury accessories business. As a director I had a number of them to give away as promotional gifts.'

Three dozen of them, thought Song, disappointment again kicking him in the guts. 'Can you recall the recipients?'

'Maybe. But what's this about?' Song bluntly told him where this one had been found. Fernandez stilled, as if a predator were walking by the nest, his face cycling through a range of emotions, all of them bad. 'And you think this is how Paine knows me? But I've never seen him before, I swear! And I didn't give these lighters out like Halloween candy; they were reserved for people of influence. I gave one to Reagan's Chief of Staff, one to Howard Stern, William Saffire, and I'll recall the others if you give me time. Never to anyone like Paine!'

'I'm sure you didn't, but maybe one of them did?'

Fernandez's mind was warring with itself, part thinking an approach to them would appear vulgar, the other appreciating how this pantheon of prestigious names could be woven into his upcoming book. It just got better and better. 'You'll have the list tomorrow.'

'Thanks, and there's one other thing. The lab found prints on the Consulate one, so would you be willing to supply yours for elimination purposes?'

'I'm only too happy to oblige', the reporter beamed. 'But would it be possible to have a photographer present while I'm doing it? For my book, you understand....'

'Bruce Willis' hands look smaller than I'd guessed, and Clark Gable's bigger. You know Alan Ladd used to stand on a box with his leading ladies, so you never can tell', drawled the badly dressed tourist, his belly drooping over his plastic belt.

His middle-aged Texan wife wished her husband would shut up with his incessant chatter. She wanted to drink in her moment outside *Graumans Chinese Theater* on the Boulevard. Ranged along the sidewalk were the hallowed prints of men and women who had accompanied her down an imaginary red carpet all her adult life. Her mind filled with a thousand *Technicolor* clips, flourishes of opening scores, and a pastiche of black and white stills. She panned her budget video camera around this living set, as Spielberg might have done.

'Where's Brad Pitt's, or do you have to be dead to be here? No, wait a minute, that wouldn't be possible would it – stupid head', her husband blathered, committing his latest idiocy to posterity as the camera's view-screen registered the time as exactly noon.

There was a sharp crack, pedestrians jolting to a stop in a bizarre reversal of a starter's pistol. In her eyepiece, slabs of paving erupted from the sidewalk, tumbling theatrically as if *Godzilla* had tossed them skyward before falling to the ground with a dull thud, as *King Kong* had done. Dust and silence filled the air for a long moment before the real-world's screaming began.

'Cut', she said.

———

Song was on the hotel's running machine catching up on the miles he had lost these past four days when Oppenheim called about Hollywood. Three people taken to hospital, one with serious injuries. Another inspired positioning Song conceded, cranking up the speed to burn off his frustration. A hundred yards west and Paine would have destroyed cement memorials to the nation's celluloid royalty. For celebrity watchers it would have been like bombing Arlington.

That evening Song sat in the Marriot's dimly lit bar area listening to Saint Etienne's *Sound of Water*. For the whole day Paine had remained in his room barricaded by newspapers and magazines, crenellated with hours of news TV. The pattern was unchanging, Kamamalu reporting his demeanor as more one of appraising how the story was being covered rather than seeking gratification from the acts themselves. When the Los Angeles story broke, Paine had nodded once before switching channels for follow-up coverage of Georgia and Tucson. Meanwhile, thousands of agents were hunting down the fragile skeletons of red herrings as the man responsible for their wasted labors ordered chicken salad from room service.

Paine's truck had been located in a parking lot eight blocks from Precinct 19. Unable to impound the vehicle for the usual legal reasons, tests had been performed in situ without opening the doors. White ants crawling around, scraping samples of soil and debris into plastic bags, photographing every square inch of its waxed chassis, all to no avail.

'So, California, what did you find out about Fernandez?' Nevada asked in her silky voice, easing herself into the bucket chair opposite. Song pointed to the four inch stack of printouts Oppenheim's team had generated, just in case there had been any danger of him getting to bed before midnight.

'That there's nothing obvious linking him to Paine. A couple of references to the Basque Separatists, Maoists in Latin America, and something on McNamara and Tet. Not enough to cover the modesty of a fly. His prints match the ones found on the consulate lighter, which means it's one of the thirty six he gave away over a twenty year period. Big help, huh? He's putting the names together so we'll have thirty six more dead-ends to rush down tomorrow', sluicing hot coffee around his mouth. 'Personally I think Paine got the lighter directly from Fernandez. How, where, and why he then entombed it in the wall – now there's the prize.' Song paused for a second until Townsend had passed her order to a waitress who never wrote anything down.

Townsend reciprocated with what she had learnt that might help Corbyn handle Scott. 'He had a shitty childhood raised in orphanages and foster homes around Bakersfield. After graduation he went to a seminary college in Wyoming courtesy of night shifts working at the Golden Arches. I spoke with the government agency that paired up with Bradley's church group in California. A lady there – the marvelously named Doreen Alabaster - remembered him. He'd come in every week sporting a beard and long hair like John the Baptist to pick up food parcels for people living in the storm drains. Do you think we should tell Brad people see him as John the Baptist, or would that go to his head – pardon the pun? Once over the holidays he'd played guitar for some kids at a cancer hospice, cementing Alabaster's high opinion of him. Since then he's been with the *Fishermen* in North Carolina running soup kitchens, supporting clean-needle exchanges, and being a thoroughly decent guy.'

'And how does any of this help Corbyn to manage him better?'

'Michelle Denny thinks we should keep Brad busy with work to avoid slides into melancholia. Embrace him and show some of that soulful FBI love we're so famous for. Most of all, be available to listen. This is a guy who's not always had that in his life.'

Chapter 6

If you are distressed by anything external, the pain is not due to the thing itself, but to your estimate of it; and this you have the power to revoke at any moment

: Marcus Aurelius

THE JOURNEY FROM THE MARRIOT TO MOUNTAIN LAKES was unremarkable, Song dozing for most of it. He had been up until two with the whispering TV running repeated pictures of the Chinese Theater incident. Someone from the *Bruce Willis Fan Club* was saying how John McClane would be kicking ass now if he were on the case. The news bar confirmed a man had lost his leg in LA and that a fifteen-year old injured in the soda shop had received a liver transplant too late to save his young life. Song had looked through a staggering amount of information regarding possible church targets. Denny had ventured which denominations Paine might be most vengeful against, but to Song's watchful eyes Paine didn't seem set against any in particular. So far his targets had a planned randomness, if that were possible. What unified them was the preciseness of the terror they caused, irrespective of whether they detonated or not.

Mountain Lakes sat amongst a wreath of hills, adorned by a mantle of lustrous trees all strutting to best display their vital April foliage. Clusters of well appointed houses flashed through the tree line along the verdant road. After a few minutes they were through the so-called built up area of the town, rising again before turning down a succession of narrow streets choked with conifers and dotted sporadically with signs of human habitation. Finally they turned off Crestview Road into a *cul de sac* where the van pulled into the driveway of their new home.

It was an imposing 1990's two storey building at the front, with a third basement floor opening up to the back. It had a long frontage full of angles and architectural protuberances successfully hiding a labyrinth of rooms and stairwells. The wood-shingled roof looked like an organic blanket thrown over uneven stacks of natural stone blocks. A manicured lawn made Song wonder if anyone had told the contractors that the previous owners wouldn't be paying their bills for the next nine-hundred and ninety-nine years. The front door led directly into a spacious communal area opening onto an elevated deck overlooking the dense wood beyond. In the communal area stood a towering stone fireplace that could brace the sturdy backs of several Kamamalus standing side by side.

Song's bedroom boasted a teenage boy's taste. A miniature hoop fixed to the door, posters of *Skrillex* and *How to Destroy Angels* taped lopsided to the wall. Paine had been given the en suite master bedroom whose windows conveniently had a fifteen foot drop to the woodland below. Kamamalu had super glued them all shut anyway. The Hawaiian had bought a padlock which he had fixed to Paine's door like a plague warning. In the town's hardware store he had struck up a casual conversation with its owner, accidentally letting it slip that activity at the house was part of a Mob witness protection program. Nothing to worry about, as he was being protected more from the paparazzi than the Sopranos.

'I'm reading this bit about Rockwell', said Townsend nursing a coffee in Song's adolescent room.

'Rockwell?'

'Haven't you seen it? The editorial in yesterday's *Post* described the bomber's choice of targets as a tour through the portfolio of Norman Rockwell.' She pointed to the headline, *Norman Rockwell's Dystopia*, on her PC.

> "*Like a nightmare journey down a dilapidated Route 66, the current spate of bombings seems intent upon expunging a hallowed memory of America from a time long since passed. Disfiguring a nation captured with such aching vivacity in the thoughtful brushwork of Norman Rockwell. Americans eating hot dogs whilst watching football; Americans accompanying their children to school; American's caught in casual symmetry with their police force; and now Americans in soda shops where those Prom Night teenagers once sat in 1957.*
>
> *Things change, life moves on. But as Americans we cherish that which we were yesterday, for it is part of who we are today. Our modern anti-Rockwell fractures this unbroken timeline and must be caught before we lose sight of that which we wish to become tomorrow.*"

'And this is a *Tribune* article today calling Paine "Rockwell", and on *Letterman* last night some movie star called him that too. Finally,' she toggled between minimized pages, 'take a look at this'. She called up a photo-shopped image on *4Chan* of Rockwell's famous *After the Prom*, but on this one the wholesome teenage couple had been mutilated, their clothes spattered in gore and blood.

'Our very own Unabomber now has his own moniker.'

As the April morning warmth enveloped Mountain Lakes, David and Nevada strolled chatting through the woods where Kamamalu had already assigned patrolling agents. Scott picked his way tentatively across the light scrub to join them. Walking quietly alongside as they swapped speculations about Paine, he seemed happy enough just to share their company.

'How are you getting on with all of this, Bradley?' asked Song, remembering Denny's advice from the night before.

'It's the Lord's way, I guess, but I hate the waiting. In Durham I'd be working in our kitchen about now, instead of walking around a shitty wood waiting upon the fancy of a murderer. And all because he remembered that fucking argument we had a ways back!' his voice rising operatically.

'Nevada and I are used to it, but for you - and the special work you do - this must be awful. I guess you can regard it as either a dreadful waste or a great opportunity.'

'What sort of opportunity?'

'To search the web – fish as it were – for what people are saying about God during this difficult moment for America. Find pastoral communities on-line and hear how they're dealing with the problem.'

Scott's eyes betrayed a mind grating noisily into second gear. 'But I don't have a computer.'

'Karen Oppenheim can get you one', volunteered Nevada.

Scott nodded his thanks as his heavily compartmentalized mind began to review the possibilities. Townsend winked at the Californian.

'Meanwhile, Brad, I saw Kamamalu tasking an Agent to buy some food for tonight. I'm wondering if those kitchen skills of yours could save us all from being poisoned by the FBI this evening?'

That afternoon Song was sitting out on the deck when, as per the plan, Kamamalu brought Paine out to stretch his legs. Song nodded, pretending to focus on his iPad. It remained a deeply frustrating curiosity that he had not spent more than an hour in total with this man since his enforced removal from California. It was like having been summoned from some distant rural community to serve in the dark bowels of the Emperor's kitchens, barely afforded the opportunity to glimpse his regal countenance.

'I know you're in no mood to speak, Thomas', he said as rehearsed with Corbyn, 'but can I ask you a question?'

'Try me', the old man replied brightly, pulling out a garden chair.

'If it'd been Nevada making the call from your porch, would you have endangered her as well?' At that moment Townsend came through the sliding doors on cue, a recorder whirring in her pocket.

'Of course', replied Paine, pushing a chair out for her. 'I regard you as equally resourceful.'

'And if I hadn't solved the puzzle?' asked Song.

'Then I'd have been wrong about that equality.'

'But why do it anyway? Why invite us here then try to kill us?' Townsend picked up the baton.

'You're thinking's too linear. Think fractal', he said with one of his broad grins, refusing to add more.

'Is a mosque the same as a church?' asked Song as a nest-building bird wheeled overhead.

'Are they the same in Vietnamese or Mandarin?' he grinned. 'Is apple the same as pear? Is Rockwell the same as Kandinsky?'

They lapsed into a stalemate silence as a cotton bud of cloud moved across the sun. Townsend opened her PC, flicking it round. 'Have you seen this picture of the little girl in Georgia?'

Paine looked at the image as one might regard freshly varnished wood, checking for the evenness of coverage. 'They won't show this on the networks. She looks dead. Isn't it interesting, the younger the victim the greater the horror? As if the integer isn't identical.'

'It's more about the loss of a life not yet led', suggested Townsend, Song watching intently from across the table.

'A life not led, a road less trod.' Paine held out his hands as if for exculpation.

'Why send the letter to the Sports Desk?' Townsend posed her next allocated question.

'Because I'm naturally suspicious. That reporter had announced he'd be on holiday so I could rely upon it only being opened after my surrender. Telling the Bureau about devices doesn't mean you'll tell the American people, so that was my insurance. And St. Bartholomew's proved me right, didn't it? Governments can patronize from time to time, you might have noticed.'

'Have you ever smoked?' re-directed Song.

'No, not even when I was...' but Paine caught himself, giving his wrist a theatrical smack of self admonishment. '...in need of it. That's why I returned the lighter to Gabriel.'

'When did he give it to you?' Townsend nursed the lead's fragile thread through a wavering needle.

'He didn't. I borrowed it, and now it's returned. Surely he can remember where?' Paine smiled. 'That's enough questions for now. In spring, David, a young man's thoughts should turn to love, not to detection', with a wink, walking towards the kitchen door. 'Just one more thing', half turning at the threshold. 'I'm guessing you already know about the lighter's fuel?'

Chef Scott's meal that night was tasty and plentiful, his gorgonzola pasta and cheesecake consumed with relish. Fernandez had been in his room since arriving that morning, emerging to peer at the evening meal with a connoisseur's suspicion. Corbyn called a short meeting to summarize the day's meager outputs. If the case's ponderous progress was frustrating for Song, it must be infuriating for the Bureau.

'Regarding the lighter fuel,' updated Benjamin, 'the first report stated the reservoir was empty. But after Paine's remark today they tested the residue and its crudeness suggests it's of foreign manufacture. So he could be signaling he took it from Fernandez outside the U.S..'

'But Gabriel's travelled to over forty countries across every continent these past thirty years, so that's not much help', picked up Corbyn. 'He's given us a list of twenty-eight lighter recipients he can remember and we're onto them.'

'Wherever it was', added Song, 'we can assume he didn't meet Paine on adjoining sun loungers in Cancun. Somewhere more challenging than that I think.'

'Precisely' agreed Benjamin. 'And if there's no passport on record for a Lane or Paine matching his description, then there must be a third identity as well. Hell, it could even be Rockwell for all we know.'

<hr>

The next day a tense group of people met in the cottage's operations room prior to their big meeting with Paine. A bank of fold-up tables pressed against the far wall supported a row of Oppenheim's PC's and printers. Two video cameras screwed to the ceiling offered Quantico a live feed.

'This is it, people', buzzed Corbyn. 'Our first real opportunity to get ahead of the game.'

'I'm feeling pretty nervous', murmured Scott sitting low in his chair, the Special Agent putting a hand upon his shoulder. Not just you Bradley, thought Song.

A circle of comfortable chairs had been arranged in front of the communal area's towering stone fireplace, a bright fire burning in its grate to see off the early morning spring chill. Paine was already seated by the window, elevating his face to catch the sun's thin rays.

'We have one simple objective, Thomas,' began Corbyn confidently. 'To identify the exact location of the next device, and any others that might follow. I've been authorized to open negotiations with you once again, so how would you like to proceed?'

'With a prayer. Over to you, Bradley', responded Paine without a care in the world.

Scott's face was all vinegar. 'Oh Lord, we ask You to care for the soul of the little girl slaughtered in Georgia. May her father find peace looking after her in Heaven and feel no remorse that he was unable to do so on this Earth. Amen!'

'Thank you; very thought provoking. Now let's move on to the introductions.'

'Start by introducing yourself,' replied Townsend mischievously.

'David, take the lead please', Paine ignoring her.

'Sure, but what's in it for us? Are you just going to tell us about the next device, or is there a larger bounty in the offing?' picked up Song, erring again from Corbyn's instructions to let Paine lead.

'Now, now; don't let's spoil the moment, David. All in good time.'

'But if we don't know the rules, how can we play the game?' the Californian persisted.

'So you want something up front?'

Song smelt the whiff of an opening and went for it. 'What do you think of William Golding?'

'Golding?' Paine stirred from his reverie. 'A great novelist. What's your favorite work?'

'*The Spire*, which I noted you have in your own collection back in Pender', answered Song, and then for everyone else in the room. 'The story of a priest building a towering spire to be as physically close to God as possible. Have you read it, Gabriel?'

Fernandez looked up jerkily from his notepad. 'Eh, yes, I have. Jocelin was his name. It ends in failure as its height makes it too unstable.'

'I'm intrigued, what's your point?' asked Paine.

'I'm thinking about other endangered spires. Can you help us with that?'

Paine moved onto his left haunch, a fleck of pain ghosting across his face. 'Okay, that was a little contrived, David, but not a bad sortie. So as a reward to start the day, you needn't concern yourselves with the spires, but look to Jack instead.' At this point Paine declared he had forgotten to pee, asking for a short adjournment.

'So who's Jack?' asked Corbyn in the break, knowing Quantico would be all over it.

'It's too obvious,' replied Townsend. 'For "Jack" read "knave"; the bomb's hidden in the nave of a church.'

'Can it really be that prosaic? It's a child's puzzle', observed Song.

'Maybe it's a coping strategy', she replied. 'He can't just say, "The bomb's in a nave", because to his self-image that's too pedestrian.' Fernandez and Scott hovered at the edge of the conversation.

'We're totally lost, Alex', interrupted Fernandez. 'What was all that about?' Corbyn had no choice but to tell them about the church threat. Fernandez looked delighted, scribbling maniacally on his pad. Scott in comparison looked absolutely stricken, returning to his chair white faced, wobbling like a lunch-time drunk.

'David, you must have been asking yourself "Why me?"', picked up Paine as he returned, 'and of course the Bureau have also been asking, "Why him?" So let's begin with your story.'

Song coughed, reminding himself not to cross the room to crush this man's trachea.

'I was born in San Francisco in 1979 to a Vietnamese Mother and a Caucasian American father', he began brightly, as Denny had advised. 'My mom left Vietnam in '76, one year after the fall of Saigon. Her husband at the time was Song Xiao Win, a Chinese name as his family originated from the border area. After the fall, the Communists were liquidating so-called war criminals and he was on their list. So using the last of the family's money he bought two tickets on an émigrés boat secretly leaving Da Nang. They were travelling separately to avoid suspicion but he never turned up. Years later she discovered he'd been caught and executed the same day she'd departed.

Miraculously after twenty eight days at sea she was picked up by a U.S. frigate and brought back on humanitarian grounds to resettle in San Francisco. She wrote to an American contact provided by her late husband and he financed her to set up a small hole-in-the-wall grocery store. Her letter to him needed to be in English, and the person who helped write it became her second husband and my father: Terrance May.

My father went to Berkeley and was involved in the '68 Peace Protests. Avoiding the draft on medical grounds he started work in San Francisco at a local College where he still teaches Politics and Philosophy. At night he taught English to immigrants which is where he met my mom. They married in '78 and a year later I arrived. It was my father who suggested I

take her first husband's family name – Song – in honor of him.
In Asia the birth of a boy is a big event, so for a father to make
this type of sacrifice was seen as very, very special.

Turning to me, I went to USC studying Literature and
Chinese. I applied to the SFPD and I'd like to tell you I was
accepted on my own merits, but I'm sure my ethnicity played a
large part. I moved to Homicide three years ago. I could go on,
but is this enough?'

Paine had sat in respectful silence, the gentle clicking of
Fernandez' keyboard the only accompaniment to Song's story.
'Talk to us about the *i4ni* murders.'

Song's antennae snapped to attention. 'Why the *i4ni* case?'

'It's how I got to hear of you', confided Paine, Corbyn
twisting towards the camera as if telepathically ordering the
case files to be summoned.

'Two years ago', complied Song, his mind racing, 'my partner
TK Bloomfield and I took an anonymous call about a body
found in an alley. He was a software engineer with multiple
blunt force traumas. His left eye had been gouged out but was
nowhere to be found. Resting against the body was a book titled
Comparative Religion. Four days into the investigation a jazz
saxophonist was murdered and again a copy of the book was
found and the left eye gouged out. But this time an eye *was* found
at the scene, however it wasn't the victim's. It was the eye taken
from the software engineer four nights earlier. Then the body
of a dog walker was discovered, again with the book, and this
time with the saxophonist's eye. Hence the case's name "eye for
an eye", written in text-speak as *i4ni*. Over the next few weeks,
three more bodies turned up: a teacher, a retired security guard,
and a plumber. All with the book and the left eye of the previous
victim. Eventually we got a break and identified a man named
Holden Webb, a sales assistant at *The Scarlett Ink* book shop in
Lower Haight. We found a bloodied scalpel taped underneath

his kitchen chair with DNA traces from all his victims. Webb claimed the scalpel had been planted – probably by me - hinging his defense on an unidentified partial print on the tape. Anyway, the jury's verdict was unanimous and he's now on Death Row.

'But you never discovered Webb's motive, because he contested his guilt', stated Paine.

'We put a few to the jury, but nothing definitive, and the crushing weight of evidence was enough.'

'So were you worried about the missing motive?' pressed Paine, Corbyn looking on, riveted by the exchange.

'Not particularly', he lied. It was true the evidence had been enough, but Song had the yin and yang thing in him. He needed symmetry: Method, Opportunity, and Motive. It didn't feel right when one of the triplets was AWOL.

'The evidence against me is already overwhelming', pursued Paine, weaving his sticky trap. 'I could be tried and convicted right now, without discovering motive, just like Webb. Would you be happy with that?'

Song considered the question, no one in the room seeming anxious to interrupt. 'No, I wouldn't. I need to understand your motive for my own sake, not for the jury's.'

'So the reason you invited David to join us', stirred Corbyn from his watchful pose, 'was because you've studied the *i4ni* case and admired his investigative abilities?'

'Correct. My case is going to need all the help it can get, and David's proven his talent on *i4ni*. Plus he has a hunger to discover motive.'

'Both undoubtedly true', pressed Corbyn, 'but those are weak reasons to involve a stranger in your case. The U.S. is full of complex cases cracked by detectives equally as able as him. And you've already mentioned his father. So let me repeat, why involve David?'

'Well there may be an additional reason, but if it exists you're going to have to find it for yourselves.'

Townsend explained she was thirty years old hailing from Phoenix, Arizona. Doing the math on her family tree, her Apache heritage amounted to two thirds of her DNA profile. To those looking on, she was a wiry entanglement of bones and athletic muscle, maintained by a menu that would have struggled to feed a savannah's scavengers. She had graduated with a decent degree in Psychology and Criminology from Arizona state. Her mother's name was Sky, her ancestral line the major contributor to Nevada's Apache inheritance. At the time Littlefeather had been accepting Brando's Oscar, Sky had been participating in peaceful protests about the injustices perpetrated against her people. She had met Nevada's father at college in 1975 and he too had distant fragments of Apache blood in his veins. They had married straight after graduation and Nevada was born a few years later having been conceived on a Labor Day trip to Ruby Lake - *Nevada*.

He had been a middle manager in an American oil business, killed in an industrial accident at a pipeline assembly in Venezuela when she was very young. Nevada's most vivid memory of him was his funeral, the somber oil men patting her head saying they would look after her mom. Someone had whispered an open casket hadn't been possible because he had been "pulped like a watermelon" under the fallen pipe.

Nevada wasn't really sure why she had chosen criminology at college, but there was something about a churning feeling of displaced justice. Her mother's stories about three hundred years of grievous marginalization, but also the passing of her father. Was anyone ever prosecuted for their appalling error in that distant nation? Her grades had been good, but she was no prodigy, submitting a badly completed FBI application form when drunk one night. Like David, she suspected her employment had been more to do with her ethnicity than her limited accomplishments.

'Tell us about *Operation Thunderbolt*', requested Paine as she stumbled to a halt.

'*Thunderbolt* - really? It's pretty straightforward.' Townsend was as surprised by the question as Song had been with his. 'We'd received an anonymous call that a Native American gaming business was involved in weapons trafficking. The case leaked to the press and there were some inflammatory headlines published about how "they" were behaving irresponsibly with the land rights "bestowed" upon them by the U.S. government. I got hold of a recording of the informant's call and picked up his distinctive Apache accent. So, while the rest of the world was lawyering-up and grandstanding about whose land it was anyway, I worked the local Native community in my '98 Dodge and moccasins. It led to a nineteen-year old kid with a grudge about being refused work at the casino because he was a weed-head. It was lightweight stuff; you couldn't even make an *Ocean's 19* plot out of it. Anyway, because of the politics and shit, I was publicly commended for breaking the case. The CEO of the casino business is also a tribal Chief and he singled me out as a shining example of how members of "our" community can make a contribution to society. Total bullshit, but my people have learnt a lot from Madison Avenue these past few decades. That's it. No gouged eyes or planted books.'

'And once again,' commented Corbyn, 'nothing remarkable in that story to explain why Nevada's here over anyone else.'

'And once again, you're missing parts of the picture', reprimanded Paine, never breaking his constant smile. 'In their own ways, both Nevada and David have explained why they're here. You just have to work out the specifics.'

Corbyn called for a fifteen minute comfort break, beckoning the two storytellers over and putting his cell onto speaker. Agent Michelle Denny from the Behavioral Unit came online.

'We didn't notice anything in particular; almost as though Paine'd heard it all before. However, he reacted a little when David mentioned his father, Terrance May. And we're pulling the *i4ni* and *Thunderbolt* cases to see if we can figure any angles there.'

'Can you think how Paine might know your father?' asked Corbyn. Song shook his head, his stomach churning at the thought. 'We need to get the two of you back home quickly now to interview your families', the Special Agent stated before sliding off to make his usual column of calls. Song and Townsend looked at each other.

'What the fuck is going on? My *Thunderbolt* Case was pure crap.'

'What about your mom and dad?' enquired Song.

'I can't see how. My mom watches daytime TV and feeds stray cats. My dad was an anonymous middle manager, crushed under a two ton section of pipe ages ago. Mr. and Mrs. Suburbia. It *has* to be something else. You look as though you're thinking the same about Paine and your dad.'

Song didn't know what he was thinking, except that the hairs on the back of his neck were steadfastly refusing to lay down.

Bradley Scott ran through his story looking the picture of discomfiture, eyes zigzagging to all compass points except straight at Paine. A less than fluid account of his fractured life correlated to Nevada's report before coming to a sudden end, as if he were exhausted by the telling of it.

'Well, Brad,' laughed Paine, 'when we met again at the Marriott I called you a credulous God-fearing asshole, and now I understand why. Your story's a powerful advocacy for eugenics. So how are you going to feel this Sunday when one of God's houses burns to the ground?'

Song's ears pricked up - so it *was* this coming Sunday! People in Washington would be diving for their phones. Scott's chin burrowed into his chest, a hedgehog looking to ball-up and escape the misery.

Fernandez held the room like the only person there with nothing to lose, and with a multi-million dollar book deal in the pipeline, that was close to the truth. With every erratic twist and vicious turn in the case, the value of his work rose precipitously; a grinder sharpening his blunted career.

Gabriel was born in 1960 and was privately educated at a select Spanish school in New York. He professed no interest in commerce, acting instead as a very silent family board member, his share of the profits affording a comfortable lifestyle ensconced in the better part of Lower Manhattan. He had fallen in love with words courtesy of Cervantes, and writing had been his only love ever since. The efficient but monotone dissection of his reporter's life quickly over, he brought his monologue to a close, his chest far too inflated for Song's liking.

'That's an impressive catalogue', offered Paine in congratulation. 'As this team's scribe, you now have the opportunity to record our work for posterity. Did you get your lighter back from the Bureau? Now if only you could remember where we last shook hands.' Corbyn stirred to say something, but Paine stilled him with a finger. 'And I know what you're going to ask; why choose Gabriel? Well, I was looking for a writer who could fulfill several criteria.

First, he had to be of below-average talent. Someone with no works to rival the one he'd be writing about this case. Second, he should have an excruciatingly ponderous style of prose so as not to distract from the grandeur of the unfolding story. Finally, he needed to be someone whose mediocrity meant he had no other pressing work commitments. I'm happy to say Gabriel admirably fulfils all of these criteria.'

Fernandez melted into the paleness of the walls around him, his face a lime-wash white. The man so replete with words a minute ago, was now lost for them. Song couldn't contain his smile.

Paine rubbed his eyes and shifted his weight. 'So, that's the team's introductions over. Earlier on I was asked to explain the rules of the game, so here they are. I'm prepared to offer commentary on the remaining devices based solely on our interactions. Work well with me and you'll be rewarded. Misbehave, and regrettably people will die. However, some of the devices will detonate no matter what you do, so no sulking or pouting in their aftermath please. I haven't seen anything in the media yet about the church, so I'm guessing someone in the command structure is weighing the pros and cons of warning the feckless. Personally I favor discretion so that one lucky congregation can get closer to God faster than they'd anticipated this week-end.'

'So how can we get at this information you're willing to share?' probed Corbyn.

Paine turned his palms to the ceiling, 'Ask me a limited number of questions and see what you get. And try not to be too clumsy about it.'

Now it was Corbyn asking for a ten minute adjournment. He was searching for his cell when it rang with Jack Greene and Michelle Denny. Song listened in as the questions were chosen, his mind recounting: Motive, Opportunity, Means. The pressure of time meant they were always focusing on Means – on getting ahead of each device - but he felt sure the case would be broken on Motive.

And if the Bureau didn't have the luxury of focusing upon that critical point, he would have to take the initiative for them.

———

'Question one: will you give us the exact location of as many devices as possible, including the one due to detonate today?' read Corbyn off the hastily scribbled list.

'Only today's' replied Paine with finality. 'In the ceiling of the Orpheum Theater in Wichita, Kansas, and get there before 10 p.m..' At the other end of the video link Jack Greene would again be running up his phone bill thought Song.

'Question two: will you give us the general location of other devices?'

'One only. Let's put it this way, I wouldn't be taking my family to any theme parks over the next couple of weeks.' This one hit Song hard. As a Californian he had lived with the parks all his life, still hearing the joyous screams of Charley and Gary as they had careened together down near-vertical slopes under transparent blue skies. And Paine had just said "over the next couple of weeks". How long was this dark pantomime going to last?

'Question three: can you confirm your real name to us?'

'You still don't know that?' Paine looked up at the cameras. 'What the fuck are you guys back there doing to help this team out? Are you expecting them to carry the whole fucking load?' in mock irritation, arms theatrically wide awaiting an answer that could not come. He shook his head to indicate they should move on.

'Question four: are you acting alone?'

'There's no need to look any further, your nemesis is before you', Paine's simple reply.

'Question five: will you clarify the time frame over which the remaining devices are due to detonate?'

'Not in its entirety, but after the church this Sunday you'll have a four day break, followed by one explosion every day after that for the following five days. No more questions for now; you've had your quota.'

Corbyn looked up from his pad, mind cart wheeling with thoughts of a chain of devices stretching into the distance. The situation was steadily deteriorating. 'Thank you Thomas, we'd just like to take a short break, and -'

'Yes, we're going to take a break, but it won't be a short one', interrupted Paine. 'I want to meet again at 1 p.m. tomorrow. But before we finish, I have one more thing to say to the people outside of this room', pointing directly at the cameras. 'There are a lot of folks out there getting mighty worried about how big this case is getting. So let me tell you this for a promise: if you move Alex aside to make room for some gutless-wonder from higher up the food chain, I'll fuck you over. If you try to interfere with the other people I've chosen, I'll fuck you over. And if I sense any loss of spontaneity in this team as you oblige them to start running things through senior management, I'll fuck you over. If you want to see a swift and successful resolution of this case, *trust in this team*', his pointed finger raking the Mountain Lakes' room. Set piece speech delivered, the silver-haired man rose stiffly from his chair.

'Just a second', said Song. Something had been gnawing at him since Pender County and here was the opportunity to test it within Paine's elaborate game structure. 'Don't you have any questions for *us*?' Corbyn arrowed a *what are you doing* look over at him. 'How about if I supply you with one?'

Paine turned, Kamamalu at his shoulder. 'So let me get this right, David. You want *me* to ask you some questions? Starting with one *you're* going to supply me with, is that right? Man, I thought I was a convoluted son-of-a-bitch!' He paused for a few seconds. 'Okay, I'm intrigued. Let's play.'

Song strained to moisten his arid mouth. 'Ask me how many devices you've planted in total, and I'll give you the answer.'

Paine's silence mastered the room. 'How could you possibly know the answer to that?' he asked, which was exactly what everyone else was thinking. In D.C. and Quantico a light murmuring had burst out in over-packed rooms, shushed quiet by the ranking person in each.

Song inhaled noisily through his nose, 'Ask me the question and you'll find out.'

For only the second time since they had met - O'Brian being the other - Paine wasn't in full command of the situation. A series of expressions passed fleetingly across his wizened face. 'Alright, I will'. Paine cleared his throat. 'So then, Detective Sergeant David Song, how many devices have I planted in total?'

The cameras hummed noisily, the only sound in that Mountain Lakes room. Song laced his fingers together and rocked forward. 'One-hundred and sixty-seven.'

Paine was rigid for a moment, before his face melted into a warm grin as he began a slow hand-clap of congratulation.

Chapter 7

Our doubts are traitors and make us lose the good we often might win by fearing to attempt

: Jane Addams

THERE WAS A NOISY PANDEMONIUM IN D.C. AND QUANTICO, everyone speaking at the same time. There was a quiet pandemonium of thoughts too in the interview room in Mountain Lakes as the team demurely filed into the kitchen, Kamamalu leading a smiling Paine back to his bedroom. Once through the swing door, their veneer of self control collapsed with everyone jostling Song.

'Son of a bitch, David!' shrieked Townsend, her voice high and shrill. 'How the fuck did you work that one out?' Corbyn had one appreciative hand on Song's shoulder, his other speed dialing Greene. Fernandez cursed at a pen that couldn't keep up with his fevered writing. Scott looked on in shock. The back-office staff had poured in from the cottage, partly to take instructions, partly to share in the intensity of the moment, gawping at Song in amazement.

'It'd been bothering me ever since I saw it at his house. It seemed a strange thing to have scratched one-hundred and sixty-seven into the door frame. When he'd asked Nevada to prove she was personally there at the airport it was about the position of the gum. Simple. And he could have done the same at the house: what's the color of the drapes, how many steps are there up to the porch? And if you're going to do it with numbers, why not scratch a single digit rather than three, unless they mean something. So when Michelle made the point about Paine's preoccupation with order, it occurred to me he might have felt compelled to number his work. Finally, I took the view that even Paine wouldn't want to sit at home with explosives lodged under the front of his house, so it was likely to be the last he'd set before turning himself in. Which is why the scratch was fresh; his one-hundred and sixty-seventh device.'

'Kudos, David, kudos!' bubbled Fernandez.

'It's the worst of news, I take no pride in it. And now someone in D.C. has to decide whether it's true or not.'

'And that's precisely what's going to happen,' answered Corbyn coming off the phone. 'Tomorrow morning at 0800hrs we'll be meeting them, and this time they're coming to us.'

———

It was warm for spring in New Jersey, the team sitting on the deck with the remnants of an evening meal before them. Benjamin had gotten hold of a proper coffee maker, bringing everyone a cup.

'That was restaurant quality pizza, Bradley', offered Townsend, exaggerating the size of her stomach. 'No wonder there are so many people on the streets down there if this is what you're serving up.' Scott blushed as people echoed her praise.

'May I propose a lemonade toast to David', suggested Fernandez, the frosted glass incongruous in his manicured hands. 'For a stroke of detective genius the likes of which Conan Doyle would have been proud. Even if it has yielded an extraordinarily bitter harvest.' They clinked glasses, minds still on the topic that had dominated their dinner conversation.

A staggering one-hundred and fifty-eight devices still to come.

Their worlds had changed in that instant. The theater, the church, the theme park - each in themselves enormous pre-occupations – had been vanquished to the margins by those three digits. Corbyn had been characteristically discreet about the particulars as they ate, only sharing with them the general tsunami of panic that had crashed over Washington as Paine had stood to applaud Song's insight. Since then he and Benjamin had been on phones for six hours straight to an ever growing array of agencies and political elites. Case strategies were being deleted on hard drives, PR game- plans lay in thin strips alongside paper shredders, diaries were being zeroed. The President had elevated the status of his briefings from once every twelve hours to every four, and the team's once anonymous names now graced the rarified air of the Oval Office.

As they sat around this ageing garden table with its wobbly leg, hundreds of miles away in DC it was as though Normandy was being planned all over again.

—————

After an early morning run Song and Townsend were quaffing juice and perspiring in the kitchen as Scott shuffled around preparing food, whistling a hymn the Californian half recognized from his childhood. The lightness of the mood that morning as the toast pinged and the bacon sizzled struck the detective as odd.

It was down to one thing: at last they had scored a victory. At last they had won something on their own recognizance rather than having it dangled in front of them by their adversary. And although the number of devices was immense, it was fathomable at last.

An hour later in the operations room, Song shook the hand again of Homeland's Deputy Director Dawn Sharper and met a new face, Calvin Adamski, Chief Press Officer of the FBI. Together they had the appearance of unlikely Siamese twins. 'Today it's them who've come to visit; tomorrow it'll be the President and Elvis', whispered Townsend.

'Four days ago when you first met Deputy Director Sharper, the situation was extremely serious', opened Adamski. 'Now it's close to crisis. Given yesterday's disturbing revelation of the enormity of the problem', shooting Song a pale grin, 'our respective agencies have offered the President identical advice, with which he has concurred.' Song looked over at Fernandez, realizing this speech was mainly directed at him and understanding for the first time the incredible power over history that this man now held. The performance of politician and bureaucrats alike measured in this man's choice of a handful of syllables. 'The advice from Jack Greene is that a more aggressive approach to Paine could result in the withdrawal of his cooperation, so the President has heeded this advice. Hence Paine will remain un-charged, cited only as helping with our investigations.'

Song conjured up the vision of a flip-chart in the Oval Office, a thick black line down its center: arguments for appeasing Paine on the left, arguments for tearing out his fingernails on the right. The lists were probably more equally balanced than Adamski would admit.

'Commensurate with this approach, the Bureau will host a press conference to announce the credible threat made to one of our nation's churches.' Townsend and Song looked at each other and then at Corbyn who resisted their gaze. 'Do you have any questions?' Song had dozens, but now was not the time.

'Excuse me, Mr. Adamski, but can I go back to the *Fishermen* in New York?' asked Scott. 'With all these bombs still to go off, we could be here for ages! I've worked it out and if Paine's setting off, say, twenty bombs every month, we could be here for another eight months. That's like a Pearl Harbor or a 9/11 lasting over half a year!'

Song saw Sharper shiver at Scott's brutal mathematics, but in his own simple way the Fisherman had deftly placed his finger on the gut-wrenching point they had all privately been considering: months and months more of this? If it wasn't war, what was it?

Adamski deflected, desperate not to have this irritating ballast of a man draw him out in front of the equally irritating journalist. 'One more thing. Deputy Director Sharper will meet with Paine today under the aegis of this team to reaffirm our cooperation.'

'I'm not sure that's such a good idea.' It was Nevada who courageously said what Song and everyone else were thinking. Corbyn's eyes counseled silence to her.

'The decision's already been made', replied Adamski. For the first time Song was thankful for Fernandez's presence, otherwise the FBI's Chief Press Officer might have chosen other words.

'Who by?' she continued unabashed, closing in on the circled wagons. Fernandez noisily flipped to a fresh sheet, pen scratching across the verdant page.

'It was a joint decision taken at the highest level, Agent,' interjected Sharper at the very edge of her patience.

'Well whoever made that "joint decision" must have their heads up their butts. Whenever Paine's been faced with someone he hasn't personally selected his behavior's become erratic. Given the shallow time frames we're dealing with, we shouldn't run that risk.'

'Nevada,' said Adamski using her first name for better connection,'the decision has been made. Period. And in deference to your excellent point about the critical importance of time, can we get a pot of coffee in here pronto before Dawn meets him?'

Paine and Sharper entered the communal room from different doors at the same time, Song seeing Corbyn's hand in even this small piece of stage timing. She perched on her chair like a length of cold steel articulated in two places and covered in a thick winter frost. Paine immediately stole the floor.

'We always start each of our sessions with a moment of prayer. Over to you, Bradley.'

The Fisherman at last reacted as though he had been expecting it. 'Dear Lord, we ask that you grant Deputy Director Sharper the wisdom to solve this case quickly, just as we ask you to deny Thomas Paine the resolution to prolong it.'

Sharper wasn't sure what to do now, so she just ploughed on as she had always done in her pile-driving career. 'Mr. Paine – or whatever your real name is - the reason you've not been charged yet is because you've indicated this would lead to your non-cooperation. We have unwillingly agreed to this request as it's our desire to minimize the loss of life at your despicable hands. However, when this investigation is completed, rest assured we will pursue the case against you with extreme prejudice.' Sharper stopped, as Paine vaguely held up a hand to attract her attention. For Song it hadn't come a moment too soon. It was as if a drunken gunfighter had stumbled out of a saloon firing a six-shooter up at the mission bells, the bullets ricocheting amongst the peaceable townsfolk down below. Across the circle Townsend stared fixedly at the floor.

'Just a moment please, Ms. Sharper. Tell me, do you have any children?' Again she seemed unsure how to respond.

'Two sons.'

'Excellent. I was never so lucky. And where are they now. *Right* now?'

'One's a freshman at Penn, the other a senior at Rutgers.'

'Rutgers?' Paine sat up a little. 'Oh, I am so sorry. I hope he'll be okay.' She looked at him long and hard, instincts working the way any mother's would. He's jerking the puppy on its lead, thought Song.

'Pursue the case against you with extreme prejudice', she picked up again, her maternal mind still flashing images of the unthinkable. 'However, if you tell us your demands we might be able to negotiate some arrangement.'

'My demands? You mean like ten million in unmarked bills in an attaché case? Or the release of political prisoners from an Israeli jail? Or a public statement about Roswell, is that what you mean? But I've already told Special Agent Corbyn as many times as you've visited an *Armani* store, I don't have any.'

'Then what is the purpose of all this?'

'Dawn, shouldn't you be leaving this line of enquiry to the investigative team?' Paine coached her.

'Sure, sure,' she backed off, 'and we have great faith in the people you've assembled', mumbled unconvincingly. 'However, if at any time you wish to access more senior personnel in the hierarchy, please feel free to contact me direct.'

Song's interpretation of this was, "We have to support this team of rank amateurs because we were the ones who fucked up by putting them in place before we knew where this staggeringly huge case was going. Now it's blown up in our faces because you're insisting that they stay." Corbyn's face was unreadable.

Paine's eyes were on the coffee table, head nodding slowly. 'Will your family be taking a vacation this year, Ms. Sharper?' again with dinner party small-talk delivery.

'Possibly', caution dripping from her voice. 'It depends how busy we are through the summer.'

Paine's face showed he sympathized with the difficulties of balancing career and family. 'Well if you do, I'd suggest you don't travel via any U.S. airports in September, and I don't just mean the eleventh. Whoever said flying was the safest way to travel may need to re-look at those statistics this fall - 'fall' being the operative word.'

Fortunately Sharper showed the sense not to respond, making her cold apologies before leaving. Slowly but surely this man was ticking every box of the nightmare scenario. Which sane American would choose to fly Russian Roulette Airlines in September when this became known? And what about the Rutgers quip? The situation was truly unbelievable.

'We have confirmation that all the bombs were placed within the fabric of the buildings', summarized Margolis by video conference that morning. 'LA's was in a length of sewer piping with a spur off the street lights for power; the Gator stadium in a retaining wall. So it's definite now that Rockwell must have had access either at the time of build or during maintenance. We're talking about bombs being *in situ* for years, perhaps decades.'

Billy-Jo Spearing updated them on the forlorn hunt for his real identity. 'We've drawn a complete blank. Agents have interviewed the remaining twenty-six Paines and Lanes, and they all check out.'

'So what's your thinking on how he got his driving license?' asked Greene via a link from his D.C. office.

'Simple - he's got very good forgeries. He might have the real one in his billfold, but we're not allowed to look.'

Song twirled his pencil not having captured one note, because once more there was nothing meaningful to write. He pinched the bridge of his nose with a ferocity born of frustration. This was still going nowhere. If something in the natural course of events didn't happen soon, he would need to initiate something unnatural himself.

At noon, everyone crowded around the TV to watch Adamski's D.C. press conference. 'Although the United States does not bow to terrorism, neither does it willfully risk the lives of its citizens in their own communities', he concluded his opening speech. 'As such, we ask church leaders to work closely with us to search their places of worship. The first two exercises will be at the President's own churches, one here in Washington, the other in his home state of Wisconsin. However, if despite our joint industry we are unable to locate the device, then the prudent action will be to close all churches this coming Sunday.'

'Close the churches on a Sunday? It's *Revelations*', croaked Scott in disbelief. Adamski went on to offer caveats and warnings against independent searches, mindful of the near anarchy that had prevailed after St. Bartholomew's.

'Where will the President's family be worshipping this Sunday?' shouted a man from *AP*.

'Hopefully at his D.C. church if the device is found in advance. If not, there will be a private service in the White House this Saturday.'

'When you say church, does that exclude other places of worship?' asked a man from the *BBC*.

'Yes', said sternly, Adamski affecting to appear in control.

'But if your source close to Rockwell can't tell you which church it's in then maybe it's a mosque, or a temple?' Adamski dodged the supplementary, a minder at his elbow whispering urgent advice.

'Is America at war with someone and the Commander-in-Chief just forgot to tell us?' called someone acerbically from the back, Adamski pretending not to hear.

'Did your source tell you if the church would be the end of Rockwell's campaign?' asked a woman from *Time*. 'And, after St. Bartholomew and the crematorium, can this Administration really be trusted to disclose everything it knows anyway?'

'We prefer not to call the perpetrator Rockwell. He's a terrorist, plain and simple', backed up Adamski, not commenting on the rest.

'Will this church look like one from a Rockwell painting?' asked the woman from *CNN* choosing not to have heard his last entreaty. Adamski dropped anchor on this and every question thereafter, the turbulent media ocean growing steadily rougher. Corbyn flicked the uninformative screen to mute.

'How the hell are they going to search every church in America between now and Saturday night?' asked Townsend.

'Or search them thoroughly', added a miserable looking Scott.

'The national and state guards, local police, and field agents from all agencies are being briefed', said the voice of Margolis from the video link, 'and all leave has been cancelled, as have all restrictions on overtime budgets. It's the closest thing to a national mobilization since the British were still in Boston.'

'Well,' said Townsend matter-of-factly, 'if it's true that God rested on the seventh day, he can sleep in again this Sunday because he sure won't be getting many calls to the office that day.'

Chapter 8

Question with boldness even the existence of a God; because, if there be one, he must more approve of the homage of reason, than that of blind-folded fear

: Thomas Jefferson

SONG WAS GRABBING SOME NOODLES BEFORE THE ONE o'clock meeting when Paine walked in carrying an empty mug. 'What did you think of Adamski's performance? If I didn't know exactly what was happening, I'd be scared shitless myself.'

'I thought he did okay', replied Song, keeping it conversational. 'And technically speaking it's not Adamski who's scaring the shit out of people.'

'Fair point,' responded Paine slathering butter onto slices of white. 'Are you going to have some lunch with me? For some reason no-one else can ever find the time.' Stepping onto the deck, they cleared the chairs of yesterday's well-used newspapers. Once again Song was struck by the utter calm of the man; by his ordinariness.

'Again, nice job on the one-six-seven! I'd expected that would take the team a lot longer. I'm glad because if everything kept going as I'd planned it'd get very tedious. I learnt that from Monsignor O'Brian. What did you think of Sharper's performance this morning?'

'I think she was in a difficult position. Top brass had to reach out to you and what exactly was she supposed to say? She probably wanted to rip your liver out through your dick. And I thought that shit about Rutgers was a really cheap shot.'

Paine snorted through a mouthful of chips. 'She's bright enough to weigh the odds. But then again I guess this is all about probabilities, isn't it?' He clapped his hands together to remove some crumbs. 'How do you think it's going in general?'

'I'd say you've effectively maintained control by brushing enough scraps from the table to keep the begging dogs interested', reflected Song. 'You've warned off the Washington boys and you've kept this team in play – *your* team that is. You have the undivided attention of the nation, which you won't be losing any time soon. Your most unusual omission is the motive, while the most unusual commission is why you gave yourself up in the first place. Everything that's happened so far could have been done anonymously so I'm assuming there's something in the future which requires you to be physically present?'

Paine carefully dabbed his lips with a paper napkin. 'Sort the motive mystery and you'll unlock the case. And as to why I gave myself up, it's a bit like watching the Super Bowl. You *can* do it on your own, but it's much more fun to do it with others.'

'How are you fixed for medicines?' Song asked, veering off.

'I've got pills for high blood pressure I bought on the net, and the inestimable Kamamalu is keeping a record of how many of those I take. Just in case I decide to OD, I guess.'

'How bad is it?'

'It's controllable. But if I don't stay on top of it my head could blow off like a cartoon champagne cork, and none of you would want that, would you?'

'Not at the moment, but in the future I know some people who'd pay good money to watch. So you don't need any other medication?' continued Song on his fishing expedition.

'Why would I?' asked Paine, pushing grapes around the plate with his finger. The man knew there was a hook in the water, circling underneath it for fun.

'I'd noticed you wince sometimes when you're sitting. Is there a pain prescription we can refill for you?'

'I'm fine, thanks, and let me save you some investigative time. I've never been to see a doctor about it, so there'll be no records through which you can trace my real identity. I guess you've worked out the Paine/Lane duality by now, and if not, shame on you.'

Song let silence erase the slate for a few seconds. 'Why did you try to kill me in Pender?'

Paine had started on his third sandwich. 'Christ, David - I've already answered that!'

'No, you gave me *an* answer.'

'Spur of the moment thing. Maybe just to check that you really are your father's son.'

Again Song felt as though someone had turned his skin inside out. 'How do you know my father, Terrance May?'

Paine popped the remainder of the sandwich into his mouth. 'It's just an expression', he smiled, rising with his empty cup. 'I'm going to freshen my coffee and head back to the TV coverage. Earlier on the head of a dumbass religious group in Arkansas was incorrectly quoting *Revelations* to a *Fox* reporter too dense to notice.

It's interesting: you bomb one church, but look how the others burn too.'

Ten minutes later everyone returned to the interview room, Fernandez having spent the rest of the morning on his PC, Scott spending the remainder of his in quiet prayer. Nevada had been for a lunchtime run passing the town's churches, their doors flung open by stern faced parishioners still in their office clothing. A curious mixture of determination and helplessness etched into their shattered faces.

'Last night David suggested you might want to share some questions for us, Thomas', opened Corbyn at their *faux* team meeting.

'Yes, but I won't take too long because – frankly – all of the excitement is on TV right now. You'd think someone had spotted the Iranians landing. I've concocted four questions and if you can answer them I'll divulge the locations of a limited number of devices as an incentive. Additionally, if any of the team's members can figure out why I invited them, I'll give you fifteen locations for each one. So, here are my questions.

One, why hasn't anyone snuck into my bathroom yet while I'm taking a shower? Two, if you want to find out who I am, why don't you follow the splinter? Three, how many gallons of water are there behind the Hoover dam? Four, in 1996 when Melissa Davidson spoke at Withers Hall, who was the most approving member of her audience?'

Shuffling his papers to buy a fragment of time, Corbyn spoke first. 'What splinter are you talking about?'

Paine rose, stretching his arms and shaking a leg, 'That's not an answer, that's another question. You had yours last night; this was supposed to be my turn.'

'I get that, but it really would help if you could be more specific,' he persevered.

'Alex, really!' Paine railed in mock disappointment. 'You want me to write the answers down, wipe Sharper's ass with it, and then fold it into an origami swan for you? For fuck's sake, show some ingenuity! David and Nevada are the only ones consistently hitting the ball while all of your PhD's at the end of this feed are adding jack-shit. Come back to me when you have answers, otherwise I don't want to see you again until after Sunday's ecumenical barbeque.'

Paine retreated to his room under Kamamalu's watchful eye, leaving a puzzled audience. 'What did he mean about the Hoover Dam? He's not saying – he's not saying - ', stuttered Scott as if even to finish the question would be sacrilege.

Fernandez darted in front of David and Nevada as Corbyn rushed out to start his long list of calls. 'I appreciate you have a lot to do given this intriguing new information, but could we carve out some time for our background interviews?'

'What interviews?' asked Townsend, forehead wrinkling.

'Part of the arrangement is that I be given access to the key players working the case. Indeed one of the angles I'm thinking about is to have parts of the story written through your eyes.'

Townsend arched an eye brow, 'No one's told me, but as a member of the FBI I will of course do as instructed. Let me discuss it with Corbyn.'

Fernandez smiled. 'And that goes the same for you, David?'

'No it doesn't.'

'You mean you won't be discussing it with Agent Corbyn?'

'I'm not a member of the FBI, my command structure resides in San Francisco. If I'm ordered to cooperate, I will. But until then I'm not available for comment.'

Fernandez's customary coolness descended again. 'I see, so I'll make the necessary enquiries. But might I ask why you wouldn't want to contribute? After all, this can only enhance your fame.'

'Gabriel', Song barked at him. 'Already a score of people have died, and the country's been placed on a nationwide alert. I'm not looking to get rich through other people's misery. Anonymity will do me just fine.'

───────────

Oppenheim swiveled round as the team strode into the operations room. 'For question two on the "splinter" we're searching the DB now. Could be a political splinter group, but there are thousands of them. Ditto for religious groups. Paine said "the" splinter, not "a" splinter. Probably a noun, rather than a verb or adjective.

On question three, the worrying answer is that Lake Mead, the reservoir behind the Hoover Dam, backs up for 110 miles. *Wiki* says eight and a half thousand cubic *miles* of water. Fuck! Greene's in touch with the field office and they're pulling together the Disaster Recovery documents. For sure they'll be telling the White House soon. This is monumental.

Question four, the name Melissa Davidson is generating thirteen million *Google* hits, and Withers Hall a further five million. But there's a teaching facility with that name at North Carolina state which seems too much of a coincidence. We'll try to link the two for intersections, but if it was something happening in 1996 the infancy of the Web at that time means it's unlikely we'll find much.

On question one, the "why haven't you been in while I'm taking a shower", we have no frigging idea. Does it have a sexual connotation, is it a euphemism, a metaphor, is there something we're supposed to see?' she gave an exaggerated shrug.

'Any ideas about the shower, David?' Townsend asked, partly because she was interested and partly because she didn't want to think about the situation developing at the Dam in her home state.

'No, but Paine just gave us the invitation to find out.'

'I'm not comfortable with this', protested Special Counsel Samantha Franks across the video link. Her face looked green, Song blaming the screen's color balance rather than the way she was probably feeling. 'I know this is broken-record but once again, we have no right of access to his room, let alone his shower.'

'What about publishing his photo for this splinter thing?' pressed Song. 'I'm sure we could find an image of him somewhere in Pender County. Can't we circulate it and see what's thrown up?'

'Absolutely not, Detective. We knew when we did this deal with the Devil that it would cut both ways: we get vital intel on the bombings and he gets to escape the manacles for a while. It's a shitty arrangement but it's already paid dividends. Anyway, I've seen the tape and he said, "Why hasn't anyone snuck into my bathroom yet when I'm taking a shower?", and that's equivocal. It's completely different to what happened at his home where he'd authorized David's entrance.'

'Hang on,' piped Nevada. 'Since we've been here, no one's cleaned any of the rooms, right? So if we asked to service his room, couldn't we gain access while he's showering?'

'As long as we only looked for things in plain sight', rejoined Corbyn while Franks weighed the cost-benefit equation.

'Okay,' she said at last, 'I'm going to authorize it. Do it the way Nevada suggests, and if he agrees – and only if he agrees! – get your rubber gloves on.'

'And as it was my idea, I want the job of servicing the Paine Suite', said Townsend in a voice that would brook no challenge.

———

Kamamalu broached the cleaning issue wrapped up in some other hum-drum questions about laundry and toiletries, Paine barely stirring from the TV to grunt his assent. The Hawaiian sat on the deck with the team that night; jacket off for the first time since Song had met him, his Glock 22 buried under a trunk-like arm.

'David, I want you to fly home tomorrow and speak with your father', said Corbyn across the slatted wooden table. 'Nevada, the same for you with your mom after you've completed your strategic cleaning duties.' Song's stomach lurched at this mixture of sweet and sour: it would be terrific to see his family again, but the conversation's agenda filled him with dread.

Benjamin and Oppenheim had piles of paper arrayed before them. 'The church searches have started', explained the Homeland Agent, 'and it's *the* news item on every channel. It's like the day after 9/11; the nation is walking around stunned. On Melissa Davidson, we think we've found her. She's a professor of political science at the University of Bath in England. Divorced, 46, a British citizen, written extensively on the topic of violence against the state. The British spooks are trying to find her for us but she's hiking somewhere. With regards to the Hoover, local Bureau are coordinating a search under the cover of an emergency drill. The President's been informed and is in discussions about contingency plans. You can guess the implications. On Paine's oblique reference to the theme parks next weekend, Deputy Director Sharper will be calling you personally to discuss this, Alex.'

'Interesting counterpoint', said Townsend. 'Keep people out of their otherworldly places one weekend and their worldly places the next. Almost as though he had a plan...'

'The DNA results from Pender are in but we're getting no hits. Surprise, surprise', continued Benjamin. 'Meanwhile, the Chinese Consulate has excellent records of construction work because everyone entering has to be security checked. That's the good news. The really bad news is that the last time structural work was done in that room was 1983.'

'So we're saying Paine planted that device thirty ago?' asked Townsend incredulously.

'It's still difficult to believe', said Song, contemplating the magnitude of the idea. 'A man sets himself upon a course of action over a quarter of a century ago, using the time in-between to seed upwards of 167 devices, waiting until now to execute it. The pathology's incredible.'

'But if he doesn't have accomplices', added Townsend, 'he must have set the mechanisms at the same time. Is there anything that can last that long?' Everyone shrugged, bemused that clearly there must be.

'I need to raise something again', stated Song, leaning onto the table. 'Can we distribute his photo to the media?'

'But you know the answer to that', interceded an exasperated Benjamin. 'Special Counsel Franks explicitly told you again today that we can't!'

'Yes, but we're a week into the investigation and we still don't know who the fucking guy is! Nothing from DNA or prints, no one spontaneously emerging to finger him – nothing. So what's going to change between now and bomb 167? Can't we at least *think* about taking this one risk? It might open up the whole case.'

'I understand your frustration', picked up Corbyn. 'We all feel it too, but that avenue is closed.' The tension sat for a while before they broke up, Corbyn signaling for Song to wait around while he went to the bathroom.

Alone now on the balcony, Song looked up at the darkening sky. On balance he was pleased to be going home tomorrow, even if the purpose disturbed him. He thought back to Greene's comment in Quantico about needing to get ahead of the curve. But the fact was that they hadn't. Paine had given them four new channels to investigate, but once again it was his handout and none of them were clear. No different to Scott ladling out soup to those who were equally helpless. There really was no point in getting ahead of the curve if it was just part of a shape over which Paine was exercising full artistic control.

No risk, no reward: Paine had implied as much himself. But with everyone in the Bureau pirouetting on legal egg shells, that really just meant no risk at all. But Song wasn't Bureau. He had options the others didn't have. If anyone on this team was going to bisect that curve it could only be him. The outline of several covert plans had already begun to coalesce in his mind. Plans with very great risk, but equally great reward.

He looked down at the table, empty now except for Corbyn's cell. Throwing a glance into the house, he saw the man making his way back to the patio doors. Song snatched up the agent's phone and slipped it into his pocket.

'This is awkward, David, 'began Corbyn upon his return, 'but I have to raise it with you. When you're down in San Francisco, I also need you to speak with your mother about -'

'About whether Terrance May is really my father. Yes, I know.' Song rested his elbows on the balcony rail peering into the darkness blanketing the woods. 'When I asked Paine why he'd tried to kill me he said it was to check if I was my father's son. I then asked him if he knew Terrance May and he backed off. There are many interpretations of that but one of them – the ugly one - is that my mom conceived me with another man. And if that's so, maybe he's my link to Paine.'

'It's just one possibility', Corbyn said softly as a silence descended upon them. 'One hundred and sixty-seven', the special agent whistled, shaking his head in admiration.' Wow! It's entirely changed the character of the case, and that's down to you alone. People will be eating out on that story for years to come. I can truly say it's my honor to have you on the team, David.'

Song thought of Corbyn's stolen phone, heavy and angular in his pocket, glad that the thickening night hid the reddening of his face.

Song, Townsend and a gaggle of agents embarked upon a 4.30 a.m. run the next day. Just before a sharp bend along a deserted road Song pulled up, telling the others to continue while he took a leak. As they moved jerkily round the corner he extracted Corbyn's phone from his sock, wiped it clean of his prints and placed it under a stone at the cusp of the tree line. The evening before he had accessed what he needed from it, so now was the time to lose it for good.

They jogged past the Mountain Lakes Baptist Church just as dawn yawned across the sky. Townsend caught sight of something and called a halt, the ragged group panting to a thankful stop. She skipped up the steps to a huddle of three people half sleeping on kitchen chairs. Candles were hung from makeshift lanterns, guttering in the light morning breeze. 'Hi, what's going on?' her breathing not betraying that she had just run five hilly miles.

'It's a candlelight vigil, ma'am. The congregation's taking it in turn to watch over the place until the bomb crisis is over. If you'd like to wait the next shift's bringing bagels and coffee soon.'

'That's kind, but we need to be getting on. Are all the other churches in town doing this?'

'Sure. And if there aren't enough people for a shift, we're splitting our resources and helping each other out. Clement here's a Catholic, and he strolled over in the middle of the night so we could take a comfort break.'

'Is this happening everywhere?'

'Yes, ma'am! We were listening to talk-radio until our batteries went. We called the New Jersey radio stations at three this morning, but all the switchboards were jammed. *At three in the morning* – can you believe it? Seems like the whole of America was up last night. I had a call at midnight from my son at his church in Pennsylvania. He says there are candles on people's porches, in windows, with people just walking the streets holding them. There's a rumor the First Lady will take a shift watching vigil at the President's church tonight. And it's not just the churches; the Muslims are at their mosques, the Buddhists at their temples. It's as if Rockwell's attacking God, not just His houses.' Townsend shook her head in wonderment, most of it genuine.

The runners gratefully accepted the water proffered and with a wave continued on their way. As their weary legs climbed the final hill back to the safe house, Song thought of the Athenians battling courageously at Marathon against an overwhelming force of Persians, and of a runner bringing news back to the city of a great victory.

———

Like clockwork, Paine showered at eight a.m. every day following a light breakfast and a ritual trawl through the news channels. Agents were seen incongruously with dusters and spray polish, but no contract cleaner need fear for their job that morning. Nevertheless, Corbyn had told them this wasn't just a cosmetic clean anymore as he was searching for the cell he had misplaced last evening. Townsend was running the vacuum cleaner repeatedly around the same area of the communal room when Kamamalu nodded her in.

Paine's bedroom was immaculate, with fresh clothes laid out upon an already made bed. She turned off the cleaner just in time to hear the muffled rush of the shower nozzle and the light clunk of the cubicle door as he stepped inside. She took a deep breath and eased the bathroom door open.

Immediately to her right were a mirror and two sinks set into a marble topped unit bearing his toothpaste, razor, and watch. At the far end a long shower cubicle, frosted glass on the left hand side, a transparent sliding door to the right, his towel thrown lazily over it. In a heap on the floor lay Paine's dressing gown and pajamas. She stepped lightly into the room stopping in the center, breathing shallowly. Through the hissing shower Paine was humming some 70's tune she half recognized. Townsend turned 360 degrees on the spot peering through the growing cloud of warm vapor.

Nothing. No Dick Tracey marks on the mirror, no ghostly dripping words on the cubicle's glass, no clue etched out in toothpaste. She spun again, raking the scene with eyes powered by adrenalin.

Still nothing. With her toe she prodded at the pile of clothes. "Only those things in plain sight", that was the rule. Fuck it, she thought, bending down to rifle the pockets, eyes on the shower.

Still nothing. Paine was humming louder now. She thought of a tattoo, or the idea of a message within the cubicle itself, both too ridiculous to be credible, but she was desperate. She took a long step towards the sliding door, steam condensing upon it as she craned round to peer in.

Paine was facing away, head bowed, massaging shampoo into short, spiky hair. He had the skin of someone in his sixties, but the muscle tone spoke of a man who looked after himself. She saw some moles, grey hair flattened under the cascade of water, some small scars, but no tattoos - no luminous arrows pointing the way out of this investigative maze. The seconds ticked by and eventually he turned, raising closed eyes to the ceiling, allowing the spent shampoo to run down his back. The first thing she noticed was his erection looking strong and hard. Apart from that, nothing.

She quietly shuffled back into the middle of the room, statuesque. Not long now before he would finish. Once again she turned 360 degrees, willing herself to see the invisible. *Why had he specifically mentioned the shower?* Something he did there allowing the team to see something not visible at any other time. Townsend ran her eyes across the articles on the marble surface. Brushing his teeth? Shaving his face? What could it be? He had stopped humming.

Then she saw it.

Leaping towards the sink as the shower turned off, she swept up Paine's antique LCD watch. What was the one thing you wouldn't take into the shower that you'd wear at all other times? An old- fashioned electronic watch.

She flicked it round as though it were scalding to the touch. The time was correct, antique red numerals burning out from a black face; the date correct too. She heard the towel rustle as he pulled it into the cubicle. The strap? Cheap black plastic, no markings, no writing. She flipped it over, as out of the corner of her eye she saw Paine's edging towards the cubicle door, toweling his hair.

There! She had found it! Throwing it back onto the marble, she dashed towards the door.

'Don't you want to join me in here, Nevada?' she heard him playfully shout, as she snapped the door shut behind her.

Taking a deep breath outside, Townsend realized she was blushing redder than the numerals on Paine's watch.

'It was on the back plate', she told the team in the cottage, a video link open to Quantico. 'An engraved *JH352*. It was pretty basic work though.'

'And there was nothing else? No marks on his body, nothing more obvious?' asked Benjamin.

'No, it's the watch, I'm sure of it.'

'When I was looking through the CSI's inventory of his house, there was reference to an engraving kit', noted Song. Oppenheim nodded to one of her analysts who started clicking through the files.

'So what could it mean?' asked Benjamin. 'Initials and part of a zip code, or a map reference? Maybe March 1952?'

'Any ideas, Quantico?' Corbyn said into the ether. Several different disembodied voices generated answers around the same theme: the date of an event, uses of these numbers in history, death of a loved one. All interesting, but entirely speculative without a context.

Corbyn looked at the paper handed to him. 'Here's a copy of Paine's inventory: *One electric engraving tool. Well used.* Okay then, let's assume the *JH352* is what he wanted us to find. Now we just have to work out why.'

By eleven that morning, Song and Townsend were in an FBI jet speeding west. Her mother was visiting friends in San Jose just south of San Francisco so they were both heading there.

'Have you *Googled* the case today?' asked Song, deftly choreographing information across his iPad. 'It's like being out in a blizzard. I've got eighteen million hits on the situation with the churches alone, and if you go onto any home page of any church the screen is obliterated by calls for community action.' There was a clip of one of the funeral processions in New York, shocking Song that he could have so soon forgotten about that first attack.

'Take a look at this, David. Remember those "Vigilante Angels" at Rosa Parks? Well this guy has set up a website called *Vigilangels* and there are already thousands of postings on it. He's even got a *Vigilangels* Gift Shop with profits going to Paine's victims. Every item is sold out.'

'When you were looking at Paine in the shower, you mentioned seeing some scars, yes?'

'Don't remind me,' she shuddered. 'A few scrapes here and there. When he was facing me I wasn't paying much attention to the scarring! I think I saw an incision around the appendix area, something above the right buttock, and a red patch around the left kidney which was probably a skin irritation.' But for Song this was the confirmation he needed to perfect his plan. A very dangerous plan indeed.

'What are you thinking?' she enquired, scenting something from his manner.

'I'm not sure yet. But I know how to find out.'

Walking into Arrivals, Song asked if the Bureau had arranged a car to take Townsend over to San Jose.

'Yep, they'll be swinging past your place tomorrow to pick me up.'

Song stopped on the spot. 'What?'

'Didn't I tell you? I'm staying at your place tonight. You'll be introducing me to your family and taking me out for some Vietnamese food.'

'Oh I will, will I?'

'Most definitely. And if you decline that would be a grave loss of face', she said in the musical tone he had already come to like. 'But don't read anything into it. The only thing you'll be jumping tonight are the hoops I'm gonna put you through in front of your family.' Before Song could respond he was almost knocked over by the flailing arms and legs of the woman who had just launched herself at him.

Charleen Tran Dok, community lawyer extraordinaire, delivered a deliberately wet kiss on his cheek. 'Welcome back, little brother! Where's my *Louis Vuitton* bag, you cheap son of a bitch?'

Gently disentangling himself from this American-Vietnamese spider woman, Song introduced Charley to Townsend. Watching them both as they shook hands, his eyes wandered to his childhood friend, the life-long cause of his heart's arrhythmia. Within a minute he was forgotten as the two women instantaneously bonded. He heard snatches of conversation about how in fourth grade he had got Charley's head caught in the school railings and charged boys a quarter to kiss her. How she had exacted her revenge by melting his *GI Joe*. Amongst the torrent of words and laughter from the back of the car Song heard fleeting references to luxury consumer goods he had only seen on billboards.

Charley had been chauffeured to the airport by her real brother, Gary, down from MIT to undertake some research with a company in Silicon. 'We saw you outside the consulate on TV. Not there just for your Mandarin, I'm sure', Gary said, guiding his BMW onto the freeway. Song let it hang in the air as Nevada and Charley talked about Pier 39. 'I'm tutoring a doctorate student who's tracking the impact of social

networking at times of crisis. That should be interesting, huh?'
he added, smiling mischievously.

Song deflected by looking out of the window at glimpses of
the Bay through passing buildings. 'I'm currently working on an
unnamed case that I need your help with, Gary', Song smiled.
'Can we talk about it some more later?'

'What's in it for me?' his old friend sparred back.

'Knowing you'll be contributing to the demise of a classic
power hegemony. One insufficiently nimble to survive the
attrition caused by emergent information paradigms.'

'Wow, you sure know how to treat a boy!' whistled Gary.
'Vencer - fucking - amos! Count me in, buddy!'

They drove directly to Song's mother's store where they
dropped him off. Charley had signed a pact with Nevada to
show her the town, agreeing they would all meet for dinner
at seven. Standing outside its entrance Song drank down the
late April air, surprised by the wave of home sickness rising in
his chest. It almost overpowered the other nausea he felt when
thinking about the impending conversation with his mom.
Entering, a vanilla K-pop tune oozed out from speakers he had
fitted a decade earlier.

'David, can you untangle those baskets please', his mom
called in Mandarin from behind the counter as if he had just
popped out a few minutes earlier. She was speaking with Mrs.
Zhou about something personal so he waited out of ear shot
for the consultation to finish before walking into the vice-like
embrace of his diminutive mother.

'Your father says Charley showed him a film of you outside
that consulate. We shouldn't have to wait for Charley to show
us, David. That's your responsibility as our son.'

'I know mom, I'm sorry', he apologized, knowing how the ritual went.

'Anyway, I'm glad you're back because tomorrow evening there's a Rockwell vigil at the Buddhist temple and I'm making one of the speeches. It'll be good to have you there - people want to see police in the community at times like this'. Song didn't volunteer that he would be leaving well before then. 'Your dad's out at a fundraiser for the communists. The Annual Democrat Softball Tournament, but he'll be back in an hour or two.'

There were many contradictions in his parent's union: their ethnicity, their physiques, their musical preferences. But the biggest was their political choices. For as long as Song could remember there'd been an annual competition as to who could raise the most money for their respective parties. "For every buck she raises to fund those GOP reactionaries, I need to raise five to support the common people" he had heard his father say half a dozen times every year. But despite the apparent fracture lines between them, Song had never seen a more devoted couple, with boyhood memories replete with examples of daily tenderness and hourly kindnesses.

Song sat down on the old wicker bar stool where virtually every Asian butt in the locality had camped-out at some time over the past thirty years. Today, aimlessly grazing through the multi-lingual newspapers on the counter, drinking hot green tea, exchanging tidbits of small talk with the shop's regular customers, he whiled away the most relaxing two hours he had spent in over a week. Finally his father limped into the store still wearing his catcher's mitt.

'Toss me that can of bean sprouts, son!' he called from the entrance, Song happily obliging. Can lodged squarely in his glove, Terrance May advanced to give his son a huge hug.

'Why are you limping?' asked his wife as he leant across the counter to peck her on the lips.

'Teddy Ellingham bunted with a man on second. Seems I can't run like a gazelle anymore and I felt something pop in my calf. I always thought Teddy was a closet Republican, and now I know for sure!'

'If he was a Republican he'd have hit it out of the park, my sweet!' she replied. They continued this happy banter, Song marveling at their enduring affection.

'Stop it now or I'll arrest the pair of you for public indecency.' He took the deepest of breaths. 'Listen, I need to speak with you.' They looked at him, the same picture of concern. His mother was immediately on the phone to her Taiwanese friend to cover the shop. Soon the three of them were ensconced in the tiny stock room, fresh cups of tea in their hands, Song steeling himself for a conversation he had been rehearsing in his head but for which he still had not found the right words.

'You know I'm working on these bombing cases, yes?'

'On Rockwell. Yep, we'd thought as much', offered his dad.

'So whatever I share with you today stays within these four walls. Not even Charley or her mom, you understand?' he looked in mock accusation at his mother. She nodded, touching the silver Buddha hanging from her neck-chain, a tenth anniversary present from her loving husband. Song took them through the parts of the case they needed to know. The question of his parentage he mercifully could leave out for now.

'But isn't it possible that Rockwell really did come across your name because of that *i4ni* case, and that's all there is to it?' asked his mom, proud her son was playing on this vast stage.

'Possible, but unlikely. And with the references he's made to dad, well ...'

His father remained quiet, a puzzled frown on his brow. Clear that no amount of words could adequately describe Paine to this audience, Song pulled out his phone. 'Dad, do you recognize this man?' showing him the image of Paine he had secretly and illegally sent to his cell from Corbyn's. His neck prickled as he thought of that phone now buried in the Mountain Lakes woods. 'Take a good look and try to imagine him as a younger man.' Song's mind flicked to an image of Special Counsel Franks and a SWAT team bursting into the stockroom, packets of noodles and cans of water chestnuts tumbling before them.

Terrence May peered at the image for a long while. 'I'm so sorry, son - nothing. Is this Rockwell or the man who's helping you out? But he's as old as me!'

Song handed the phone to his mother. 'The name we have is Thomas Paine but he's also known as Thomas Lane. Maybe from your college days, from the party organization, from teaching?' Again they both shook their heads, disappointed at letting their son down.

'The only Thomas Paine I know is the philosopher,' offered his father. 'I know a Thomas Jefferson teaching history over in Fillmore, but that's it I'm afraid.' The secret photograph now shown with no tangible result, Song surreptitiously turned on the audio recorder in his jacket pocket as others would need to hear what was about to pass. The time he had been dreading had come, like walking into a minefield wearing snow shoes.

'When we were talking to Rockwell he said he wanted to check that I was – quote - "my father's son"', shifting uncomfortably on the plastic garden chair. 'That's a curious thing for him to say if he doesn't know you, Dad, don't you agree? You've been in some scrapes in the past: the anti-nuclear stuff back in the 70's, the anti-war protests on Iraq – twice! I respect you for your courage, so is that what he's comparing me against? Does he know you from that?' Again the old man blankly shook his head. Song was sweating hard in the coolness of the stock room. He was going to have to ask the question that would break his mom's heart. But it was her that spoke first.

'Rockwell is smart, yes? And he's playing some kind of game with your team. So you're hanging on his every word and trying to interpret their meanings, yes?' she said slowly, Song nodding in agreement. 'So when he says "are you really your father's son", your detective's mind starts to consider all the possibilities.' She straightened her back, her voice cooling as the half-idea in her sharp mind flowered into deadly nightshade. 'And one of these possibilities is that this is not your real father, is that correct?' reaching across to take her husband's hand, Song's choked silence her answer. Then, with an iciness Song had never experienced before, she locked onto her son's gaze.

'David Terrance Song, I can tell you that I have only ever loved four men in my life: my dear hard working father, bless his sacred memory; my first husband, Song Xiao Win, whose precious bones were tumbled into an unmarked Saigon grave; you, my dearest, dearest son; and this man whose hand I'm now holding.

This man who took me under his protection when I first arrived, frightened and alone. *This man* who taught me his language so that I might survive in a strange world. *This man* who throughout his life has been fearless in his defense of people who cannot defend themselves. *This man* who raised you to be the fine young man you are today. *This man* who's never let me down in my hour of need. *This man* whose star has been constant for me - forever. And you ask me, David Terrance Song, *you ask me if he is really your father?*' She shuddered to a jolting halt, straining to contain her rage. 'Look away in shame, boy! Look away in shame!'

Song sat on that scuffed plastic chair feeling more wretched than ever before in his life. As his mother spoke, thin fingers had tightening on his father's large hands until her knuckles resembled white marbles. Her eyes had moistened but not wept. Twenty-eight days adrift on the South China Sea had tempered her soul to the strength of steel, only to have it tested again now by her prying son. Song felt a deep, deep misery that by playing Paine's sick game his own insinuations had now brought his beloved mother to this wretched place. With a trembling voice and head held low in abject humiliation, he spoke.

'My dear mother, it is I who am dishonored and ashamed. It was never my intention -, I would never knowingly hurt you -, I humbly, humbly apologize to you and to my father. A son could never ask for better parents. I beg you both for your forgiveness.'

His father gently lifted his loving wife to her feet, extending a hand to help raise Song to his.

Together they stood the three of them, arms wrapped tightly around each other, eyes wet with love.

———

Song had already planned to walk the three miles from the store to the restaurant. There was something he needed to do, and any doubts about his resolve to do it had just evaporated in that tiny room. He took the long route, reacquainting himself with San Francisco's architecture and gardens, allowing his burning anger with Paine to dissipate, trying to put a physical and mental distance between himself and his disgrace. As he walked, Song passed beleaguered churches teeming with people, each wearing a mask of defiance. Across the city sirens gave out their distant wail as the bomb searches were repeated, church by endangered church.

But even now Song's mind was only half there, the other portion processing the case so far, pouring over the things Paine had said, trying to get a grip on what was happening and - most importantly – why. This session with his parents had been his lowest point in the case so far. He would rather be standing on that porch in Pender County than go through that miserable experience again. He despised Paine for creating the circumstances where not just Song was under suspicion, but his loved ones too.

Meandering his way towards the restaurant, Song took the opportunity to linger at street corners that afforded him good visibility in multiple directions. He looked at the reflections of passers-by in shop windows and kept a running memory of license plates, just in case. In an hour of zigzagging counter-surveillance he saw no FBI tail. Relieved, Song dodged into the Chinese herbal remedies store he had been circuitously making his way towards.

There was something he needed to buy.

Chapter 9

In skating over thin ice, our safety is in our speed

: Ralph Waldo Emerson

AT THE VIETNAMESE RESTAURANT SONGS THREE friends had already been there an hour, and four empty bottles of wine attested to them not having wasted a minute of it. Song quickly embraced the spirit knowing that both he and Nevada needed to unwind. Waiting for a taxi at midnight, Gary and Nevada discordantly sang *Born to Run* for the benefit of the odd passing car. Charley pulled Song aside, her night-black hair swishing against his cheek as she slurred into his ear.

'She's one hell of a girl, Davey. You can bring her back anytime, okay? She's sleeping at your place tonight, okay, so you make sure she's okay. Okay?'

'Don't worry, I will safeguard her honor', he responded with a baritone seriousness excited by the alcohol.

'I wasn't meaning that, you dick. I meant make sure she gets up to see her mom tomorrow. You don't seriously think you have a chance with her, do you?'

'No, no, I have no feelings for her that way', he stammered, knowing exactly who he *did* have feelings for. 'I was just saying that, well - '

'Well she certainly has no feelings for you. You're not her type, if you know what I mean.' Song looked blankly at her. 'You're not her type. And nor is Gary, nor anyone else with a penis, you idiot.'

Looking stupid, and now feeling stupid, Song mouthed an 'Oh' and winked. He thought he had understood, but maybe he had better wait until morning when his brain was back in its skull to be sure.

In the morning Song found a scribbled note on the spare room's pillow: *Left with FBI at 0600hrs. See you at jet later. Thanks for the bed, partner. Nevada.*

Song thought about what Charley had said last night as he moved quietly around his studio kitchen, trying not to bump into the hangover that was following him everywhere. He was just finishing the bacon and eggs, which had fried way too noisily, when the house phone rang.

'Is that Detective Sergeant dickhead Song? I don't know if you remember me but I used to be your partner one week ago, asshole. Now I accidentally find out that you're back in town, you fucking dip-shit!'

'Hi TK,' grinned Song through his pain, 'I was gonna call you this morning but - '

'Don't give me that shoulda, coulda, woulda shit. How about some breakfast?'

'I'm just finishing some, but maybe coffee later?' Song's doorbell rang.

'Great idea, so why don't you answer that doorbell I'm ringing so we can swap some spit and I'll walk you down to *Zeta's* for her Saturday morning special. Meanwhile, make like an anorexic and stick a finger down your throat. I hate to eat alone.'

At *Zeta's* Song ordered the 'full works' along with TK, more out of camaraderie rather than hunger. Bloomfield did most of the talking, bringing David up to speed alternately on the cases they had been working and the single women he hoped to be working. He talked about their last case of the bubble in the concrete with the wrist-watch found in it, and Song's mind involuntarily leapt back to the *JH352* on Paine's.

'Though we ain't done any real police work these past two days. Everything's on hold while the whole fucking department searches churches. Even Romero! I've seen more crosses than a Klansman these past forty-eight hours. It ain't worth shit of course. You need trained dogs to do this work and there ain't enough to go round. So we stand there looking down at the pews and up at the cherubs, and we say everything looks okay, but it's horseshit.' The time passed as TK ate and talked his way through an impossible amount of food, carefully avoiding making the link to why his partner had been called away. It wasn't until his fourth cup of coffee and his third muffin that he nudged the subject onto the table.

'How about the attack on that school, huh? Terrorizing adults is one thing, but when they start to mess around with the kids,' Bloomfield waved his fork menacingly to underscore the point. 'The churches, well that's a bad thing too, except for the overtime that is. It's disgraceful. Don't you think it's disgraceful, Davey?'

'I can't talk about it, TK. You know that,' smiled Song. Disgraceful wasn't a word Big Bird used a lot given that his vocabulary contained so many more colorful phrases, none of which he had ever been able to use in his daily crossword puzzles.

'Sure, sure, I totally get it. Anyways, I know you agree, bombing the cops, schools, churches, and now the libraries, it's as bad as it gets for regular folk.'

Song dropped his stirring spoon into the mug. 'The libraries?'

'Don't you know? Last night there was an explosion at the *Ronald Reagan Memorial Library*. No casualties, but half of it went up in smoke.'

On Corbyn's instructions Kamamalu had marched into Paine's bedroom to wake him the night before. Paine had wiped the sleep out of his eyes and acknowledged the library was one of his, but that it had gone off earlier than expected. Paine had immediately switched on the TV to watch live footage of flames shooting into the California night sky, fuelled by tons of irreplaceable archives and memorabilia. The old man was now destroying the past as well as the present.

On the way to his parents Song dropped in at Gary's, walking him down to a nearby community garden. Yesterday he had put the first phase of his secret plan into action, now he needed to complete the next. Song picked up on the short conversation they had had in the car, explaining in hushed tones what he wanted from his MIT friend.

'That sounds dangerous.'

'Which is why we'll still be good if you say no', replied Song, cautiously scanning the main road for signs of surveillance.

Gary thought for a moment. 'I have my reputation to consider.'

Song moved uneasily on the garden bench below a majestic acer. 'Yes, that why I'd fully understand if you declined.' Knowing that if this was indeed Gary's answer then his ambitious plan would collapse in ruins.

'What? You misunderstand, I meant what about my reputation if I said *no*! Shit, I could never look any of my nerdy crew in the eye again. I'm in, brother! So how are we going to make it work?'

Mightily relieved, Song squeezed his friend's elbow. 'Here's my cell. I want you to copy the image file on it and then return it to my parents' by noon.' Explaining further what he needed Gary to do, Song handed over a paper bag bearing his mom's store logo. 'I bought a couple of burners yesterday – here's yours. I'll ring you from my one when it's time to execute. Fuck social networking – it's back to just the two of us again, bro.'

Brunch with his parents was difficult for Song, even though they behaved admirably. But them having to work so hard to maintain the conceit just made him feel even worse. Not soon enough Song's phone trilled with an agent telling him ten minutes. His mother disappeared into the kitchen to wrap up some *banh bot chien* to go. Song's father beckoned him to the side making it clear he didn't want his wife to overhear.

'There wasn't time to say this yesterday,' whispered his father, squirting looks towards the kitchen door, 'but I understand why you had to ask the question.' Song made to say something, but his father squeezed his shoulder. 'Let your old man finish. Your mother was hurt, but she's also very practical and I'll make sure she gets over it.' Song stared down at his shoes, his face betraying the misery he still felt. 'But having your mom say those things, no matter how impassioned, doesn't really help, does it? You still need cast-iron proof that I'm your father.' The old man opened a cabinet drawer, passing Song a padded envelope. He cupped his hands around his son's, gripping hard. 'I wasn't sure how to do it, but inside this envelope you'll find some of my hair and a jar containing a cotton-swab that I ran around the inside of my cheek.' Song's face filled with horror as he made to thrust the package back. 'No, take it! Think about it, son. What if they don't believe us? Are we going to have some FBI stranger knocking on our door questioning your paternity? This is the best way to protect your mother's honor.'

Song's struggling stopped. In truth he had been pondering the same problem during yesterday's long walk to the restaurant. The two men embraced now with as much affection as they ever had. Outside, Song ripped open the heavy envelope containing his cell that Gary had just returned through their door as arranged. Climbing into the FBI car with a greaseproof bag stuffed with his mom's food in one hand and his father's padded envelope in the other, Song had in their different ways the most precious gifts possible from his beloved parents.

At the airport, Nevada explained that her mother had dug out the much thumbed photos of her dead father. But now the FBI agent had been looking intently at everyone else in the frame rather than him. After three hours of detailed inspection there was still nothing there, and Sky had expressed no memory of ever knowing a man fitting Paine's description.

Oppenheim called Song as the jet's wheels came up to confirm that the British Melissa Davidson was being flown out for tomorrow's Quantico meeting. Also that in the nationwide search of the churches, some congregations had found dry rot, some had discovered pipes with slow leaks, and some that they needed to improve the quality of their insulation. But of the officially estimated 98.3% of churches covered these past two days, there was no sign of the sinister object of their frantic efforts.

So for the first time in recorded history, the churches of America would be open for worship that Saturday night and closed on the Sunday.

———

The roads around Quantico were deserted that Sunday morning just as they had been the previous week. But this time the silence of the highways did not speak of a day of rest, but instead one of bleak anticipation. As their SUV sped along the empty roads, Song snatched glimpses of churches where at discreet distances knots of people drank coffee, sang hymns, and hugged new arrivals to the thronging crowds. On the hotel TV, Song heard the same sound bite on three stations of a black Presbyterian preacher speaking from a makeshift pulpit atop a grassy hill in Vermont the night before.

> *"Today my brethren, we shall not despair; for this lonely hill is not our Golgotha. No my brothers and sisters, for this gentle rising of the land merely lifts us closer to our God. He has not abandoned us in the inky blackness of our hour of need, for what He says to us is this:*
>
> *It is true that tomorrow was My day of rest. But you must remember that on the Saturday I had created. Just as this Saturday the people of America are creating a new spirit of resistance. And with this thought, we understand that our Lord has given us His permission to bend in the choice of our day of worship. To bend, but not to break. So let us bend but not break people, in the face of Rockwell's evil taunts. Bend, don't break! Hallelujah, hallelujah!"*

The weekend emptiness of Quantico's entrance hall gave way to offices crowded with people working the phones, and staring at Song and Townsend as they walked together across the floor.

'Good job, guys,' someone shouted from a cubicle as they moved towards the conference room. 'We'll get the SOB', shouted another, and one last voice as they approached the door. 'Bend, don't break.'

Senior Analyst Margolis confirmed the C4 found at the theater dated from 1973. 'We'll be pre-dating Pearl Harbor if this continues', quipped a bemused Greene. 'If Paine is deploying an average of six pounds per device, and he has 167 of them, that's a ton of ordnance in total. That's a lot of fireworks to go missing without anyone noticing.'

Benjamin confirmed the dates of structural work at other locations: 1992 for the Ben Hill Griffen Stadium; 1990 for the Orpheum Theater; 1988 for the soda shop; 1991 for the Ronald Reagan. There was still no information on the timing mechanisms atomized by the blasts.

'I was working a case back home of a body interred in concrete', interrupted Song. 'After winding, the vic's watch still worked 25 years later. We've been focusing on the *JH352*, but maybe it's not the engraving that's important, maybe it's the watch itself. Could this be the timing mechanism he's been using?'

'But he's been wearing it', chimed a bemused Margolis.

'You mean he's been using *similar* watches to trigger the detonators?' clarified Townsend. 'But that sucker's really old. Can they work that long without any servicing?'

'Paine's does', picked up Margolis, intrigued by the thought. 'And if you were planting devices that needed accuracy and durability over a few decades, it would have to be something like this.'

'So his watch might have been the timer intended for bomb 352 if he had gotten that far. So what does the *JH* stand for, and why is Paine wearing that particular one?' asked Benjamin, posing the questions on everyone's mind.

'We've researched the phrase 'splinter' and can't find anything that helps us', reported Billy-Jo Spearing. 'The Algiers Trotskyite Splinter Faction, the Free Catalonia Splinter Group, and the Splinter of Christ anti-abortion group in Tennessee. Nothing likely to yield rich pickings apropos Paine.'

'So, nothing whatsoever on the splinter clue', concluded Greene darkly.

'I even have a couple of guys reading the walkthrough of a console game called *Splinter Cell*. We're that desperate.'

'This whole case feels like a video game at the moment' opined Greene. 'Because it sure doesn't resemble any reality I know.'

Professor Melissa Davidson looked as though she had been abducted in the middle of a backpacking holiday, deprived of any sleep for twenty-four hours, and then thrown from a moving jeep into a place where no–one spoke her language. All of which were not far from the truth.

'The Rockwell case, that's why I'm here? Oh wow! And you're interested in what I was doing in 1996? That's an incredibly long time ago, Mr. Corbyn. Let me think.' Song thought she had a quintessential British accent, like Keira Knightley.

'In '96 I was working at the University of London, and was a Visiting Lecturer at Clemson. I'd just written my second book and was on the road publicizing it: *Acts of Terror – from Byzantium to Baader Meinhof*. It asked whether terror really has been a successful strategy for changing the status quo over the past three thousand years.'

'Can you remember where you went on that publicity tour?'

'With great accuracy. It had just started when I received news of my father's death in Australia necessitating my early departure. Let's see', she shut her eyes, corkscrewing out the memories. 'I went from Clemson to Penn State, to North Carolina, down to Miami, and I was in the airport preparing to go to A&M when I heard the news.'

'You mentioned North Carolina; do you remember the name Withers Hall?'

'Is that a person or a place?'

'It's a teaching room. Can you remember anything about your lecture there?'

Looking up at the ceiling. 'It was well attended. I remember we had quite a vigorous debate about something because I was taken by the speaker's accents. To my British ears they sounded very *Gone with the Wind*.'

'Anything in particular about that debate? *Anyone* in particular?'

'I dimly recall a conversation between an academic and one of the students beacuse he was very harsh on the young man. He'd said something typically student-ish about violence and your own War of Independence against us Brits. Then the academic said something like, "Haven't you been listening to Doctor Davidson. It's not just about terror as a force for emancipation from a foreign power, but also about the actions of a dissatisfied citizenry towards their state." Then - yes, I remember now - he'd quoted Heinrich Himmler, which I'd cited in my book.'

'Can you remember that quotation please?' asked Corbyn, betraying the growing sense of excitement they were all feeling.

Davidson closed her eyes: "*The best political weapon is the weapon of terror. Cruelty commands respect. Men may hate us. But we do not ask for their love; only for their fear*", opening them again as though emerging from a light trance. 'Sorry, rote regurgitation is a habit with us scholars.'

Corbyn smiled, flicking through his notes. 'Do you know anyone named Thomas Paine or Lane?' Davidson laughed, relaxing a little.

'My first book was on the writings of nationalist revolutionaries: Garibaldi, Danton, Bolivar, and Thomas Paine. And now you mention it, I remember we spoke of Paine that day in North Carolina. There was a student in the audience from Norfolk, Virginia and her ancestors were from Norfolk in England, which is where Thomas Paine was born. She quoted Paine: *"We have it in our gift to make the world over again"*, but she was corrected by someone saying, *We have it in our power to make the world over again.* And the more I think about it, I believe it was the same academic who'd chastised that other student.'

'And you're sure he was an academic?'

She shrugged, 'He was much older than the students so I surmised he was.' Corbyn patiently quizzed her for a further half hour adding little else before calling a halt.

'Good luck with the investigation, Mr. Corbyn. It bears the hallmark of a classic terror campaign, except of course for a demand. Unless you already have one and it hasn't been disclosed. Well of course, that must be it, how stupid of me. Anyway, as Thomas Paine once wrote: *"These are the times that try men's souls."*'

'It was easy for him to get onto campus from Pender', observed Townsend closing the door on Davidson. 'And he gets two bangs for his buck: a visiting expert on Thomas Paine who's also a specialist in terrorism.'

'But why did Paine specifically refer us to her? Does it speak to motive?' asked Song.

'He hasn't made any political demands, asked for any concessions. It doesn't fit the usual terrorist typology. I need to get someone reading her book from cover to cover', noted Corbyn as they made their way back towards the conference room, a new bounce in their step as they pondered this emerging lead. It remained for all of twenty seconds until they walked into the conference room to find Bradley Scott's pixilated face splashed across the huge TV screen. The logo at the top identified it as a *YouTube* posting, but the banner at the bottom said *CNN*.

'We've got a problem', said Denny muting the screen. 'Bradley's gone public'.

'These truly are the times that try men's souls', sighed Song quietly.

Devaughan Wallis from PR had dashed out as soon as Scott's face had appeared, phones pressed to each ear. Corbyn instructed Kamamalu by phone to hunt Scott down. The Fisherman had already generated 300,000 hits, but now it was on *CNN* that would increase exponentially. Denny accessed *YouTube* and hit play. Scott was speaking to camera, a makeshift *Fishermen*'s logo behind him. They watched in silence, and then read the transcript Wallis brought hurriedly back into the room:

> *[Walks into shot having turned the camera on]*
>
> "*Hello, my name is Bradley Scott and I'm pretty nervous so sorry if I dry up. I'm associated with the Fishermen of Galilee providing food and clothing for the homeless. Last week I was approached by the FBI telling me I was needed to help out with all these bombings. They took me to New York where I met with the man who's helping the government with the Rockwell case. It was him who'd asked me to be present, though I had no idea why. I wasn't alone cos he'd asked for three others too: a policeman, another FBI person, and a reporter.*

None of us knows him, or why we're here. So for the past week we've been attending meetings where he gives the FBI information on the location of the bombs. We've saved lots of lives and maybe some property too – but I don't care about that last bit. The FBI head of the team is doing a real good job and the other people are working hard like me to help out where we can. It's been a strange time personally, but through the guidance of Christ our Lord I'm coping - just. But as you know, Rockwell's about to bomb a church and that makes me mad - real mad. They lent me a computer so I know there are millions of you out there feeling the same as me.

But then I got to thinking. Perhaps that's what Rockwell wants? Why bomb a school and a soda shop, and that other stuff? It's just plain mean. Maybe Rockwell just wants to scare us, America. He wants us to hide ourselves away and be too frightened to take our kids to school, or go walking in the park, or to go worship. He wants this to be our Crown of Thorns.

And I don't think we should let him.

I can't put it any better way than that. So if you agree with me, tell your politicians, tell your neighbors, tell the newspapers that you will not give in to fear. And to show me I'm not alone in this, go onto this website called Vigilangels and leave a message there on the wall for me. And just in case you don't believe anything I've said, why don't you ask the FBI about the theme park bomb next weekend? Then you'll know I'm telling the truth.
[Walks towards camera. Final words off-camera]

Bend don't break, people. Bend, don't break."
[Off]

Everyone stared at the frozen screen. The theme park reference echoed the St. Bartholomew's cover-up. A *CNN* anchor was already interviewing a security consultant about the implications if it were true. The tickertape said a Floridian Senator had just called upon the FBI to confirm or deny the threat.

Song found a quiet nook down the corridor with a working coffee machine. He would leave the FBI to solve this latest miserable puzzle and decide what to do with Scott. He tried to clear his head of these weighty distractions and focus solely on the case. The clandestine search of the Hoover Dam complex had found nothing. And with a structure that was 45 feet thick at the top and 660 feet at its base, the pop-gun bombs Paine was using hardly warranted a run on the supermarkets.

But why choose the Dam unless you knew how to breech it? Was it really about the fear Bradley had mentioned? Song swirled the weak coffee in its plastic cup and turned his mind to the splinter. He had his detective's hunch, but hadn't shared it with a soul so far. If he did, a heavy curtain of objections would drop cripplingly upon his bold idea.

No, he had already taken the first steps to test his hypothesis and needed to get back to Mountain Lakes to put it in play. In the meantime there was the other work he had set in motion with Gary, with Scott's little exercise today underscoring how important the timing of that would be.

Greene had said they needed to get ahead of the curve. Song was about to do just that, in fifth gear on a mountain pass, burning rubber perilously close to its crumbling edge.

'Mary! Are you out back?' shouted the verger leaning outside the creaking back door of the Hammon Lutheran Church just north of Elk City, Oklahoma. It was noon and he and his wife needed to be in the car soon if they were to have any chance of arriving at their son's in time for Sunday lunch. The chalk-white of the quaint clapboard building dazzled in the midday sunshine, the smell of curing paint wafting in the air.

First constructed in 1845, burnt down by lightning in 1886, and again by a misplaced kerosene lamp in 1905 the plucky little building had done battle with the multiple tests of time. Again over the past few days the small Lutheran community polka-dotted around the area had gathered to protect it once more. Then late on Friday afternoon two of the Sheriff's boys had arrived and taken a dog inside for a full eight minutes before waving their goodbyes and hurrying off to the next location, already two hours behind schedule. Yesterday, on the Saturday, the verger had never seen the little church so crowded. It had lifted his spirits almost as much as the sermon itself. Now he and his wife were just bagging up the rubbish in time for Monday's collection. She emerged from behind the backyard wall, overfilled bags in each hand.

'Let me help you with those, sweetheart. You know you shouldn't - ', but the verger never finished his marital sermon. The blast caught him from behind, hurling him out of the back entrance, taking its newly painted door with him. Ten thousand roughly hewn toothpicks and countless shards of shattered planking first engulfed and then accelerated beyond him as he flew wingless through the crackling air.

The last thing his wife saw as she stood rooted to the dirt was the limp body of her husband arrowing towards her: a torn angel amongst a cloud of slivered death.

With the Scott tape commanding the airwaves and now the live feed from Oklahoma, the Quantico meeting was delayed indefinitely. Song watched Greene and Corbyn bouncing around between phones as they handled their political masters. Two air traffic controllers attempting to land a thousand tons of investigative metal on the evidence of a few incoherent blips on a darkened screen.

With a resolute face Song opened his case to retrieve the burner, punching in the number he had written on its cardboard packaging.

'Gary, it's me. The situation's deteriorating. It's show time, my friend'.

Chapter 10

Don't be afraid to go out on a limb. That's where the fruit is.

: H. Jackson Browne

THE LUTHERANS HAD SET UP A RE-BUILDING FUND AND IN just six hours they were already three thousand times over-subscribed. On a major astrological site its chief reader was predicting where the next bomb would explode, allowing of course for some troubling perturbations in the aspect of Venus. It seemed that everywhere Song surfed, someone had something to say.

'Where the fuck did you get to?' asked Townsend, easing her way into his hotel room six hours later.

'Everyone else had a job to do, whereas I was merely required to wring my hands.' Song raided his mini-bar for two shots of whiskey.

'I was liaising with the Oklahoma field office, but what can you do when the guy at the end of the phone is walking around a field picking up body parts.' She cracked the lid and downed the amber liquid in one. 'Have you had the TV on?' switching to a *CNN* recording of FBI Chief Press Officer Adamski speaking again to the media.

'... Turning now to the issue of the theme parks, our people only recently discovered the threat and are investigating its veracity', he explained, dishonestly.

'In his *YouTube* video, Mr. Scott said three other people were working with your intelligence source. Can you tell us about them?'

'All I can say is that their participation has proven critical in averting further carnage at the Consulate, St. Bartholomew's, the theater etcetera.'

"*Etcetera?*" There have been so many he can't remember them all, thought Song. And he'll get whacked for using the word "carnage". Too emotive, too graphic.

'*ABC* has learned the Hammon church was checked by a police dog yesterday. So what confidence can the American people have in future searches?' Song muted the screen to avoid Adamski's own PR carnage.

'Oh-my-God! Bradley's an internet star!' Townsend was on the *Vigilangels* site, to be greeted on its front page by a large button bearing the words:

Click here if you agree with Bradley Scott. "Bend don't break, people. Bend don't break."

She passed it to Song and he clicked, unfurling a flashing central lozenge. On it was written:

Thank you for clicking your agreement with Bradley! You join a total of 42,367,892 pledges. And remember: "Only the unknown frightens men. But once a man has faced the unknown, that terror becomes the known." - Antoine de Saint-Exupery

'Son of a bitch! Look at that number! If Paine's goal was to get everyone's attention, he'll be pissed that he's running head-to-head now with lil' ol' Bradley Scott. Is it too late to get Monsignor O'Brian back?' Townsend laughed, disappearing into the washroom. Song noticed a document minimized on her screen. Shocked, he read it quickly before shrinking it again at the sound of the flush.

He would speak with her about its contents, but not just yet.

Monday morning in Greene's Quantico office and if the senior team had clocked more than ten hours sleep between them Song would have been surprised. The early news highlight had been an interview with Florida's Attorney General assuring viewers that the state's theme park operators were 100% behind closing all of their facilities this coming weekend, when everyone knew they could do nothing else. First the churches, then the theme parks. What would be next to close – the hospitals, wondered Song?

'We need to update you on another unwelcome development', said an unusually grim-faced Jack Greene. Devaughan Wallis swiveled her PC and staring back from the *Vigilangels* site was a large photograph of Thomas Paine. Underneath it the words: *Do you know this man?*

'Oh shit!' exclaimed Townsend. 'Where the hell did that come from? And it's been *Photoshopped*, hasn't it?'

'Yes', confirmed Wallis. 'This shows Paine against a white backdrop but the edge-pixels reveal colors from a different original. And the whole image looks as though it's been 3-D'd and CGI rotated thirty degrees by some top-of-the-range software.'

'More importantly,' interrupted Corbyn stemming the technical evaluation, 'it was uploaded along with a statement about this being the mystery man helping us with our investigations. That site's fast becoming a clearing house for anything to do with this case. Already the image's been cut and pasted thousands of times. Someone's even created a spoof *Facebook* site for him!'

'So where did it come from, and who uploaded it?' asked Song, a tumor-sized lump of guilt sprouting in his throat.

'We're speaking with North Carolina to see if their Pender canvass threw up any photos', responded Wallis. 'But this one's an exceptionally professional job. When we checked for the source of upload, we drew a complete blank.'

'That's impossible,' stated Townsend. 'Everyone leaves an electronic signature, we all know that. You can't walk across the snow and not leave footprints.'

'Well there *are* footprints, but whoever made them ensured we can't determine the shoe size. Our techs say it's a real expert; someone they want to shake the hand of before we cuff it.' An expert indeed, thought Song, looking at Corbyn who was staring fixedly at the screen. Even allowing for Gary's superb image manipulation, had the Special Agent recognized that the photo's origin was from his own cell?

'For now we offer no comment', took up Greene. 'It's just internet chatter, but soon some folks in Pender will post the name and then someone will tell the story of Paine's house search. Samantha is blind with rage. But since it's out there, let's pray it now gives us the break we need.

We're now into a good old-fashioned manhunt, the twist being that we already have the guy in custody.'

———

Corbyn instructed Townsend to stay in Quantico working angles with Benjamin whilst Song was to return to Mountain Lakes to manage Paine and Scott. 'They both seem to relate to you, so be my eyes and ears while I'm pinned down here. We don't know how Paine will react to the photo's publication. Bradley's under lock and key and told he's looking at a multi-year sentence for impeding an investigation. See if you can drill some sense into that dense skull of his.' They all made to leave. 'And you know we never did find my cell. There's an image file on it I'd really like to see again', Corbyn said flatly.

'I think he's talking about his illegal photo of Paine', whispered Townsend as they walked out. 'So he still can't find his cell, huh? Yet another set of footprints in the snow.'

Michelle Denny rang as Song's SUV entered the airport's concrete expanse. 'The tests are back on your father's DNA.' Song's throat collapsed, his breathing temporarily suspended. 'I'm pleased to confirm that Terrance May is your biological father. I'm so sorry you've had to put your family through this, David.'

Song saw his plane on the runway, but from the lift in his heart he could have flown to Newark unaided. Thanking Denny for her professionalism and care, he repeatedly punched the vehicle's roof, drawing a quizzical rear-view glance from his driver.

After a flight full of reflection and planning, Song waited by the car as the agent went to find his partner. Powering up the burner Song dialed the single number on it. 'Saw your impressive work on *Vigilangels*. All okay?'

'No problems. Adjusted the image courtesy of a badass *Photoshop* clone on steroids. Someone took it down, but I put it back up again. Guess they were hoping I'd leave a trail this time - so I did.'

'Where to?'

'The IP address of Homeland Security, and in particular to the account of Deputy Director Dawn Sharper.'

'You're an anarchist.'

'True that', guffawed Gary. Song wiped the number and then the handset. Bending to tie his shoelace, he slipped the dead unit unseen into a Newark storm drain.

Song sat on the deck as Paine emerged with a pot of coffee. 'Cup o' Joe, Detective Sergeant?' Song held out his empty mug, eager to draw the man into conversation. 'Shame about the library. All that history. Poof! But what about the church, huh?

It's amazing what 20lbs of C4 can do to a wooden superstructure. And Quantico will want the year of manufacture so you can tell them 1979. I don't think Nevada was born then.'

'When did you set it?'

'September 1991. The Elk City Regional Business Airport is south of there.'

'When did you fly in to it?'

'Who said anything about flying in? I merely said there was an airport nearby, just as the Black Kettle National Grassland is to the west of it, but I didn't arrive by buffalo.' Paine swigged his coffee and made to leave. 'By the way, how did my picture get onto the net?'

'The FBI genuinely has no idea', replied Song, mirroring the words tutored to him by Wallis. 'None of the agencies involved in this case were responsible, it's deeply regretted and Alex hopes you won't rush to judgment.'

'It's still in breach of our agreement and there will need to be consequences', replied Paine peeling a banana. Song guessed as much, so it was critical that there now be serious payback from the gamble he had taken. If you take the curve in fifth you need to factor in the potential to spin violently off the track.

'One last thing. Did you set the church's device before or after the dam?'

'Ha! You're indefatigable, David! It's good to have you back. How's your mom holding up? So as a welcoming present, the answer to that question is after the dam, but before the baseball stadium.'

————

With chilling images of crowded bleachers panoramic in his mind, Song delayed his meeting with Scott as he handed over this new urgent recording to Oppenheim. And Paine mentioning his mom now rather than his father was beyond irritating. Karen offered Song a large oatmeal cookie which he devoured in two frustrated bites as she typed in and red-lit the new baseball intelligence.

On *Vigilangels*, support for Bradley's clarion call now stood at thirteen million, cycling up further as they watched in real time. Her screen chimed with someone attempting to connect.

'The wristwatch theory we discussed yesterday', said the blurred image of Margolis, 'we've got some interesting results.'

'You found another antique watch to experiment with?' enquired Song.

'The glory of *eBay*! We pulled it apart and jury-rigged it onto a dummy explosive device, and - to cut the geek-stuff short – it worked! Our watch was manufactured in 1983 but it proved way good enough to activate a detonator here in the 21st century. Service requirements are nonexistent, you just need a regular power supply and the technology does the rest. Bill Nye would be proud.'

Outside Scott's bedroom, Song was given a barely audible assent to enter. The Fisherman sat awkwardly on his bed, sheets tucked in tightly as though awaiting inspection. Had this been the regime in Scott's catalogue of orphanages?

'You can fuck off if you're going to rag on my ass like everyone else.'

'Nope, I'll leave that to the Feds', shrugged Song looking to establish himself as the trusted neutral. 'I'm not working any agenda, Brad, so just tell me why you did it.' Scott folded his arm, eyes averted. 'Okay, so let me have a go then, yes?' and receiving no answer either way, Song continued.

'You've been dragged away from your important work by some guy who you can hardly remember, and by being here it's like you've become part of the destruction he's wrought. You feel sullied by his acts. Then you borrow a PC and see all the fear he's creating out there. So you just try to rebalance the scales in your video, and you give up the theme park for authenticity - not to cause any problems. Am I right about any of this?' Scott's defensiveness melted with a single nod. 'Okay then, so that's exactly what you tell Corbyn.'

'I'll do just that', Scott replied, rubbing a hand across red-ringed eyes. 'I'm so tired. I'm just a cook who helps people, that's all. All of this Paine shit is frying my brain, man', lapsing into a brooding quiet. 'And anyway, what can Corbyn do about me? I'm untouchable. Take me off the team and Paine won't tell them nothing no more, will he?'

No, he won't, thought Song. You're learning, Bradley. As have I.

'Good job on the baseball park, David, but it's another gut-wrencher', sighed Corbyn on a poor cell line that night. 'Norman Rockwell will indeed be turning in his grave. I'm coming back tomorrow evening once the ship's steadied here. The White House is baying for blood, but they don't know whose. Now we have to mention America's Game too. Hitchcock couldn't have written it better – or maybe Lynch. You're in charge of Paine until I return.'

'I'm in charge?'

'You've proven yourself more than capable. You have my complete trust.'

Song reddened, knowing that tomorrow he was going to betray his leader in the most shameful fashion.

The next morning as the joggers lumbered past Corbyn's buried cell, Song thought of Poe, driving the breathless pack forward lest its electronic telltale heart give away what he was about to do. After a shower he joined Paine outside for breakfast in the spring sunshine, his repugnance for the man acting as an appetite suppressant. 'What do you know about quartz?' Song asked, draining his juice.

'Silicon dioxide, a super-abundant crystalline mineral. On the beach it's between your toes in the form of sand.'

'And the uses of quartz in time-keeping?'

'Ah, that's a specialism of mine!'

'I want to hear more; let's grab a coffee and take a spin around the woods.' Paine went inside for a sweater while Song refreshed their mugs. Walking into the shade of the greening canopy, Song was peripherally aware of the patrolling agents adjusting their orbits discreetly around them.

'Quartz vibrates at a predictable speed when an electrical charge is put through it,' continued Paine, 'so by counting these you can calibrate a watch to keep time.'

'Explain.'

'Quartz is an ideal oscillator because it loses very little energy, so it's incredibly accurate. Typically it vibrates at 32,768 times per second when it receives its electrical charge. A processor is attached to count off the 32,768 to represent one second before starting over again. It just goes on and on for as long as there's a current, adding the seconds into minutes, hours, days, and – real importantly - years.'

'How do you know all this?' Song asked, finishing his coffee as they passed under a spreading oak.

'I've been working on these beauties for over thirty years. I believe Nevada's already seen my old Texas Instruments watch,' he grinned. 'So incredibly accurate, they might lose or gain a few seconds over a year, but across many years the pluses and minuses even out. No maintenance, just that constant electrical supply.'

'So a quartz mechanism can be adapted to act as a timing device with multiple applications?'

'Multiple applications? Ha! There's one in particular we're both interested in, yes? Bomb making back then was easy if you had a little knowledge of solid state, explosives, detonators, and power sources. The Reagan Library fiasco was an error in my math, not the mechanism. Nowadays you can pick it all up on the net, as I'm sure you already have, but thanks anyway for listening to an old man's stories. Bomb making today is all courtesy of mouse clicks and memory sticks. There's *Dr. Strangelove* poetry for you. Though you still need to get your hands on all the components. C4 for instance. You can't get that on the… on the… inter…' The old man leant against a wild cherry, its pale green buds peppering the sky as he stared down at the brown froth of last year's bounty, his breathing labored.

'Are you alright?' asked Song's urgent voice, taking the man's elbow.

'I feel….. light headed. Going dark now - ', Paine's legs buckled, sliding him down the trunk of the awakening tree. Song ditched his mug, calling out an alarm as he held the man's sagging body off the floor. The agents were there within seconds, hauling Paine towards the house, his body limp and cold. Through the basement's sliding doors the knot of agents laid him on the carpet, skin white and clammy, saucer pupils under heavy lids.

Kamamalu barreled in as Song ripped open Paine's shirt spraying buttons across the floor. Pressing an ear against his chest the prickles of the older man's sweat merged with his own. 'Did he take his blood pressure medication this morning?' probed Song. Everyone felt sure he had as Paine's pulse accelerated to *Indi 500* speeds. 'We need to get him to hospital. The closest is in Denville a few klicks away.'

'Maybe we should call the local doctor instead for reduced exposure?' suggested Kamamalu, his unflappable poise wilting in the moment.

'Too dangerous. We can't risk under-treating him.' Kamamalu made to disagree, Song raising his hand to cut the Hawaiian off. 'Stop! Corbyn's put me in charge so it's my call. I'm taking full responsibility for the situation. Let's get him into a van – now! Go, go, go!'

That settled, the agents jerked into life, hauling Paine's deadweight off the floor and dashing off like battlefield medics. Engines were already gunning, air filling with the acrid tang of exhaust as Paine's prone figure was hurled into a vehicle, head cradled in Song's shaking hands.

Flying around the winding roads of Mountain Lakes in the SUV convoy, blues and twos screaming, Song called the operator. Shouting his identification over the din, she patched him through to the hospital's emergency line as an SUV flashed past to secure the location. Song welded his ear to Paine's blanched chest, the man's heart beating a military tattoo in stark counterpoint to his desperately irregular breathing. Song himself took a breath for what seemed like the first time in ages.

Paine's limp body, eyelids fluttering like a window blind caught in a gale, was hauled in through the hospital's back entrance. The shouted imprecations of panicked agents scattered the medical staff waiting to lend their assistance. A secluded room had already been cleared, a bemused mother and her adenoidal daughter unceremoniously tipped into the corridor. In double-time, Paine was half-hoisted, half-thrown onto a gurney where a quad of doctors and nurses frantically closed in attaching clips and drips. Song shouldered his way into their claustrophobic midst.

'I want him scanned – now!' he barked to the gowned circle, not sure who was the most senior.

'Are you family?' asked a doctor whose tag announced him as Anup Patel.

'Fuck the family. That's a direct order from the FBI. Give him a full body scan – now!'

Patel was undeterred, his colleagues buzzing round their stricken patient reeling off pharmacological abbreviations. 'We have to stabilize him first. I don't think a scan will be necessary. Now if you'll just -'

Song grabbed Patel's arm, physically spinning him round. 'You don't understand', he yelled, jabbing a finger close to the man's face. 'I'm not *asking* you to scan him, I'm fucking *ordering* you to. You can run every other piss-ant test you want while we're moving him, but you *will* do it - now! Otherwise your whole fucking hospital will find the FBI, the NSA, and Homeland Security parked so far up its fucking ass that your most gifted proctologist won't be able to find them.'

'BP's dangerously high,' said one of the nurses unperturbed. Patel was wavering. Song squeezed the man's arm taking a pace towards him.

'Don't fuck around with me now, Doctor, because I have the power to make Lord Shiva and all his shitty minions look like the fucking *Mouseketeers*.'

Patel hesitated a second longer and then pronounced. 'Okay people, let's keep the medication coming on the way to radio for a head scan', nurses simultaneously mobilizing the trolley.

'No, not just a head scan,' interjected Song, tightening his grip further, 'make it a whole body scan.' Then to seal the deal, 'We suspect a systemic physiological problem engineered by a hostile foreign government. Do the whole fucking body.'

Patel's eyes widened. 'Marian, phone ahead. Tell them we'll need an emergency scan and to get quarantine protocols in place. Code Orange.' Paine's prone body was strapped to the gurney as medical staff and agents catapulted it out of the room almost taking the doors off their hinges. Shouts and expletives emptied the corridor as the vibrating contraption bulleted towards the waiting elevator. Breathlessly piling in, Song looked back down the now vacant corridor at the colossal figure of Kamamalu standing outside the examination room.

As the sliding doors swept across, Song saw the questioning look on the Hawaiian's face: *What the fuck do you think you're doing?*

———

Paine awakened to a brilliantly white hospital room, crisp linen tucked firmly into a cream framed bed. 'How are you feeling?' asked Song, unfolding himself from a leather seat tucked into the corner. Paine turned his head slowly, vision swimming with the movement.

'Out of kilter. How long have I been here?'

'Seven hours.' Song popped his head out the door to speak with one of the guards. 'Corbyn will be along momentarily.'

'I thought he was away until tonight.'

'That was the plan, but then his key suspect took a dive so he hightailed it here by helicopter.' The door opened to admit a serious looking Corbyn, Benjamin, and Townsend, accompanied by a man in a doctor's coat.

'Alex, you came back for me!' uttered Paine, his mordant sense of humor undiminished. Corbyn introduced Doctor Ashley Rope, a senior FBI medic. 'So, Doc, will I live long enough to be executed?'

Rope flipped open a buff medical file. 'You suffered a blackout resulting from extremely high blood pressure, Mr. Paine. It wasn't quite a stroke, but that was just your good fortune. Your recovery from the blackout was,' he paused to search for the right words, 'hampered by high levels of sedative in your blood. Benzodiazepine to be precise, an ingredient used in many sleeping medications. And while the hospital was conducting your panel they also found evidence of other chemical elements affecting your blood pressure.'

'Well they would. The FBI already knows I take medication to reduce it.'

'No sir, I didn't make myself clear. The chemicals they found are known to *increase* blood pressure.' Paine looked up at the matt white ceiling, deep in thought. 'Which is why we're concerned you may have tried to take your own life, sir.' Paine started a low chuckle. 'Is there something funny about that, Mr. Paine?' asked the confused Rope.

'We're just about to find out, Doctor. And as for suicide, it wouldn't make much sense in the circumstances, would it? But what do you think, David?' Simultaneously, Paine's visitors swiveled round to look at Song still sitting in the corner.

'I'm sure there was never any intention for you to be harmed', the Californian's enigmatic reply.

'When you arrived it wasn't clear what the precise nature of your ailment was, so it was decided to conduct a full body scan', said Rope in a voice barely concealing his professional dismay.

'A full body scan when somebody my age faints? No wonder my insurance premiums are spiraling.'

'It's unusual, I agree, but it was suggested your condition had been created by... by hostile agencies working against American interests', Rope explained, unable to hold Paine's eye.

'Hostile agencies? Well, well. And what did the scan reveal?' In answer Rope pulled out a torso X-ray, holding it between Paine and the window he pointed at a thin black line on the film.

'It's a foreign body lodged just behind your second and third lumbar vertebrae, and I would hazard it causes you considerable pain from time to time.'

'Yes, it does. So, David, are you going to tell them, or shall I?' smiled Paine. Surprised again, everyone turned to Song who had moved now to the end of the bed. The detective coughed and took a deep breath.

'It's my belief that this foreign body is the "splinter" we've been challenged to find. My hunch is that a metallurgical analysis will provide us with a critical clue in the hunt for Thomas Paine's real identity.'

'Is this true?' asked Corbyn in hushed tones.

'I told you, this is the guy you want on your team, Alex', smiled the wan faced patient.

'So how did all of this come about, David?', asked Corbyn, sensing he was about to get very angry. Song took another deep breath, knowing it might prove to be his last on this case.

'From the start I'd observed the problem Paine was having with his lower back when seated, and then Nevada reported seeing scar tissue around his lower right abdomen in the shower. It occurred to me this could indicate an old wound. Then when he challenged us to find the "splinter" I thought about its synonyms, of which 'fragment' and 'sliver' are two. I knew from Homicide these are terms used to describe shrapnel left in a body after a shooting, but how to test this out? I guessed Special Counsel Franks would jump on any suggestion to enforce a full physical, so I decided to go it alone by creating a medical emergency.' Song paused but no one moved an inch.

'While in San Francisco I bought some *tan shen* from a Chinese Herbalist knowing that its blood thinning properties would counteract Paine's high blood pressure medication. But I knew this wouldn't be enough because - if he passed out – he might wake up again before the scan. So I stole three of my mother's sleeping pills which when mixed with the *tan shen* simultaneously knocked Paine out and raised his blood pressure at the same time. Finally, I massaged the facts to Doctor Patel to have him to conduct a full scan. I think that's about it, Alex.' No one said a word. Paine was smiling, his eyes closed.

'I don't know what to say', spluttered Corbyn after a long silence, not lost for words, just having difficulty selecting the right ones.

'How about saying, "Thank you, David!"', proffered Paine. 'Or am I the only one impressed by its simple brilliance?'

'He could have killed you, sir', commented Rope, still processing this fantastical story.

'There'll be people queuing up in Court to do that soon enough, Doc, so hold the melodrama. If it means anything, I won't be pressing charges. Hell, I'll even pay for the CT myself!'

'But will you consent to us going all the way?' interjected Song, knowing there was little time left before the world collapsed around him. People looked on quizzically.

'He means we still need to extract the splinter in order to prove his original theory', answered Benjamin. 'Otherwise it remains a hypothesis. No splinter, no lead.'

'Not bad, Agent Benjamin. Welcome to the game - at last', remarked Paine, smiling beatifically.

'Speaking purely as a physician,' said Rope picking up the theme, 'removing it would alleviate your pain. Medical practices have advanced significantly since you picked up that injury, sir.'

'Okay, let's do it straight away!' answered the sprightly patient. 'I bet there's an impoverished metallurgist out there who could do with some overtime tonight.'

Corbyn took Rope outside to discuss the medical way forward, after which he was immediately on the phone to Greene. Back in Paine's room Townsend and Benjamin were staring at Song. He shrugged back at them.

'The San Francisco street cop spanks the combined forces of the Federal government. He's very impressive don't you think, Nevada?' observed Paine.

'Unless of course he already knew', added Benjamin, giving voice to the thought they had all been fostering. 'If he keeps getting things so very right, so very quickly, people are going to get very suspicious.' Song looked down uncaringly at the blue linoleum tiles. He was sick of double-guessing what people might be double-guessing about him. He knew this had been a huge breakthrough and that was enough.

'That's a good point, Agent', opined Paine. 'But brilliance always has its price. It's a feeling the less talented amongst you will never know. Now, before you all leave, can you please make sure that Deputy Director Sharper isn't on my surgical team?'

'It's just so – so – fucking irresponsible', raged Townsend in a changing room down the hall. 'With one swing you've managed to crack a key part of the case and your own head at the same time!' Song was prepared to spend as long as necessary with Nevada to hear the venting of her justifiable frustrations when to his dismay the door cracked open and Corbyn entered.

'Well, Detective Sergeant, once a man begins on this path – let alone a police officer – he can justify almost any course of action. Whatever happened to the rule of law?'

'I have no excuses, just my rationale. The two are not the same.' Corbyn gestured for Song to continue. 'Paine intends to see through all 167 steps of this charade. Meanwhile Federal have to play by his rules: you can't take his fingerprints, you can't look in his wallet, you can't haul his ass down to a hospital to conduct a body scan. Even though he's sort of winking at us saying, "go on, I dare you", you just can't do it. But I don't have to play that game, and I think it's time we acknowledged it.'

'But no sane commanding officer could ever agree. The upsides of what you're proposing may look huge, but the downsides could be enormous', huffed an exasperated Corbyn.

'Shit, I've just administered two potentially lethal drugs to the guy and what was his reaction? He laughed and congratulated me! I implore you, use the difference I bring to our best advantage, that's all I'm saying.'

Corbyn sucked in air and vigorously shook his head. 'Answer me this, detective.' what's the difference between the reckless individualism you've demonstrated today and what that simpleton Bradley Scott did on the net?'

'That's the irony, Alex. Nothing much at all.'

Townsend and Song leaned back in their hospital chairs, the large pizza between them almost totally devoured. The patient had been prepped for surgery within two hours of giving his consent. Above them the scrolling banner of the muted TV proclaiming: *Owners put people above profit. Parks to remain closed as nation braces itself for more terror attacks.*

'You keep this up and whatever Paine says, they'll bust you off the case. You're becoming more of a liability than the Fisherman,' she commented in earnest. 'And what about your career back home?'

'I'll worry about my day job when this is over. And don't forget, there's always Fernandez.' She looked quizzically at him. 'Gabriel's already worked out our dollar value,' he explained, 'and I've just become his new house in Malibu. So if they fuck me over, how do you think he'll write that? Everyone tells me I'm a goddamn American hero, so who's gonna screw over the guy wearing the cape?'

'And do you *want* to be a key player in his story? You brushed Gabriel off the other day like he was a defecating fly.'

Song smiled knowingly. 'What do you learn in high school when someone asks you on a date? Even if you're interested, it's best to decline their first overture to further heighten their desire. Anyway, since when do you get off advising me on my career given your own situation?'

'I don't know what you mean,' she replied, succumbing to the residual pizza crust.

'In your hotel room you let me use your PC. I saw your letter resigning from the Bureau. So what's going on?'

'Well, David,' she replied with mock seriousness, 'the one thing I learned in high school is that if someone asks you something, it's best to refuse their first overture to further heighten their desire.' Smiling, she wandered off to find the bathroom.

A weak sun was pushing up against the horizon as a bleary eyed Song read that the site manager of the consulate's last building work couldn't recall anything odd about that job. However he had also spontaneously volunteered that he didn't recognize the picture of "that old guy on the net" either. Song smiled feeling sure it was only a matter of time before the risk he and Gary had taken uploading the photo would be rewarded. Corbyn strode up waving an evidence bag aloft like a kid who had bagged a squirrel with a catapult.

'Ladies and Gentlemen, behold a fragment of munitions, otherwise known as a splinter. The patient is sleeping, which is what I suggest the both of you do too. This is going off to metallurgy.' He made to leave before turning to Song. 'Doctor Rope has called you a son of a bitch in his official report, and he's damn right about that. But the fact is that you're *my* son of a bitch, and I'm still grateful to have you on this team.' As he strode off whistling, Townsend peered at Song, shaking her head in disbelief.

'Let's go home, Lazarus.'

Chapter 11

Fear not for the future, weep not for the past

: Percy Bysshe Shelley

THE SEARCH OF THE HOOVER DAM WAS PAINFULLY SLOW. THERE was just so much ground to cover – or rather vertical surface - that the two hundred personnel assigned were like ants scurrying around their oblong farm. Paine's pirated image could now be found on over fifty thousand websites, and his unofficial *Facebook* site boasted a full spurious biography accompanied by postings full of hopes and fears. The number of hits on *Vigilangels* now stood at over one billion.

'Basically', said Oppenheim in the operations center, 'we've passed information meltdown and are in to – well, we don't have a metaphor for it. Movie attendance is down 30% because the TV news is more interesting. Paine is the only attraction in town. And maybe Bradley too.'

As Corbyn beckoned Song out of the cottage wearing a stern frown, the detective was preparing to receive his punishment, thinking how good it would be to spend time back with his family again. 'The senior team has been apprised of yesterday's outrageous events and predictably everyone went orbital. After intense discussions that included White House personnel, I've been asked to convey that you should consider yourself warned.'

Song wrinkled his brow and shuffled his feet. 'Warned?'

'Yes, warned about future behavior', responded Corbyn economically, as if there were suddenly a tax on the spoken word. They locked eyes, each choosing to say nothing more before Corbyn nodded and walked away.

Song smiled. It looked as though the Suits were going to let him ride point after all.

Paine's hospital room sported three vases of flowers, all from Gabriel Fernandez and the *New York Times*. The reporter had been in and out more times than the nurses these past two days. Song and Townsend had driven over to spend the rest of the morning with Paine in case he wanted to speak. Upon their arrival Benjamin summoned everyone to meet with Corbyn in a commandeered nurses' restroom.

'The bullet splinter was from a Kalashnikov, and was manufactured between 1979 and 1984', shared the Special Agent.

'Uncle Sam's been on virtually every continent since '79, so he could have picked it·up anywhere – Desert Storm, peacekeeping in Africa, black ops in places we don't even know about', observed Fernandez who had arrived with the dawn that morning.

'The good news is that it removes the Vietnam possibility given it ended in 1975', confirmed Song, glad to have that shadow removed from the equation.

'On the issue of Paine's photo upload,' added Benjamin, 'eighty-two people have rung from Pender County reporting that it's Thomas Lane. Several thousand more identified him as Frank Zappa, Kurt Cobain, or some other metaphysical MIA. However, there were some interesting leads that deserve our attention. It may have been illegal, but whoever posted that image has done us all a favor.'

A live-feed to D.C. and Quantico had been set up when the team filed into Paine's recovery room as if it were a crowded elevator. Finally the old man was looking his age, the scrubland on his graying chin adding fifteen years. Scott anticipated what was coming, reaching across the bed to take the recuperating man's hand, hospital identity band hanging limply around a thin wrist.

'Oh Lord, we pray for the complete recovery of Thomas Paine. You have sent him as a trial for us, and we ask that You make him strong in constitution so he may be executed in good health. Amen!'

'Who needs pain killers when there's this for a soporific?' croaked Paine. 'Can someone help me up? That's great, thanks. I promised the FBI a reward for questions correctly answered. Well, the FBI didn't, but David did. So for the splinter I'll give you the locations of ten devices. And for half-solving the shower problem, here are a further five.' He rattled off fifteen addresses spread across eleven states and a range of public and private targets. There was a general surprise in the room. So far they had fought so hard for every infinitesimal scrap of detail, but here were fifteen golden eggs laid in quick succession. It was a bounteous harvest, the elation of the team hard to mask, Song glowing privately inside. Fifteen devices, and how many innocent lives saved?

'No need to grin so much, Benjamin – it's very gauche', reprimanded Paine. 'If you've met Melissa Davidson, you still haven't worked that one out or I'd know, so you're fucking up there, Agent. And as for the Hoover, keep looking – not much time left now.'

Still 142 more to go, thought Song, but this had been a marvelous victory nonetheless. Still he couldn't help but ask another question. 'Only solved half of the shower puzzle? How so?'

'You found it, but do you know the relevance of *JH352* yet? Now if you don't mind, I need to get some sleep and you kids have some champagne to open.'

Corbyn was straight on to D.C. while the others headed towards the hospital's back entrance, Fernandez not knowing which self-congratulatory conversation to push his recorder towards first. Scott was talking excitedly to Townsend about the veteran's home in Boise that was amongst Paine's fifteen sites as they pushed through the doors towards their SUV.

Two teenagers wearing *Bradley Scott – we believe!* T-shirts rushed forward. 'Hi Brad, oh wow, can we have your autograph, man?' Scott gave a strangulated scream as they lunged towards him, before breaking into a run. Song and Townsend closed in to protect him as two agents shot out of the van to scoop the Fisherman up.

'Please, man. Some people think you're not real, but, like, here you are, man. Come on, dude, just an autograph?' One was shooting phone video throughout and, as the door with its darkened glass slid firmly shut, Song heard the other one shout.

'Bend, don't break, Brad.'

The TV news was a feeding frenzy as fifteen operations from Washington to Maine, and from North Dakota to New Mexico played out in front of a transfixed viewing public. A ranch house, a sewage works, a saw-mill, an elevated highway amongst others, each vaulted into the spotlight for their fifteen minutes. For the networks it was like all the pipes in a house bursting at the same time, they didn't know which gusher to cover first. The discovery attracted plaudits from all quarters, Wallis and her team spinning the story for all its worth in the certain knowledge there would be rocky times still to come.

In the mid-afternoon, Corbyn pulled Townsend and Song from their calls to meet in his Mountain Lakes bedroom where Special Counsel Samantha Franks sat looking out of the window. After congratulating them all on this huge but risky victory, she launched into the reason for her visit. 'As part of the *Times* deal, Fernandez has the right to speak with anyone – included me. David, I've spoken with your Police Commissioner Hamilton so he's squared off. We know it's an extraordinary request, but these are extraordinary times.'

'My answer is yes to the interview, but with three provisos', replied Song. 'One, that I be allowed to see any material in advance of its publication. Two, the interview takes place at the very end of the investigation. Three, that in return Fernandez answers any questions I may have of him.'

'What questions might they be?' asked Corbyn, his interest stoked.

'I'll tell you when I have his answers.'

'Okay, that seems reasonable', replied Franks. 'What about you, Nevada?' the young agent perched on an office desk too big for the room.

'No, I won't cooperate.'

Franks pulled a face. 'I see. Can you tell me why?'

'Because I joined the Bureau to serve my country, not the Fourth Estate. Fernandez already has a terrific story, he doesn't need anything more from me.'

'You do realize the Bureau can compel you to cooperate?' Franks turned up the heat.

'Yes, which is why I resign', she said calmly, extracting a letter out from her battered linen shoulder bag. Corbyn and Franks looked stunned; Song gazed out the window. 'Normally this would be with immediate effect. But given Paine requires me to perform in this circus, please accept it as notification of my intention to resign at the case's conclusion. At which point, as a private citizen, I will tell Gabriel Fernandez to go fuck himself.'

Scott's culinary skills weren't available for dinner that night as he was back under wraps with the New York chapter of the *Fishermen of Galilee*. Nevada's hair was still wet from the lone run she had taken around the lake. Song caught her eye across the countertop, inclining her head she beckoned him over. 'We've agreed to keep it quiet. Franks will tell Fernandez that I've consented to speak later, just like you.'

'Do you know what you're doing, Nevada?'

'Absolutely. I've been looking for just this opportunity – or maybe this excuse – for some time now. But it's some weird shit that it's Gabriel fucking Fernandez who's handed it to me. I've never really felt comfortable in the Feds. All those wrap-around shades and Bluetooth ear pieces. It's all Bond, Bauer and Bourne. Sometimes I swear we scare the good guys more than we do the bad. Anyway, I'm sick to death of the Alpha Male bullshit so I'm getting out.'

'But Greene and Corbyn aren't like that.'

'Statistical anomalies. Trust me, they're massively outnumbered by the Sharpers and the Benjamins.'

'What will you do?'

'Remember *Operation Thunderbolt*? Well the Native Americans running the gaming operations down there have offered me Deputy Director of Security. The money pays multiples of what I'm earning now.'

'And how do you feel about working in the gaming sector?'

'Better than working for Lehman or Enron, and I don't accept the implication. The guys I'll be working for haven't water-boarded anyone lately. Can Uncle Sam say the same?'

It was inky black outside when later that night someone reached into the depths of Song's unconsciousness to shake him awake. 'Excuse me David,' breathed Karen Oppenheim, 'I'm sorry to disturb you, but Special Agent Corbyn urgently needs you downstairs.'

Through the swirling smog of sleep Song's watch confirmed it was just after three a.m.. 'What's the hurry?' grumpy at the imposition.

'D.C.'s taken a call from a guy saying he can identify the photo on *Vigilangels*, and they think he's the best hit yet.'

'And he's on the phone at three o'clock in the morning?' coughed Song, wide awake now but unable to get up for his nakedness under the sheets.

'It's not three where the caller is. Its eleven hundred hours.'

'Eleven? So where exactly is he?'

Oppenheim paused to ensure she had his full awakening attention. 'He's in Iraq.'

The *Skype* connection to Baghdad was superb. It wasn't a secure line, but there wasn't time to get him onto one. Iain Devlin sat six thousand miles away in a construction site office, a large calendar festooned with *Post-Its* behind him next to an aluminum stand adorned with hard hats. Devlin was in his late fifties, the signs of middle age spread evident in both chest and neck.

'I've been in-country two years with Halliburton. The Rockwell bombings are big news over here, which is pretty ironic some would say. This morning I get a web-link from my son to that *Vigilangels* site I read about in *USA Today*. So I'd just clicked the button saying I agree with that Bradley guy, when I scroll down and – shit!. - there's a face I know staring right back out at me.'

'So Mr. Devlin, who do you think it's a photo of?' asked Corbyn in a croaky voice more to do with his excitement than the early morning hour.

'I don't *think* - I *know*. It's Iain Paterson. That's Iain with an "a", like my own name.'

Oppenheim was straight onto the net while shooting out one line mails to the extended team also tipped from their beds. Song imagined a bedraggled Billy-Jo Spearing at her kitchen table rousing people across the country to once again check births, deaths, and marriages.

'And why are you so sure?'

'Because he saved my life back in '81. He's lost a lot of weight, and he doesn't have a beard in this shot, but I'd bet my overseas bonus it's him, and if you knew how much that was…..' The screen blurred as Devlin moved a little too quickly for the camera's liking. 'I only spent a day with the guy, but in addition to him saving my ass, we have the same first name.'

'1981? But the first Gulf War wasn't until 1990?' clarified a spiky-haired Benjamin.

'Not in Iraq; we met in El Salvador. It was bandit country back then - probably still is. Commie guerillas and right wing military groups using the place as a shooting gallery. Anyway, one day in June '81 I was sent to a town outside of San Miguel. Someone had blown up a generator substation and the electrical boys – all American contractors - needed a civil engineer to assess the infrastructure. I arrived with my security detail from the National Guard to be met by a posse of armed locals, and when I turned round my so-called bodyguards were driving away at speed! So I get manhandled into the compound at the muzzle of an AK, and the Americans were all squatting in the corner shitting themselves on account of the two Death Squad motherfuckers poking M-16's into their faces. Meanwhile their leader's arguing in Spanish with another American in the middle of all the debris and crap. And that guy was none other than Iain Paterson.

Even though I don't speak the language I could tell there was some serious, serious shit going down. After some shouting, the leader walks towards me putting a round into his pistol breech, but Paterson he gets between us, staring the mother down.

Eventually, they both calm down as though nothing's happened and Paterson tells us to get on with our work assignments. Man, you've never seen guys do a quicker assessment of a job! Paterson even helped me do my site review. He was a civil engineer himself, and a pretty good one at that. He said the whole argument had been about the trickle down of kickbacks to the little guys outside the capital. We finished our jobs and a truck arrived to take us back to our hotels.'

'Did Paterson tell you anything about himself?'

Devlin paused as a door opened at his end and he sent someone back out in broken Arabic. 'I think he mentioned getting his degree from a college in the north east but I couldn't swear to it, and that he'd picked up his Spanish in-theater.'

'Did he mention getting shot in the past?'

'Shot? No, he looked pretty healthy to me.'

'Did he say how long he'd been there?'

Devlin paused to claw back the memories. 'No, but he seemed to have a good handle on what was going down, so he'd been there a while.'

'Overall how would you describe his behavior?'

'Hmm, interesting question. Confident, purposeful, a leader of men. And even though he and the pistol guy were screaming at each other, I never felt Paterson had lost control of the situation.'

'What happened when you got back to the hotel?'

'The truck dropped us off but he stayed in it. Come to think of it, it must have been him who arranged the ride, and the driver seemed to know him.'

'Do you know who the truck belonged to?'

'Sure, didn't I say earlier? It was U.S. army. One of those used by the military advisors.'

After the call no one had any intention of returning to bed. Phones and PCs hummed as briefings were given and instructions issued. The name of Iain Paterson needed to replace those of Paine and Lane in every single enquiry made so far. Additional checks would be added on the civil engineering lead, and the military angle would be blitzed one more time. Agents across the land wouldn't be seeing their families again for a while to come. Song said a silent prayer to Gary and the god of Photoshop. But huge though the Paterson news was, vying for their attention that morning was the teenager's *YouTube* clip of Scott taken outside the hospital. By the end of the day tens of millions would have noted its address. Preemptively, Corbyn had decided to evacuate Paine, but there was a problem.

'He's refusing to leave. Says he doesn't want to jeopardize his recovery', reported Benjamin with a cynical smirk.

'Jeopardize my ass. He's jerking us around', grumbled Song.

'Oh, for sure. But since it was you who put him there, we can't really complain, can we?' Benjamin's barbed reply.

'But then we wouldn't have the AK-47 lead, would we?' snapped Townsend. 'Overall I think we've got the better of the deal, so shut the fuck up, Benjamin.'

'Anyway,' bulldozed the Homeland man flushing red, 'we're locking the place down. There are already two-hundred Bradley Scott autograph hunters outside and the switchboard's jammed. And if someone finds out there's also a guy there who looks like the image on the net, it's going to go all *X Files* on us real fast.'

Oppenheim confirmed there were just eight people named Iain Paterson within Paine's age profile, though five of these were spelt 'Ian'. Most had been contacted by field agents within the hour and ruled out. The military were cross-checking their records for a Paterson with a lower abdominal wound.

Meanwhile, *CBS* had a breaking news story about a surprisingly long anti-terror drill running at the Hoover Dam. Townsend and Song looked knowingly at each other. If there had been no other news, this would definitely have been the lead, but editors didn't seem to know where to focus nowadays. Bizarrely, it was the Scott sighting at the hospital that seemed to be winning the day.

'It's Ali versus Foreman all over again', observed Song engrossed in his iPad.

'What do you mean?' asked Townsend, not a big sports fan.

'*Google* rope-a-dope.'

'Okay, I get it. We're on the ropes taking a blizzard of big hits, sucking them up preparing to deliver our killer punch', she summarized. 'Well let's hope the referee doesn't step in before we get the chance.'

With thoughts filled with the morning's events, Song grabbed a bottle of *Evian* from the refrigerator and went for a lone run in the weak dawn light. Familiar with the route now, his body was guiding him around the lake and back up again, allowing his mind to wander freely through the case. Worryingly, Paine's image hadn't generated any other mention of the name Iain Paterson from callers. A dark voice at the back of his consciousness was already questioning whether the information from Iraq had been accurate.

The lake was still, an un-seasonally cold snap leaving a froth of mist on its surface, the thin trickle of commuter traffic gently rising as the town's sparse inhabitants set off for work in New York. Song was on the final punishing incline back to the house, lungs protesting at the outrage, as an SUV with darkened windows rolled slowly past. Agents returning from the hospital he thought, pulling over now to offer him a lift.

The door opened and a figure emerged. He was dressed in a dark blue one-piece wearing a full-face red ski-mask, an oblong gash across the eyes. In his free hand an Uzi swung menacingly back and forth. Song was fifteen yards away as his tired legs filled with lead.

'Detective Sergeant Song, you're in no danger. Please get into the vehicle.'

His lungs struggled to suck in air, the reptilian part of his brain shrieking the fight-or-flight reflex. 'The Uzi says otherwise', Song gasped, playing for time to jump-start the depleted oxygen in his leg muscles.

'If we'd wanted to harm you, we would have done by now. This is about Iain Paterson.'

Song wheezed a cry of surprise as his curiosity auto-piloted him into the back seat. Inside were two analogues, bright red masks out of place next to grey executive trim. The man in front swiveled round. He wore sunglasses too, rendering him completely anonymous.

'Thank you, David. We're going for a five minute ride so as not to raise any concerns at your safe house. You need to listen very carefully and then I'm going to recommend a course of action. It'll be your choice what to do after that, but I must warn you'll be in great danger if you choose incorrectly.'

'Danger from you?'

'No, not from us. Danger from the people trying to stop you discovering the true identity of Thomas Paine.'

Song sprinted past the agents guarding the house to find Corbyn in the kitchen, coffee in one hand, toast in the other. 'Outside – now!' he ordered his boss, half pulling the Bureau man into the woods, trampling its delicate spring growth.

'Listen, I know I've broken your trust several times, but I need it again now - big time.'

Corbyn threw his coffee dregs onto the leafy ground. 'David, you're a loose cannon, not a knife in the back. So what is it?'

'I've just been told something and, if it's right, not only will we be able to confirm Paine's identity, but also why he chose one of the people in our team.' Corbyn's cell rang seven times over the next ten minutes but he was immured to them all. At points he stopped to stare in amazement at Song's story, exhaling loudly when the narrative had finished.

'You're asking a lot from me, David. It's a huge gamble for the case.'

'And for you personally.'

'Not just me', retorted Corbyn, eyeing the detective. Their conversation continued for another hour discussing options and plans before Corbyn rescued his neglected cell and rang Oppenheim. 'Get me the number of Deputy Director Mark Ladd. No, hang-on Karen, you won't find him in the Bureau's data base. It's a different branch of the tree.

The CIA down at Langley.'

Chapter 12

Too many people are thinking of security instead of opportunity.
They seem more afraid of life than death

: James F. Bymes

The security officer from the Federal Bureau of Reclamation stood atop the 45-foot wide ribbon that was the pinnacle of the Hoover Dam. Looking along Lake Mead he could see but a fraction of the water snaking back for 112 miles. The multi-agency team was just finishing its night shift as thirty yards away the media vultures turned in their tight, hungry circles behind the hastily erected barrier. He peered out over the still water, an early morning desert sun reflecting brightly off its meniscus.

The first thing he noticed was a puff of smoke spurting into the air six hundred yards along the lake's left bank, quickly followed by the firing of a large caliber gun. After several seconds of eerie silence, a shout rasped out, 'Point the cameras over there!' as other voices screamed down phones for producers to take live feeds. Without instruction, the security officer ran with fifty other men towards a balloon of grey cloud that was quickly inflating itself above orange tongues of fire.

'It's an electrical substation', someone cried above the staccato stamp of feet and wailed invocations to a god that had long since replaced Neptune.

———

Deputy CIA Director Ladd was off-site at a strategy conference that week. Corbyn had asked for his cell only to be deflected by his secretary's thin obfuscations. In normal circumstances he would have gone up the hierarchy, but it was important for his and Song's plan that this stay low-key for now. Meanwhile Song rang San Francisco and asked to speak with his commanding officer, Captain Romero. He explained what was needed, handing the phone over to Corbyn for confirmation. Next, Song rang Townsend at the hospital.

'It's under control at the moment but it has the potential to get really difficult', she observed. 'There's a thousand people here. Grans and Pops plus a lot of teenagers. There are groups singing hymns and someone's stretched out a bed-sheet bearing the words *Have my babies, Brad*. Unbelievable, huh?'

'How's Paine?'

'Spent the morning complaining about the amount of saturated fat in his breakfast. He knows about the crowd from the TV coverage. Benjamin's also shown him Scott's internet epistle and he laughed so hard the nurse had to re-insert his catheter.'

No sooner off the call than Song's cell vibrated again with Agent Burke in Charlotte. 'The local paper's running a story today naming the mysterious image on *Vigilangels* as Thomas Lane. A slightly panicked Sheriff Le Bon is getting extra cars down to secure the house. It had to happen once the picture was posted. Strange times, David.' Song turned as a ball of paper hit him on the back of his head. Oppenheim, one hand pressing a phone to her ear while the other jabbed at a TV screen filled with the majestic presence of the Hoover Dam.

No one injured; an explosion in one of the many electrical substations along the reservoir; a small fire now under control; power re-routed through the network of other stations; the efficient operation of the Dam totally uncompromised, confirmed the official press release. Nonetheless, the media gyroscope worked itself into a whirling dervish with Song's favorite morbid sound-bite coming from a *CBS* stringer: *"unleashing a skyscraper high tsunami, presaging a flood of Biblical proportions"*. The Governors of Nevada and Arizona had announced a joint press conference for early that afternoon, but their calming advice had not stopped thousands of downstream citizens from uselessly packing their cars and jamming the roads. Paine watched all this from his sick bed, but his laughter could be heard echoing all along the hospital's antiseptic corridors.

That afternoon Song caught a ride with three shift relief agents. A mile away from the hospital Townsend called. 'Someone on the medical staff's dropped a dime to *ABC* about their patient being the mysterious man on the web, and it's just breaking on the other networks as we speak. If you want to get anywhere near the building before the masses descend, better punch the *Millennium Falcon* into hyper-drive now.

Hey David, now I *really* get rope-a-dope!'

The cooperative crowd had respected the entrance path for ambulances, Song watching from Paine's floor as their headlights swept across the faces of the eight thousand people camped outside the hospital's besieged entrance. Townsend sat next to him in the dark, her face ghostly illuminated by her PC screen.

'It's weird. I'm watching people through this window while reading their real time *Vigilangels* postings here. A teenager just uploaded a picture of herself standing – there.' Townsend pointed to a patch of darkness over by the hospital's entrance just as a wedge of light burst forth, a news team preparing to carry another bulletin "live from the scene". Was there any part of America not caught up in this monstrous saga?

Later that night inside Paine's bleach scented room, the old man lay on his stomach, his TV muted. Corbyn had given Song a job to do as a final test before the two of them executed their Langley plan. Ideally Song would have preferred Nevada not to be present, but he couldn't find a good enough reason to shake her.

'Not watching TV?' she asked the patient, speaking to the back of his head.

'Boring. There's the excitement of the event, then the interviews with some fuck-wit bystanders, then the ex-military guys who talk as though they know what's going on, and finally the rapidly decomposing corpse gives up its politicians. Did you see the Governors' press conference on the Hoover? Demosthenes would have been ashamed to watch. How's the Cult of Scott the Messiah coming along out front?'

'The great man himself is back at the Lakes in his swaddling clothes' replied Song. 'Pontius Pilate has him in the cells. But I think you might be seeing more of him on TV. It appears he exercises a calming influence over the American people.'

'Bradley - a calming influence? You should show them clips of him ranting at me!'

'That would probably elevate his reputation further', retorted Song. 'Can I ask you some questions?'

'You can ask what you like, but I'm unlikely to answer.'

'Where did you learn your Spanish?' Song asked in Spanish.

There was a slight hesitation before Paine's reply. 'No comprendo.'

'Were you in El Salvador in June 1981?' The old man cleared his throat, his face averted. Song smiled knowingly.

'Why put the second "i" in "Iain"?' pursued the Californian. Paine sniffed.

'Cry "Havoc!" and let slip the dogs of war, That this foul deed shall smell above the earth, With carrion men, groaning for burial', quoted Song at his quarry.

'Julius Caesar', noted Paine, drawn at last. 'But why specifically that passage?'

'Dogs of War. You know why', replied Song wearing his poker face. Paine twisted round to look back silently at his inquisitor. The detective had learnt what he needed from the enigmatic exchange, and rose to leave, a furious Townsend clipped to his side.

'What the fuck was that Dogs of War shit?' she spat, snapping at his heels.

'Mercenaries. Or something close to it', Song conceded, pained that he was not allowed to tell her more. 'Sorry, about the cloak and dagger, but I can't say more. Corbyn's orders.'

Pursing her lips she stalked back to her PC, jabbing down hard upon its innocent keys.

The investigative team had returned to Mountain Lakes before eight that morning, electing to escape the hospital before the crowd had swollen to Woodstock proportions. Fanning himself in the musty air of the operations centre, Song wafted a *FedEx* envelope containing the secret document Romero had promised to send. On the TV, Calvin Adamski looked like a man who'd been caught cheating on his wife by his mother-in-law.

'Can you clarify the relationship between Bradley Scott and Thomas Lane – the photo on the internet - both of whom have been seen in the same New Jersey hospital?' piped a reporter from *Time*.

'As Mr. Scott stated in his video, he is working alongside our team at the specific request of Mr. Lane, who I can now confirm is the person helping us with our work.'

'Supplementary, sir. Mr. Scott's mentioned three other people. Can you confirm their names as Nevada Townsend, David Song, and Gabriel Fernandez?'

'Oh shit!' exclaimed Townsend. On screen Adamski appeared to be thinking the same thing.

'No comment on that. Next question please.'

'Is the Bureau withholding any other locations from the public?', asked the *Washington Post*.

'No, we aren't.'

'Then can you explain why a terrorist drill was been conducted at the Hoover *before* yesterday's explosion?'

'You've answered that one yourself. It was a timely drill. Next question.' You're going to pay for that lie when Fernandez publishes his book, thought Song.

'We understand the President's children have hit Bradley Scott's *Bend, don't Break* button on *Vigilangels*. Is this indicative of how the President is feeling too?' shouted the *Baltimore Herald*.

'I don't know if that's true about his children. Next.'

'*The Economist*. In the early hours of this morning our London office opened a letter accurately stating the target of each of the bombs so far, including the Hoover Dam. It indicated another device detonating tomorrow, Sunday, with the target being "telecommunications". Given your answer earlier, are you still saying you know nothing about this?' Even on this average connection, Song could hear the general uproar at the other end.

'I strongly urge you to hand over to the authorities any information you may have', spluttered Adamski. 'In the meantime - '

'We already did, sir - yesterday. To both the American Embassy in London and to the FBI representative in New York.'

'Eh, thank you,' said Adamski lamely, the torpedo hitting amidships. 'As I was saying, in the meantime….'

Song turned the volume down. 'Well, I'm not a media specialist, but that looked to me like a fucking disaster.'

"More importantly,' added Benjamin, 'if they only received the letter yesterday, who posted it to them?'

The sergeant from the Kentucky state guard swiveled her binoculars across the brightly colored metal chutes of the *Gushes Galore* water park just outside of Frankfort. The eerie silence reminded her of the *X-Box* zombie apocalypse game she played with her kids. Anything to get some face time with them nowadays. Usually this time of year at *Gushes* there would be carnival music competing with country rock, punctuated by screams of anticipation and joy. But today only silence, except for a flock of noisy crows perched on the ride that dropped passengers like a falling elevator. Behind her a radio in one of the cars cordoning off the area squawked the turn of the hour.

The slap of the blast sent the death black birds cawing and circling maniacally over-head, just as it wrenched a scream of surprise from the sergeant's slackened mouth. Both sounds eclipsed by the lurching screech of metal on metal as the coaster's central support flopped in slow-motion onto the sun-hardened ground, dragging tons of snapped and twisted rail along with it.

It became clear what had happened. In London, *The Economist*'s call was languishing on the voice mail of the Head of Station who was out sick. In New York, the magazine had couriered a copy of the letter to the wrong Bureau department.

Devaughan Wallis looked the picture of misery on the video call as she explained the unfortunate double screw-up. 'We can't seem to catch a goddamn break. And now you guys need to be careful about your net-presence too', she complained. 'You've just had your names exposed at a major press conference on the hottest story in the world. Now every crackpot, crack head, and crack shot knows who you are.' By the time Song logged on to his sites there were already thousands of messages from strangers waiting for him. For simplicity he purged everything and contemplated what type of cave he might want to live in for the next few months.

'It was posted to London from the U.S.A. when Paine was already in our care. And – get this – those bozos over at *The Economist* can't find the original envelope', grumbled Benjamin at the afternoon team meeting, 'so we don't have any prints. Meanwhile every business that thinks itself as being in telecommunications is jamming FBI lines. Even the hardware store here in Mountain Lakes called in because it still sells ink for fax machines!'

At dinner time that evening, Song was purging his cell of another tranche of nuisance calls when he found Scott perched on a kitchen stool picking over a plain cheese. 'I want to go back online again in an hour', the Fisherman said flatly.

'Go online. You mean access the net?' clarified Song, glancing up from his temporarily empty phone.

'No, I mean record another video and post it on *Vigilangels*.'

'I'm not sure that's such a good idea. If you'll wait until Alex and Devaughan are back from the press conference I'm sure that –'

'No, I won't wait. I'm not a fucking prisoner here. So if you don't help me I'm gonna knock on every neighbors door until I find someone who will. And as everyone seems to know me nowadays, there'll be plenty of them.'

'Okay, Bradley – calm down, I'll help. But can you give me an idea of the content?'

———

Song read the hastily typed transcript with Townsend and Benjamin peering over his shoulder.

[camera turned on; Bradley Scott walks into shot]

"It's me again. The team's working real hard so please remember us in your prayers. What started off bad has gotten worse since we last spoke. And tomorrow there's something to do with telecommunications and shit. Sorry, for cussing, but I I don't know how to edit it out.

I'm guessing it's gonna get worse before it gets better. That's the way life seems to work. Well, my life anyway. [Grins].

There's a saying that in spring a young man's thoughts turn to love. But for me in spring, my thoughts turn to God when I see the beauty of His awakening creation. And this year that thought's meant more to me. So tomorrow after church I'm not gonna stay inside and watch His beautiful day through a dirty window. That would mean I've given in to Rockwell. No, I'm gonna be finding me a phone booth somewhere and I'm gonna dial a number at random and say hi to a complete stranger. I'm gonna show Rockwell his telecommunications threat ain't gonna deny my free speech. And maybe that way I'll get to know a stranger a bit better, and at the same time get to know myself better too.

So, why don't you do the same tomorrow? Find a phone booth and just punch in any ol' number to ring a stranger too. It seems to me that fear is at its greatest when you're alone. So tomorrow, America – don't be alone.
[walks to the camera. Heard off-screen 'Bend don't break, people. Bend, don't break']

Song navigated to *Vigilangels*. Nevada had helped Scott post the new video half an hour earlier and already it had 160,000 hits. 'Care for any side action on this, gentlemen?' asked Townsend. 'We each guess the number of *Vigilangels* hits in millions by ten o'clock tonight – in two hours' time. Loser does the dishes.'

At midnight that evening Benjamin placed the last washed saucepan on the drainer. He had guessed the lowest at eighteen million, the highest guess being Song's at forty-two.

The actual number had been two hundred and thirty five million before it crashed.

Early Sunday morning, Corbyn and Song were in a helicopter heading towards Virginia, Song streaming interviews with people on their way to church. One man held up a roll of quarters, intending to ring people from the phone outside his breakfast diner. Later in the car, a few blocks from their destination, Song caught site of a phone booth outside a *Starbucks*. With the advent of cells he had grown to regard each of them as small open-air museums. But today there were seven people waiting in line at this one, talking freely, wearing smiles that masked a steely determination. He nudged Corbyn's elbow and pointed.

'Bradley's turning out to be a Prophet in our time.'

At the Langley offices of the Central Intelligence Agency, Corbyn and Song were led along a carpeted corridor to a windowless meeting room dominated by a large round table. Deputy CIA Director Mark Ladd greeted them in dark blue suit, ultraviolet white shirt, and a pair of golf-tee shaped gold cuff links. Alongside him were Paulo Alvarez, head of the Agency's Central American desk, and Mitchell Waits, Assistant Head of Strategic Operations. Alvarez was in his late thirties, Waits looked close to retirement.

'It's a good thing the Agency doesn't have to rely upon civilian telecoms alone today!' Ladd said with a wide smile as his guests took their leather trimmed seats. 'Paulo has the information you requested on Central American operations dating back the last thirty years. He'll fill in the details we're at liberty to disclose. Mitchell here is in charge of Agency interface with FBI operations, so he's interested in helping out too. Now, if you'll excuse me, there are some crises *outside* of these shores that need my personal attention. Regrettably our fanatical friends don't sleep on a Sunday.'

'Could we trouble you to stay a while longer please', requested Corbyn. 'Thanks for the file but we don't need it.'

'So what *do* you need?' asked Ladd, curiosity vying with irritation.

'We need to ask Mitchell a few questions.'

'You mean Paulo, don't you? Mitchell's only here in his liaison capacity.'

'We felt sure that when Mitchell heard of our visit he'd want to participate too. It was him who suggested he attend, wasn't it?'

'I don't know what you're talking about,' interjected Mitchell Waits before his boss could respond, 'but for the record, yes, I was surprised to only learn of your visit a couple of hours ago. Protocol requires the Bureau to contact my office well in advance.'

'That's because I only notified my own Bureau contact first thing this morning,' smiled Corbyn. 'We didn't want you to destroy any more evidence than you already have.'

'Explain,' barked Ladd, more as an order than a request. In response, Song placed a thin folder on the table. Waits alternately stared at him and the file in rapid succession. Paulo Alvarez looked on blankly.

'Mr. Waits, you were based in El Salvador from 1980 to 1983, is that correct?' picked up Song.

'Hold on, people!' shouted Ladd, raising both hands. 'What's going on here? There's no way we're going to tell you about the specific duties of Agency personnel. And what was that shit about destroying documents?'

'In David's folder we have overwhelming evidence that elements in the CIA have been blocking progress in our case,' answered Corbyn. 'My coming here today was intended as a courtesy to allow the Agency time to prepare its damage limitation. Alternatively, if you prefer not to cooperate, I can hand this file over to the embedded *New York Times* reporter in our team. I'm sure Gabriel would love to add a chapter about how a serving member of the CIA aided and abetted domestic terrorist elements.'

Ladd turned blankly to Waits as if for advice, but the other man's eyes were tracing the whirls of his fingertips. The silent Alvarez looked as though he had been caught delivering pizza to a brothel when the cops busted in. 'You've got one minute with Mitchell, then I throw you both out', stated Ladd at last, his face dark with anger.

Corbyn having done his job in creating the opening, Song leapt into the fray. 'Mr. Waits, in El Salvador did you work with anyone named Thomas Paine or Lane?' Waits shook his head. 'What about an Iain Paterson?' Again a shake. 'And do any of those names relate to your time in Nicaragua in 1977-78?'

'You seem remarkably well-informed about the background of Agency personnel', observed Ladd acerbically, poised to bring these bizarre proceedings to a skidding halt. 'It's a felony to obtain information of this nature.'

'And it's a felony to withhold information pertaining to a homicide investigation', Song snapped back, touching the folder lying before him like it were a loaded pistol before turning again to his quarry. 'Mr. Waits, I've asked you two questions and you've lied twice, so you leave me no choice'. Song rose, pulled out the paper he had secretly received in yesterday's *FedEx* package, and strode around the table. 'Mitchell David Waits, I have here a warrant for your arrest issued by the state of California with regards to your complicity in the bombing of the *Ronald Reagan Memorial Library*.'

'Corbyn, what the fuck does your boy think he's doing?' screamed an incandescent Ladd, springing up and nearly spilling his chair.

'I'm afraid there's nothing I can do about it. Detective Sergeant Song doesn't work for me, and this warrant was issued under Californian jurisdiction to David's captain. There's a press conference scheduled there in two hours time where documentation on the CIA's involvement in Rockwell will be published and Mitchell's arrest announced. A summary of this meeting will also be available', Corbyn hesitated. 'Unless of course… David, have you actually served your warrant yet?'

'No Alex, you interrupted me. Shall I continue?' Song's gunslinger eyes leveling on Ladd's. There was a long pause filled and the sound of grinding teeth before the Deputy Director nodded once. A white faced Mitchell Waits poured himself some sparkling water and began.

'In 1977 I was a U.S. military advisor to Somoza's Nicaraguan forces, coordinating covert operations against Sandinista insurgents. We poisoned the wells of rebel villages, burned their crops, bombed their public places – you know the score. Iain Paterson was one of our top explosives contractors. I can confirm he also undertook similar demolition work for me in El Salvador in the years you stated.' Waits opened his palms to indicate that this was the sum total of his knowledge.

'Gentlemen, clearly Mitchell should have alerted you when Paterson's name came up in the Rockwell reports', conceded Ladd, 'but it's hardly high treason. So is there anything else you need from the Agency?' flicking a furtive look at his watch.

'I'm afraid there is', answered Song flatly. 'When your operatives requisitioned C4, were there any checks on its usage?'

'Inventories don't have a lot of currency with contractors in operational environments', sneered Waits.

'And because "contractors" enjoyed quasi-diplomatic positions, could they send packages home without customs inspection?'

'Sure - that's how I ended up with a five year supply of Cubans', Waits smiled mockingly. 'So, yes, it's possible that Paterson retained and repatriated portions of C4 using his diplomatic immunity, if that's what you're driving at.'

'What do you know about Paterson prior to Nicaragua?'

'I'm not in Human Resources, Detective, but I can tell you his real name isn't Paterson. Every operator has a handler who gives them a fake name to create a new personnel file, and then another name that's used in field documents. It's a double-security cover to protect their real identities. So in Nicaragua he would have gone by the field name of Paterson, but I can't remember the name he was given for his new identity.

I can tell you that Paterson had been in Nam, but then so had nearly everyone else working at that time, me included. After Nam he'd been hanging out with some other tortured souls around Tijuana, sacrificing his liver to Saint Tequila. It was great recruiting territory for the Agency. Not surprisingly, none of those guys ever made it onto my Christmas list.' Waits' story stopped suddenly, as if he had hit a buffer.

'Where is the file confirming Paterson's real, birth name?' pursued Song, privately pondering the Vietnam specter that had just opened up once again.

'We'd have gotten that from his Defense file, but the Agency doesn't have that anymore.'

'How can you be so sure?'

'Because I checked this morning,' grinned Waits. 'There's an operations note submitted by his handler confirming that the file containing Paterson's real name had been lost in San Salvador in 1984.'

'You checked this morning? What a coincidence. So what does "lost" really mean, Mitchell?'

'As I said, Detective, a lot of these guys came to us pretty damaged by their combat experience. Nowadays we'd call it PTSD, but back then they were just fucked up. So when a guy managed to turn himself around it was sometimes known for their real file to "disappear" - if their handler was of a mind to help them out. Like gifting them a new life.'

'So maybe the handler will remember Paterson's real name?'

'He's dead', replied Waits with a crisp certainty.

'That's a shame. Okay, so what was the handler's name?' pursued Song changing direction, but Waits looked at Ladd to signal this was a question too far.

'Okay,' said Song hurriedly, sensing that the door might be shutting. 'So if you won't confirm the handler's name, please write down privately for Deputy Director Ladd the year in which he died.' Bemused, Waits scribbled a date and carefully slid it across to his boss. As the Deputy Director privately read the slip of paper, Song lifted the palm of his hand to reveal a date he had previously written on it. The two dates were identical : 1987.

'As you can see, Deputy Director, we already know a lot,' commented Corbyn, 'and Mitchell here is in danger of exposing the Agency – and you – to some very damaging scrutiny.'

The survival skills that had carried Ladd to his current position of great authority finally kicked-in. 'Continue with your questioning, Detective', he said coldly as the collegial distance between himself and Mitchell Waits yawned open. Alvarez, the forgotten man, continued to watch in complete silence.

Song went for the bloody kill. 'Again, what was Iain Paterson's handler's real name?'

Waits picked up his glass, but it was as empty now as his previous words had been. 'His name was Edward Michael Townsend.'

'The same Ed Townsend whose cause of death was notified to his family as an industrial accident in his cover role at an oil facility in Venezuela?' harried Song.

'Correct. Whereas in reality he'd been shot in theater by an unstable Agency contractor named Billy Storey, pissed off that Ed had refused to "lose" his real file.'

'So when you saw the names of Nevada Townsend and Iain Paterson paired together in our Rockwell case reports, didn't that ring any alarm bells?' asked Song, Ladd now watching stony eyed.

'Townsend's not an uncommon name', squeaked Waits.

'Indeed, but several years ago you lent your private support to the FBI's recruitment of a graduate from Arizona state whose grades wouldn't normally have attracted the Bureau's attention. What was her name?'

Waits smiled. 'And you have all of this in that itty-bitty file, Detective? Losing your father at such a young age can be tough, particularly if you don't know that it was in the proud service of his nation. I've kept an eye on Nevada ever since, and this was a simple way for me to give her a helping hand up.'

Corbyn leant forward threateningly. 'I've only worked with Agent Townsend for a fortnight, Mitchell, but I can tell you, sir, that she needs no one's helping hand.'

'Well that's one name you've remembered, Mr. Waits,' Song drove the knife in further, 'so I wonder if you've had the chance now to recall the name of Paterson's other identity? The one Ed Townsend gave him.'

Waits went to take another sip of water from the empty glass, feeling the rough noose close around his *Ralph Lauren* collar. He shot Ladd a look that pleaded for help, but his boss was staring impassively down at the table. 'As I recall, the new identity that Ed Townsend gave him was Thomas Paine.'

Although Ladd was too experienced to gasp out loud, Song fancied he heard one that morning. Silence mastered the room. No one moved. Eventually Corbyn cleared his throat to address the group. 'Mark, the Agency clearly has some serious internal matters to address here, so we'll withdraw now. The details disclosed to us today can be shared "as new" in writing tomorrow in order to avoid the Agency any embarrassment: the fact that Paterson and Paine are the same person; that you cannot confirm his real name; that his file was destroyed as a simple humanitarian gesture by Nevada's father. What happens now to Mitchell I'll leave to your internal procedures.'

Ladd nodded his mute gratitude at the generous offer. 'Just one question if I may', he said, unable to resist the pull of curiosity's tide. 'Where the hell did you get all this classified information from?'

'Hawks and doves', replied Corbyn. 'Thirty years ago when Ed Townsend hid Paine's real name by destroying his file, maybe he was a Dove in that sense. The men who gave us the information we've shared today expressed a concern that Hawkish ghosts from a darker period in the Agency's history should not be allowed to haunt its present.'

Ladd quickly shook their hands, clearly eager to get some personal time alone with Waits. His PA silently escorted the visitors down empty staircases, past the famous memorial wall of stars commemorating the Agency's fallen. Song wondered which of them was for Nevada's father.

In the car the two men stayed alone with their thoughts for a while, peering instead at the long queues at each payphone they passed. One caller wore a T-shirt bearing Bradley Scott's screen-printed face, a halo above it. But Song had no appetite for calling a stranger today, ringing Charley instead.

'Give Brad a hug for me', she sang, in her intoxicating voice. 'The guy's kind of crazy, but he's offering a moral leadership that reassures people. And how's Nevada doing?'

'She's good', answered Song, knowing that in a few hours time she was going to be decidedly worse.

'Can we go see the anniversary *Matrix* triple-bill over in Clarksdale?' he pleaded on that warm Mississippi Sunday. Unpaid cell bills had recently forced him to use the grubby payphone across from the grocery store where he worked. But today he was under the reproving glare of four idiots who had decided to do that dumbass Bradley Scott thing. All impatiently looking at their watches, frustrated that someone might actually be using the phone for any reason other than a speedy *hi, just calling at random to give Rockwell the middle finger.*

'What about the new Eddie Murphy? The adverts look good', his girlfriend whined at the other end.

'The last funny thing he did was *48 Hours*. He never got out of the 80's, girl.' This last sentence said louder, hoping someone in the queue might agree with his critical evaluation. But they just glowered and then suddenly flinched, adjusting their gaze along the sidewalk.

He heard a loud metallic snap, like a firecracker in a tin can, followed by a splintering noise and the whipping sound of wires pulling taut before breaking. Outside the hardware store a telegraph pole had been snapped off around five feet off the ground and was now leaning across the road at a precarious angle.

'....or the new Jamie Foxx', completing her litany of preferences just before the pole's two remaining wires gave way, slamming the mortally wounded column into the startled street.

<hr />

'Now we know where his false documentation's come from. The Agency has an army of forgers at their disposal. But we don't know where he stored the smuggled munitions, and we still don't know his real goddam name', observed Song at the airport.

'And we shouldn't forget the re-emergence of the Vietnam link', added Corbyn, though Song was already nervously aware of that fact. Nevada's selection was now clearly nothing to do with the *Thunderbolt* case, so what was the likelihood that *i4ni* was the reason for his? Corbyn had just come off the phone having heard that the great telecommunications threat had turned out to be a simple pole carrying some phone lines in Ruleville, Mississippi. Now it rang again with Ladd on speaker phone.

'This past hour we've keenly impressed upon Mitchell the need to ensure there's no further embarrassment for the Agency.' Song imagined what that "keenly impressed" approach might look like. 'There's one new piece of information, but it's only something Waits *thinks* he heard.'

'Thanks for the warning. So what is it?'

'He thinks Thomas Paine had a child.'

Chapter 13

Let us not look back in anger, nor forward in fear, but around in awareness

: James Thurber

BILLY-JO SPEARING WAS TASKED TO HUNT DOWN A CHILD bearing the Paine, Lane, or Paterson names already knowing the improbable arithmetic of the request. The period of interest was vast - somewhere between 1966 and 1985 - but with precious few clues offering sustenance to the investigation, they would take whatever leads they could scavenge. Meanwhile Song was on the phone to Benjamin asking the ballistics team to check whether the devices could have been detonated remotely by a younger accomplice.

'So review all the CCTV footage at every fucking scene for someone holding a James Bond look-alike detonation kit?' growled Benjamin making his prejudices obvious. 'Right about now we're supposed to be narrowing the case down, not blowing it back out again. Fuck!'

As they meandered through the wood, Song and Corbyn couldn't see Nevada's face, but when she spoke it was through tears. 'So my father gave the gift of a new life to Paine, and his way of saying thank you was to commit these heinous crimes and then involve me in them?' relayed in a trembling voice. 'Is there any suggestion my dad received payment for destroying his file?'

'Your father acted out of simple humanitarian compassion', answered Corbyn evenly.

'Well that was a fucking mistake, wasn't it?' she spat. 'I need to see my mom. Then I need to speak to that Paulo Alvarez guy in your meeting about what happened to Billy Storey – the bastard who killed my dad. After that I need to find a way to kill Waits, but I'm sure there'll be a long queue for that privilege. As for Paine, I'll let the Constitution take care of that motherfucker.' And with that she dissolved into the arms of her boss, spilling a river of salty tears into his white silk handkerchief.

Earlier that day, Scott had made good on his promise to make a call to a stranger, though agents had driven him forty miles north of Mountain Lakes to obscure the trail. A woman in Kansas City had since gone on TV proclaiming that she had been its lucky recipient, but then again so had several hundred others. In reality, agents had listened into Scott's conversation just in case, and they alone knew he had spoken to a deaf, ninety-seven year old World War Two veteran in Parnassus.

The man had hung up, thinking it was a crank call.

At dawn the next morning while the thronging crowd slept fitfully outside the hospital, an ambulance arrived, its blues and twos inactive. Two paramedics, baseball caps pulled down, entered the building. Five minutes later two paramedics and a driver emerged, eyes towards the ground. One of them needed help climbing into the cab.

Paine walked unaided through the Mountain Lakes door shouting a hollow *Honey, I'm home!* before agreeing to a quick meeting with the team later that day. Townsend was arranging her flight home, Benjamin called Song over. 'We've been reviewing Gabriel's notes from his private meetings with Paine.'

'Gabriel's been meeting with Paine?' repeated Song, surprised.

'It's in the agreement we made with him', as if talking to a slow child. 'Both here and at the hospital – just him and Paine. Corbyn wants you to look at the notes.'

'And are we sure Gabriel's showing us everything they're discussing?'

Benjamin frowned into his chest. 'That, Detective Sergeant, is a good question.'

'I think Gabriel and I need a little chat. I have something he wants, and now I know what I want in exchange for it.'

Paine's seat had been padded with extra cushions, Kamamalu trailing behind carrying tea in an elegant cup and saucer. 'I think we can skip the prayers Bradley as I'm sure I've been in everyone's these past few days. I hear you've answered one of my puzzles?' Nevada took him through the story of Ed Townsend as Paine's handler, his benevolent destruction of Paine's real personnel file, and his death at the hands of Billy Storey.

At the end of its telling, she drew herself up. 'So if my presence here was for you to judge whether I'd lived up to my father's name, how do I measure?'

Paine chugged two pain pills. 'First, you have correctly identified my link to the Townsend family, so I'll give Corbyn fifteen devices as promised. As to my expectations - you have exceeded them. Your father was a decent if not simple man, and he'd be proud.' Nevada's phone vibrated : *We R all thinking of U. Quantico.* She looked towards the camera, nodding once, her cheeks drained of color. Corbyn took an immediate adjournment to receive the fifteen locations.

'Congratulations, Nevada. I admire your courage and that of your father', oozed Fernandez, sidling up to her with Scott and Song.

'I'm not sure what I think about all this CIA covert shit', squawked Scott haughtily. 'Paine bombs people indiscriminately and we're pissed, but when our government does it abroad it's okay?' The uncomfortable silence spurred him to stumble on. 'You never said what happened to that guy who shot your father.'

'We don't know yet, Bradley', Townsend forced a pale smile. 'We're waiting for Langley to confirm.' Excusing herself, she moved off to the washroom just as Agent Burke rang Song to offer a general update on their Pender trawl. Song tried hard to listen but in truth his mind was raking over something else.

Something so important, he almost forgot to breathe.

With instructions fanning out to the fifteen new locations and with the media already trumpeting the exciting news, Paine restarted the meeting. 'David and Nevada are going to add to their air miles once again. Let me just get some fruit from the kitchen and I'll tell you where the next device is located.' Corbyn offered to have it brought, but Paine was already on his way citing doctor's instructions to take regular light exercise.

'So Gabriel', said Townsend, 'with Bradley on the net enjoying the media glory, how are you going -' There was a loud metallic crash from the kitchen followed by the percussive smash of tumblers and plates. Everyone dashed through the swing door to find the prostrate body of Paine surrounded by fragments of glass and china.

'He keeled forward and caught the dirty crockery', explained Kamamalu trying to lift his ward safely out of the jagged debris.

'I'm fine, I'm fine', wheezed a winded Paine. 'I tripped, that's all.' The outside door flew open, people rushing in from the cottage. 'If I could trouble someone to bring me an apple, we can restart.' His clothing was checked for shards of glass as he cleaned his hands of spent ketchup. 'There are people looking forward to my fall, but only if it involves a short rope and a long drop', Paine joked as they retook their seats. All except for Song whose stomach for the second time in just a few minutes was churning violently.

Something was definitely wrong. He was looking directly at it now, and it had changed. Corbyn was saying something but Song wasn't paying any attention. He wanted to run from the meeting to check the tapes.

'Okay, Alex, here it is.' Paine's voice dragged Song back from the panic deadening his veins. 'I'll tell you where the kids need to be by seven a.m. tomorrow, but we shouldn't hang around here too much longer.'

'*We* shouldn't hang around here?'

'Yep, this time I want to come with you. And that's non-negotiable.'

'So where are we going?' asked Townsend in a resigned tone, wondering when she would finally get the opportunity to tell her mother their family's painful news.

'We're going to Birmingham', exclaimed Paine with his trademark executioner's grin. 'I'm giving you plenty of time to organize the trip given that I'm coming too. Such wonderful people; I'm looking forward to returning.'

———

At last released from the meeting's torture, Song burst into operations, grabbing Oppenheim. 'What do we do with the recordings from Paine's interviews?'

'Burn them to disk', looking at the hands gripping her arms.
'What about recordings from the kitchen camera?'

'It's on a sixteen hour loop.'

'I need to see that and the interview room's for the past hour', with the insistence of a man buying the last ticket out of Gomorrah. Song was soon slipping the kitchen's recording into a PC, moving directly to what he was looking for. He played it several times, admiring the simplicity. Swapping to the interview room he moved through to their mass exodus into the kitchen. *Son of a bitch!* whispered to himself with a mixture of awe and glorious relief.

Nevada strode in, 'We need to prepare for Birm - '

Song manhandled her to the screen. 'I'm going to blow your Bureau mind', shaking his head at how incredible this was going to sound. 'I think Scott is now working in league with Paine.'

'What?' she exploded, dropping into the seat next to him.

'Did you tell anyone exactly how your father died? No. So how is it that Scott asked who *shot* your father?'

Townsend thought back. 'That's true, he did, but it was an intelligent guess, that's all.'

'Or maybe Scott has links to the CIA – or maybe he *is* CIA! I can accept that. So let me move to the critical evidence', Song grabbed the mouse. 'Did you notice what Paine brought to the table today?'

'Eh, some tea, in a cup and saucer? You're losing me, David.' Song forwarded the interview room tape to the point where they all rushed into the kitchen. All, except for Scott.

'By now everyone had swapped their camera view to the kitchen because of the almighty crash.' On tape, Townsend watched Scott wait in the vacated room before advancing towards the table. He bent down and did something, his angle obscuring the cameras, before moving off to the kitchen to join everyone else.

'It all looks the same to me', said Nevada peering at the grainy image.

'Except for one thing. The tea cup handle is facing the other way. Scott picked it up.'

'Maybe he spat in it. Paine and him don't get on too well, you might have noticed. Or maybe he spiked it with some Chinese medicine – that's happened before you know.'

'I believe Paine hid a written message underneath the cup and Scott retrieved it after Paine's noisy diversion.'

Townsend looked impassively at her Californian colleague. 'David, we've all come to respect your instincts, but isn't this all a bit too – well – bizarre? You're inferring a fuck of a lot from a little. I'll grant you it's unusual, but Scott's not the sharpest knife in the drawer, is he? It's a considerable leap of deduction to link the angle of a tea cup to the passage of a secret note. All a bit Cold War, don't you think?'

'Remember, Tom Cruise got Jack Nicholson because the victim didn't pack his suitcase the night before', retorted Song. 'That ain't any less bizarre than this!'

'So are you saying Scott's always been Paine's accomplice, or that he's fallen under his influence since arriving?'

'I don't know, but look at this tape of Paine's so-called fall in the kitchen. See, he's deliberately pulling stuff onto the floor and he's extended his arms to break the fall before he's tripped. This decoy alone points to some form of prior organization. But the only way to know for sure is to set them a trap.'

'We'd need something more tangible if we're to speak with Alex', she observed. 'He has enough on his plate without this conspiracy theory crap. And there's one obvious thing we haven't looked at yet.' They stared wordlessly at each other.

'We haven't checked Scott's DNA or prints', completed Song.

'Because he's been "one of us" there was never any cause to. So how could we do it now without attracting attention?' she asked.

'I think I have an answer, but I'll need some time. The DNA is particularly important.'

'I'm ahead of you for once', she interrupted. 'Because - if you're right about this – then maybe Bradley Scott is Thomas Paine's missing child. Christ! Someone call the Reality Police – I think I've been abducted to an alternative universe.'

The atmosphere was tense on the jet journeying to Birmingham. The news was all about the fifteen devices discovered the day before: in a grocery store, an apartment block, a post office, and multiple other humdrum sites. The media were equally jubilant but horrified all over again.

Townsend had been steeling herself for an emotional meeting with her mother and this Birmingham delay heightened her anxiety rather than postponing it. Partly as a refuge from her anguish she had re-opened her files on Scott. Song too was mulling over a Paine–Scott axis. He had worked cases where stronger minded individuals had bullied weaker ones into uncharacteristic actions. But what would Paine be asking Scott to do?

In the front seat Paine sat blocked against the window by Kamamalu's titanic frame, while Benjamin sat growling next to Fernandez, walling him up against the fuselage. Song pressed his head back into the seat, wondering what critical information the dapper reporter might be holding back from them.

At 6.45 a.m. the team assembled in the parking lot of Birmingham's police headquarters, Benjamin ensuring that everyone knew he was the key liaison. Paine and Kamamalu were handcuffed together in a windowless surveillance van, while Fernandez moved nonchalantly amongst the local officers gently stroking them into unguarded comments. There was a fog of tension in the air as if everyone were awaiting news on a loved one's surgery.

'What's the weather like?' asked Paine jauntily over a two-way.

'Warm and muggy', observed Song.

'I'd have expected different this time of year. No matter. The bomb's at the central railway station, detonation due at 6 p.m. local time today.'

Their cavalcade was there within ten minutes, coinciding with a live press conference hosted by Birmingham's mayor and police commissioner. Song thought of all the trains brought to a halt somewhere along the lines from New York to New Orleans, and from Orlando to Las Vegas. If you wanted to press a heavy finger on the carotid artery of a rail network, this was a fine way to do it. Glancing up at the rooftops, he caught glimpses of black garbed men carrying rifles on tripods. *Why had Paine given them so much time to look for the device?* he wondered. Maybe it was just another part of his ritual humiliation of them if in eleven hours it hadn't been found.

Dogs and their handlers progressed along the station, a curious mixture of intense professionalism and amateurish truffle hunting about their approach. By noon nothing had been found except empty rats' nests and ancient newspapers. The area around the police cordon had become a dense second perimeter of media vans and gawking civilians as once again a riveted nation looked on. Fernandez called to say Paine wanted a word with them.

'You've been searching in the wrong place', Paine advised. 'So if you get me out of this van for a coffee I'll show you exactly where to look.' Benjamin put a call through to Corbyn who reluctantly agreed to the deal. Police cars were raided for a baseball hat and a high collared jacket to mask the identity of the man whose face was plastered across the United States. A police helicopter chased off the circling media as a tight bolus of bodies surrounded their ward. The odd party took a corner seat in a downbeat coffee bar, Paine facing an oversized TV screen hanging precariously on one screw. No surprise what was on it.

'Okay, where is it?' asked Townsend slurping down a mouthful of bottled water.

Paine tucked into a toasted sandwich, rivulets of melted cheese running down his fingers. 'Patience. Undue haste isn't good for the digestion. Everyone enjoy their coffee and take in the atmosphere.'

'You've done it again', commented Song. 'I'll bet people everywhere are canceling their train journeys, no matter their destination. You get a big bang for your C4 buck, Thomas.'

Paine's tongue chased a fugitive dribble of cheddar along the heel of his hand. 'You don't need to crash a plane into a building to catch the attention of our great American public. In fact I'm going to ask Corbyn if I can publish something about that very topic in the *Times*.'

Everyone looked sideways at each other. 'You - publish something? What exactly?' enquired Benjamin.

'Re-publish would be more accurate', Paine corrected himself, noisily stirring the coffee in his daffodil yellow mug.

'Oh my God! Look!' Fernandez was staring wide-eyed at the muted television, trembling finger raised. Everyone but Paine turned to the crooked screen. To Song the picture looked unchanged from the one shown for hours now: a distant shot of the station taken from a static camera stationed at one end of the barricaded street.

'Not the picture. The tickertape', gasped Townsend seeing it for herself now.

Breaking News: reports of an explosion at Birmingham railway station, England, Great Britain

'That sandwich was delicious', observed Paine. 'Can I get another?'

Early reports were of many casualties. The screen changed to a live *BBC* feed of British police encircling their railway station in perfect symmetry to the scene a hundred yards away from Song.

'You son of a bitch', exclaimed Benjamin as the elderly man drained his coffee. 'You said 6 p.m. local time and that's when the detonation occurred in England. You said "Birmingham", but you didn't mention Alabama – we assumed it. This morning you said you'd been expecting different weather - the weather in Birmingham, England? And when you said you'd show us where the device is, you knew the news would break while we were in here. You piece of shit!'

'Having calmed the Chinese down, it's the Brits who're going to be pissed now', smiled Paine. The *BBC*'s feed showed stretchers bearing blackened bodies.

'So now gone really global', stated Song.

'I went global when I was in Central America, detective. Everything after that has been essentially the same work - except now it's *pro bono*.'

The bomb had detonated in the women's washroom, killing eight. Secreted behind the wash basins and then tiled over, the flying shards of razor-sharp ceramic causing the most injuries. In all the media, home or abroad, the fiasco of "the wrong Birmingham" was already playing out. The team looked like imbeciles.

On his subdued drive back from Newark airport, Townsend called Song from her own journey back to her mother's. 'I've had an idea about Bradley. *Amazon* will be delivering something tomorrow; you'll need to sign for it.'

'Sure,' aware that Benjamin was in the car listening, 'what is it?'

'I can't tell you. Too many strings attached,' Townsend hung up.

It immediately trilled into life again. 'Paulo Alvarez here. Remember, from the Langley meeting? The Agency has further information it would be useful to discuss privately with you.'

Song recalled the quiet man who'd been relegated to observer status in that tempestuous meeting with Ladd and Mitchell Waits. 'Sure, but I won't be able to get down to Virginia for a few - '

'No, I'm coming up to you.' There was the slightest of pauses before the Agency man continued. 'It's a red ski-mask situation.'

———

In the woods next morning, the patrolling agents adjusted their routes as Alvarez confirmed that Waits' interrogation had not yielded much further information. Song expected as much, but if that was the case, why the special visit to New Jersey? And how did Alvarez know about Song's brush with the men in the red ski-masks?

'Your Rockwell case has everyone on a hair trigger' picked up the Agency man, who was now very talkative. 'My own parents are getting all their groceries dropped off and eating more takeout than ever before. If you could wear broadband out my dad would have it down to a few microns thick by now, he's constantly surfing for news. If they knew we were talking they'd chew me out for not getting your autograph.'

'My autograph?'

'Sure! *YouTube* has you at the consulate and Birmingham. My dad looked for your *Facebook* page but couldn't find it.' Alvarez stopped with his back to the safe-house, lowering his voice until barely audible. 'Normally I'd frisk you for wires, but I've read your file and you seem like a decent guy, so can we speak off the record?' Intrigued, Song nodded his consent. 'From the Agency's uneducated view it's clear Paine will only give up the locations if you can solve his torrid little puzzles. So our job is to help wherever we can, but there are some residual Agency elements not happy about Paine's re-emergence. As you already know from your red ski-mask friends, there's the Old CIA and the New CIA.'

'And which of those two tribes does Deputy Director Ladd belong to?' asked Song, making sure the patrolling Bureau agents were keeping their distance.

'Indeterminate. But if there's a sleeping dog in this case, it's not in his interests to tweak its tail. For my part, it's only when Paterson's name emerged that the red light flashed on my desk. From the paperwork it was clear someone had destroyed geologic layers of data before I'd gotten there.'

'That would have been Ed Townsend', completed Song.

'Correct, but we didn't know precisely what. That's why I needed your help in outing Waits - to fill in the details. Sorry about the ski-masks, but I didn't know how you'd react', Alvarez smiled wanly, 'though red isn't really my color. And now I want to share some new information that wasn't in the report Ladd submitted after your visit. Prepare yourself for a shock, detective.' Alvarez handed over a thin file that had been folded into his jacket pocket.

Song looked at the CIA logo at the top and then at the person's name typed just underneath it. 'Oh shit!' his stomach performing a wild somersault.

'Oh shit indeed', echoed Alvarez. 'That's one sticky web you're caught in, detective.'

Song was in the kitchen still reeling from the sight of that file when an Agent brought him Townsend's *Amazon* delivery. The package size covered his torso, though it was light and the multiple *Fragile* stickers just fuelled his curiosity further. He spent the rest of the afternoon lying on his bed deep in thought about Alvarez's file, when at dusk Townsend burst in wearing more makeup than usual.

'Too much foundation? Damn! I spent eight hours blubbing with my mom last night. This was supposed to hide my feminine vulnerabilities. Fuck *L'Oreal!*'

'How did it go?'

'She had no idea whatsoever. My mom has pictures of him wearing hard hats and carrying tools and stuff, then I pitch up and tear down every emotional construct she's ever had about her husband. She was so proud, then so angry, then proud again, and then – oh, I don't know.'

'And where are you?'

'Me?' she shrugged, looking up at the ceiling as if to see the stars beyond. 'Settling somewhere between pride and realism. I've always thought well of my dad, but I guess I'm walking a little taller tonight.' To change the subject she snatched up the *Amazon* package, tearing off its wrapping. 'I told you it had "some strings attached"!'

'It's an acoustic guitar', he said, matter-of-fact.

'Wow! I can see why you got those sergeant's stripes, boy.'

'How does this help work out whether Scott's in league with Paine, or if he's Paine's son?'

Townsend played a few bars of Mazzy Star's *Fade into you*, one string slightly off-key. 'Back up a second, flat-foot. This can't prove either of those things, but it *can* prove whether he's really Bradley Scott or not.'

Before that evening's meeting with Paine, Fernandez had hastily returned from a dinner hosted by his editor. With Paine's permission, the taciturn Scott had returned to Durham for a few days low-profile work with the *Fishermen*, a hefty Bureau escort in tow. Song and Townsend were uneasy about his departure, but couldn't say anything without raising suspicion. News that day had been dominated by the gracious way the British were handling a bombing on their sovereign soil, proving that some vestige of the Special Relationship was still intact. 'Our generation remembers twenty years of IRA bombings', said their Prime Minister, 'so we have mettle enough to see off the likes of Rockwell.'

'Birmingham was belated pay-back for 1814', quipped Paine to his non-appreciative audience. 'That's three members of the U.N. Security Council down – two more to go. Or should that be the Insecurity Council? So now on to the next locations! David, you're going to Boston, while Nevada's off to Philly because there are two devices tomorrow. I'll call each of you at nine a.m. eastern time.'

'You mean Boston, Massachusetts, and Philadelphia, Pennsylvania?' clarified Corbyn.

Paine laughed. 'Ouch, yes! You must be smarting. And are you any closer to solving the remaining puzzles - JH352 for instance? Oh dear, more body-bags and flags yet to come.'

It was agreed that Benjamin would accompany Song, while Fernandez would go with Townsend, though she wasn't sure which was the shortest of those two straws.

Like everywhere Song had travelled these past two weeks, he had never visited Boston before. He considered the parallels between this current emergency and that of the city's bloody marathon, seeing only outrage and fear as their common denominators. After the Birmingham debacle, a slightly more contrite Benjamin was handling the local liaison, allowing Song to gratefully blend into the fringes. Nonetheless, the Homeland man was still making it known he was the new sheriff in town. Benjamin's phone rang, silencing the anticipatory conversations of the fifty officers gathered around him.

Benjamin listened to Paine before surprisingly hanging up without passing the phone over to Song. 'It seems our friend is also willing to speak with me now, not just yourself and Nevada. We're heading for *Flannery's Old Book Store*.'

Song didn't really care. In fact he was relieved that Paine was diluting his focus. Yesterday Birmingham, today Boston and Philly; where would he dispatch his marionettes tomorrow? And *still* no idea of motive, and *still* no clarity on why Song was there. He would welcome the time to ponder these questions again while Benjamin developed sunburn from his day in the limelight.

Flannery's was a few minutes away, Song knowing that yet another governor and his police commissioner would be on-air anytime now. Spilling out of their vehicles, the first TV crew soon rolled up along with a gathering crowd of Bostonians awaiting their city's latest detonation. For Song the routine had already become stale, but for America it remained hypnotic. Office work stopped as people crowded around PCs and TVs, mainstream programming surgically altered to insert live coverage from whichever Rockwell occurrence on that particular day. Like baseball, it seemed there was always a Rockwell game playing out somewhere.

Song strolled along the deserted street, the bookstore's turquoise-on-black sign proclaiming the *Flannery's* name. Paine had identified noon as the time of detonation and the bomb squad's bulky forms were already prowling its aisles. 'The target here's a local fast-food joint at noon', confirmed Nevada from Philadelphia, 'so all the burgers will be well-done this lunch time.' A passing sniffer dog growled at Song, its handler jerking him back to the business at hand. Song wished Townsend luck and headed for the store.

The squad moved methodically up and down, elbows brushing Frost and Kerouac, eyes searching cream walls for signs of new brickwork and errant cables. Song browsed a new McEwan and a biography of FDR that looked interesting. He ran his finger along the spines of the greats as if administering their last rites. For the next three hours he watched the smooth dissection of the premises only to hear it declared 'clean or unseen', meaning it was either a hoax or too well secreted. It looked as though Paine would have his day - again.

'City Architect's office says it was refurbished in 1996, right in Paine's activity slot', reported Benjamin, the two of them now standing behind sandbags well back from the store. The approach to noon saw the withdrawal of all remaining personnel, leaving the area as silent as any downtown street post-looting and pre-National Guard. The networks had the luxury of leisurely fitting in their allotted advertising slots and coiffuring their anchor's hair before the mayhem. An agent called over, pointing to a well dressed man in his late forties: Michael Flannery, the store founder's great-grandson. It was agreed he could spend the remaining time with the Bureau's team to be there at the end.

Just a few minutes left. Song edged over to the solitary figure of Flannery looking ungainly in the ill-fitting Kevlar vest he's been issued, Benjamin peeling off to update Corbyn. 'I'm sorry for your loss', Song murmured.

'You feel it too? It's not the store itself — we can rebuild masonry. It's the books. They're just paper and ink, I know, but.... The industry predicts books as artifacts will be dead in twenty years as everything goes soft-copy. It's still literature, and that's the important thing, but can you imagine a bookstore empty of books? Pasternak in pixels, Bronte in bytes?' Song let the man talk, just as you do relatives at funerals.

'You have a good selection in stock', Song complimented. 'The modern works people seem to want: the celeb bios, the kiss-and-tells, the beach fiction; but you've got a strong back-catalogue too.'

'I try to keep the door open both ways. In terms of profit per shelf yard, the classics don't punch their weight, but it can't always be about the buck, can it?'

Song nodded both his agreement and his appreciation. 'Where do you keep your rarer works? I couldn't see them on general display.'

'We don't have any', answered Flannery, sad eyes riveted to his silent storefront.

'You mean you've stopped selling old books?'

'We've never sold them. Since my grandfather's first store we've only ever stocked contemporary publications.'

'*First* store?' repeated Song.

'Yes, we moved to these premises in 2005.'

Song gasped, shooting past Flannery to man-handle Benjamin. 'Nate, the message you got from Paine. He said *Flannery's Old Book Store*, yes?'

'Yeah, what's your point?' in high irritation. There were under two minutes left.

'Oh Christ, Nate! He didn't mean "Old Book Store", they don't stock any. He meant the book store before they moved here!'

Benjamin's face drained blood, his voice high and tight. 'Where?'

'Just three blocks from here', Flannery pointed. 'It's now a pre-school toy shop called *Lilliput*.' Song was off and running before the last syllable was out, Benjamin screaming for people to follow as he too set off at a sprint. No time for Song to look at his watch: maybe a minute or so to go, bawling at pedestrians to get out of his way, parting like a Biblical sea as a dozen burly men charged towards them.

Grateful now for those early morning runs, Song streaked into the third block parallel to *Flannery's* cursing his own sloppiness. When Benjamin had said Paine didn't need to speak with him, Song had felt a sense of relief. All this channeling of bad news through him and Townsend was bone-achingly wearying. But now Paine had deliberately played Benjamin's arrogance. This wasn't another mistake, it was another trap. That stinging thought spurring another furious burst of speed as protesting shoppers dove out of his way.

Definitely less than thirty seconds left. *Lilliput's* pastel shaded sign and colorful windows were soothing to the eye as Song bulled his way through the entrance, tearing an antique doorbell from its hinge.

'FBI! Get out - now!' The bevy of young mothers looked back at him blankly. Didn't he know all the fuss was three blocks over? Nothing happened in kids' stores that didn't involve unicorns and soft-hearted pirates. Consequently, no one moved.

'F.B. fucking I.! There's a bomb in the store. Go!' yelling now, as three wheezing agents charged in through the flapping entrance. Just as there had been silence and bewilderment before, now there was panic and din. A dozen frantic shoppers hurtled towards the door, stroller wheels crashing with *Ben Hur* intensity, sustainable jute bags flung aside, pyramids of primary colored bricks toppling to the rainbow ground. Song and the agents half lifted, half-pulled the bung of frenzied people through the door, propelling them towards a hastily erected perimeter. Shoppers poured out of adjacent stores, agents shoving them towards safety. The first camera crew to have spotted the commotion had raced round to relocate themselves a mere thirty yards away.

Fragments of seconds left now thought Song, the store almost emptied.

'There's a lady with a kid out back!' squealed a shop assistant clinging to the day's takings. Song leapt to the back of the store slamming through slatted shutters decorated with fantastical animals and in one flowing movement used his momentum to kick-in the changing room door. With no time to explain, Song tore a baby girl from her mother's grip, fleeing the room yelling 'Bomb! Get out!' His lightning reasoning was that a parent watching her daughter's abduction would instinctively pursue the kidnapper, and the wailing banshee now snapping at his heels was proving him right.

In a few triple-jumper's strides he was into the street, the screaming child locked in his arms, Benjamin snagging the trailing mother to whip her off to the side. Song stumbled past the edge of *Liliput's* plate glass window etched with circus animals just as its surface bulged grotesquely and erupted spewing a vicious torrent of shattered glass across the deserted street. The quartet were hurled to the ground, Song desperate not to crush his precious cargo. Next to him he heard the woman yelp under Benjamin's weight accompanied by the unmistakable sound of snapping bone. Then there was only the silence of the aftermath, and a manic whistling in his damaged ears.

Song wanted to get up but couldn't. His last ounces of strength channeled into maintaining the cage of arms containing the fragile bird beneath him. Momentarily he was hauled up, his hands being gently unhinged from their grip around her. Then he was dragged away, his body not wanting to do anything about it.

The last thing he noticed before blacking out were the acrid fumes of sponge-filled books melting in the corona of a street-level sun.

Chapter 14

A timid person is frightened before a danger, a coward during the time, and a courageous person afterwards

: *Jean Paul Richter*

He refused admission to hospital, the ER doctor shining lights into his ears, a nurse dressing his grazed knees. The job finished and assurances of a complete recovery given, Song drifted out into the corridor while Benjamin underwent the same. Earlier Song had seen rings of moisture in the agent's eyes, knowing it had been his own hubris that had led to this catastrophe. On TV, Song saw rerun footage of their hurried exit from the store followed a split-second later by the window's detonation. He had to admit it looked extremely dramatic. Song's phone vibrated again but there was no point answering, his ears still whistling like a wind tunnel. He had texted he was okay to people, and amongst their many good wishes a message from Nevada: *Glad ur ok. Philly bomb at 1159. Fries all over our SUV.*

Song's device had been hidden in the shared back wall between *Lilliput* and a coffee shop. With no warning possible there, the blast had shattered their steel espresso machines spraying shrapnel into the faces of two baristas, killing them instantly. In the dull fog that still occluded Song's mind he felt the sharp bitterness of despair. Paine had given them five hours notice, yet still people had died. It was unimaginable. The girl Song had saved was named Hope Faith. He shook his head towards the heavens, partly with the irony of her parents' choice, and partly in anger at her Maker's perfidy.

An Agent touched Song's arm to catch his attention. 'Corbyn's on the line. We've cranked up the volume for you', he said with exaggerated enunciation.

'David, thank God! Nathan's briefed me. It's very, very unfortunate.' That was one word for it, thought Song. 'I hate to ask you this, but are you fit for another assignment?'

Song looked down at his bandaged knees and listened to the whistling sonata in his ears. 'Sure. You need me back at the Lakes now?'

'No, I need you in Pender County. I know you're not hearing too well, but listen hard to this: in the early hours of this morning the cops down there arrested Bradley, and he says you're the only one he'll talk to.'

By the time the FBI's jet landed at Raleigh-Durham that evening, the deafening forte in Song's ears had diminished to a light legato. Agent Ezekiel Burke looked as smart as ever, flanked by the full figure of Sheriff Le Bon, regulation sweat patches seeping from his underarms. Song greeted them, conscious of the tears in his pants hastily sewn up by a helpful nurse in Boston.

'We moved Scott to the Bureau's office in Charlotte', explained Burke in the car.

'We were keeping an eye out for souvenir hunters at Lane's', explained Le Bon, 'when at eleven p.m. last night an officer saw someone cut across the orchard towards the house. He told the

intruder to raise his hands, which he did without no fuss. It's
only when we got him back that the duty officer recognized him
as the celebrity from TV. I've locked the place down. My guys
have been told to keep their mouths shut otherwise I'll have
them painting white lines up the Interstate without closing off
the traffic. Since then Mr. Scott has confirmed his identity but
refused to speak with anyone but you.'

Song's mind was half listening and half concocting the
Fisherman's motive, an image of Scott holding an innocuous
cup of tea repeatedly streaking across his memory. 'And what
was he carrying?' prompted Burke.

'Oh yeah, two cans of gasoline and a box of matches. We
found his stolen car at sun-up and in the trunk was fifty yards
of twine, a screwdriver, and a spade. The car's owner says none
of it's his.'

'So, gentlemen, what are we thinking?' asked Song.

'Looks as though he was about to torch the house. Soak the
twine in petrol and feed it through a broken window. Would've
gone up as quick as that church Rockwell targeted in Oklahoma.'

'Exactly as Zeke says', chipped in Le Bon, 'or maybe break in
and soak the furniture.'

'And the spade?' asked Song.

'Maybe to dig his car out the mud?' offered Le Bon. 'We've
had rain lately and those back roads can turn into bogs real
quick. He'd know that.' Song agreed with their general direction,
but why burn down the house? If he and Nevada were right
about a Paine/Scott connection, were there clues here that
needed destroying? And, if so, why hadn't Paine done that
before surrendering himself in New York?

'So Bradley, what the fuck were you doing?' asked Song
in the cool white of the Bureau's interview room. Before his
suspicions had been aroused, Song would have just given

Scott a parental shellacking before bundling his morose ass onto a plane back home, but now he wanted to play the game differently.

Scott gave his trademark shrug. 'Dunno. Guess I was so pissed off I wanted to get back at Paine some way.'

'But he's never coming back here. He'll serve five thousand years in a federal penitentiary at best.'

'Still, he would have known it was gone. Taking away from him in spirit what he's taken away from people in blood.'

Song left a silence on the table. 'How did you lose your agents?'

'Told them I weren't feeling well, then scooted out the window to the hardware store and to boost a ride.'

'So what was the plan?'

'Bust in Paine's door, spread the gas around some, light it and leave.'

'So why the other stuff: the screwdriver, the twine, the spade?'

Scott looked confused at the question. 'Just in case I couldn't get through the door. Break a window, soak the twine and use it as a wick in the cans, just like a Molotov', his lower lip growing over its counterpart. Song thought he was about to cry.

'Is this why you asked Corbyn to come back down here?'

'Oh no, the intention was to get back to the *Fishermen*. The New York chapter folk are okay, but too big city for my tastes. It was on the plane down when I made up my mind.'

'And do you plan to talk about your attempts at arson in your next pop video?'

'Shit, no way, man. I'd be too ashamed. Sometimes I just lose control of my judgment.'

'Interesting', said Song leaning forward onto the table. 'Because the people in Children's Services in Bakersfield have nothing but good words for you. Responsible and calm, they said.'

Scott grinned. 'You've been talking to Miss Alabaster. I did some chores and helped her out when I could.' Song was disappointed by his accuracy, Townsend's budding theory that this man was not the real Bradley Scott taking a bruising.

'Plausible,' offered Burke as Song joined him and Le Bon behind the one-way mirror, 'but I have my doubts.' Song looked at the sheriff for his opinion.

'Horseshit. Can't put it any plainer. Boy comes all the way down here one day, and the next he's fixing to burn a place down? And him working with homeless folk and all - razing somewhere people can live? It don't square.' Le Bon's radio squawked and he made his apologies.

Buoyed by these new suspicions, Song took a deep breath and launched into his next reckless plan. 'Zeke, I'd like you to process Scott's fingerprints off that can of soda in there, and also get these DNA tested.' He handed over a phial containing hairs he had lifted from Scott's bathroom back at the Lakes two days earlier.

Burke scrutinized the tube as though looking for some miniature hallmark. 'Are you saying you want Scott processed for this incident?'

Song moved his feet awkwardly. 'No.'

'Then why would you want his prints and DNA? And why not do that in New Jersey? You must have the nation's resources at your fingertips.'

'I think it'll be done quicker here. We're overloaded.'

'U-huh,' replied the Agent slowly, still eyeing the glass container. 'But you're not asking me to say we took these hair samples today?' he asked cautiously, brow furrowed.

'No sir, I'm not.' Song waited for the man to make up his mind. It was a big thing he was asking, and Burke might want to pick up the phone to Corbyn just to check.

'So if we did the DNA test,' Burke said slowly. 'We wouldn't put a rush on it, because it's just a regular background check, right? We wouldn't want to attract too much attention to it, would we? If I were to do it, that is.'

'Correct. Just put it in the system, that's all.' Song waited for what seemed an age, sweat gathering on his upper lip.

'That was a good thing you did in Boston with the little girl. Bravery like that should be rewarded, don't you think?' said Burke eventually, snapping his hand around the phial. 'You know, your visit today's got me to thinking. This is the first time I've worn this jacket since that first day at Paine's house, and - heaven forgive me - I've just recalled I found hairs just inside the door there and a used soda can underneath the stoop. They've been in my pocket all this time. Still, no harm done, as it's accepted that Scott visited Paine's house at least once, yes? Promise not to tell Corbyn I screwed up?' smiled Burke.

Wanting to hug the man, Song offered his hand instead. 'Promise.'

· Back in the interview room, Scott looked up from his empty soda can as the two men entered. 'So what happens now? Am I gonna be charged?'

'I doubt it very much, Bradley', opined Burke. 'You being a national hero and all.'

Song was re-painting *Lilliput's* pastel yellow walls helped by a score of three year olds, each with a roller. They were constantly bumping into each other, paint slopping everywhere, on account of the fact that their eyes had been bloodily sewn shut with coarse fishing line. Across the room featureless baristas were trying to escape rats gnawing at their shoeless feet. A hand alighted on Song's shoulder and bade him to follow.

Eyes snapping open, Song found Nevada sitting on his bed, juice in one hand, bagel in the other. 'Bad dreams? My mom says nightmares are our ancestors' way of sending us dark messages. But surely that's why we have *Fox News?*' she threw a wodge of morning papers onto his chest. 'You're all over the front pages. There are a dozen kids eating their *Lucky Charms* today because of you.' She played a *YouTube* clip of him falling on top of the little girl set to *Born in the USA*. It had been viewed thirty million times.

'Enough already,' protested Song, 'get out of my room so the national icon can shower his selfless body?'

'Sure, but I wanted to be the first to show you this headline.' She held up the *Times'* front page for him to squint at through sleepy eyes: *The UnSong Hero.*

His head collapsed back into the pillow as he emitted a low, painful groan.

'Good afternoon, everyone', intoned Paine. 'Yesterday's *Oscar* can only go to one man! I admit that when I saw that fuck-wit Benjamin lining everything up in the wrong street I could hardly contain myself. Even *my* heart was in my mouth watching you save that kid, David. Superb television!'

'And what about those young baristas who died? Nothing superb about that', replied Song evenly.

'True. But you know how the media like its heroes so that's just an irritating detail, isn't that right Gabriel?'

'I think the media want to report the news as it is. And at times when it's so very dark, it's not uncommon for editors to alight upon the brightest point of illumination in counterpoint to the midnight that prevails.'

'Extraordinarily eloquent, Gabriel. Quite humbling. Well tomorrow it's my turn to publish an article, so here it is.' It had been agreed Paine would be allowed half of page three in the *Times* in return for the locations of ten devices, and as long as his text passed FBI muster. The paper was happy to oblige at no charge, knowing the cost would be paid back tenfold in PR for its forthcoming serialization of Fernandez's book.

Corbyn scanned the note's neat handwriting with trepidation. '"*No one man can terrorize a whole nation unless we are all his accomplices*". Is this it?'

'Isn't it enough?'

'That's Ed Murrow', interjected Fernandez. 'I recognize it from my journalism classes.'

'It most certainly is', confirmed Paine. 'I'd like it published in 96 point, *Times Roman*, black on white. Nothing fancy.' Paine rattled off the ten addresses, Song trying to keep up. What stuck in his mind was a wall in Missouri, an electricity pylon in Florida, a mall in Virginia, and a car park in Wisconsin. Nondescript, everyday targets, but that seemed to be the idea most of the time. Song thought of the significance of the Murrow quote and the fact that they still weren't below a hundred in remaining devices.

'That's only nine locations', observed Corbyn, Fernandez's shorthand confirming the count.

'That's because number ten has already detonated', replied Paine.

'Where?'

'The *World Trade Center*, New York City'. Anyone could have spoken, but no one knew what to say. Song imagined the same tableaux repeating itself in offices taking their digital feed.

'What are you implying?' asked Townsend at last.

'I'm simply stating I placed a device in the North Tower and that it detonated on September 11th, 2001.' Bright minds were working as fast as they could.

'It goes without saying we know that date', said Corbyn levelly. 'So either you're suggesting you played some part in it or – or what exactly?'

Paine laughed to break the crystalline silence. 'I'm just saying I'd placed a four pounder there back in '89. So when the Tower came down that day, I'm guessing my own humble device detonated early. I can't say for sure, of course.'

'Fuck you, Paine', shot Townsend.

'Light through a prism, Nevada. It's refracted into a rainbow of colors, but it's still light.'

'Thanks for the *Pink Floyd*, but fuck you again anyway.'

———

That evening, Townsend organized a get-together for the agents in the basement's rumpus room. They were careful not to depict it as a party, there was too much not to celebrate. Corbyn had been lukewarm about the idea. 'It's a Friday', argued Townsend, 'and the guys are tired. Let them kick back a little.' So that night, while in nine cities teams were determinedly hunting down the day's bounty trailed by an equally determined media, Corbyn sanctioned a low-key social event in the safe house's rumpus room. After a small thank you speech for the team's efforts so far, Corbyn called to Kamamalu who emerged hefting six trays of non-alcoholic beverages. In total, with all the Bureau's security staff and Karen Oppenheim's team, there were over two dozen people present. The smiling Scott was sitting on the floor, back braced against the external sliding doors, jammed between two agents gently joshing him about his videos. Even Fernandez had loosened his tie a little.

Townsend slipped upstairs and returned with something concealed behind her back. Before Scott had the chance to spot it, she thrust the guitar onto his lap. 'Come on, Brad, liven the place up with a little music just like you used to do back in Bakersfield.'

Scott held it like the used diaper of someone else's child. 'I don't play much anymore, and then only church music.'

'Okay, I understand. Could you just check it's tuned properly please, then I'll have a strum myself. My hearing's out of whack from getting too close to the blasts'. She swung round to continue her conversation with Oppenheim making it impossible for Scott to decline.

'Seems fine to me now', he concluded handing it back after a while.

Later, Song sidled alongside Townsend. 'Well?'

'He didn't tune it, he just twiddled the keys.'

'How do you know? You haven't played it yet.'

'I absolutely fucking know he didn't, because this afternoon I restrung it to be played left-handed. If he knew anything about guitars he'd have mentioned it. I tell you, this guy has never played one before in his life.

Whoever this fucker is, he's not the Bradley Scott that Doreen Alabaster knew back in California.'

———

At two a.m. that morning, sleep was still playing hide-and-seek with Song. Surrendering to the shrieking of his bladder, he crept along the darkened corridor towards the bathroom. He could hear the gentle splashing of a faucet as some other reveler said farewell to their cola. Karen Oppenheim emerged, Notre Dame T-shirt pulled down baggily just below her butt. 'Good night, detective', she whispered with a smile. As he turned to close the door, he saw her slip quietly into Nevada's bedroom.

It was the best turnout yet for the dawn run, including Corbyn for the first time. After a couple of miles the group had strung out to reflect the comfort of each runner, Song's sore knees pairing him with Corbyn whose age dictated a more conservative pace. Song wondered whether he should take this opportunity to mention Scott's DNA and fingerprint search, but if Corbyn were to have a heart attack now, Song wanted it to be attributed wholly to his exertions and not anything that had been said. As had become the custom, the group stopped halfway round by the old church. A lone parishioner still sat out front surrounded by candles and bunches of flowers. Corbyn looked quizzically at Townsend.

'Churches everywhere have committed to stand watch until the crisis has ended. See those flowers?' she pointed. 'It's one bunch to commemorate every attack.'

Corbyn wiped the sweat from his eyes. 'They're going to need a bigger vase.'

Song grabbed some toast and cereal, heading down to the rumpus room to catch the morning's TV news. The efficient Kamamalu had detailed some of the agents to play Martha Stewart and it was already almost spotless. Two cases of cola lay unopened in the corner. 'Where do you want these putting, guys?' Song asked, keen to lend a hand. They indicated the facilities room along the basement corridor. Hauling them toward it he swung open the door to be greeted by an ear-piercing wail as it screeched ajar. At that delicate time in the morning it sounded like a hundred kids dragging their nails down a blackboard. 'Son of a bitch! The drug lords who used this place used hundreds to light their Cubans but they couldn't afford a spot of oil for these damn hinges?' He slammed the facilities room door shut to another eye-watering rasp of metal on metal.

Slumping onto the couch with his granola, the news was glut coverage of yesterday's operations. Already the devices in Missouri, Virginia, Maine, and Oregon had been made safe.

There were clips of Americans celebrating these 'victories' as though they were Okinawa, while others saw the discovery of this current crop as an even better reason to remain behind closed drapes, hoarding rice and bottled water. Song was distracted by the sight of Big Bird's caller ID.

'Hi TK, let me guess. You're in *Dunkin* and you can't decide whether to get sprinkles or jelly.' There was a moment of silence before his partner answered.

'I can't fucking believe it, but I've just checked and it's confirmed. Fuck me. Fuck me. It's just huge.'

Song had never heard his partner so upset. 'For Christ's sake, what is it?'

'I've just had a call from the lab. They've had a hit on that partial we took off the tape strapping the scalpel to Holden Webb's chair in *i4ni*,' lapsing again as if reading from a faulty auto-cue.

'Are you saying they're from another perp?' Song's mind racing through multiple options, each of them equally bad.

'This is totally fucked. You know the system automatically compares old case files with freshly entered fingerprint records. Well today's hit is from the ones just uploaded for Bradley Scott in North Carolina.

It's your internet guy. It's his prints on the *i4ni* tape.'

Chapter 15

Worry gives a small thing a big shadow

: *Swedish proverb*

S<small>ONG COULDN'T REMEMBER DISCONNECTING THE PHONE</small>, but there it sat in front of him as lifeless as he now felt. He walked to the nearest toilet just in time before his legs gave way, dropping him unceremoniously onto the bowl. Gradually the Catherine wheel rotating in his head slowed and he righted himself.

Song's mind crawled across the various possibilities before he hit the ugliest one of all. Scott was the *i4ni* killer and had framed an innocent Holden Webb. Someone tried the locked door, but Song said nothing – he couldn't. And now the monolithic question. Did Paine know that Scott had been involved, thus confirming *i4ni* as the real reason why Song had been invited into this cabal? But then why all the theatrics of O'Brian's dismissal to create the opportunity for Scott to join them? Still so many questions starting with the word *why* and Song's head was exploding from them.

One last desperate hypothesis flashed across his mind. What if the murders had been perpetrated solely to provide a reason for Paine to issue his invitation to Song? He reeled with motion sickness. It was like some tortured version of *The Truman Show*: all the deaths arranged around him.

Ezekiel Burke! If TK had already seen the results, then so might Burke. Song fished out his phone and - as if endowed with special powers – miraculously it rang.

'Zeke, thanks for calling, don't worry, I'm just about to speak with Alex about the match.'

'I'm sure you are! I'm now personally camping out at the lab. No-one's taking a leak until I have the DNA results in my hand, but it'll still take around three more days.' Song sped into the kitchen to find Nevada, dragging her out to the deck, a yogurt drink six-pack swinging limply from her hand. Drawing close, peering through the wooden boards to check no one was below, he rifled off everything he had just learned.

She stood thin lipped, a v-shape deepening in her forehead. 'We need to tell Corbyn now or we're toast', she stated, tossing the drink over the balcony. They burst through the door into the operations room, Corbyn looking bemused, Benjamin wearing a vacant frown, the Homeland man's arrogance still cowed by the humiliation of Boston.

'I've seen you both in this hyper-energetic mode before', observed Corbyn. 'It's usually either extremely bad news, or extremely good. So which is it this time?'

After they had told him, Corbyn still couldn't work out which it was.

———

At Corbyn's instruction, the pair took Greene through the story: Scott's quip about Ed Townsend's death, Paine's kitchen fall, Nevada's guitar test, and finally the devastating fingerprint match with the DNA check still awaited.

Greene peppered them with questions about facts and suppositions before agreeing a plan of action. 'In addition to sorting out the critical Paine-Scott link, Devaughan needs to give a view on the damage this'll cause when it gets out. Scott's face has become the flagship of this case; his words a source of comfort to millions. Christ, my nephews have his photo on their screensavers! This could rate as one of the greatest confidence tricks ever. Madoff looks like a rank amateur!' Greene tailed off, his shaking head blurring the video. Song thought of Holden Webb lying fitfully on a hard mattress tonight, a cluster of family pictures stuck haphazardly on his wall. He was suddenly aware Greene had mentioned his name. 'It's becoming a habit, but I want to thank you again, David. I can't say your methods are conventional, but they're certainly effective.' But for Song the shadow of an innocent Holden Webb blotted out any pleasure he might otherwise have taken from these words. 'And to you, Agent Townsend. I can see that guitar test finding its way into a Quantico case study. The Bureau can be proud it has young, talented people like you coming through its ranks.'

Nevada nodded her silent thanks, Corbyn's face a study in inscrutability.

Corbyn gave instructions to Benjamin for a covert shadowing of Scott. David and Nevada were to return to California to dig deeper into the Fisherman's background. 'You've also got Paine's Vietnamese link and the Holden Webb-Bradley Scott entanglement to sort out while you're there', he instructed. 'But please remember that the Scott investigation's a sideshow unless it generates tangible links to Paine. Let's hope that following Bradley's trail – past and present – will give us the edge we need.'

Song was pleased to be returning home again, because he also had the file Paulo Alvarez had secretly given him that needed further investigation.

Song felt nauseous just thinking about it. For it was the CIA's report on his father's visit to Nicaragua in 1980.

———

Walking into the San Francisco arrivals hall that evening with Townsend, Song wore a baseball cap pulled down tight to avoid 'Boston' recognition. Big Bird barged through the bevy of waiting Bureau agents, scraping them aside as he did the unwanted salad on his burgers. 'Okay guys,' he boomed holding up his badge, 'this motherfucker's wanted in connection with a series of canine sodomy charges. The douche-bag's coming with me.' Never a quiet man, Bloomfield spent most of the journey shouting and gesticulating at his partner. It took him three hundred yards to realize he was driving with the handbrake still on, and another mile before he stopped hitting the horn as if it were a faulty soap dispenser. Townsend sat quietly in the back, trying not to hear.

'Why are we going to HQ at this late hour?' enquired Song calmly.

'Because some cocksucker Fed rang Commissioner Hamilton and told him we'd arrested the wrong fucking guy in *i4ni*, that's why! So he sends a black and white to bring me to his fucking office, all humiliating like! But he wasn't really concerned about my fuck-wit apology, because he was just interested in how far he could insert his foot up my ass. Then – just as he's bending me over - he gets a call saying you're coming home and instructing him to extend his full departmental support to whatever the fuck you ask from him. And this is at the specific request of the Secretary of State, the Department of Justice, and George fucking Washington who's been specially disinterred for the occasion. So there I am witnesssing Hamilton's getting royally shit on, for fuck's sake. *That's why we're going to HQ, you fucking dickhead!*'

'Thanks for clearing that up,' smiled Song, patting his partner on the arm. 'I've missed you Big Bird.'

Bloomfield was still for a moment, flicking a quick look at the gently smiling Townsend in his rearview. 'By the way, Davey; good job on that kid in Boston. I was real proud of you, man,' offered the big man quietly, his face set in a mask of iron.

———

Song found himself in a crowded room headed by the Commissioner and joined on the phone by the disembodied voices of Greene and Franks. The actions agreed, people drifted away after midnight leaving Song alone with Hamilton and Captain Romero. He felt surprisingly calm, almost uncaring as to what might now happen, the trials of these past few weeks having thickened his hide.

'Detective Sergeant Song – may I call you David?' started Commissioner Hamilton. 'We've received glowing reports about your Rockwell contribution and seen with our own eyes the heroism you showed in Boston.' Song wanted to open the window to dilute the bullshit. 'The Webb case was an impeccable piece of investigative work given the information available at that time. Absolutely impeccable. If it's now proven you were misled, I want you to know the City of San Francisco doesn't hold anything against you personally.'

If this was the man's idea of exculpation, it smacked more of PR than of authenticity thought Song. And anyway, the only forgiveness he would be seeking was from Holden Webb, the victim of that "impeccable" piece of work.

The FBI's San Francisco conference room was packed with people. In addition to Song and Bloomfield, there were three prosecutors and two of Holden Webb's defense team. The paneled door opened and Webb himself entered flanked by two prison guards. He looked thinner than Song remembered, but his eyes still shone like a man standing at a slot-machine. He looked directly at the detectives, nodding an acknowledgement as if to old friends.

'Mr. Webb,' began Song, 'thank you for meeting with us, we -'

'Just a moment, detective' interjected the orange suited man. 'I wanted to ask how you were.'

'Eh, I'm very well. How are you doing?' Song spluttered, blushing crimson. How did he expect a man who had been wrongly incarcerated to be doing?

'I saw Boston and I wanted to say how much I admire you.' If Webb's intention was to make Song feel even worse, he was unerringly hitting the mark. Bloomfield's chair complained as the big man shifted his weight.

'Do you recognize any of these people?' Song took out a large envelope containing the photographs of some known criminals, innocent people, minor celebrities, and tucked in amongst them the unassuming face of Bradley Scott. Donning reading glasses that made him look even more vulnerable, Webb studied the first page.

'I think I've seen this man in a TV drama.' Song confirmed he was right. Webb looked confused but continued without further comment. This happened twice more before he turned to the page with Scott's picture. Webb smiled, tapping the photo.

'This is Bradley Scott.' Both Song and Bloomfield brought all their years of investigative experience keenly to bear upon that moment, looking for the slightest wisp of a prior association, a micro-hesitation, the faintest smear of complicity. But all they saw was an innocent man. 'Interesting,' Webb lent back, luminous jumpsuit stretching over a thin ribcage. 'You're working on the most important investigation since 9/11, but you come all the way back here to show me a picture of Bradley Scott. Are you implying there's some link between *i4ni* and Rockwell?'

'Your imagination's working overtime, Mr. Webb. We put these shots together at random, and one of them happened to be Bradley's', answered Song, mustering as much plausibility as he could manage.

'Forgive me, I may have lost my freedom but I haven't lost my intelligence. One of the people in this folio is the target of your interest, and - given your proximity to Scott - I'd guess it's him.' Song shaped to deny the claim, but Webb held up his hand. 'Detective, please, I really don't care either way. I'm innocent, and if Bradley Scott was involved in *i4ni* I want you to catch him for the victims' sake as well as for mine. So – once more for the record – I have never met this man before. I can look you in the eye and say that I did not murder those people, and I don't know who did.'

The Clutterbuck Foundation Orphanage lay on the outskirts of San Jose, built in the 1930's as a philanthropic gesture by the wife of a local businessman. Its white masonry paintwork looked fresh, the lawns well tended with borders densely stocked with spring blooms. Song and Townsend were met by its Principal, James Agnew, who was the type of man that exuded goodwill. In his office two comfortable sofas sat opposite each other in a cut flower strewn bay window.

'You like the flowers? We have a greenhouse our boys tend under the tutorage of local gardeners. Doris!' Agnew shouted. 'Can we have three coffees and an equal number of your double fudge brownies.'

'Coming right up!' the disembodied reply from along the corridor.

'On the phone we'd confirmed that Bradley was with us between '86 and '88, and again for short periods in '92 and '94. We've since checked for other records, maybe something from a sporting event, a photo taken on a day out, that sort of thing. There wasn't much left, but we did find this.' Agnew presented the picture of a happy group of boys crowded around a basketball, scrawled writing on the back capturing their names. Song saw a wiry Scott smiling at him from down the years, but nothing that proved or disproved a likeness to today's Bradley Scott. A tall woman entered carrying a tray stacked with drinks and cake.

'Now', she said in a thick Nigerian accent, 'I'm not leaving until I've seen the both of you taste my baking.' The visitors meekly complied, at which point she bent down and kissed Song full on the lips. 'That's for the life of the little one you saved in Boston. Leave me your numbers under the plate', she beamed, exiting the room.

'Ah, the life of the modern hero!' smirked Agnew.

Song coughed his reply. 'Is this all you have?'

'We have fragments of documents but they're too blackened to be of use. After the smoke and the water damage, they're more artifacts than information sources now.'

His visitors exchanged glances. 'Scott's records have been burnt?' enquired Townsend.

'Not just his. I thought we'd told you? There was a fire in the basement archive. Arson. We were lucky not to lose the whole building, but a passer-by called it in.'

'When was this?'

'June 19th, 2009. It's not a date I'll easily forget. A security guard stumbled across a broken basement window one night. Someone had poured in cans of gas and put a match to it.'

'What happened then?' she pressed.

'It's very sad. The guard was overpowered trying to apprehend the arsonist and ferociously beaten with his own nightstick. He was in a coma for a fortnight and then ill-health retired.'

'I meant the investigation.'

Agnew shrugged. 'There was no evidence left to investigate. No eyewitnesses, and the guard had no recollection of events other than he was sure it was a man, not a boy.'

'So what's your theory, James?'

'Maybe a disgruntled graduate from Clutterbuck's past looking to torch the place. The archives would have been a great place to start given the combustibles down there.'

'Any other ideas?' asked Song pursuing the theme.

'Only one. There was something down there that someone wanted to hide.'

'What do you think?' Song asked as their driver steered their car out of Clutterbuck's grounds.

'I'm not a big fan of coincidence', proffered Townsend. 'If our Bradley Scott isn't this place's one, we need to find the point where he swapped identities. As for the fire, it's excessive, but if our Bradley didn't know what was down there then best incinerate the lot. Wrong time, wrong place for the security guard. But then if secrecy was important, why not finish him off with the nightstick?' she added as an afterthought.

'Maybe disturbed before he could finish the job', replied Song. Townsend's question sat with him a while longer before the goose bumps reared once more across his neck. 'Oh shit! Surely not', he speed dialed Bloomfield. 'Get out the *i4ni* file and look up Stacey Kepler,' he barked without explanation before hanging up in a daze.

'Who's Stacey Kepler?' asked Nevada.

Song looked at the gift box full of brownies perched incongruously on his lap. 'I mentioned in the telling of my story to Paine that one of the *i4ni* victims was a retired security guard. His name was Stacey Kepler, and I'm just hoping that it isn't – well, you know.'

Townsend reached across to hold his hand. 'It's gonna be him. You know it.'

And he did.

Doreen Alabaster, Deputy Director of Bakersfield Child Services, sat behind a tired municipal desk in her postage stamp of an office. At just over sixty years of age in a printed flower dress the seasoned African-American was doing her best to keep the lumps and bumps of advancing years under control. 'I remember Bradley well. We get lots of his ilk passing through, sometimes as transitory as the people they're helping out.'

'You'd mentioned to me his guitar performance. Is there any video?' fished Townsend.

'Not that I recollect, but I'll check', she committed, making a note on a sheet already festooned with actions. 'And I remember him because of that *ZZ Top* beard and his long hair. All you could see was a letterbox of pasty flesh between his eyes and nose. It was *yes, ma'am* this and *would you kindly, ma'am* that. Never heard him say a cuss word or act up.'

'What about Bradley's new found fame - does that surprise you?' asked Song.

'Not in the sense of the goodness we experienced here, but yes in how his confidence has grown. I'm proud of him - of what he's become. He's quite the People's Hero. I've sent him a *Vigilangels* email to wish him well.'

'Anything else you'd like to share with us?' Song was in a hurry, and this woman did not appear to have much else to add to their existing knowledge of the man.

She drummed her fingers thoughtfully on the desk. 'Well there's the gift he gave me, I suppose.' Townsend involuntarily squeezed her cardboard cup, slopping coffee onto the scratched linoleum floor. 'I'd been on *eBay* one lunchtime browsing for antique crockery, me being a part-time collector, when Bradley walked in. We talked some, then a while later he handed me something wrapped in tissue paper. It was an 18th century Delft dinner plate he'd found during a charity house clearance. I knew it was rare and I offered him money, but he declined saying it was a thank you for the work I did with the kids. I have it on display at home.'

'So he'd cleaned it himself, and you've had it on display without anyone else touching it?' clarified Townsend as calmly as she could.

'Honey, I wouldn't *let* anyone else touch it – it's that rare!'

'Ms. Alabaster, I wonder if we get hold of it, along with your fingerprints?' asked Song.

'Why on earth would you want my plate? Did Bradley do something illegal?'

'No, we don't think your Bradley did anything wrong, but we suspect someone else did.'

Alabaster took them home, dutifully depositing the plate into a sealed evidence bag. They were on their way back to San Francisco when Bloomfield rang. 'Kepler's career history's a string of half-starts ending with a security gig. He was pensioned off after being clubbed into a coma during an arson attack. D'you want me to find out where?' But it was Song that told his partner the answer. 'Son of a bitch's bitch!' exploded Bloomfield. 'That fucker Scott capped the others vics in *i4ni* just to mask Kepler as his primary target? It can't be, it's too fucking elaborate. And the *Scarlet Ink* link to Webb was a solid lock. I'll check back to see if the store fits in to Scott some other way. Man, I'd take a serial killer anytime compared to this convoluted shit!'

Dinner was planned at Song's parents' for seven, having arranged to meet his father for coffee beforehand. Through the pastry shop's etched window they watched a stream of San Franciscans making their relaxed way home from work.

'This editorial in the *Journal* suggests Rockwell's campaign may have more lasting domestic consequences than 9/11. That old Ed Murrow quote is making people think about how fearful of life Americans have become. Where's our old Lewis and Clarke spirit?' lamented his father over a triple espresso. But Song wasn't up for a philosophical discussion right now.

'Dad, we know Rockwell spent some time in Central America and while pursuing that lead I came across a CIA file saying that you visited Nicaragua in 1980. Is that correct?'

His father's face split into an elliptic smile. 'I have a CIA file? Oh boy, that's great, I can't wait to tell the guys!'

'So you *did* visit Nicaragua?' spluttered his son at this revelation.

'Sure, where I met with Daniel Ortega himself. Very charismatic, very driven.'

'You've never told me about this before! What the hell were you doing in Managua?'

'Chill out, son. I guess it never came up between us. Congressman Bill Benson from the 8th organized a fact finding tour funded by the local party. He was looking for people to accompany him and I volunteered. We were there three nights. Do you know who the Sandinistas were?'

'I've got your *Clash* vinyl of the same name', his son snapped sarcastically.

'We met the Deputy U.S. Ambassador at an official dinner along with our Commercial Attaché - who was clearly a military stooge - a few U.S. businessmen living down there, a handful of contractors, and some CIA spooks dressed up as non-combatants.'

'Those contractors - anyone in construction?' Terrance May shook his head indicating he couldn't remember. 'Did you say anything that might have attracted anyone's attention?'

'Nope, I was pretty quiet because I'd had god-awful diarrhea from the morning we arrived. But the atmosphere was charged at times and I do recall a bust-up Benson had with a local reporter at that embassy dinner.

The guy was pushing Bill hard on Reagan's zero tolerance approach to communism, blitzing him with facts and figures, until Bill let the youngster have it with both barrels. He said something like, "the Domino Theory has now become Reagan's Domingo Theory here in Central America. Fifty-six thousand dead American boys will tell you it wasn't relevant in Vietnam, and it ain't relevant here either". I haven't made it sound very eloquent, but at the time it really shut that local newshound up.'

In their ten minute stroll back to the apartment, Song tried again but his father genuinely seemed to have nothing further to say about the trip. If he had been as unobtrusive during it as he was suggesting, and assuming Paine had met him there, what possibly could have warranted his interest in Song now?

After dinner that evening Song sat down alone with his Mother, resolute in his intention to squeeze more out of her than he had just managed with his father. 'Mom, please tell me more about the relationship of Song Xiao Win with the Americans in Saigon.'

'I don't know much. My first husband and I had - how can I say – a traditional marital relationship', she replied, again uncomfortable with the past. 'He just told me what he thought I should know.'

Song circled the topic like a coyote advancing upon dying embers. 'I guess I'm not asking you what he said, but rather what you worked out for yourself.'

She let out a deep and troubled sigh. 'Well I knew he wasn't just working for the government. No one back then was just doing that. We were at war, and it wasn't always clear whose side the people around you were on. Sometimes he'd leave a file around the house and it was clear from those that Xiao Win was working liaison with the Americans. There were times he'd accompany them on trips - very dangerous ones. Once, after being away for twelve days, he came home wearing a bandage on his arm. He laughed and said he'd cut himself falling against a tree. Though after the dressing was removed, it looked more like a bullet wound to me.' Song mulled this over, not sure where to go from here. 'The only American Xiao Win ever spoke about was the one who lent me the money to start my store', she added as an afterthought.

Song kicked himself for not thinking of it earlier. 'Can you remember his name?'

'Of course! How could I forget the man whose generous gift to everything this family has today? His name was Oliver Henry, and he lived at 38 Acacia Drive, Bloomington, Illinois. Xiao Win made me memorize it, even though I didn't speak English. Now the number 38 is lucky for me. And I can already guess what you're thinking! Is Oliver Henry the crazy man you're investigating? Well I can tell you he isn't, because he died in 1981. I sent repayment checks to him every year but they were never cashed. It was driving me crazy, so in 1986 I hired a private detective to track him down.'

'You hired a private detective!' Song gasped in incredulity.

'What, you think your old mom's too dumb to do that? Anyway, he investigated and found that Mr. Henry had died in 1981. The next week I sent flowers to his grave. He was a great and generous man, don't you think?'

Walking back to his apartment the night was cool but not unpleasant, and Song wanted to think through what he had learned these past few days. He tasked Oppenheim to have local agents run a full check on Oliver Henry, also giving her the *Domingo Theory* phrase to search. Townsend had just emerged from the shower when he got back, having earlier met up with Charley for pizza. The TV was hosting two professors of philosophy debating the pervasiveness of fear in modern America, Paine's Murrow quotation interminably cycling along the bar: "*No one man can terrorize a whole nation unless we are all his accomplices*".

'You should ask that girl out', pronounced Townsend toweling her hair.

'Which girl is that?'

'Charley, you dumbass. You're made for each other. Yin and Yang, Jay Z and Beyonce. But you've been friends for soooo long now that neither of you can see it. And maybe you're both scared about what might happen?'

Song pretended to type on his iPad. 'Charley and I don't have that sort of relationship. We're like brother and sister.'

'Except you're not, are you? Barely a day goes by where you don't reach out to each other half a dozen times. It's called love, dude.'

'Thanks for the insight but this time, Agent Townsend, your instincts are wrong.'

'If you say so. But it seems odd that a guy who has the courage to put himself between a child and an exploding plate glass window can't find the balls to ask a girl out.'

Song didn't reply. His fingers dancing across the pixilated keys, pretending to look at the gobbledygook they were creating.

They rose just after dawn taking a hilly jog across the city, the Golden Gate their compass. Song's phone rang, Townsend jogging on the spot beside him as the voice of Gabriel Fernandez gilded with an uncharacteristic early morning cheer greeted him. 'I'm in California helping my writing team on the Reagan Library angle and wondered if the two of us could meet for dinner tonight?' Fernandez made it sound spontaneous, but the detective recognized that his performance in Boston had ramped up the reporter's need to consolidate their relationship. For Song's part, the time was now right to exact his own price for cooperating. Agreeing the venue, Song immediately took another call from the forensics team in Bakersfield. Alabaster's Delft plate had yielded two distinct sets of fingerprints; the first were hers, but the second were for a person not currently on record.

At last it was official: their Bradley Scott was not the same person as hers.

Oppenheim broke her own surprising news during the team's video conference. 'We ran the *Domingo Theory* and got a hit from a student's doctoral thesis written at the University of Mexico in 2006. The quotation was fully attributed by her to its original author, which was…. Gabriel Fernandez!'

'My dad described Congressman Benson's argument with a Nicaraguan reporter who had pretty good English, but I think he got it wrong', explained Song making the link. 'That reporter was Fernandez, and dad confused Gabriel's hint of a Spanish accent with that of a local. We know Fernandez advised the Reagan Administration and that he visited in-theater. So, unbeknownst to each other, a young Fernandez shared a dinner with my father that evening, and I'm guessing that also around the table that night was Thomas Paine in his capacity as a spook. Maybe my dad said something that was meaningful to Paine?'

Everyone spoke at once, Corbyn tasking Benjamin to find out if
any record of invitees to that event has survived down the years.

'Oliver Henry served in Nam and died in Illinois in 1981',
announced Benjamin. 'That confirms why your mom's checks
were never cashed.' Song sighed aloud, another possible lead
perishing under the FBI's withering scrutiny.

Corbyn wound up the conference with a warning for Song.
'When you meet Gabriel tonight, don't scare him off. If he was
already aware of the Nicaraguan link between him, Paine, and
your father, we need him to play out his next move.'

'What do you mean?'

It was Benjamin who answered. 'Because maybe it isn't just
Bradley Scott who's been helping Paine out from the start.'

—————

Fernandez was staying at *The Fairmont*, whose hefty bill
Song assumed would find its way onto a *Times* expenses claim.
He half rose to shake the Californian's hand at a quiet table
towards the back of the restaurant. Song ordered straight from
the menu whereas Fernandez's selections required ancillary
instructions: the green salad without the greens, the honey
barbeque dressing without the honey, the sparkling water
without the bubbles.

'I'm prepared to cooperate with an interview at the end of
the investigation,' explained Song as their bartering began. 'But
in advance of that I need something in return. Information.'

Fernandez's smile betrayed how delighted he was. 'Surely -
anything I can do to help you out, David!'

'Well that isn't strictly true, is it, Gabriel? I know you haven't
been straight on everything your writing team's discovered.'
Song sensed that his dinner companion's appetite for crispy
skinned chicken had just vanished.

'I don't have a clue what you're talking about.'

Song glanced into the heart of the restaurant, most of the tables empty with people staying home just in case Rockwell had paid a visit a few years earlier. 'You shouldn't think because you've been watching us that we haven't been watching you too, Gabriel.' Their drinks arrived, Fernandez oblivious to them now.

'You've already conducted background checks on me, so you know I have nothing to be ashamed of', bluffed the reporter, a film of sweat forming on his wide forehead.

Song waved his hand in acknowledgment. 'Two of your writing team have records for possession of marijuana, so I had my buddies in California Highways conduct a random stop and search this week, and guess what they found in their luggage? And then what do you think they traded to us in order to dodge the bullet?' The light levels were low over their table, but Song felt sure Fernandez was about to cry. 'So how's it going to look when it emerges you told your reporter buddies to withhold information in order to prolong the case and multiply your book sales? It won't be Matthew Arnold you're compared with then - it'll be Benedict Arnold.' Song attacked his starters with relish, Fernandez yet to raise his fork.

'Who else knows about this?' shot Fernandez. The imaginary crowd in Song's chest punched the air in victory. His creative bluff had worked. Song had no idea how many people were working in Fernandez's team, let alone who and where they were.

'Only me – so far. In this respect neither you nor I have been entirely honest with Alex.'

'So if I confirm there are some things – very small things – I've learnt that I haven't shared with the Bureau, you'll keep it to yourself?' Song nodded his agreement, comfortable with the lie for now.

'So, what have my colleagues already told you?' through a mouthful of duck liver pate.

'It doesn't work that way, Gabriel. There's no guarantee your pothead friends gave us full disclosure, so you take me through everything in your own words.' Seemingly relieved to unburden himself, Fernandez spent the remainder of the meal laying out their discoveries, taking two hours to embellish a story that could have been told in one. Most of it was low level intel, but there were three details in particular that arrested Song's attention.

As their coffee arrived, he picked his way back through Fernandez's narrative. 'You mentioned Bradley's Spanish?'

'He's not a very communicative man, as you know, but he's spoken a passable Mexican-Spanish to me. What's strange is that my team can't find out where he learnt it. There's nothing in his academic records and it would have been an easy pass for him.'

'And you said something about munitions licenses?'

'The Bureau's investigations have been directed almost solely at the military explosives angle, but little on civilian construction. So I had my team dig up a list of people issued with industrial licenses to use explosives over the past eighty years.'

'Eighty years! Why so long?' Song interjected.

'I was thinking sociologically. In the past it was quite normal for a son to follow in his father's professional footsteps. So I was looking for the same name to occur twice on the list and in the same location. The older name would be Paine's father, and then – presto! - we'd have more leads to follow.' Song smiled noncommittally, though inside his interest was snapping like popcorn. The investigative team had considered the construction angle but the discovery that the explosives were military had prematurely collapsed that line of enquiry. Begrudgingly, he applauded Fernandez on his foresight.

'The license records are not easy to come by, but so far we've found a lot of duplicate names which suggests my theory is correct. What I can tell you is that Paine didn't have any reaction when I showed it to him.'

'You showed him the list?' repeated Song, surprised. 'What did he say - exactly?'

'He just flicked through a couple of the pages and made some trite point about the number of women who were trained to use explosives. Here, take a look yourself.' Fernandez extracted a document from his briefcase for Song to phone-snap.

'One final point. You mentioned Paine's neighbors spending time with him?'

'Yes, but neighbor singular. A little girl named Louise England; her parents farm the land adjacent to Paine's orchard. My team were interviewing the mother when the little girl piped up that she hoped Mr. Lane and her could pick peaches again this summer. Her mom was just as surprised as us. Louise had climbed over Paine's gate to gather windfall fruit a couple of years earlier and he'd offered her some milk. She'd been back several times since.' Song could see how the girl would have been missed in Le Bon's canvass, but she definitely needed to be interviewed. Crazy as it was, the seven year old seemed to be the only person who might add something material to their current knowledge of Paine's life in Pender County.

Fernandez called for the check to signal the evening's end. 'One last thing, Gabriel; have you ever been to Managua?' Song enquired lightly.

'Not in the past twenty five years. Why?'

'Paine spent time in Nicaragua, and we're trying to understand it. I was just wondering if you knew the place.' The reporter obliged with a detailed review of his thoughts on the country and his various embassy visits there. 'Wow, you ate in ambassadorial circles?' schmoozed Song. 'Did you meet anyone of interest?' Fernandez was only too happy to oblige, reeling off a list of people until the name Benson was mentioned. 'Is that Congressman Bill Benson from California? My dad worked on his election team back in the day. He tells some stories about that guy.'

'Bill was always good for a sound bite or two', confided Fernandez, as though the man were a life-long friend. 'At one embassy dinner in Managua he and I had a robust exchange about something or other. He was wrong, of course. I had my suspicions about some of the other guests present that night. Too many Agency and military types there for my refined sensibilities. Dangerous places tend to attract dangerous people.'

Not wanting to alert Fernandez to his theory that Paine had also been there that night, Song made his way to the waiting Bureau car, Fernandez accompanying him as a courtesy. 'Isn't there something else you want to tell me?' asked Fernandez awkwardly as the concierge swept open the door. The detective looked back blankly.

'No. Should there be?'

'It's just that – well, no matter. Thank you again for a memorable evening, David. And may I say somewhat portentously, "Good night, and good luck".'

Back in Song's flat, Townsend was stretched like a cat on his IKEA couch. He shared Fernandez's dinner revelations, her chin resting on its arm. 'The mendacious piece of shit! Though admittedly we should meet that England girl. Maybe she can identify Scott as a visitor?'

'Then as I was leaving – it was curious – Gabriel acted as though he was expecting something from me. A request from Corbyn maybe?'

'Or Paine?' she snorted.

'Probably just a misunderstanding – forget it. I'm going to take a shower. And anyway, Fernandez will have free access to pretty much everything in the Bureau's case files. So what extra information do I have that he could possibly want?'

At eight a.m. the next morning, Townsend and Song were approaching the jet chartered overnight to take them to meet little Louise England. Scott's DNA results from North Carolina were still some way off. Song's phone rang with Fernandez. 'Morning, Gabriel. How's breakfast at the *Fairmont?*' he shouted above the din of planes buzzing noisily around him on the airport's apron.

'I wouldn't know, I'm in Sacramento, aren't I', Fernandez's frosty reply

'You must have risen extra early. What's over there for you?'

There was a pause. 'I was hoping you'd answer that. Don't you have something to tell me?'

Song heard the distinctive roar of a Harley at the other end. 'I don't believe so', he replied in a reprise of that curious moment yesterday evening.

Another pause. 'Paine said you'd tell me at eight this morning, but I thought you might have saved yourself the trouble and told me last night when you were departing.'

'Told you what?' Song pressed a free hand to his other ear to minimize the roar of a passing aircraft, Townsend urging him to hurry so they could get away.

'Paine said I should call and you'd give me the exact location.'

'Paine said that?'

'Yes, when I was visiting him at the hospital. He said it must be frustrating having to share the detonations with the other media, so he'd be providing the exact location of a bomb in Sacramento to you alone. He said you'd keep it away from the FBI to guarantee me some exclusive pictures. He told me to go to the forecourt of the *Exxon* station on 4th for the best view of the target. So that's where I am now with a photographer looking across the road at a printers, an opticians, and a timber yard. So which one is it?'

In a blink Song knew with nauseating certainty what the next target would be.

'Gabriel, get out! It's a trap! No questions, just run!' Song heard the foreshortened revving of the Harley once more, followed by a hissing rasp, then nothing. The phone felt like a brick held uselessly to his ear.

Townsend stood in front of him, eyes clouded with concern. 'What's happened?'

'It's Gabriel. He's dead. Paine's latest target - it was a gas station.'

Chapter 16

Fear is the main source of superstition, and one of the main sources of cruelty. To conquer fear is the beginning of wisdom

: Bertrand Russell

PAINE'S HOUSE LOOKED DIFFERENT TO SONG STANDING outside it now with Burke, Le Bon, and Townsend. That first time here, Song had almost lost his life. Now Fernandez had lost his.

The drapes had been closed, and the grass was in need of a hard cut. Tarnished peach blossom speckled the ground in every direction. Song tried to keep this image in his mind in order to blank out the maelstrom of fire and pitch black smoke he had seen on early news coverage of Sacramento. Numbed, he had flown to this opposite side of the country, feeling disembodied somewhere in-between.

On their way to visit the England's, Song had wanted a detour to view Scott's nocturnal route to the house. Sheriff Le Bon took the party deep into the orchard before theatrically pacing to the spot where Scott had been apprehended. Song pushed for details of Bradley's car as they had found it, hoping that recounting it might illuminate a dark space where an important fact still lurked. Le Bon obliged without referring to his notes.

'And the trunk of the car Scott stole had been left open', Song stated as confirmation. 'Was there a moon that night?'

'A moon? I don't rightly recall. I'll find out', replied Le Bon crestfallen that he didn't already know.

'I ask because there was no flashlight in the inventory', explained Song.

'That's right, there wasn't. I hadn't thought about that. Maybe he just plum forgot?' offered the sheriff. Or maybe he knew the place well enough not to need one, thought Song looking across the backyard lawn, a dip in the ground the only thing left to mark its canine graves. He strolled over to the kitchen door, the party following in silence as Song conducted his investigative pilgrimage around the site.

'Do you see anything with those fresh eyes of yours, Nevada?' Song rattling the handle.

'Nope, but it's interesting about the flashlight. This website confirms there was no moon that night.'

Song gave a voice to the puzzle bothering him. 'So Scott parked the car four hundred yards away, and hauled two full cans of gas across a strip of uneven field, a hedge line, and an orchard on a pitch black night.'

'What's your point?' asked Townsend, growing evermore familiar with his thinking style.

'I'm just wondering why he didn't bring the twine with him too. He said he might have needed it as a wick to make a sort of Molotov. That way he'd only need make the one difficult trip.'

His audience exchanged quick glances. 'Maybe he was too nervous to think about the pesky ergonomics', suggested Burke in a manner implying Song was focusing on marginal detail. Le Bon reminded them all that Cerise England had arranged for her daughter to miss an hour of school so they shouldn't be late. Song looked down the garden once more.

There was something else he was missing, just out of his mind's sight, its blurred shape casting a long and deep shadow.

The England's house was not dissimilar to Paine's except it needed of a lick of paint. It was agreed that only Song and Townsend would meet with the girl and that Nevada would take the lead. Cerise England would be present to protect the interests of her daughter. The three of them were sitting in old wicker chairs sipping apple juice on the porch when the Bureau car rolled up. A little girl wearing a white cotton dress emerged, its color in stark contrast to the rich ebony of her skin, the multi-colored beads in her hair bobbing up and down as she ran towards her mother.

'Well, is this really Louise, or is it her older sister? She looks so grown up, I can hardly believe it!' sang Townsend, beaming her brightest smile, staying half crouched so as not to tower above the tiny girl. Over the next quarter of an hour Nevada wove a meandering conversational path through the colorful world of a child. Song learnt about the scariest character in Harry Potter, why Louise wanted to sing like Mariah Carey, and exactly why beets were worse than sweet potatoes. He sat smiling until his jaw ached, marveling at the accomplished manner in which his partner developed the child's trust.

'When I was a little girl hundreds of years ago, I used to like swinging on a tire my daddy fixed to a tree. Did you ever swing on the tire in Mr. Lane's orchard?' Nevada asked. Song half remembered seeing it before, but not having put two-and-two together.

'Oh yes! He pushed me real high, but stopped when I got scared.' But now Louise had some enquiries of her own. 'Are you an Indian squawk - eh, squaw?' Cerise England interjected explaining it was a rude question, but Nevada said it was fine. 'You look just like Pocahontas in the *Disney* film. She's pretty too.'

'Well thank you, Louise! So if I'm Pocahontas', she said pointing over to Song, 'is he John Smith or Captain Ratcliffe?' All four of them laughed, though Song wasn't quite sure at what. 'When the Pilgrims arrived in Virginia, my people offered them peach juice, just like the glass that Thomas offered you.'

'He used to add cinnamon to it. Yummy! We would sit at his big table in the yard and he'd bring the juice and cookies out.'

'Did you ever go into his house?' asked Townsend sweetly. Louise shook her head. 'What about any secret places? You know, where you could play pirates, or circuses, or maybe princesses?' Another shake. 'Did Thomas ever give cookies and juice to any of his friends?'

'No. Thomas lives on his own'. Song was hearing the girl, but still finding it difficult to keep his mind here in the warm sunshine of Pender County, and not on the billowing smoke of Sacramento. 'Am I in trouble?' warbled the little girl, tears welling. Nevada and Cerise lent forward to reassure that she had done nothing wrong. 'I sent that letter for him all secretly like he said I should. Did I do a wrong thing, Mommy?'

'Which letter was that, sweetheart?' honeyed Townsend.

'To a place called London in a town called England – like our name. He said if I sent it secretly he'd send my mom flowers on her birthday last week. And he did!' Cerise England confirmed she had received a bunch from an anonymous source which her husband had joked about ever since. 'Thomas said I should post the letter he gave me one week before her birthday if I wanted her to get the magic flowers, but I couldn't tell anyone about it, so that's what I did.' Townsend and Song looked at each other. This must have been the letter to *The Economist*. If the envelope had not been lost they would have discovered the fingerprints of a seven-year old girl on it. 'Is Thomas in trouble?' Louise asked, her voice still cracking. 'Some of the kids at school say he's done bad things. They say his house will be knocked down and his trees chopped up, he's been so bad.'

Townsend squeezed the girl's tiny hand. 'No one's going to do that. Don't you worry.'

'Good, because that would make me sad. And the big tree out back is very shady. We had our drinks at the big table under it.'

Song had been so effective at melting into his chair that Townsend was surprised when he jerked forward. 'Is that the big tree to the right as you look out from the back?' The little girl seemed to have forgotten his presence too, his direct question silencing her.

'I think what John Smith means is whether it's the tree closest to this hand', gently taking the girl's right hand. Song was embarrassed not to have factored in a child's confusion about left and right. The little girl nodded.

'And Thomas had a big table there and some chairs,' Song continued, more carefully now, 'just like the ones that kings and queens sit in.'

'No, not like them at all. Those chairs are all covered in jewels and diamonds, and made out of gold and silver', she answered, Nevada and Cerise suppressing their grins. But for some reason Song had grown agitated and clearly wanted to leave. The two interviewers rose with Townsend promising to send Louise a pair of beaded moccasins that would look great with her hair.

Song ran to the waiting car instructing Le Bon to take them back to Paine's. 'Zeke, do you remember we sat on the garden furniture in his back yard while we were waiting for the bomb squad?'

'Sure. Over to the left looking out from the back of the building.'

'Exactly, on the left, not on the right.'

'They were set on a sort of wooden platform', added Burke as they bumped their way along the dirt track. 'I remember we had to step onto it.'

Song was out and jogging before they had come to a complete halt. Townsend was the next to run after him though she had no idea why. Song looked again down the vista of Paine's backyard at the graceful beech tree to the right, festooned in fresh leaves. Underneath its arches lay the empty grave of the two Labradors. Over to the left stood the garden furniture. 'So why did Paine move the platform and the furniture all the way from there over to there? They're heavy, he isn't a young man, and they're now in full sight of the noonday sun.'

'Maybe he just wanted to bury his dogs under a beautiful tree?' ventured Le Bon, attempting to be helpful. They stood in silent contemplation for a while, before Townsend squeezed his arm, her fingers like talons. Song looked down at the revelation on her face.

'Paine's hidden something *underneath* the dogs!'

They jogged over to the disturbed ground. 'Ritchie,' said Song excitedly, 'are there any spades around we can use to - ' he stopped mid-sentence.

'The spade!' erupted Townsend finishing the thought. 'The one in Scott's trunk!'

'And that's why he left the twine in the car', shouted Song as the mysterious shape that had been evading him came into sharp relief. 'He had to go back anyway to pick up the spade because he couldn't carry everything else and the gas tanks in one journey!'

'I can get some of my boys down here pronto, and we can dig right through to China if we need to', offered Le Bon.

'Yes, but not some of your men - all of them!'

'Whatever's hidden down there, he kept it covered with that wooden platform', Song pointed to the cedar wood construction that Paine had dragged over to the orchard. 'He guessed we'd turn the place over and find the disturbed ground under the platform, so he killed and buried his dogs there to disguise it. No one thought about digging any deeper, and if he does have explosives down there, two decomposing dogs would have masked the odor.'

'And he gave that little girl juice and cookies right on top of it', observed Le Bon with white-lipped anger. The space for excavation quickly became cramped so they widened the cut to allow two men in shifts to dig. The four foot deep marker and then the five came and went. 'Are you sure there's something else down there? I was joking when I mentioned digging through to China.'

Song was standing on the lip looking up through the arboreal grace of the beech when the gravelly sound of the spades beneath him was interrupted by a metallic thud. 'Stop!' yelled Le Bon as if the two sweat-soaked diggers hadn't thought to do so. The tall one stood to stretch his back, at six feet tall his head barely coming level with the surface.

'What do you think it is?' asked Townsend in a half whisper. 'Some type of munitions box?' Soon they had uncovered a section of metal almost a yard square. 'Jesus! What the fuck is that thing?'

'I know', answered Le Bon. 'It's an old septic tank. Folks round here aren't on the municipal network. And there I was worrying about explosives and shit, when actually it was just shit!' Song peered into the cavernous hole. This was not what he had been expecting.

'Can you clear away the soil right underneath you', Song asked. The tall deputy jabbed his spade into the earth where he stood to be greeted by a different type of noise. Everyone craned their necks.

'This section's about six inches higher, boss. It looks like a manhole's been welded onto the tank.' Arms were offered to the exiting officer, others extended to assist Song's descent.

He and the remaining digger revealed a crude keyhole in the cover. Using one end of a tire-iron the lid popped open on its catch. Irrationally, Song thought of Howard Carter in the *Valley of the Kings*.

Lifting the heavy metal disc exposed a circle of blackness underneath, natural light barely illuminating the tank's floor eight feet below. Song dropped to his still bruised knees and used the screen light of his phone to penetrate its darkness.

A table, a chair, shelving, equipment stacked in one corner, all coming into shadowy vision. The light in Song's head came on just as the light on his phone went out.

'Agent Burke, get on to the North Carolina Bomb Squad. Tell them they're going to need the biggest truck they've got.'

Police flashlight in one hand, his other on a ladder discovered just inside the cylinder, Song lowered himself into the converted septic tank. The Bomb Squad had declared it packed with explosives, all inert. Paine had boarded out its curved bottom to create an even floor. Fifteen feet in length, mostly lined with handmade shelving, half of which was jammed with wooden boxes filled with C4. Labels on others identified their contents as detonators, coils of electrical wire and other paraphernalia. One shelf held eight car batteries and next to these a large cardboard box. Peering inside, Song saw a couple of dozen antique LCD wristwatches. He took one out and turned it over. There was nothing inscribed on its back. In another box he found six hundred thousand dollars in freshly banded bundles. Lying in plain view on a small desk was a notebook. Hardly daring to look, Song lifted it as though it were as delicate as the Dead Sea scrolls. On the left hand side of the first page was written the number one, and alongside it a string of unfathomable letters and numbers. Underneath it was the number two, followed by a similar cipher. The pattern continued through the pages up to the last entry.

It was numbered one hundred and sixty seven.

———

Song stood on the Mountain Lakes deck, an empty mug dangling from his fingers as he gazed into the lustrous wood. Leaving the ground yesterday in San Francisco he had peered into the distance searching for a ribbon of choking smoke tethering a lapis lazuli sky to the scorched earth below.

At the gas station there had been significant collateral damage to adjoining buildings, some of which had burned out of control for upwards of twelve hours. The gas station itself was still alight this morning. Every fire vehicle within a thirty mile radius had been summoned to the scene, ambulances ferrying an endless convoy of casualties to local ERs. On TV a trembling driver who had left the *Exxon* forecourt ten seconds before the detonation told his story to a rapt nation.

'I felt the blast before I heard it. I've got an SUV and I swear it was lifted off the road for a second. I looked in my rearview and I saw Hell – that's the only way I can describe it. Brimstone and sulfur were coming through my AC. There was a guy behind me at the register with two young kids getting them a slushy. Did they get out alright? I sure hope so. God, I sure hope so.'

The patio door squeaked open, Townsend emerged carrying fresh mugs of coffee. With a forced smile she handed him a one page update. The Sacramento body count was thirty seven, with another seventeen unaccounted for. This last number included Fernandez and his photographer. The charred skeletons of six vehicles at the pumps were still being tortured by angry flames. A provisional assessment suggested the ordnance had been placed adjacent to the subterranean fuel store, such had been the blast's ferocity.

The first Song was aware of Corbyn's presence was when he touched him on the shoulder. 'Are you okay?'

'No, not really', Song's honest reply. He had been at the end of the line listening to Fernandez's horrific death. Corbyn motioned for them all to sit, including Benjamin looking as grim as Song had ever seen him. It was agreed that Scott – or whoever he was – should now be treated as hostile. The evidence against him had become overwhelming, irrespective of whatever link the DNA test proved or disproved. To maintain their upper hand he would remain free, but if he stepped out of the house, a detail of twenty agents were on call to covertly shadow his every move. At Corbyn's request Song took them all through his last dinner conversation with Fernandez.

'Have you had time to think about Paine's motive for executing Gabriel?' asked Corbyn.

'I've thought of nothing else. Either it was always in Paine's plan to entrap him, or it was a tactical adjustment because he was close to finding something out.'

'And which do your instincts prefer?'

'The second. I think Paine was scared of something Gabriel was doing. We need to get hold of all of his team's notes and fine-sieve them. Fuck the 1st Amendment.'

The Lakes interview room felt completely different as Song took his customary place in the circle. Fernandez's chair had been removed, constricting the loop like a hangman's noose. And although Scott was physically present, in Song's mind his too was now an empty chair.

Paine sat down without greeting anyone. 'Before we begin, lead us in a moment's prayer for our fallen soldier, Brad.' Song thought again of the crackling white noise at the end of his phone, Townsend crossed her legs, Corbyn pursed his lips.

'In the circumstances, that's not called for', said the Bureau man coldly.

'If you say so, Alex. But let me know where to send the flowers, as Gabriel so kindly did when I was under the surgeon's knife. David, I know you've met Death before, though probably never heard the arc of the scythe in real time. What were his last words?'

'As he was a Catholic, I'd like to think he was asking God to forgive you.'

Paine nodded in appreciation. 'Look, I understand you're all pissed with me, so I want to make it up by offering the general location of my next device. I know it can never replace Gabriel – there isn't enough shit in the world to do that – but it's a gesture.

You'll find it underneath a mobile home somewhere in America, due to go off in the next two weeks. I was surprised to learn just how many people live in those rodent boxes. The authorities couldn't evacuate the trash in New Orleans in time, and this problem's going to be *much* bigger!' Corbyn tried to extract more details but Paine stopped him with a raised hand. 'Have you all noticed that your team's now down to four? Not a very auspicious number is it, David?'

'In Chinese culture, the number four, or *si*, is considered bad luck', explained a tired Song, 'because when pronounced with a different tone in Mandarin it also means death.'

'And let's add the Four Horsemen from our own culture too', Paine peered at him, waiting. 'I guess you haven't worked it out yet?'

Song stared back, eyes narrowing. Had he missed something obvious?

That night Song slept as badly as he could ever remember. Padding down to an empty kitchen at five a.m. he grabbed some milk and turned on the TV. The Sacramento fire had been wrestled under control and it was confirmed that the station's fuel reservoir had been built in 1990.

At seven a.m. he was cooking eggs for Townsend and Oppenheim. 'One interesting thing for you', Karen said overseeing the toast. 'The field guys tracked down the death certificate for a Henry Oliver in Illinois, but your mom said his name was Oliver Henry, yes?'

Song beat the eggs with ferocity. 'Remember she didn't speak English. She might have inverted them I suppose.'

'That's unlikely. If you learn something rote, you remember the phonetics. If you teach a foreigner the word "disappointment", they don't say "pointadissment" do they?'

Song thought about it for a moment. 'Get them to check again. Whether it's relevant or not, I'd still like to have an accurate name for my family's benefactor.'

Later, Song was in the Ops Room trawling through the first batch of notes subpoenaed from Fernandez's team when Oppenheim dropped into the seat next to him. 'The death certificate was definitely for Henry Oliver, which means your mom either swapped the names around, or-'

'Or,' said Song finishing, 'Xiao Win passed his own pronunciation mistake on to her.' He thought some more. 'Or-'

'Or Xiao Win's American friend *deliberately* gave him the wrong name', completed Oppenheim.

'I can answer that - neither of them was technically right', interjected Townsend joining with a freshly printed sheet in her hand. 'One of the Illinois Agents with OCD dug a little further. The house was transferred into the ownership of an Oliver Henry *Buchanan* upon the death of his father in 1972. It was Buchanan who was your mom's benefactor. Then, in

1978, that Oliver Henry Buchanan legally changed his name to Henry Oliver. But this newly christened Henry Oliver was himself declared dead in 1981 after his clothes were found on the Lake Michigan shoreline, though the body was never found. All confirmed by the family's attorneys who still act on behalf of the Buchanan family.'

The three of them exchanged looks. 'So what are we saying here?' asked Song. 'That Henry Oliver didn't die in 1981, but became Thomas Paine instead? And that he deliberately gave Xiao Win his name incorrectly and in reverse? But why be so convoluted?'

'We're not saying anything - yet', clarified Townsend, 'but let's look at how the arrow flies. You're named by Paine onto the investigative team. We don't know why. We speculate it's something to do with your family's past, not *i4ni*. Is it something to do with Terrence May's visit to Nicaragua, or your mother's first husband? If it's the latter, what could have happened in Vietnam that would have made the man Paine/Lane/Paterson/Buchanan/Oliver so indebted to Song Xiao Win?'

'That's shot through with holes', countered Song about to enumerate them.

'I know, I know, but I'm just sharing. And anyway, just how much did that indebtedness translate into in hard cash? How much did he loan your mom?'

'I've no idea; it's not the type of thing you ask an Asian parent.'

'Well you're going to find out, because Henry Oliver's attorneys still have his bank statements on file and they're sending them over.'

Song hadn't made much of a dent in Fernandez's private notes when the first batch of the Oliver financials arrived in his in-tray. At the desk next to him Benjamin was speaking with FEMA about the impossibility of relocating everyone from

America's mobile home community, while Oppenheim was still trawling DBs for Melissa Davidson references, just in case. Using his finger as a makeshift ruler on the screen, Song ran methodically down the blurred scans of thirty year old financial documents.

After two hours and seventy-six eye-aching pages, one entry stopped him dead.

It contained five of the same digit, and it had been a cash withdrawal made by Henry Oliver. Song leant back and stared for a full minute at the dimpled tiles stretching in serried ranks across the ceiling.

'Ladies and gentlemen' he announced loudly to the busy room, 'I now know the true identity of Thomas Paine.'

Chapter 17

Be not afraid of life. Believe that life is worth living, and your belief will help create the fact

: Henry James

CONVERSATION STOPPED AS THE ROOM STARED BACK AT SONG. Benjamin hung up on FEMA, Corbyn on Franks. iPad to his chest stabbing his finger at the offending line, Song rose slowly to his feet.

'Look at the amount of this withdrawal.'

Only Benjamin standing next to him could see the numbers clearly, sucking in his breath. 'Fuck! Four hundred, and forty-four dollars, and forty-four cents. All fours. The Chinese number for bad luck that Paine teased us with.'

'Why are you calling me in the middle of the day - are you okay?' Song's mother said over the speakerphone for the benefit of an entranced operations room, Corbyn looking as tense as Song had ever seen him.

'I'm fine, mom. Listen, I have another question for you and I know it's sensitive.'

'Go ahead, but I may not answer!' she replied as a passing vehicle tooted an errant jaywalker.

'How much money did Oliver Henry lend you back in 1977?'

'That's my affair, just like I never ask you about all those dead bodies you see.'

'And normally I'd never ask such a private thing. But this is really important, Mom – really, really important.'

There was a pause at her end. 'Well I can't see why, I'm sure. But I trust you, son.' Song heard the mid spring traffic rolling by her store in stark counterpoint to the deathly silence in the operations room. 'Mr. Henry sent me four hundred and forty four dollars, and forty four cents. It's a number you can't easily forget.'

Everyone punched the air accompanied by strangulated yelps of success. 'Why do you think he chose that amount given its difficult connotations?' continued Song through the haze of joy.

'Mr. Oliver explained why in his accompanying letter. He said he understood I'd suffered a lot of bad luck when Song Xiao Win had been lost. So by sending me this exact amount I should daily remember that with perseverance the human spirit can always prevail against unlucky circumstances. Those words have shone like a lantern to me ever since. If he were alive today people would benefit from listening to his wisdom, don't you think, David?'

The team congregated in the middle of the room, shaking hands and hugging. Nevada let out a Native American battle whoop as Oppenheim high fived Benjamin. Corbyn was just about to speak when Song stopped him. 'Hold on, I've just thought of something' he said excitedly. Accessing his phone he pulled up an image, enlarging it to the section he needed. 'In the aftermath of Gabriel's death I almost forgot. This is the photo I took in the restaurant of his list of fathers and sons with licenses to use explosives. Look – Oliver Henry Buchanan', pointing to a blurred name on the screen. 'And above it James

William Buchanan, both of Illinois, who I'm guessing was his father.' Song inclined his head. 'If you're looking down on us from up there, Gabriel, that was one great last piece of investigative journalism.'

Song was scrapping the last morsel of food from his plate when Oppenheim stuck her head into the crowded kitchen. 'You're wanted in ops. They've broken Paine's notebook's code!' The murmuring of agents at the full lunch table dropped further, the rumor that Paine's identity may have been discovered already widespread.

'Well, well. Paine's real name and a broken cipher all in one day! Who needs Morse anyway?' grinned Song, scooping up a drip of ketchup. There was laughter as one of the agents started tapping out something, quickly echoed by someone else until everyone in the room was repeating the same beat. 'My knowledge of Morse isn't so good. What are they signaling?' Song asked Oppenheim at the door.

'It's *VJ*', she smiled, the Californian departing to a crescendo of drumming on tables, plates, and pans.

In the packed Ops Room, Song approached a gaggle of people bent over a PC. Townsend turned, disappointment on her face. 'It's been cracked alright, but it's a puzzle within a puzzle. For instance, look at entry number seventy-six: *Peloponnesian War*. Paine coded an aide memoir for himself rather than a clear description of the target. It could mean anything: Athens, Georgia; Sparta, Tennessee; or any one of the thousands of Greek restaurants across America.'

Song's eyes ran down obscure references on every line: *Dan Fouts, Black and Tans, Juno, New Deal, Cherry Tree*. Then, at number eighty, the font had been changed to emboldened red. 'What's happened here?' looking at the translation *Steel Black Chrysler*.

'It's in red because that entry was the only one circled in Paine's notebook', answered Benjamin. 'Could be a reference to a guy called Black who runs a dealership?'

'Or an African-American car mechanic. Or, or, or……' complained Townsend. 'Once again we open one of Paine's Russian dolls only to find another inside gaudier than the last.'

Corbyn had been up most of the night rehearsing his next interaction with Paine. They were going for broke, intending to lay before him everything they had learned in the hope it would unlock the Mother lode of devices. Meanwhile, urgent plans were being laid for the evacuation of an estimated twenty million people living in mobile homes across the country. Song had been shocked by the number. Emergency plans for the use of school halls and stadia were advancing apace, the shrewdness of Paine's targets still drawing the begrudging respect of his pursuers. If the creation of fear had been one of his primary intentions, he had proven himself its master practitioner.

At the team's morning meeting, before Paine could invite Scott to say prayer, Corbyn commandeered the agenda in no mood for any more of this farce. 'Thomas, you set us the challenge of discovering your identity and the reasons for inviting David, Nevada, and Gabriel to participate. If we do that now, you'll give us all of the remaining locations, is that correct?'

'No, that's not correct. It's fifteen each for David and Fernandez – a posthumous decoration – and twenty-five for discovering my identity.' Song had been expecting as much. There was still much to discover: what was the purpose of

Scott's role, and what was the overarching motive for this whole deadly charade? Paine wouldn't be giving away all of his collateral until he'd worked through his whole plan.

'So how do we get access to the remaining fifty six devices?' enquired Corbyn doing the quick math.

'That's Phase Two, which we haven't spoken about yet.'

'Phase Two? How long does that last for?'

'That'll depend on the White House. But the worst case scenario is another four years. That's when the last of those fifty-six devices will detonate. That'll mean my campaign would last longer than World War Two and span the terms of two Presidents. How will they deal with *that* at their televised debates, I wonder?' Corbyn tried to squeeze out more but Paine remained his adamant self. The FBI man cleared this throat, while Song considered the new meaning of the *Four More Years!* chant.

'Your real name is Oliver Henry Buchanan, a.k.a. Henry Oliver, a.k.a. Oliver Henry, a.k.a. Iain Paterson, a.k.a. Thomas Lane, a.k.a. Thomas Paine. You returned to Illinois to stage your own suicide at Lake Michigan in 1981 but were actually in Mexico and Central America from the late 70's through to the early 80's. You and your father were civil engineers by training, both at Penn State, both with licenses to use explosives in civilian work.

Your association with Gabriel was from a dinner you attended in Nicaragua in 1980 where you relieved him of his cigarette lighter. We don't know exactly what happened between the two of you, but it was clearly enough for it to leave you with a negative impression of him.

Your association with David is through your friendship with his mother's first husband, Song Xiao Win or perhaps through his step-father Terrance May, who you also met in Nicaragua.' Corbyn paused to check that in his nervousness he had not missed anything out. 'Is all this correct?'

Paine sat iceberg still for a moment. 'Yes, all of that's correct. With the exception of the Terrance May reference. I've never knowingly met the man so that's news to me. A freak of happenstance if it's the case.' He looked over at Song. 'I can assure you he's not half the man the person who *should* have been your father was. Congratulations, team! As your reward, here are the locations I promised you. This is going to drive the great American People delirious with pyrrhic joy. First, go to....'

'Sorry, sorry', interrupted Song to Corbyn's palpable irritation. 'That's it? All this shit, all this death? And now you're going to hand over half of the remaining locations without further explanation? So you met Gabriel at a dinner party and had a tiff over the hors d'oeuvres, – so fucking what? Shit! It's as though we've just given you directions to a *7-11* and you've decided to reward us with your life savings. There *has* to be more to it.'

Paine looked through him. 'No, that's it for Phase One. You shouldn't be so literal. It's just a transaction, that's all, David.' With this he recommenced his litany of locations, giving up a tool-hire in Albany and a public baths in Providence before Song interrupted again.

'We know about *Steel Black Chrysler*', he blurted into Paine's monologue. Corbyn, aching to complete the list, gave him another withering glare. 'You may have written everything in cipher in your notebook, but your accomplice wasn't so smart. We don't have everything, which is why we need your confirmations now, but we're not nearly as fucked as we were two days ago. That's the problem when you trust others, Thomas, they invariably let you down. *Steel Black Chrysler*. That's what all this has been about.' Song stared fixedly at Paine, keeping Scott's movements in his peripheral vision. The two of them couldn't confer nor look to each other for guidance. Neither of them moved.

'Nice bluff, David. If you're right, I'll soon find out', smiled Paine at last, picking up again with a public lavatory in Pocatello, Idaho.

'Fuck this waiting around, I need a piss', interjected Scott in that whiney voice he used when sulking. 'You can carry on this bullshit without me, yeah?' Scott looked imploringly at Paine whose shrug indicated he didn't care either way. The lugubrious man dragged himself off his chair, sloping towards the stairs, Song wondering what role this traitor would play in whatever Phase Two was about. As the Fisherman rounded the half-turn stair down to the basement he looked back, squirting Song a half-smile.

'Eight. The roof of the ticket hall at Logan Square on the *L*', continued Paine, looking at his watch as if there was somewhere else he should be. Audible above the sound of Paine's liturgy, Song heard something that set his teeth on edge. He filtered out Paine's voice as something began to gel in his mind, but what was it? Then he heard the same horrible noise again. It was the shrieking hinge on the basement's facilities room door as it had opened and then closed, still not oiled since that day after the party.

But Song knew there was no bathroom in that part of the basement. His mind pulled up a virtual map of the building with the interview room at its center: in the basement a couple of single bedrooms, a multi-purpose area, the rumpus room, and directly underneath where they all sat – the facilities room.

No, surely not.

The moment was caught in aspic as his senses surged tenfold. It was Boston all over again. Every iota of his being snarling that something was terribly wrong. He wasn't aware that he had risen from his seat until he heard Corbyn saying something to the silenced room. But he couldn't respond, his lungs were welded shut. And then he was off, raw adrenalin fuelling his spastic legs as he spurted towards the stairs knocking Scott's vacated chair clear across the room.

'Kamamalu — with me!' leaping down six steps to the half-turn, he heard Paine's voice booming from behind him. 'Now! Now! Do it now!'

At the bottom in another giant leap Song flung himself around the corner in a sprint, grappling the facilities room handle, shoulder thudding into the door. The lock half opened, half tore away from the frame as he lunged into the room, the telltale shriek of the hinge replaced now by the tearing of ply-wood. Song lost his footing, quickly transforming his spilling body into a tucked roll. In this last physical act his hand had instinctively moved to his shoulder holster, the Smith & Wesson slipping fluidly from it. From roll to crouch in one easy motion, Song disengaged the safety and swept the room in a smooth arc.

Scott was standing to the left of him four yards away, face etched in disbelief, his right hand tucked into the blanket of yellow insulation encrusting the wall.

'Move away and lower your hand!' barked Song as the shadow of Kamamalu closed in on the door behind him. Through the ceiling he heard the invocations of Paine for a second longer until they were cut short mid-stream.

Scott's face morphed to that of the innocent little boy before that veneer burnt away to reveal eyes vicious with contempt. 'Fuck you, gook', rasped the real voice of the man known as Bradley Scott, fingers still hidden in the insulation striving to complete their work.

Song fired six times into a four inch diameter around Scott's heart.

The impostor's body was punched away from the partition into a concrete wall, head slamming sickeningly against it. Song looked to where Scott's hands had been, not at the prone body now spurting hissing blood onto the powder grey floor.

No time to investigate.

'Clear the building – now!' he screamed, pushing past a shocked Kamamalu, bumping into Corbyn who was just reaching the basement. 'Bomb! Get Paine away!' and then Song was off again, three steps at a time. The interview room revealed a scene of toppled chairs and scattered paperwork. Paine curled fetal-like next to his chair, his breathing distressed from Townsend's punch to his solar plexus, now sitting on top of him, gun barrel to his temple. 'Get him out!' yelled Song. 'You in the cottage', he shouted into the cameras, 'there's a bomb! Get into the woods as far as you can. Quantico: call 911!' before spinning round to continue his upward journey. Some of the agents working shifts would be sleeping. He sprinted along the corridor banging on doors, screaming at bleary eyed men to run.

Across the front lawn twenty seconds later, he and a bevy of half-dressed men fanned out like a punt-blocking unit, hurdled the flower beds and hurtling across the street to perform quarterback slides down a grassy bank. Grunts and yelps filled the air as skin was shredded from unprotected parts, before all those sounds were eclipsed by a colossal blast that rent the air around them.

A chaotic bundle of roofing, wood, and glass fountained into the spotless heavens. The front side of the house vomited across the street, sleeting through the branches above Song's head. He closed his eyes imagining chunks of fireplace raining down upon his broken body, thinking of Ed Townsend crushed under that illusory pipe in Venezuela.

Thankfully, the worst debris Song experienced were a few scraps of smoldering drapes, and a snapped leg off the interview room's coffee table. Quickly the drizzle of aerial flotsam ceased and he crept forward to peek over the bank.

The house was no more. Two stunted and bedraggled towers of splintered wood stood at either end, their structural integrity holding for the moment. In-between them through the smoke there was nothing except a half-toppled chimney and some gushing water pipes. Song now had an unimpeded view of the wood-top to the rear of the house, and trees swaying gently in the warm spring air.

Chapter 18

Never fear shadows... that always means there is a light shining somewhere

: Jonathan Santos

CHECKING INTO THE WASHINGTON D.C. MARRIOT THAT night, Song found new clothing laid out on the king-size bed. It was eleven p.m. and the smoldering ruins of New Jersey felt like thousands of miles and days away. That had been the third time in two weeks where Paine had nearly killed him, and the man had been in custody throughout. The hotel foyer had been filled with Agents staring at him as he had dragged his tired body into the elevator. As the doors closed, Song had heard the distinctive sound of someone tapping out two familiar letters.

At three a.m. he was dragged from the violent clutches of Morpheus by the insistent ringing of his hotel phone. 'It's me', confirmed a tired Nevada, 'we just got the DNA result back. The man we knew as Bradley Scott was Thomas Paine's son. Have we been played, or what?'

Paine's new safe house – the previous one having proven not to be - was in a quiet Bethesda cul-de-sac, a few miles north of FBI headquarters. He had received the news of his son's death with no apparent concern, returning quickly to his reading of the *Washington Post*, barely missing a beat. Media coverage was uniformly about the search for the fifty-five devices he had still rewarded them with, which had seen every enforcement agency across the nation fully exercised these past twenty-four hours. Joyful delirium mixing again with a stunned disbelief at the magnitude of the day's haul. *How much longer is Rockwell's nightmare going to last?* buzzed the editorials, echoing the thoughts of panicked citizens barricaded into homes across the country. War and rumors of war.

The team - now down to three – met Paine in the house's mock-Georgian dining room dominated by a large teak dining table and eight scalloped chairs, with the ever-present video camera jammed in behind the door.

'What a son he turned out to be. This is not the first time I've had to adjust my plan because of that imbecile', railed Paine, shaking his head at his own stupidity rather than the passing of his child. 'One overly motile sperm and you pay the price for life. So how did you figure out who he was?'

'He knew more about Ed Townsend's death than was possible, he didn't conform to the real Bradley Scott's profile, the moonlight escapade at your house, all confirmed post-mortem by his DNA', replied Corbyn flatly.

'So – just to be clear – he really was my son? As I said, a total fuck up. So let me tell you for free how he got involved with me. I spent time in Mexico post-Nam and I got hooked up with a woman there doing the rounds on her back. She said the bastard she was carrying was mine, but it could have been any one of ten vets sharing her at the farm. After I disappeared to Central America she attached herself to another vet who eventually followed me down south himself, drawn by the big money and free blow. A few years later the woman and her brat went up to the Ozarks with that guy. Oh, by the way, his name was Billy Storey - the man who killed your pop, Nevada. Six degrees of separation, huh? Billy will be my age now, so he shouldn't prove too difficult a kill if you're up for it, girl. Just you remember that it's him who's responsible for bringing Bradley up the way he was – not me. Anyway, three years ago the runt turns up at my place saying I'm his real pa and calling himself Thomas Paine. Ironic, huh? Billy always had a wicked sense of humor to go with that wicked temper of his. I contemplated killing him, my son or not, but he was a vicious little bastard with a borderline personality so I decided to put him to the test.

I needed to give myself a bogus reason to invite David into the team anyway, so I challenged him to kill a man. But first he needed to inherit an identity so I told him to cruise the soup kitchens for some anonymous hobo about his size who he could off. But oh no, the idiot had to go for one of the guys ladling out the food instead. The real Bradley Scott was physically very similar to him, up until the time we cut off his hands and head that is. It's not just the hearts that are left in San Francisco, you know. The real Scott had a big, bushy beard which added to the cover as no-one had really seen his face for years. We tortured him to get his life story – drilled through his knees with a Home Depot special, dislocated his fingers, set fire to his beard. Whoosh! It didn't need any accelerant. When we'd gotten everything we needed, the new Bradley pushed a screwdriver through old Bradley's ear and scrambled his brain. After that, our Bradley boned up on all that religious guff which helped refine our plan to present him to America as a country boy apostle. The plan was for him to continue my good work after I was gone, but by then as *Saint* Bradley Scott.

We needed to get rid of the real Scott's history, and my son
had a hankering for some arson. I warned him it was getting too
flashy, but he wouldn't listen. That ended messily with Kepler
who he thought he'd finished off that night. Fucking amateurs,
eh, Alex? However, demonstrating a flash of his old man's
creativity, he then came up with *i4ni* in order to solve the Kepler
issue as well as roping in David, so in the end my boy did good,
I guess. And he wasn't squeamish about taking out those eyes
with a dessert spoon either. He got a job working at *Scarlett Ink*
specifically to jam someone up, and it was his idea to leave that
religious book next to the bodies as a breadcrumb trail. He chose
Webb as the fall-guy because he didn't like his iPod playlist.
Actually, David, your colleague Bloomfield interviewed my boy
during the investigation under the assumed name of Charles
Watson – one of the Manson Family members - but he'd fixed
the shop's shift schedules to make it look as though Webb was
your only suspect. Bradley even left a partial print on the tape as
a teaser, but you found a way to ignore it, didn't you? That was
pretty lazy, detective. I hope you'll be more thorough with me.

I was going to gift Brad my house in Pender as a final act
of repentance later on, and along with it a third of a ton of C4
still left in the old septic tank. So what are those fuck-wits on
Vigilangels going to say when they find out he's Beelzebub, not
Billy Graham? More disillusionment, more despair – I can
hardly wait.

His biggest mistake was getting caught with the gas cans
in Pender. I'd given him the order to do it hidden under a cup
just after David had mentioned that *Dogs of War* quote to me in
the hospital. I thought you were onto something about my two
Labradors and I was kicking myself for not moving the ordnance
and torching the tank before turning myself in. Looking back
on it now, I guess you were referring to the mercenaries working
for the CIA, yes? Damn! Too much morphine dulls the brain.

Anyway, although Bradley fucked up that arson, he did convince David to take him back to his crib at the *Fishermen's*' before returning to Mountain Lakes. That's where he kept his personal supply of C4 which was the source of the thirty pounds used to level the safe house yesterday. Didn't you notice the weight in his backpack, detective? Sloppy work again.

So, from those humble beginnings in the Ozarks, to global internet star, to chunk of meat on a coroner's stainless steel table. He's no loss to the world.'

'So what brought about yesterday's fireworks?' asked Corbyn evenly, disturbed by the absence of any jot of emotion in Paine's story.

'Boredom. I wanted to move on. The plan was to set the timer so I'd be in the kitchen with Bradley getting some water while you all died in the interview room. I'd find a way to take the fall for it once Bradley had courageously apprehended me trying to escape. Another Bradley miracle.

'Bullshit', said Song tiring of the superficiality, his face progressively souring as the explanation had unfolded. 'You risk a quarter of a century's planning on the whim of involving a putative long-lost son? You're *way* bigger than that. And we still don't have your motive, and what about Melissa Davidson, and JH352 and *Steel Black Chrysler*? *Boredom*, seriously?'

Paine shrugged his indifference. 'You can believe what you like. And as for motive, you'll need to wait for the trial. So let's turn now to Phase Two', Paine rubbed his hands together. 'If I walked outside now, I'd be dangling from a streetlight within the hour. Rockwell on a rope. Alex, do you remember my question about justice versus mercy when I interviewed you? Well I've decided to put America to one last test on that very point.' Song looked at Townsend, fearing the worst. 'As of this moment, all cooperation between us ceases. The only way you'll find the remaining fifty-six devices will be to execute me. In the hour before they administer the lethal dose I'll give them all to you – or rather the ones left by then. The longer you take for my trial and sentencing, the more uncontrolled detonations there'll be. Delaying my death will multiply the deaths of others.

So let's see how civilized America is now, shall we?'

After a few hours of dizzily senior conversations, Corbyn finally charged the man they knew as Thomas Paine. For the Devil's deal to be secured, Paine insisted that he be held at San Quentin State Penitentiary and that his execution – should it take place – be by lethal injection. 'That's the state in which Bradley and I committed our first murders so it's only right, and this way David can come and visit too!

I don't have any family now, so friends will have to suffice', he added with a smile.

There followed yet another extraordinary week bursting with incident. A concrete block supporting a mobile home outside St. Louis blew up catapulting its load onto two adjoining plots, killing a disabled man. Released from its contract by Paine's arrest and Fernandez's death, the *Times* had already run three jaw-dropping stories that had transfixed the nation, with ten more promised to come. The book itself was nearing completion, with advance orders already above twenty million. It's title: *Rockwell – a portrait of fear*.

Meanwhile, anyone in the general public with a working keyboard was offering an opinion about Rockwell and the still hazy link between him and Bradley Scott, the martyr. *Vigilangels* had placed a sepia-tone picture of the Fisherman on their site, a black mourning band across one corner. Sales of Norman Rockwell prints were booming, psychologists casting them as a salve healing the nation's most egregious wounds.

But the most violent discussions were reserved for the bitter division about what to do with Paine himself. A group calling itself the *Association for Justice* had formed with a simple manifesto calling for the pursuit of due process and establishing a sensible timeline for his trial. The *Association* acknowledged that further lives might be lost this way, but this was eminently preferable to a bastardization of the rule of law and a return to the quick justice of Dodge.

The *Citizens for Public Safety* on the other hand argued the diametrical opposite, believing the rule of law itself to be founded upon a higher order concern for the protection of the population. Their own single-point manifesto was to arrange Paine's trial today and to execute him tomorrow.

Arguments between the two camps raged like windblown wildfires with politicians screaming themselves hoarse, fights breaking out in bars, running skirmishes occurring on campuses, and in Vermont a short-lived gun battle between the groups that saw three people die.

Four days after St. Louis, there was an explosion at a movie theater in Jacksonville killing seven. The arguments intensified, with an A-list celebrity pulling a gun during a talk show to demonstrate he was prepared to administer summary justice himself. This pressure cooker forced the President to give an Oval Office address counseling calm, while at that very moment outside the White House's gates a *Citizen* threw acid into an opponent's face.

Reclining in his San Quentin cell, Thomas Paine smiled up at his grey ceiling.

———

Eight days after Paine's formal arrest the Department of Justice in concert with the state of California announced that the trial would commence in two weeks. Its swiftness was unprecedented, carving swathes out of the normal timetable.

People roamed the streets chanting *U.S.A.! U.S.A.!* , cars cruising through the night sounding horns and flashing lights. While in other homes people drew their drapes before the sun went down and went to bed early.

'Nuremberg took longer to organize than this', wrote an Auschwitz survivor in her blog.

Townsend had returned to Vegas to clear her desk despite the fervent ministrations of senior Bureau personnel. Corbyn and Benjamin were pinned down in Washington with the prosecution team, Paine giving notice that he intended to marshal his own defense. Song was ordered back to San Francisco and two months well-deserved leave. Now he was merely required to visit Paine twice a week as any 'family member' might do. Arriving back at the airport hidden under a cap and oversized sunglasses, Big Bird had taken him straight home with barely a word exchanged.

On the night of the Vermont gun battle Song sat morosely in his flat with Charley. 'Missing the buzz?' she asked quietly, ladling French onion soup into bowls.

'Something's terribly wrong', his anguished reply. 'We're missing investigative pieces all over the place, but now we have Paine between the crosshairs all the resources have been shut down. No one wants to hear about the proper motive, or why he really got Scott to blow the place up, because I know it wasn't fucking *boredom*, that's for sure! Or what Melissa Davidson has to do with anything, or the true nature of Paine's link to Song Xiao Win, and on and on. It's a jumble of unanswered questions, and I hate it.'

'Like when you lost a month's sleep fretting over Holden Webb's missing motive?' Only Charley could get away with a comment like that.

'Yeah, and look how well that turned out!'

'But this time you *have* got the right guy', she continued, placing a tossed salad on the table.

'But maybe for the wrong reason', Song snapped back, flicking from Paul Desmond to Charley Parker on the Bose. 'He's segregated in San Quentin as no one wants him taking a shank before the trial and the closure it will bring. After that it'll be okay to execute him without finding out why he really masterminded all of this as no fucker will be interested. When I visited him last, we ended up talking about the Giants' pitching depth. It was surreal, and he knows that I know.'

'So why don't you investigate the case', she said bringing warm bread to the table.

'What do you mean?'

'You're still on it, aren't you? You have privileged access to the files and you're sat on your ass here doing nothing but whining like a little bitch, so pull some all-nighters and find out what everyone's been missing. Pace of the case was so fast and the manpower so multi-focused, maybe they couldn't see what they were looking for.'

At eleven o'clock Charley kissed him on the cheek and was about to disappear into the elevator. 'That's why you mentioned me losing sleep over Holden Webb, wasn't it?' Song mock-frowned at her. 'You were teeing me up for this private investigative thing, you manipulative cow.' As the doors glided shut she blew him a featherweight kiss. Immediately he was on the phone to Oppenheim. 'Can you *FedEx* a complete set of softcopy files to me?'

'It runs to over three terabytes, and that's just the digest. What exactly are you looking for?' she asked.

'Peace of mind.'

Chapter 19

Ultimately we know deeply that the other side of every fear is freedom

: Marilyn Ferguson

AT THREE THE NEXT AFTERNOON AN AGENT DELIVERED A package with five external drives crammed into it. Song was watching the contents list of one unfurl on his screen when the doorbell rang again.

'Move out of the way, *Beach Boy*', quipped a casually dressed Nevada Townsend striding past him, a large carryall draped over her shoulder.

'I thought you were in a casino somewhere?' he called after her.

'I've got three weeks furlough, so it was either a sun lounger in Florida with a flaccid beach ball all to myself, or a studio apartment on the Bay sharing a hard drive with you.'

'Oppenheim rang you last night, huh?'

'Nope, it was Charley. You're like silly putty in her hands, boy.'

By midnight the next evening, there wasn't much space on any of Song's walls not covered with mind maps, insane scribblings, and multiple layers of Post-its. Each distinct area was dedicated to islands of questions teased out from the oceans of data in which they swam. Exhausted, they both slumped onto the sofa, crushing empty pizza boxes as they went. Amongst all of their networked thinking and all of their logic towers, Song kept being dragged back to *Steel Black Chrysler* and *JH352*.

'I'm sure it was my reference to *Chrysler* that triggered Scott's actions that final day.' He rubbed his fatigued eyes.

'Fuck him and fuck all this deduction shit. Why don't we just *ask* Paine?' Nevada said, shaking out her hands and assuming the lotus.

'Exactly', agreed Song. 'Time to pimp out our history with him. He owes us one.'

Every time Song visited Paine in San Quentin he couldn't help thinking about the newly released Holden Webb. And now he didn't want there to be two reasons why this place haunted him for the rest of his life.

In their secure meeting area, Paine read the *San Francisco Chronicle*. 'It says here the *ACLU* are challenging my legal process. How presumptuous - they never asked me', he smiled as Song reclined in a plastic seat. They exchanged thoughts about how politicians were aligning themselves in non-partisan configurations on either side of the argument. 'Did you see that *Association for Justice* rally where that balloon burst and everyone ducked under the table? Bleeding heart liberals scared of their own bleeding heads', Paine chuckled.

'I guess there's no use me asking about the next device?' redirected Song.

'You know the rules of Phase Two. But – since it's you - let's just say some time in the next two days, and close to the Mason-Dixon line.' Song would get that straight to Corbyn.

'Nevada sends her regards. She's back at my apartment still working your case. Neither of us buys your capitulation. Not while *JH352* and *Steel Black Chrysler* remain unanswered.'

Paine cracked his knuckles. 'Is this that thing you have about motive? Man, it'll be the death of you. Can't you just accept the victory? In a short while I'll be forgotten and on some teenager's ketchup-stained T-shirt.'

'You get bored easily so you must be going insane in here. So how about we play one last time between the three of us?'

Paine rubbed his chin as he made up his mind. 'Alright. You kids should focus on Nicaragua, but you'll need to improve your Spanish.' Clear he would get nothing further out of the prisoner, Song made his excuses and speed-dialed Townsend as he hurried along the corridor.

'Nicaragua, huh? Okay, let me find the files.'

'No,' interrupted Song, 'he's worried about us continuing to dig, I could see it in his eyes. Nicaragua is a misdirection. Let's concentrate on Vietnam instead. I've been trying to avoid it throughout the case – but now it's time for me to go home.'

The next two days were spent exclusively in Song's flat, empty takeouts vying for space with dog-eared papers and used printer cartridges. In the afternoon of the second day news broke of an explosion at the *Gettysburg Visitor Center*, with three more names to be added to the roll of honor at that poignant site.

That same evening an *ABC* debate saw two eminent commentators come to blows on the topic of the hastened legal process. "And my great-great grandfather didn't fight at Gettysburg for his descendents to toss the Bill of Rights aside like a used condom", its most memorable sound bite, quickly followed by the snapping of spectacles as his adversary's fist connected with them. In Alabama a hardware store sponsored a Cadaver Tree in its yard where every day it strung-up another Rockwell manikin.

Focusing on Vietnam was a gamble but it helped cut the paperwork more than a thousand fold. Even then there were still myriad lines of investigation to follow. On the third day Townsend's *Skype* chimed into life with the familiar face of Karen Oppenheim.

'I'm taking a vacation so send me some stuff over, but don't tell Corbyn or I'll be tarred and feathered.'

'Are you two, still – you know – together?' asked Song coyly after the call.

'Nope. It was just about the sex', Nevada replied matter-of-factly. 'Not like you and Charley where it's all about the relationship and nothing about the sex, because you haven't had any.'

Song regretted the foray, turning instead to the five gigs of files destined for that afternoon's perusal.

Paine's trial was more about *Barnum & Bailey* than it was about justice. He had told the prosecution he would plead guilty as long as he could make a short statement to the court – and the watching hundreds of millions – and with a guarantee that the lethal injection would be administered on his birthday, August 10th. After a day's fevered calls between the President, constitutional lawyers, and the Governor of California, the deal was agreed with any residual moral considerations relegated to the classrooms of Yale. At San Diego Zoo three civil rights lawyers set up a mock courtroom outside the kangaroo enclosure, while in Washington *Amnesty International* burned copies of the 8th Amendment outside the Lincoln Memorial: "nor cruel and unusual punishments inflicted" read the words crinkling in the flames. The *Post* had run the headline *The Department of Joustice*, likening the fast-food process of trial, sentencing, and execution to that of the Dark Ages.

On the day of the trial, August 3rd, static TV cameras inside the courtroom conveyed images to the estimated half a billion audience worldwide. Song watched with Townsend from his apartment, both having declined invitations to attend the spectacle.

As Paine showed his face for the first time, the commentator noted how much he really did look like Norman Rockwell. On entering, Paine had offered the judge one of his trademark quips. 'Relax, your Honor. We're safe in this building – well, for today anyway', worried eyes in the packed courtroom instinctively scanning the ceiling.

The prosecutor ran through the litany of charges and Paine was asked how he would plead. There was a second of silence in which America held its collective breath: 'Guilty' he responded, greeted by a whoop of delight from half the crowd assembled outside the courthouse. The judge said she would now sentence him, greeted by a louder howl of derision from the other half. Death by lethal injection, to be carried out at the pleasure of the state of California on August 10th. 'Eight-ten! Eight-ten!', chanted half the baying crowd.

Paine was invited to read his statement, which he pulled from the back pocket of the same Chinos he had surrendered himself in just four months earlier.

'I offer no apology for the lives I've taken, just as America has never apologized for those it has illegally taken on foreign shores. Once I used the skills *you* taught me to kill anonymous people in places anonymous to most Americans. Now I have used those same skills to butcher Americans whose names you will never forget. My challenge to America was how it would react in the face of my assault. And so here we are today, the due process of law fast-forwarded at your explicit will in order to expedite my death. So what then is the difference between you and I? Which of us the Hunter and which the Prey? Perhaps you should ask the ghost of my accomplice, Bradley Scott, the Media Messiah in whom millions of you credulous fools placed your faith?

Some of you likened my targets to those captured in the sentimental art of Norman Rockwell. Are you so wedded to this flawed vision of a halcyon past that you cannot see the ugliness of the present? Of the arrogance of your presumption?

America, I leave you alone with your conscience. You deserve each other.' With that he sat down. There was a moment of unscripted confusion in the court, as if *Macbeth* had not returned for the last act, before Paine was led away smiling.

Song looked over at Townsend. 'Are you buying this shit? *Of the arrogance of your presumption?* That's not the way he usually talks. The fucker's still laughing at us.'

'Agreed. So let's press on and see if we can leave him crying.'

———

It didn't take more than a day for the *Citizens'* first campsite to be set up outside San Quentin. Each morning the red painted tents at its center were rearranged to spell out the execution's countdown from six days to one for the helicopters' aerial cameras. On a nearby parking lot the *Association* established their base, lighted candles arranged at night to spell out those same numbers. Meanwhile Paine's speech had stirred the discussion to even greater passion. A Buddhist monk in Nebraska had immolated himself in protest at this summary justice, while the grandmother of one of the Boston victims was raising a petition that she be allowed to administer Paine's lethal dose.

All of this played out on Song's muted TV as through tired eyes and fogged minds the trio ploughed through the heavy clay soil of information overload. Oppenheim was testing to destruction the *Steel Black Chrysler* angle, Townsend taking *JH352*, while Song concentrated on any link through to Vietnam. Doric columns of printed data had sprouted across his apartment floor.

'We should go and see him again', Nevada said at last, rubbing eye sockets with the backs of her hands. 'He's spilled important stuff to us before when we've done it together.'

'Back then he wanted to. Now I have the impression he doesn't.'

'Look, we've been at this for days and got jack, and I have no confidence that'll change before he's slipped the needle.'

'Okay', said Song at last, drumming fingers on his iPad, 'One last bossa nova with the Devil.'

Two days before the execution their vehicle was escorted through football crowds of protestors and promoters alike. Paine greeted Nevada with a small hug, her body rigid beneath his arms.

'Have you found anything? No, well I did tell you.'

'Haven't found anything *yet*', her tenacious reply.

'It's not as though you have a lot of time', he grinned back, spending the next hour deflecting questions that were growing evermore pointed as the minutes ticked by. Paine appeared more interested in discussing the tortuous soul-searching his speech had sparked. There were even rumors that two Supreme Court Justices were pondering their resignation.

'The next time I see you both will be through bulletproof glass', Paine observed, beckoning the guard to open the door.

'I don't think I'll be coming to the execution', responded Song. 'My job's to catch the bad guys; I leave the delivery of justice to someone else.'

Paine gave him a long hard stare. 'Remember, David "These are the times that try men's souls"', humming *Paint it Black* as he left.

'So that's all we get', railed Townsend afterwards. 'That same fucking quotation from Thomas Paine.'

Song balled his fists in excitement. 'Actually, no. More recently it was a re-quotation from Melissa Davidson. Paine's given us his final clue.'

———

Melissa Davidson had been a part-time player in this theater, almost overlooked as the slew of other leads overwhelmed hers. Plucked from obscurity she had offered them context about the nature of fear, its echo down the years through Ed Murrow becoming clearer since. In the car back to Song's, Oppenheim had been tasked to review every syllable of their Quantico meeting with the British Professor. No sooner were they in the apartment than his Skype chimed.

'She's not British, she's Australian', shouted Oppenheim making tea at her end. 'Remember she cut short her speaking tour because her father had died in Australia? We assumed he'd been on vacation, but he was actually an Aussie. Her parents divorced when she was six and her British mom took her back to England. Not sure if this helps us though.'

'Oh shit!' exploded Song rushing to his tablet. 'What was her father's full name?'

'Barry Alan Davidson.' Song typed in one of the hundreds of URLs he had already scanned in his desperate attempt to find inspiration. He and Townsend gasped with surprise.

'What are you guys looking at?' shrieked the unsighted Oppenheim.

'The Australian Government's Nominal Roll of their Vietnam veterans', answered a fevered Townsend. 'Barry Alan Davidson was one of the 61,000 Australians who served in the war, listed here as being in their Engineering Corps. Somehow Paine knew Melissa Davidson's father.'

Suddenly, oceans of Vietnam data had shrunk to puddles, the tyranny of the clock now the trio's extra spur. Song rang Alvarez to ask one last favor, judging the CIA man would be able to move faster than Corbyn in the murky world where military overlapped with intelligence. And anyway, Corbyn wasn't even aware they were still working the case.

By the early evening it had been confirmed that Davidson was on a Mediterranean cruise without her cell. 'Christ! Who the fuck does that nowadays?', shouted Song, slamming his fist down on the table, almost masking the sound of a key turning in his front door lock.

'I've brought take out', announced Charley waving bags at her unshaven childhood friend. She looked around the room's messy warzone, one eyebrow raised. 'Interesting', her only comment. Charley prowled along the walls taking in their brickwork of paper postings, her own capacious mind ordering it into clusters of logic. 'What's this *JH352* thing?' Song explaining what Nevada had found on Paine's watch. 'Okay, I want in. Give me something to do.' Charleen Tran Dok eased herself onto the sofa, scooping off pizza take-out boxes as she went and plugging a stick into her port. Seven hours later with the moon high in the sky and Song *Googling* Barry Davidson's Army Company, she coughed.

'*JH352* is Jimi Hendrix', she said, as if it were obvious.

'And how did you work that one out?' asked a *Red Bull* powered Oppenheim over Skype.

'Because of Song Xiao Win.' Charley looked at their blank faces, aggrieved at having to point out something so simple. 'What does the Mandarin word Xiao mean in English? *Little*, it means *little*. Which gives you Song Little Win which leads to the song *Little Wing* by Jimi Hendrix - hence JH.' Her audience looked back, unconvinced. 'It was meaningful back then', she continued. 'Hendrix died in 1970 and that track's a classic. Paine didn't use his own watch as a detonator because it was a tribute to Song Xiao Win. Something the man did for Paine. So we should focus now on the 352 because it's related to the both of them. Hey, it's only two a.m. - bet we can find it by sun-up.'

It was Townsend who found the 352 as dawn broke - but it wasn't related to Vietnam. It was Cambodia. 'This article says that in the early seventies Nixon launched something called *Operation Menu*, the illegal carpet bombing of Cambodia and Laos. Intelligence said the Viet Cong were avoiding raids on their supply lines by diverting them across those countries' borders. We dropped thousands of tons of munitions on them causing massive civilian casualties. *Operation Dinner* was launched on Base Camp 352. Could that be it?'

'Who knows,' replied Song. 'Maybe there's a -'

'Holy Shit!!' exclaimed Oppenheim over the video link. 'Guess who the author was of the article I've just been quoting from? Gabriel fucking Fernandez!' They crowded round the screen as she activated *Skype* sharing. 'Jeez, he's sucking Nixon's and Kissinger's dicks - completely exculpating them of the crime.'

'So maybe it wasn't just Fernandez accidentally meeting Paine in Managua, but something here too?' suggested Townsend.

Song jabbed at his phone summoning Alvarez's number. 'Paulo, I think I can narrow that Barry Davidson search down some more for you.'

A day left now before the execution, and the team could at last turn its full attention to the *Steel Black Chrysler* puzzle. Song was pursuing a tenuous line of logic down a Chrysler Imperial Sedan route when Charley sprang to answer the door bell.

'Charleen Tran Dok, I presume', said the handsome middle aged man standing outside, a sullen TK Bloomfield loitering behind him.

'He insisted on coming here straight from the airport,' the big man whined, 'and he's a fucking Fed so what was I supposed to do?' She opened the door wide with a flourish, letting Special Agent Alexander Corbyn into the already overpopulated space.

'So, where are we?' asked Corbyn, throwing his jacket onto the back of the couch and unbuttoning his cuffs. Song and Townsend looked first at him and then at each other, Oppenheim ducking below her screen camera. 'Hello Karen, no need to hide', said Corbyn into space.

'Was it Alvarez who told you what we've been doing?' asked Song. Corbyn looked at Charley, Charley giving Song a weak grin in return. The detective shook his head and sighed. 'Grab that memory stick, Alex, and start searching for relevant Chrysler references.'

Everyone went quickly back to work, with the exception of Bloomfield who stood like a thick trunked streetlight in the middle of the room. 'What can I do?' Song pointed distractedly at the Post-its on the wall, briefly explaining the *Steel Black Chrysler* clue as a focused silence descended upon the team.

With nowhere left to sit, Big Bird slumped against the window, crushing the papers taped to it. Picking up an FBI report he noisily flicked its pages back and forth drawing annoyed looks from Townsend. An hour later he levered himself straight, staring trance-like into the middle distance as nimbler fingers danced over keyboards around him. He picked up a blunted pencil and a discarded sheet of paper, scribbling something on it, the tip of his tongue protruding from the side of his mouth. After a while he thumped over to Song's bookshelf extracting a thick volume of *Twentieth Century Movie Classics*, his nightstick thumbs creasing its pages.

'How long you been going at this clue?' he boomed, disturbing everyone's concentration again.

'A month or so', replied Nevada trawling through a list of towns with names similar to *Chrysler*.

Bloomfield laughed. 'Fuck me, I should have been a Fed what with my crossword skills and all. Someone already solved it for you a fortnight ago but it got lost in all this data crap', he declared, waving a report over his head. Everyone stopped to look up at the huge man. 'One of your anonymous backroom boys went through the codes in Paine's notebook generating word alternatives. See, he wrote down that *Steel* could be *Steal*, though he missed that steal could also be *Rob*. But he got that *Black* could go to other colors such as *Red*, and that *Chrysler* could go to *Ford*', Bloomfield paused for his audience's reaction, to be greeted only by silence.

'Don't you college grads get it? *Steel Black Chrysler* is code for Rob Redford?' His unconvinced audience still looking back flatly at him. 'And the number next to *Steel Black Chrysler* in the notebook was eighty, yeah?' Bloomfield slapped Song's copy of *Movie Classics* onto the table, pointing a stubby finger at a black and white picture of a younger Robert Redford. 'So look at which movie Sundance was in that year.'

'*Brubaker?*' repeated Greene at the end of the conference line. 'That's the one where Redford's a prison governor. So are you suggesting Paine's gonna make a break from San Quentin?'

'No, why go to all this trouble to get in into it if the objective is to get out?' replied Song. 'The final answer to *Steel Black Chrysler* lies in its pairing with *JH352*, but we don't have much time to work it out.' Townsend told Greene about Melisa Davidson's father but that she was somewhere on a Mediterranean cruise.

'Time for us big boys to help you out', Greene stated, dialing a number.

One hour later, a disheveled Professor Davidson *Skyped* them from the captain's quarters of a cruise ship offshore from Ephesus, the two burly Turkish secret-servicemen who had dragged her from a warm bed now standing sentinel at her side.

'My dad didn't speak much about his war experiences. I know his specialism was demolition, but that's it.'

'Did he ever mention Cambodia or Laos?'

'Oh sure, that's where *JH352* came from', her nonchalant reply.

Everyone's jaw dropped as Davidson reached into her shirt to pull out a chain. 'He wore this St. Christopher with *JH352* inscribed on the back.' She held it up close to the PC's camera for all to see.

'Were you wearing that when we met in Quantico?' asked Corbyn, irony's pull impossible to resist.

'Sure, it's my lucky charm. Dad told me it was in honor of a man who saved his life in Cambodia, so I guessed it was probably something to do with *Operation Menu*.'

'You know about that too?' croaked Song.

'Of course - I'm a historian! And in our profession we like to say that those who do not understand their history are condemned to repeat it.'

—————

It was the morning of Paine's execution, the media choreographing the day as though it were a British royal wedding. A medley of bloody archive footage and micro stories about the perfidious Bradley Scott accompanied the main event. Song had lain awake all night pondering the team's failure at this last hurdle. Something was going to happen at San Quentin relating to a shared experience between Song Xiao Win, Barry Davidson, and Thomas Paine in Cambodia – but what? He was dragged up from the cold depths of despair by the trilling of his almost depleted phone.

'We've found it', announced an elated Paulo Alvarez. 'I'm sending you the file now!'

Song was at his iPad in three long steps, shouting to rouse his crumpled house guests as Alvarez's scanned document unfurled before them. There, in an aged confidential file about *Operation Menu*, were the three target names captured together for the first time. Townsend squeezed Song's arm in delight.

But Alvarez's file also contained the name of a fourth individual.

Bloomfield grunted an expletive, prodding at it on the screen with a greasy finger. 'That can't be the person I'm thinking of, can it?'

'He's too young', said a sleepy Charley wearing one of Song's shirts as a nightgown. Townsend typed it in and everyone read the man's Wiki-bio in silence.

'Fuck me! It's not the guy from Cambodia, it's his son!' said an amazed Bloomfield.

'At last!' sighed a smiling Song, looking like the man who had just broken the *Enigma* code. 'So this has all been about the fourth man. *That's* been Paine's motive all along! Now I can die a happy man.'

'And as a result, Paine will now die an unhappy one', observed Corbyn quietly.

Chapter 20

Fear is that little darkroom where negatives are developed

: Michael Pritchard

AT SIX THAT EVENING, 10TH AUGUST, THE EMERGENCY work Corbyn had set in train had been completed. There were six hours to go until Paine's execution. The team sat in tight anticipation spotted around Song's living room waiting for a call they knew would come. All afternoon the Detective Sergeant had sat with an immensely tired but seraphic smile of his face: the dog that had caught the cat that had caught the canary.

Nevertheless, everyone jumped as Corbyn answered the sharp ringing of his phone. It was the warden of San Quentin handing his over to Paine.

'Slight change of plan, Alex. I also want the Governor of California to be here tonight when I divulge the balance of the locations. Given he's a hot tip for the Democratic Presidential nomination next time round, I'm sure he won't object to the exposure. And rest assured, I won't be asking him for a reprieve.'

'The Governor? I'm not sure he's in state, or if he'd accede to the request...'

'It's not a request, it's a demand. No Governor, no list. Four more years of C4 surprises.' Corbyn gave assurances he would see what he could do. Hanging up on Paine, he looked at his smiling audience.

'Well, it's taken until the final day, but at last we're one step ahead of the bastard.'

Corbyn suggested that the meeting take place in the warden's office and Paine had consented. The White House had spoken to Governor Edward Ronson about the criticality of his participation and he had consented to attend, albeit with a raft of reservations.

Two hours before Paine's midnight execution, a curious mixture of law enforcement personnel and political aides were waiting in the warden's office for the condemned man. News of Governor Ronson's personal attendance had stirred the media into a frenzy of speculation about a late stay of execution. Now it was the turn of the *Association for Freedom* to chant 'Eight-ten Eight-ten!', fistfights with *Citizens* breaking out across the country. After half an hour of muted conversation the warden's thick wooden door opened to admit the source of the nation's recent agony. Striding confidently into the room Paine looked at the assembled masses.

'Everyone out except for Governor Ronson, Alex, David, and Nevada. You can leave the video running for posterity.' The room cleared, Paine lowered himself into a comfortable chair glancing up at the clock. 'Ninety minutes left until the needle. Let's get some coffee in here – I need to be awake for it. In the meantime Governor Ronson, it's become a custom in our team for people to tell us something about themselves,' Paine remaining imperious to the last.

'When are you going to give us the remaining locations?' enquired the sandy haired, forty-eight year old politician who was not used to being overmatched. Ronson gazed evenly at this creature before him – part man, part monster.

'This isn't Ways and Means, Governor, so take a pill.' Conscious of the Bureau's briefing to comply with Paine's reasonable requests, Ronson launched into a reprise of his personal history as though he were sitting before a nominations committee. Much practice had helped him shoehorn the sum total of an unimpeachable life into precisely twelve minutes.

'People have speculated that I might declare an interest in seeking the Democratic nomination for the presidency', he concluded. 'All I can say is that I'm humbled by my current opportunity to serve the great state of California. I will look after today and let the future look after itself.'

Paine had listened patiently throughout, peering alternately at the loquacious man and then at the clock, as if he was supposed to be somewhere else.

It was 10.49 p.m..

There was a hollow quiet in the room, accentuated by the absence now of the Governor's booming voice. Uncomfortable with the silence, Ronson looked worryingly to Corbyn for a lead, the Special Agent remaining perfectly still as if stalking a wounded animal. Song and Townsend looked on, almost comatose.

The second hand on the warden's clock clicked noisily to 10.50 p.m., the only thing moving in that frozen room.

Paine smiled wistfully. 'I've just noticed the smell of fresh paint. You found it, didn't you?'

'Six pounds of C4 and a small can of gasoline hidden in the Governor's ceiling right above our heads', answered Corbyn quietly, pointing upwards. 'The records say the office was remodeled in 1988.

Steel Black Chrysler. From Robert Redford to *Brubaker*, to prison, to San Quentin, to *your* choice of 10th August for your execution and your late request for Governor Ronson to be present at 10.45 p.m., added Corbyn, though Paine of course already knew all of this. The Governor looked on mystified, as though people had suddenly started speaking a foreign language. 'The builders did a fantastic job this afternoon tearing down the ceiling and then replacing it after the Bomb Squad had done their work.'

Paine shook his head accompanied by a sardonic laugh. 'I shouldn't have risen to your bait, David. It was a mistake to give you any clues once I was here, but you knew I enjoy the game too much. Congratulations, that's all I can say. I bow down to you all', at which point he did.

Corbyn explained the gist of the situation to the surprised Governor who then had the honor of asking the biggest question of all. 'Why on earth would you want to kill me, Mr. Paine?'

'After I've told you my story, you'll understand. And when people see this video it'll explain why you should never become President.' Paine steepled his fingers for the last time and told his tale.

———

'I was born Oliver Henry Buchanan, in Illinois, in 1945. My mother died of pneumonia when I was three leaving my father to raise me the best he could. He ran his own construction business using the skills he'd been taught with the SEABEEs. I learnt his trade and obtained a license to work with explosives. It was Gabriel's persistent digging on this point that confirmed his crispy departure after he'd shown me that father and son list of his. I couldn't risk the association being made before this evening's scheduled entertainment.

Uncle Sam completed the art of my munitions education, if your definition of art includes the mathematics of kill-ratios to ordnance tonnage. I was drafted in '69 and did my basic training at Fort Polk. On the Friday of graduation I was eating a celebratory pizza at a nearby Italian, and the following Friday I was on another continent slitting the throat of a VC scout. Two of my Polk class were already dead by then.

I was only twenty-four, but a month into my tour I felt like an old man. I'd seen things that changed me irrevocably. It sounds passé now, and I know Hollywood's milked that cow dry, but life's not lived in celluloid, is it?

In 1970 I was part of a four man team parachuted into Cambodia to provide ground support for *Operation Menu*, target Base Camp 352. There are assets you can't be sure of destroying with high altitude bombing, so teams like ours went in to mop up. Australian Sergeant Barry Davidson and I were joined by a South Vietnamese army liaison officer named Song Xiao Win. The fourth man - and our commanding officer - was Lieutenant Kent Ronson, your dead father, Governor.

He was a prick. Half military, half CIA; half-serpent, half-wit, with a growing reputation for cowardice and poor judgment. But his father, your Grandfather, was a decorated Iwo Jima vet connected to the brass so he was given a lot of slack – and boy did he trip us up on it. Two days into the mission we had to abort when we ran into three divisions of VC. By that time we were thirty klicks across the border with no LZ possible, so it was Jimi who led us back on foot. I say on foot, but in reality we were crawling on our bellies for most of it. We called Song Xiao Win 'Jimi' because of the *Little Wing* reference, which I'm guessing you've worked out by now.

What followed were the most frightening eleven days of my whole life. At night we slept standing up in the constant rain, and by day we crawled through the mud alongside the snakes and bugs. It was Jimi who nursed us through: hunting food off the jungle floor, gathering water from rock pools, and by calming our young nerves with the odd word here and there. That man was a player - best I ever met. I didn't see him sleep for those whole eleven days.

And all this despite the constant fucking whimpering of your father, Governor. I thought the VC would find us from the stink off his pants, he pissed himself so much. One night I woke to find Jimi on top of me wrestling with an NVA scout, spilling his bowels onto my tunic with a Bowie knife. The VC was about to bayonet me having walked right past your gutless old man who'd fallen asleep on guard. Jimi took a bullet in the arm saving my life that night, all because your piss-poor father couldn't do his duty. Eleven agonizing days later we emerged from the tree line back in Vietnam. Yep, me and fear grew real tight back then, and we've been inseparable ever since.

I gave Jimi my address but a false name – Henry Oliver. Not great thinking, I know, but we were kids caught up in all the secrecy shit. Davidson and I kept in touch for a while, that's how I knew about the birth of his daughter, Melissa. It wasn't until Nicaragua that I heard about Jimi's execution. Some of the CIA boys down there had known him in Saigon back in the day. They told me Washington had been desperate to get an ex-military South Vietnamese brass out in '76, so they'd traded the whereabouts of six "collaborators" to the Commies in exchange for his safe passage. Jimi's was one of those names, earning him two bullets in the ear that same day. And who was that person in D.C. so eager to bring the brass home at the expense of Jimi's life? None other than your father, Kent Ronson. How's that for gratitude, Governor?

Ronson had been moved into an Intelligence desk job trading the identities of old allies for new favors from Ho Chi Minh's boys. And there was the added bonus that the brass he helped get out made sizeable donations to his personal bank account. Don't look so shocked Governor, how did you think a salaried CIA man could afford that eight bedroom townhouse you grew up in? I wanted to kill him myself, but by the time I'd gotten off the bottle he was already half eaten away by cancer. I figured the pain from that was too delicious to cut short. But I still needed to even things up between me and the Ronson family, so that's why you were invited here today. It's an honor thing, Governor, though I wouldn't expect a politician to understand the concept.'

'Assuming any of this is true, you can't visit the sins of the father upon his son', said Governor Ronson with surprising grace given that he was clearly shaken by these allegations. 'I'm no Bradley Scott, Mr. Paine. I've made different life choices to the ones *my* father made. And to underscore that difference, I can tell you that I deeply regret if his actions led to the death of this man Song Xiao Win, whereas I doubt my father would ever have expressed the same.'

Paine sighed his indifference. 'You think any of that's my concern, Governor? I'm only interested in a cold and mechanical vengeance, not your sociological cant about how different you are from your dear old Dad. We're talking about a measured vendetta here, not absolution.' Paine gestured to the clock in a plea to allow him to continue.

'After Vietnam the next few years were spent in an alcoholic haze between the physical depredations of a farm in Mexico, and the spiritual ones of Central America. That's where I made the contacts who've helped me assume my many identities ever since. Have you met Mitchell Waits yet? Oh good - another one of America's fractured heroes. False identities for cash, no questions asked, that's his forte.

Back then I was the 'Angry Young Man' everyone writes about, except I wasn't so young anymore. All I knew was that fear seemed to be the constant in my life. My father hadn't been a patient man and as a youngster I'd had two broken arms to show for it. So when in my Agency career I was being paid to generate that same emotion abroad in the name of our national interest, I couldn't believe my luck. A man called Cousins once wrote, "people are never more insecure than when they become obsessed with their fears at the expense of their dreams". But for me the obsession with fear *was* my dream. So, with the assistance of forty percent proof alcohol, I reasoned that my revenge shouldn't be limited to Ronson alone and that America too should pay for what it had made me become. I must admit it sounds rather hackneyed when I say it now, but it's the truth, and clichés become clichés because they best express a situation. Anyway, that's when I started over-requisitioning C4 and sending it back home through the diplomatic post. It was all Walter Mitty stuff - I didn't have any viable plan at the time. Tequila will do that for you. I got out of the CIA game recovering from a bullet I took in a firefight in San Salvador – the famous splinter David so brilliantly tracked down - and I gradually sobered up. Then one day, rational as hell for the first time in ten years, I found myself looking at a ton of C4 in the bedroom of my rented house in Texas. My first idea was to blackmail the government, but I realized money wasn't the currency I was interested in anymore. America had paid me to create fear, so now I'd pay it back in kind.

So using construction trade publications to find the best targets and supported by false CIA documentation, I spent the next fifteen years crisscrossing the country seeding my down payments. I didn't have that Norman Rockwell targets idea in mind, but I'll admit that in retrospect it kind of made sense when the media raised it. I placed around a dozen bombs a year, so it was light work, and I generated my living expenses by selling off parcels of C4 to various private customers.

I got into the Chinese consulate using a false health and safety inspector's pass, finishing the job one morning while the men were arriving. In Birmingham I was a tourist who picked up a day's work as a laborer. Those pre 9/11 days you could put anything you liked into a suitcase. At the Gator stadium I was the job's foreman for a week, and so on. There are plenty of ways to get onto a site, and if you work over a lunch break while the hardhats are pawing their way through *Playboy*, it's amazing what you can accomplish. I had a beard, long hair, was fifty pounds heavier, and wore tinted John Lennon's. That's why no one recognized me when my photo was posted.

Then around the millennium I just stopped. I had plenty of ordnance left and I was still mad as hell, but I wasn't sure if this was what I wanted anymore. In fact, in 2009, I was contemplating sending the full list of locations to the *National Enquirer* and having done with it all, when suddenly the feckless Bradley Scott turns up on my doorstep claiming to be my son. He was equally as angry about life as me, but without any good reason.

I'd kept tabs on Governor Ronson's rise, and for the first time it all clicked together like a beautiful mechanism. Administrations had been fanning people's fears with this terror alert color-coding horseshit, so if a government can scare its own population, why not us? This way Bradley would get his own prolonged day in the sun, and I could take out the Governor. And we could have a lot of fun along the way to boot.'

Paine paused to scrutinize his audience. 'I can tell from your faces you think that the cause of my actions was not in proportion to their devastating effect' he grinned. 'But that's just the fallacious moral mathematics you keep doing in your ethical little heads. I don't suffer from those same limitations. And, yes, I can see you think I'm too calm, too detached, don't you? Well it's true, maybe I could have done the *Rambo* thing and snapped with the inequity of it all. That would have been far simpler. But in truth mine was more of a gentle separation than a tear. Revenge has proven to me that it really is a dish best served straight from the refrigerator. So, respectfully, fuck your personal expectations, and pardon me if I yawn while doing it. I think that's about it. Is there anything else you need before we say farewell?'

There were things Song desperately wanted to say, but with under an hour left in this sad man's life, what was the point?

'And the choice of San Quentin for the ambush?' enquired Corbyn.

'Didn't have to be here. I had a couple of other possibilities, but I liked this one best. I would have stipulated we meet in the warden's office but you beat me to it, and now I know why! I stupidly ringed it in my notebook and that fucker Bradley Scott stumbled you onto it. Kids huh, what are you going to do with them?'

'So our participation was about paying back old debts to my father, and to Song Xiao Win by way of David's mom. But what about Gabriel?' enquired Nevada.

'It was his interview with Kissinger and that article on *Operation Menu* in particular that really pissed me off. I saw it in *Newsweek* thirty years ago, but I also remembered him from a dinner in Managua where he made me so mad I wanted to put the fish knife between his ribs. I waited for him outside the embassy that night, but he stayed over. Saved his worthless life for a while. People like Fernandez give oxygen to rotten politicians. Kissinger is a murdering fuck, *Nobel Peace Prize* or not. The man should have been indicted as a war criminal, not inducted as a Laureate. I'd been saving up something like Sacramento for Gabriel all along.'

'So your twin motives have been revenge against Ronson and revenge against America for fucking you up, is that right?' summarized Song, the dissatisfaction clear in his voice.

'I can hear you're still not convinced, David, but that motive fixation of yours is overrated. Sometimes people just do things because they can't think of anything else. Life isn't always about one plus one equaling two; not about the shortest distance between two points being a straight line. Some days I prefer to eat peas, while some days it's carrots. Go figure. Maybe I'm just suffering from an advanced form of ennui. And, frankly, that's what I'm beginning to feel right now, so how about I give you the final locations and then you can slip me the needle? These last ones are my gift to David's mother - tell her that please. Governor Ronson, I'll let you decide what your gift to the American people should be. Let's see if you have more integrity than your father.'

As he had always done, Paine reeled off the balance of devices without any hesitation, Corbyn patiently ticking the coded notebook's list. Ronson sat quietly throughout, Song unsure whether the man was contemplating his past or future resumes.

Some days I prefer peas, some days carrots, thought Song, shivering at the vision of a little girl's bloodied legs folded across a broken soda shop window. 'There's one missing', Corbyn noted from his tally. 'Number 103. Labeled *Different Strokes* in your notebook.'

'Yep, that location I'm not going to give you. It's my final gift to America. Have a smile on your lips for me when you find out.' There was only half an hour left now, Paine sitting legs crossed on the warden's couch staring vacantly at Nevada.

'Sir, you appear remarkably calm for a man who's just about to die', observed Ronson quietly.

Paine rewarded him with a tolerant smile. 'I died forty years ago, Governor - today you're only killing my body. I'd like to tell you that was an original quotation, but actually I stole it from someone on *Oprah*.'

Corbyn made a call to summon the priest requested by Paine to administer his last rites. The room was still, no one knowing what else to say. 'Did you see the news this afternoon?' ventured the man with the dwindling future. 'Police in Wyoming found a family of five dead in their farm's storm shelter. Bizarrely the father had taken them down to escape my work, but the door had jammed shut and they'd starved to death. It's the perfect epigram to conclude my case: Fear is mankind's key driver, happiness is merely an interlude.'

Song's heart wanted to sing to Paine of something else: of the love of the parents who had defended their children at *Rosa Parks*; of parishioners safeguarding the thousands of churches they loved; of the selfless acts of millions of Americans who had loved and nourished each other through these turbulent months. Of his own love for his parents, and for Charley – *yes, his love for Charley*! He felt it more now in this room of endings than he had ever done before, and it fed the furnace of his soul. Love – that other four letter word – so absent in Paine's actions, so obvious in people's response. But as Song made to speak these words, the door opened and Paine's priest walked in.

It was Monsignor O'Brian.

'Didn't anyone tell you?' smiled Paine to the team as he rose. 'I thought I'd give the Monsignor an opportunity to get some closure. Because I certainly don't need any.'

With that he nodded once, put his hands into his pockets and walked out, whistling.

Epilogue

None but a coward dares to boast that he has never known fear

:Ferdinand Foch

ONE COLD JANUARY NIGHT FIVE MONTHS LATER, LIEUTENANT David Song rolled over to answer his insistent cell, its screen blinking 2.17 a.m.. Gently lifting Charley's hand from his chest he placed it softly back upon her pillow. If happiness was an interlude, as Paine had said, Song would ensure this one lasted forever.

The caller I.D. announced it was Corbyn. They hadn't spoken much since Paine's execution and the punishing month of end-to-end interviews that had followed. It was quieter now, the world moving on to its latest media-packaged crisis. The *Vigilangels* site had been mothballed, Bradley Scott branded coffee mugs timing out on *eBay* without bidders.

'We're getting reports of an explosion. I'm sure it's the one Paine left for us. No one hurt and the sprinklers engaged before the fire could take hold. Some exhibits were slightly damaged, but everything's going to be okay.'

'Exhibits - where was it?' Song whispered as Charley yawned. He pushed a strand of hair away from the face he had always loved. Corbyn paused, and in his mind's eye Song could see the Special Agent smiling.

'It was at the *Norman Rockwell Museum* in Stockbridge, Massachusetts.'

One need not be a chamber to be haunted;
One need not be a house;
The brain has corridors surpassing
Material place

: Emily Dickinson